FREDERIK POHL
SUPER PACK

– 2015 –

Cover Image © Can Stock Photo Inc. / Catmando

Positronic Publishing
PO Box 632
Floyd VA 24091

ISBN 13: 978-1-5154-0329-6

First Positronic Publishing Edition
10 9 8 7 6 5 4 3 2 1

FREDERIK POHL SUPER PACK

by Frederik Pohl

TABLE OF CONTENS

PREFERRED RISK

by Frederik Pohl and Lester del Rey

CONTENTS

CHAPTER ONE

The liner from Port Lyautey was comfortable and slick, but I was leaning forward in my seat as we came in over Naples. I had been on edge all the way across the Atlantic. Now as the steward came through the compartments to pick up our Blue Plate ration coupons for the trip, I couldn't help feeling annoyed that I hadn't eaten the food they represented. For the Company wanted everyone to get the fullest possible benefit out of his policies—not only the food policies, but Blue Blanket, Blue Bolt and all the others.

We whooshed in to a landing at Carmody Field, just outside of Naples. My baggage was checked through, so I didn't expect to have any difficulty clearing past the truce-team Customs inspectors. It was only a matter of turning over my baggage checks, and boarding the *rapido* that would take me into Naples.

But my luck was low. The man before me was a fussbudget who insisted on carrying his own bags, and I had to stand behind him a quarter of an hour, while the truce-teams geigered his socks and pajamas.

While I fidgeted, though, I noticed that the Customs shed had, high up on one wall, a heroic-sized bust of Millen Carmody himself. Just standing there, under that benevolent smile, made me feel better. I even managed to nod politely to the traveler ahead of me as he finally got through the gate and let me step up to the uniformed Company expediter who checked my baggage tickets.

And the expediter gave me an unexpected thrill. He leafed through my papers, then stepped back and gave me a sharp military salute. "Proceed, Adjuster Wills," he said, returning my travel orders. It hadn't been like that at the transfer point at Port Lyautey—not even back at the Home Office in New York. But here we were in Naples, and the little war was not yet forgotten; we were under Company law, and I was an officer of the Company.

It was all I needed to restore my tranquility. But it didn't last.

*

FREDERIK POHL

The *rapido* took us through lovely Italian countryside, but it was in no hurry to do it. We were late getting into the city itself, and I found myself almost trotting out of the little train and up into the main waiting room where my driver would be standing at the Company desk.

I couldn't really blame the Neapolitans for the delay—it wasn't their fault that the Sicilians had atomized the main passenger field at Capodichino during the war, and the *rapido* wasn't geared to handling that volume of traffic from Carmody Field. But Mr. Gogarty would be waiting for me, and it wasn't my business to keep a Regional Director waiting.

I got as far as the exit to the train shed. There was a sudden high, shrill blast of whistles and a scurrying and, out of the confusion of persons milling about, there suddenly emerged order.

At every doorway stood three uniformed Company expediters; squads of expediters formed almost before my eyes all over the train shed; single expediters appeared and took up guard positions at every stairwell and platform head. It was a triumph of organization; in no more than ten seconds, a confused crowd was brought under instant control.

But why?

There was a babble of surprised sounds from the hurrying crowds; they were as astonished as I. It was reasonable enough that the Company's expediter command should conduct this sort of surprise raid from time to time, of course. The Company owed it to its policyholders; by insuring them against the hazards of war under the Blue Bolt complex of plans, it had taken on the responsibility of preventing war when it could. And ordinarily it could, easily enough.

How could men fight a war without weapons—and how could they buy weapons, particularly atomic weapons, when the Company owned all the sources and sold only to whom it pleased, when it pleased, as it pleased? There were still occasional outbreaks—witness the recent strife between Sicily and Naples itself—but the principle

8

remained... Anyway, surprise raids were well within the Company's rights.

I was mystified, though—I could not imagine what they were looking for here in the Naples railroad terminal; with geigering at Carmody Field and every other entry point to the Principality of Naples, they should have caught every fissionable atom coming in, and it simply did not seem reasonable that anyone in the principality itself could produce nuclear fuel to make a bomb.

Unless they were not looking for bombs, but for people who might want to use them. But that didn't tie in with what I had been taught as a cadet at the Home Office.

*

There was a crackle and an unrecognizable roar from the station's public-address system. Then the crowd noises died down as people strained to listen, and I began to understand the words: "...where you are in an orderly fashion until this investigation is concluded. You will not be delayed more than a few minutes. Do not, repeat, do not attempt to leave until this man has been captured. Attention! Attention! All persons in this area! Under Company law, you are ordered to stop all activities and stand still at once. An investigation is being carried out in this building. All persons will stand still and remain where you are in an orderly fashion until this investigation..."

The mounting babble drowned the speaker out again, but I had heard enough.

I suppose I was wrong, but I had been taught that my duty was to serve the world, by serving the Company, in all ways at all times. I walked briskly toward the nearest squad of expediters, who were already breaking up into detachments and moving about among the halted knots of civilians, peering at faces, asking questions.

I didn't quite make it; I hadn't gone more than five yards when a heavy hand fell on my shoulder, and a harsh voice snarled in the Neapolitan dialect, "Halt, you! Didn't you hear the orders?"

I spun, staggering slightly, to face an armed expediter-officer. I stood at attention and said crisply, "Sorry. I'm Thomas Wills, Claims Adjuster. I thought I might be able to help."

The officer stared at me for a moment. His cheeks moved; I had the impression that, under other circumstances, he would have spat on the floor at my feet. "Papers!" he ordered.

I passed him my travel orders. He looked them over briefly, then returned them. Like the Customs expediter at Carmody Field, he gave me a snap salute, militarily precise and, in a way I could not quite define, contemptuous. "You should just stay here, Adjuster Wills," he advised—in a tone that made it a command. "This will be over in a moment."

He was gone, back to his post. I stood for a moment, but it was easier to listen to his orders than to obey them; the Neapolitan crowd didn't seem to take too well to discipline, and though there was no overt resistance to the search squads, there was a sort of Brownian movement of individuals in the throng that kept edging me back and away from where I had been standing. It made me a little uncomfortable; I was standing close to the edge of a platform, and a large poster announced that the Milan Express was due to arrive on that track at any moment. In fact, I could hear the thin, effeminate whistle of its Diesel locomotive just beyond the end of the platform. I tried to inch my way from the edge. I dodged around an electric baggage cart, and trod heavily on someone's foot.

*

"Excuse me," I said quickly, looking at the man. He glared back at me. There was a bright spark in his eyes; I could tell little about his expression because, oddly enough in that country of clean-shaven faces, he wore a heavy, ragged, clipped beard. He wore the uniform of a porter. He mumbled something I could not quite catch, and moved as if to push me away. I suppose I put up my arm. My papers, with the Company seal bright gold upon them, were still in my hand, and the bearded man caught sight of them.

10

SUPER PACK

If there had been anger in his eyes before, there was now raging fury. He shrilled, "Beast! Animal!" He thrust at me blindly and leaped past me, out of the shelter of the bags; he went spinning furiously through the crowd, men and women ricocheting off him.

I heard a harsh bellow: "There he goes! Zorchi! Zorchi!" And I could hear the bearded man shrieking curses as he hurtled up the platform, up toward the oncoming train, over to the edge—and off the platform to the tracks!

He fell less than a yard in front of the slim nose of the Diesel. I don't suppose the speed of the train was even five miles an hour, but the engineer hadn't a chance in the world to stop.

While I watched, struck motionless, along with all the others on that platform, the engine passed over the huddled form. The brakes were shrieking, but it was much, much too late. Even in that moment I thought he would not be killed—not instantly, at least, unless he died of loss of blood. The trunk of his body was safely in the well between the tracks. But his legs were sprawled over a rail. And the slow click-click of the wheels didn't stop until his uniformed body was far out of sight. It was shocking, sickening, unbelievable.

And it didn't stop there. A strange thing happened. When the man had dived into the path of the train, there was a sudden fearful hush; it had happened too suddenly for anyone to cry out. And when the hush ended, there was only a momentary, instinctive gasp of horror. Then there was a quick, astonished babble of voices—and then cheers! And applause, and ringing bravos!

I didn't understand.

The man had thrown himself deliberately under the train. I was sure of it. Was that something to cheer?

*

I finally made it to where the Regional Director was waiting for me—nearly an hour late.

It was at a hotel overlooking the Bay, and the sight was thrilling enough to put the unpleasant accident I had seen out of my mind for a moment. There was nothing so beautiful in all the world, I thought, as the Bay of Naples at sunset. It was not only my own opinion; I had seen it described many times in the travel folders I had pored over, while my wife indulgently looked over my shoulder, back in those remote days of marriage. "La prima vista del mundo," the folders had called it—the most beautiful sight of the world. They had said: "See Naples, and die."

I hadn't known, of course, that Marianna would die first...

But that was all behind me. After Marianna's death, a lot of things had happened, all in a short time, and some of them very bad. But good or bad, I had laid down a law for myself: I would not dwell on them. I had started on a new life, and, I was going to put the past in a locked compartment in my mind. I had to!

I was no longer an ordinary civilian, scraping together his Blue Heaven premiums for the sake of a roof over his head, budgeting his food policies, carrying on his humdrum little job. I was a servant of the human race and a member of the last surviving group of gentleman-adventurers in all the world: I was an Insurance Claims Adjuster for the Company!

All the same, I couldn't quite forget some of the bad things that had happened, as I walked into the hotel dining room to meet the Regional Director.

*

Regional Director Gogarty was a huge, pale balloon of a man. He was waiting for me at a table set for four. As he greeted me, his expression was sour. "Glad to meet you, Wills. Bad business, this. Bad business. He got away with it again."

I coughed. "Sir?" I asked.

"Zorchi!" he snapped. And I remembered the name I had heard on the platform. The madman! "Zorchi, Luigi Zorchi, the human jellyfish. Wills, do you know that that man has just cashed in on his twelfth disability policy? And not a thing we could do to stop him! You were there. You saw it, didn't you?"

"Well, yes, but—"

"Thought so. The twelfth! And your driver said on the phone it was both legs this time. Both legs—and on a common carrier. Double indemnity!" He shook his enormous head. "And with a whole corps of expediters standing by to stop him!"

I said with some difficulty, "Sir, do you mean that the man I saw run over by the train was—"

"Luigi Zorchi. That's who he was. Ever hear of him, Wills?"

"Can't say I have."

Gogarty nodded his balloonlike head. "The Company has kept it out of the papers, of course, but you can't keep anything from being gossiped about around here. This Zorchi is practically a national hero in Naples. He's damn near a millionaire by now, I guess, and every lira of it has come right out of the Company's indemnity funds. And do you think we can do anything about it? Not a thing! Not even when we're tipped off ahead of time—when, what, and where!

"He just laughs at us. I know for a fact," Gogarty said bitterly, "that Zorchi knew we found out he was going to dive in front of that express tonight. He was just daring us to stop him. We should have! We should have figured he might disguise himself as a porter. We should—"

I interrupted, "Mr. Gogarty, are you trying to tell me this man *deliberately* maims himself for the accident insurance?" Gogarty nodded sourly. "Good heavens," I cried, "that's disloyal!"

Gogarty laughed sharply and brought me up standing. There was a note to the way he laughed that I didn't like; for a moment there, I thought he was thinking of my own little—well, indiscretion. But he said only, "It's expensive, too." I suppose he meant nothing by it. But I was sensitive on the subject.

Before I could ask him any more questions, the massive face smoothed out in a smile. He rose ponderously, greeting someone. "Here they are, Wills," he said jovially. "The girls!"

The headwaiter was conducting two young ladies toward us. I remembered my manners and stood up, but I confess I was surprised. I had heard that discipline in the field wasn't the same as at the Home Office, but after all—Gogarty was a Regional Director!

It was a little informal of him to arrange our first meeting at dinner, in the first place. But to make a social occasion of it was—in the straitlaced terms of the Home Office where I had been trained—almost unthinkable.

And it was apparent that the girls were mere decoration. I had a hundred eager questions to ask Gogarty—about this mad Zorchi, about my duties, about Company policy here in the principality of Naples—but it would be far out of line to bring up Company matters with these females present. I was not pleased, but I managed to be civil.

The girls were decorative enough, I had to admit.

Gogarty said expansively, all trace of ill humor gone, "This is Signorina dell'Angela and Miss Susan Manchester. Rena and Susan, this is Tom Wills." I said stiffly, "Delighted."

Susan was the blonde one, a small plump girl with the bubbly smile of a professional model. She greeted Gogarty affectionately. The other was dark and lovely, but with a constant shadow, almost glowering, in her eyes.

So we had a few drinks. Then we had a few more. Then the captain appeared with a broad menu, and I found myself in an embarrassing position. For Gogarty waved the menu aside with a gesture of mock disgust. "Save it for the peasants," he ordered. "We don't want that Blue Plate slop. We'll start with those little baby shrimps like I had last night, and then an antipasto and after that—"

I broke in apologetically, "Mr. Gogarty, I have only a Class-B policy."

Gogarty blinked at me. "What?"

I cleared my throat. "I have only Class-B coverage on my Blue Plate policy," I repeated. "I, uh, I never went in much for such—"

He looked at me incredulously. "Boy," he said, "this is on the Company. Now relax and let me order. Blue Plate coverage is for the peasants; I eat like a human being."

It shook me a little. Here was a Regional Director talking about the rations supplied under the Company's Blue Plate coverage as "slop." Oh, I wasn't naive enough to think that no one talked that way. There were a certain number of malcontents anywhere. I'd heard that kind of talk, and even worse, once in a while from the Class-D near-uninsurables, the soreheads with a grudge against the world who blamed all their troubles on the Company and bleated about the "good old days." Mostly they did their bleating when it was premium time, I'd noticed.

But I certainly never expected it from Gogarty.

Still—it was his party. And he seemed like a pretty nice guy. I had to allow him the defects of his virtues, I decided. If he was less reverent to the Company than he should have been, at least by the same token he was friendly and democratic. He had at least twenty years seniority on me, and back at the Home Office a mere Claims Adjuster wouldn't have been at the same table with a Regional Director. And here he was feeding me better than I had ever eaten in my life, talking as though we were equals, even (I reminded myself) seeing to it that we had the young ladies to keep us company.

*

We were hours at dinner, hours and endless glasses of wine, and we talked continually. But the conversation never came close to official business.

The girl Rena was comfortable to be with, I found. There was that deep, eternal sadness in her eyes, and every once in a while I came up against it in the middle of a laugh; but she was soft-voiced and pleasant, and undeniably lovely. Marianna had been prettier, I thought, but Marianna's voice was harsh Midwest while Rena's—

I stopped myself.

When we were on our after-dinner liqueurs, Rena excused herself for a moment and, after a few minutes, I spotted her standing by a satin-draped window, looking wistfully out over a balcony. Gogarty winked.

I got up and, a little unsteadily, went over to her. "Shall we look at this more closely?" I asked her. She smiled and we stepped outside.

Again I was looking down on the Bay of Naples—a scene painted in moonlight this time, instead of the orange hues of sunset. It was warm, but the Moon was frosty white in the sky. Even its muddled reflection in the slagged waters was grayish white, not yellow. There was a pale orange halo over the crater of Mount Vesuvius, to our left; and far down the coast a bluish phosphorescence, over the horizon, marked Pompeii. "Beautiful," I said.

She looked at me strangely. All she said was, "Let's go back inside."

Gogarty greeted us. "Looking at the debris?" he demanded jovially. "Not much to see at night. Cheer up, Tom. You'll see all the damage you want to see over the next few days."

I said, "I hope so, sir."

Gogarty shook his head reprovingly. "Not 'sir,' Tom. Save that for the office. Call me Sam." He beamed. "You want to know what it was like here during the war? You can ask the girls. They were here all through. Especially Susan—she was with the Company's branch here, even before I took over. Right, Susan?"

"Right, Sam," she said obediently.

Gogarty nodded. "Not that Rena missed much either, but she was out of town when the Sicilians came over. Weren't you?" he demanded, curiously intent. Rena nodded silently. "Naples sure took a pasting," Gogarty went on. "It was pretty tough for a while. Did you know that the Sicilians actually made a landing right down the coast at Pompeii?"

"I saw the radioactivity," I said.

"That's right. They got clobbered, all right. Soon's the barges were in, the Neapolitans let them have it. But it cost them. The Company only allowed them five A-bombs each, and they had to use two more to knock out Palermo. And— well, they don't like to tell this on themselves, but one of the others was a dud. Probably the only dud A-bomb in history, I guess."

He grinned at Rena. Astonishingly, Rena smiled back.

She was, I thought, a girl of many astonishing moments; I had not thought that she would be amused at Gogarty's heavy-handed needling.

*

Gogarty went on and on. I was interested enough—I had followed the Naples–Sicily war in the papers and, of course, I'd been briefed at the Home Office before coming over—but the girls seemed to find it pretty dull. By the time Gogarty finished telling me about the Sicilian attempt to trigger Mt. Vesuvius by dropping an A-bomb into its crater, Rena was frankly bored and even Susan was yawning behind her palm.

We finally wound up under the marquee of the restaurant. Gogarty and the blonde politely said good night, and disappeared into a cab. It was clearly up to me to take Rena home.

I hailed a cab. When I made up my new insurance schedule at the Home Office before coming over, I splurged heavily on transportation coverage. Perhaps I was making up for the luxuries of travel that life with Marianna hadn't allowed me. Anyway, I'd taken out Class AA policies. And as the cab driver clipped my coupons he was extremely polite.

Rena lived a long way from the hotel. I tried to make small talk, but she seemed to have something on her mind. I was in the middle of telling her about the terrible "accident" I had seen that evening at the station—suitably censored, of course—when I observed she was staring out the window.

She hadn't been paying attention while I talked, but she noticed the silence when I stopped. She gave a little shake of the head and looked at me. "I'm sorry, Mr. Wills," she said. "I am being rude."

"Not at all," I said gallantly.

"Yes." She nodded and smiled, but it was a thoughtful, almost a sad, smile. "You are too polite, you gentlemen of the Company. Is that part of your training?"

"It's easy to be polite to you, Miss dell'Angela," I said by rote. Yes, it was part of our training: A Claims Adjuster is always courteous. But what I said was true enough, all the same. She was a girl that I enjoyed being polite to.

"No, truly," she persisted. "You are an important officer in the Company, and you must have trained long for the post. What did they teach you?"

"Well—" I hesitated—"just the sort of thing you'd expect, I guess. A little statistical mathematics—enough so we can understand what the actuaries mean. Company policies, business methods, administration. Then, naturally, we had a lot of morale sessions. A Claims Adjuster—" I cleared my throat, feeling a little selfconscious—"a Claims Adjuster is supposed to be like Caesar's wife, you know. He must always set an example to his staff and to the public. I guess that sounds pretty stuffy. I don't mean it to be. But there is a lot of emphasis on tradition and honor and discipline."

She asked, rather oddly, "And is there a course in loyalty?"

"Why, I suppose you might say that. There are ceremonies, you know. And it's a matter of cadet honor to put the Company ahead of personal affairs." "And do all Claims Adjusters live by this code?"

For a moment I couldn't answer. It was like a blow in the face. I turned sharply to look at her, but there was no expression on her face, only a mild polite curiosity. I said with difficulty, "Miss dell'Angela, what are you getting at?"

"Why, nothing!" Her face was as angelic as her name.

"I don't know what you mean or what you may have heard about me, Miss dell'Angela, but I can tell you this, if you are interested. When my wife died, I went to pieces. I admit it. I said a lot of things I shouldn't have, and some of them may have reflected against the Company. I'm not trying to deny that but, you understand, I was upset at the time. I'm not upset now." I took a deep breath. "To me, the Company is the savior of humanity. I don't want to sound like a fanatic, but I am loyal to the Company, to the extent of putting it ahead of my personal affairs, to the extent of doing whatever job the Company assigns to me. And, if necessary, to the extent of dying for it if I have to. Is that clear?"

Well, that was a conversation-stopper, of course. I hadn't meant to get all wound up about it, but it hurt to find out that there had been gossip. The dell'Angela girl merely said: "Quite clear."

We rode in silence for a while. She was staring out the window again, and I didn't especially want to talk just then. Maybe I was too sensitive. But there was no doubt in my mind that the Company was the white hope of the world, and I didn't like being branded a traitor because of what I'd said after Marianna died. I was, in a way, paying the penalty for it—it had been made pretty clear to me that I was on probation. That was enough.

As I said, she lived a long way from the Gran Reale. I had plenty of time for my flare-up, and for brooding, and for getting over it.

But we never did get around to much idle conversation on that little trip. By the time I had simmered down, I began to have disturbing thoughts. It suddenly occurred to me that I was a man, and she was a girl, and we were riding in a cab. I don't know how else to say it. At one moment I was taking her home from a dinner; and at the next, I was taking her home from a date. Nothing had changed— except the way I looked at it.

All of a sudden, I began to feel as though I were fourteen years old again. It had been quite a long time since I had had the duty of escorting a beautiful girl—and by then I realized this was a really *beautiful* girl—home at the end of an evening. And I was faced with the question that I had thought would never bother me again at least a decade before. Should I kiss her good night?

It was a problem, and I thought about it, feeling a little foolish but rather happy about it. But all my thinking came to nothing. She decided for me.

The cab stopped in front of a white stucco wall. Like so many of the better Italian homes, the wall enclosed a garden, and the house was in the middle of the garden. It was an attractive enough place—Class A at least, I thought—though it was hard to tell in the moonlight.

I cleared my throat and sort of halfway leaned over to her.

Then she turned and was looking up at me, and the moonlight glinted brightly off what could only have been tears in her eyes.

I stared.

She didn't say a word. She shook her head briefly, opened the door and was gone behind the gate.

It was a puzzlement. Why had she been crying? What had I done?

I reviewed my conduct all the way back to the hotel, but nothing much came of it. Perhaps I had been brusque—but brusque enough to bring tears? I couldn't believe it.

Curious new life! I fell asleep with the pale moon shining in the window, brooding about the life I was just beginning, and about the old life behind me that was buried in the same grave with Marianna.

CHAPTER TWO

The Naples branch of the Company lay in the heart of the city. I took a cab to a sort of dome-roofed thing called a galleria, and walked under its skeletal steel ceiling to my new office. Once the galleria had been roofed with glass, but the glass had powdered down from the concussion of the Mt. Vesuvius bomb, or the Capodichino bomb, or one of the other hammerblows the Sicilians had rained on the principality of Naples in the recent unpleasantness.

I entered the office and looked around. The blonde girl named Susan appeared to double as the office receptionist. She nodded efficiently and waved me to a fenced-off enclosure where Sam Gogarty sat, plump and untroubled, at an enormous desk.

I pushed open the swinging gate.

Gogarty looked at me icily. "You're late," he said.

He had no hangover, it was clear. I said apologetically, "Sorry, I'm—"

"Never mind. Just don't let it happen again." It was clear that, in the office, business was business; the fact that we had been drinking together the night before would not condone liberties the morning after. Gogarty said, "Your desk is over there, Wills. Better get started."

I felt considerably deflated as I sat down at my desk and stared unhappily at the piles of blue and yellow manifolds before me.

The Company had trained me well. I didn't need to be coached in order to get through the work; it was all a matter of following established techniques and precedents. I checked the coverage, reduced the claim to tape-code, fed the tapes into a machine.

If the claim was legitimate, the machine computed the amounts due and issued a punch-card check. If there was anything wrong, the machine flashed a red light and spat the faulty claim out into a hopper.

And there were plenty of claims. Every adult in Naples, of course, carried the conventional War-and-Disaster policy—the so-called Blue

Bolt coverage. Since few of them had actually been injured in the war, the claims were small—mostly for cost of premiums on other policies, under the disability clauses. (For if war prevented a policyholder from meeting his Blue Plate premiums, for instance, the Company itself under Blue Bolt would keep his policies paid—and the policyholder fed.)

But there were some big claims, too. The Neapolitan government had carried the conventional Blue Bolt policies and, though the policy had been canceled by the Company before hostilities broke out—thus relieving the Company of the necessity of paying damages to the principality of Naples itself—still there were all the subsidiary loss and damage claims of the Neapolitan government's bureaus and departments, almost every one of them non-canceling.

It amounted to billions and billions of lire. Just looking at the amounts on some of the vouchers before me made my head swim. And the same, of course, would be true in Sicily. Though that would naturally be handled by the Sicilian office, not by us.

However, the cost of this one brief, meager little war between Naples and Sicily, with less than ten thousand casualties, lasting hardly more than a week, must have set the Company's reserves back hundreds of millions of dollars.

And to think that some people didn't like the Company! Why, without it, the whole peninsula of Italy would have been in financial ruin, the solvent areas dragged down with the combatants!

Naturally, the Regional Office was understaffed for this volume of work—which is why they had flown in new Adjusters like myself.

*

I looked up from my desk, surprised. Susan was standing next to me, an aspirin and a paper cup of water in her hand. "You look like you might need this," she whispered. She winked and was gone.

I swallowed it gratefully, although my hangover was almost gone. I was finding in these dry papers all the romance and excitement I had joined the Company's foreign service for. Here before me were human lives, drama, tragedy, even an occasional touch of human-interest comedy.

For the Company was supporting most of Naples and whatever affected a Neapolitan life showed up somehow in the records of the Company.

It was a clean, *dedicated* feeling to work for the Company. The monks of the Middle Ages might have had something of the same positive conviction that their work in the service of a mighty churchly empire was right and just, but surely no one since.

I attacked the mountain of forms with determination, taking pleasure in the knowledge that every one I processed meant one life helped by the Company.

It was plain in history, for all to see. Once the world had been turbulent and distressed, and the Company had smoothed it out. It had started with fires and disease. When the first primitive insurance companies—there were more than one, in the early days—began offering protection against the hazards of fire, they had found it wise to try to prevent fires. There were the advertising campaigns with their wistful-eyed bears pleading with smokers not to drop their lighted cigarettes in the dry forest; the technical bureaus like the Underwriter's Laboratory, testing electrical equipment, devising intricate and homely gimmicks like the underwriter's knot; the Fire Patrol in the big cities that followed up the city-owned Fire Department; the endless educational sessions in the schools... And fires decreased.

Then there was life insurance. Each time a death benefit was paid, a digit rang up on the actuarial scoreboard. Was tuberculosis a major killer? Establish mobile chest X-rays; alert the people to the meaning of a chronic cough. Was it heart disease? Explain the dangers of overweight, the idiocy of exercise past forty. People lived longer.

Health insurance followed the same pattern. It had begun by paying for bills incurred during sickness, and ended by providing full medical sickness prevention and treatment for all. Elaborate research programs reduced the danger of disease to nearly nothing. Only a few rare cases, like that of Marianna...

I shook myself away from the thought. Anyway, it was neither fire nor health insurance that concerned me now, but the Blue Bolt anti-war complex of the Company's policies. It was easy enough to see how it had come about. For with fire and accident and disease ameliorated by the strong protecting hand of the Company, only one major hazard remained—war.

And so the Company had logically and inevitably resolved to wipe out war.

*

I looked up. It was Susan again, this time with a cardboard container of coffee. "You're an angel," I said. She set the coffee down and turned to go. I looked quickly around to make sure that Gogarty was busy, and stopped her. "Tell me something?"

"Sure."

"About this girl, Rena. Does she work for the Company?"

Susan giggled. "Heavens, no. What an idea!"

"What's so strange about it?"

She straightened out her face. "You'd better ask Sam—Mr. Gogarty, that is.

Didn't you have a chance to talk to her last night? Or were you too busy with other things?"

"I only want to know how she happened to be with you."

Susan shrugged. "Sam thought you'd like to meet her, I guess. Really, you'll have to ask him. All I know is that she's been in here quite a lot about some claims. But she doesn't work here, believe me." She wrinkled her nose in amusement. "And I won't work here either, if I don't get back to my desk."

I took the hint. By lunch time, I had got through a good half of the accumulation on my desk. I ate briefly and not too well at a nearby trattoria with a "B" on the Blue Plate medallion in its window. After the dinner of the night before, I more than half agreed with Gogarty's comments about the Blue Plate menus.

Gogarty called me over when I got back to the office. He said, "I haven't had a chance to talk to you about Luigi Zorchi."

I nodded eagerly. I had been hoping for some explanations.

Gogarty went on, "Since you were on the scene when he took his dive, you might as well follow up. God knows you can't do worse than the rest of us."

I said dubiously, "Well, I saw the accident, if that's what you mean."

"Accident! What accident? This is the twelfth time he's done it, I tell you." He tossed a file folder at me. "Take a look! Loss of limbs—four times. Internal injuries—six times. Loss of vision, impaired hearing, hospitalization and so on— good lord, I can't count the number of separate claims. And, every one, he has collected on. Go ahead, look it over."

I peered at the folder. The top sheet was a field report on the incident I had watched, when the locomotive of the Milan express had severed both legs. The one below it, dated five weeks earlier, was for flash burns suffered in the explosion of a stove, causing the loss of the right forearm nearly to the elbow.

Curious, I thought, I hadn't noticed anything when I saw the man on the platform. Still, I hadn't paid too much attention to him at first, and modern prosthetic devices were nearly miraculous. I riffled through the red-bordered sheets. The fifth claim down, nearly two years before, was—

I yelped, "Mr. Gogarty! This is a fraud!"

"What?"

"Look at this! 'On 21st October, the insured suffered severe injuries while trapped in a rising elevator with faulty safety equipment, resulting in loss of both legs above knees, multiple lacerations of—' Well, never mind the rest of it. But look at that, Mr. Gogarty! He already lost both legs! He can't lose them twice, can he?"

Gogarty sat back in his chair, looking at me oddly. "You startled me," he complained. "Wills, what have I been trying to tell you? That's the whole point, boy! No, he didn't lose his legs twice. It was five times!"

I goggled at him. "But—"

"But, but. But he did. Wait a minute—" he held up a hand to stop my questions—"just take a look through the folder. See for yourself." He waited while, incredulously, I finished going through the dossier. It was true. I looked at Gogarty wordlessly.

He said resentfully, "You see what we're up against? And none of the things you are about to say would help. There is no mistake in the records—they've been double and triple-checked. There is no possibility that another man, or men, substituted for Zorchi—fingerprints have checked every time. The three times he lost his arms, retina-prints checked. There is no possibility that the doctors were bribed, or that he lost a little bit more of his leg, for instance, in each accident—the severed sections were recovered, and they were complete. Wills, *this guy grows new arms and legs like a crab!*"

I looked at him in a daze. "What a fantastic scientific discovery!" I said.

He snorted. "Fantastic pain in the neck! Zorchi can't go on like this; he'll bankrupt the Company. We can't stop him. Even when we were tipped off this time—we couldn't stop him. And I'll tell you true, Wills, that platform was loaded with our men when Zorchi made his dive. You weren't the only Adjuster of the Company there."

He picked a folded sheet of paper out of his desk. "Here. Zorchi is still in the hospital; no visitors allowed today. But I want you to take these credentials and go to see him tomorrow. You came to us with a high recommendation from the Home Office, Wills—" That made me look at him sharply, but his expression was innocent. "You're supposed to be a man of intelligence and resourcefulness. See if you can come up with some ideas on dealing with that situation. I'd handle it myself, but I've got—" he grimaced—"certain other minor administrative difficulties to deal with. Oh, nothing important, but you might as well know that there appears to be a little, well, popular underground resentment toward the Company around here."

"Incredible!" I said.

He looked at me thoughtfully for a moment. "Well," he said, "it's quitting time. See you in the morning."

I had a lonely dinner at the same cheap restaurant where I'd had my lunch. I spent an hour in my room with my Company-issued *Adjuster's Handbook*, looking for some precedent that had some sort of bearing on the case of a man who could grow new arms and legs. There wasn't anything, of course. I went out for a walk... and still it wasn't nearly time for me to retire to bed.

So I did what I had been avoiding doing. I looked in the phone book for Rena dell'Angela's number. There was, it developed, a Benedetto dell'Angela at the address she'd given the cab driver; but the phone was disconnected.

So I wandered around some more, and then I went to sleep, dreaming about Benedetto dell'Angela. I saw him as a leather-faced, white-bearded and courtly old gentleman. Rena's father, surely. Possibly even her elder brother. Certainly not her husband.

It was a dull finish to the first full day of my rich, exciting new life...

*

The "minor administrative difficulties" got major. So I didn't get to see Zorchi the next day, after all.

A Junior Adjuster named Hammond—he was easily sixty, but the slow-moving, unenterprising type that would stay junior till the day he died—came white-faced into the office a few minutes after opening and huddled with Gogarty for a quarter of an hour.

Then Gogarty called me over. He said, "We're having a spot of trouble. Hammond needs a little help; you're elected. Draw what you need, take a couple of expediters along, report back to me this evening."

Hammond and I stopped at the cashier's office to draw three dispatch-cases full of lira-notes. Outside, an armored car was waiting for us, with a full crew of six uniformed expediters. We raced off down the narrow streets with the sirens wailing, climbing the long hill road past the radioactive remains of Capodichino, heading out toward the farmlands.

Hammond worriedly filled me in on the way. He had got in early to his branch office that morning, but no earlier than the first of a long line of policyholders. There had, it appeared, been some kind of rumor spread that the Company was running out of money. It was preposterous on the face of it—after all, who printed the money?—but you can't argue with a large group of people and, before the official hour of opening the branch, there were more than a hundred in the knotted line outside the door.

Hammond had rushed into the Naples office for help, leaving his staff to do the best they could. He said gloomily, staring out through the view-slits at the farmlands and vineyards we were passing through, "I just hope we still have a branch office. This is a bad spot, Wills. Caserta. It got bombed out, you know; the whole southern end of the town is radioactive. And it has a long history of trouble. Used to be the summer royal seat of the old Italian monarchy; then the Americans used it for a command headquarters in the war Mussolini got into—the first atom war.

It's been fought over time and again."

I said reasonably, "But don't they know the Company has all the resources in the world?"

"Sure they do—when they're thinking. Right now they're not thinking. They've got it in their heads that the Company isn't going to pay off. They're scared. You can't tell them anything. You can't even give them checks—they want cash on the line."

SUPER PACK

I said, "That's pretty silly, isn't it? I mean—ugh!" I retched, as I suddenly got a whiff of the most unpleasant and penetrating odor I had ever encountered in my life. It was like death and destruction in gaseous form; a sickly sweet, clinging stink that oozed in through the pores of my skin to turn my stomach. "Wow!" I said, gasping.

Hammond looked at me in bewilderment; then he grinned sourly. "New here, aren't you?" he inquired. "That's hemp. They grow the stuff for the fibers; and to get the fibers out, they let it get good and rotten. You'll get used to it," he promised.

I tried. I tried pretty hard to get used to it; I hardly heard a word he said all the rest of the way in to Caserta, I was trying so hard. But I didn't get used to it.

Then I had my mind taken off my troubles. The branch was still doing business when we got there, though there were easily three or four hundred angrily shouting policyholders milling around in front of it. They scattered before us as the armored car came racing in; we skidded to a stop, siren blasting, and the expediters leaped out with their weapons at the ready.

Hammond and I climbed out of the armored car with our bags of money. There was an audible excitement in the crowd as the word spread back that the Company had brought in enormous stores of lire, more than any man had ever seen, to pay off the claims. We could hear the chatter of many voices, and we almost could feel the tension slack off.

It looked like the trouble was over.

Then there was a shrill whistle. It sounded very much like the alarm whistle of one of our expediters but, thinking back, I have never been sure.

Perhaps it was a nervous expediter, perhaps it was an agent provocateur in the crowd. But, whoever pulled the trigger, the explosion went off.

There was a ragged yell from the crowd, and rocks began whizzing through the air. The pacifists in the mob began heading for the

29

doorways and alleys around; women screamed, men shouted and bellowed, and for a moment it looked like we would be swamped. For not very many of them were pacifists, and there were at least a hundred screaming, gesticulating men lunging at us.

One cobblestone shattered the theoretically unbreakable windshield of the truck next to my head; then the expediters, gas guns spitting, were ringing around us to protect the money.

It was a short fight but vicious. By the time the first assault was repulsed there were at least fifty persons lying motionless in the street.

I had never seen that sort of violence before. It did something to my stomach. I stood weaving, holding to the armored car, while the expediters circled the area around the branch office, firing hurry-up shots at the running rioters. Hammond looked at me questioningly.

"That smell," I said apologetically.

He said only, "Sure." True, the fetid aroma from the hemp fields was billowing all around us, but he knew as well as I that it was not the smell that was bothering me.

In a few moments, as we were locking the bags of money into the office safe, redcrossed vehicles bearing the Company insignia appeared in the street outside, and medics began tending to the victims. Each one got a shot of something—an antidote to the sleep-gas from the expediters' guns, I guessed—and was loaded unceremoniously into the ambulances.

Hammond appeared beside me. "Ready for business?" he asked. "They'll be back any minute now, the ones that can still walk. We'll be paying off until midnight, the way it looks."

I said, "Sure. That—that gas doesn't hurt them any, does it? I mean, after they go to the hospital they'll be all right, won't they?"

Hammond, twirling a pencil in his fingers, stared broodingly at the motionless body of one policyholder. He was a well-dressed man of fifty or so, with a reddish mustache, unusual in that area, and shattered rimless glasses. Not at all the type I would expect to see in a street fight; probably, I thought, a typical innocent bystander.

Hammond said absently, "Oh, sure. They'll be all right. Never know what hit them." There was a tiny sharp crack and the two halves of the pencil fell to the floor. He looked at it in surprise. "Come on, Wills. Let's get to work."

CHAPTER THREE

Of course I still believed in the Company.

But all the same, it was the first time since I went to work for the Company that I had even had to ask myself that question.

That long, long day in Hammond's puny little branch office, sweltering in the smell of the hemp fields, pushing across the mountains of lire to the grimfaced policyholders left me a little less sure of things. Nearly all of the first hundred or so to pass my desk had been in the crowd that the expediters had fired on. A few had fresh bandages to show where stones had missed the expediters, but found targets all the same. Nearly all of them were hostile. There was no casual conversation, very few "*Grazies*" as they received their payments.

But at last the day was at an end. Hammond snapped an order to one of the clerks, who shoved his way through the dwindling line to close the door and bang down the shutters. I put through the last few applications, and we were through.

It was hot and muggy out in the streets of New Caserta. Truce teams of expediters were patrolling the square, taken off their regular assignments of enforcing the peace between Naples and Sicily to keep down Caserta's own mobs. Hammond suggested dinner, and we went to a little Blue Plate in the palace itself.

Hammond held Class-A food policies, but he was politeness itself; he voluntarily led the way to the Class-B area. We presented our policy-cards to the waiter for canceling, and sat back to enjoy the air conditioning.

I was still troubled over the violence. I said, "Has there been any trouble around here before?"

Hammond said ruefully, "Plenty. All over Europe, if you want my opinion. Of course, you never see it in the papers, but I've heard stories from field workers.

They practically had a revolution in the Sudeten strip after the Prague-Vienna affair." He stopped talking as the waiter set his

Meal-of-the-Day in front of him. Hammond looked at it sourly. "Oh, the hell with it, Wills," he said. "Have a drink with me to wash this stuff down."

*

We ordered liquor, and Hammond shoved his Class-A card at the waiter. I am not a snoop, but I couldn't help noticing that the liquor coupons were nearly all gone; at his present rate, Hammond would use up his year's allotment by the end of the summer, and be paying cash for his drinks.

Dinner was dull. Hammond made it dull, because he was much more interested in his drinking than in me. Though I was never much of a drinker, I'd had a little experience in watching others tank up; Hammond I classified as the surly and silent type. He wasn't quite rude to me, but after the brandy with his coffee, and during the three or four straight whiskies that followed that, he hardly spoke to me at all.

We left the Blue Plate in a strained silence and, after the cooled restaurant, the heat outside was painful. The air was absolutely static, and the odor from the hemp fields soaked into our clothes like a bath in a sewer.

Overhead it was nearly dark, and there were low black clouds. "We'd better get going," I ventured. "Looks like rain."

Hammond said nothing, only grunted. He lurched ahead of me toward the narrow street that led back to the branch office, where our transport was waiting.

The distance was easily half a mile. Now I am not terribly lazy, and even in the heat I was willing enough to walk. But I didn't want to get caught in a rain. Maybe it was superstition on my part—I knew that the danger was really slight—but I couldn't forget that three separate atomic explosions had gone off in the area around Caserta and Naples within only a few months, and there was going to be a certain amount of radioactivity in every drop of rain that fell for a hundred miles around.

I started to tell Hammond about it, but he made a disgusted noise and stumbled ahead.

It wasn't as if we had to walk. Caserta was not well equipped with cabs, but there were a few; and both Hammond and myself ranked high enough in the Company to have been able to get a lift from one of the expediter cars that were cruising about.

There was a flare of lightning over the eastern mountains and, in a moment, the pounding roll of thunder. And a flat globule of rain splattered on my face.

I said, "Hammond, let's wait here for a lift."

Surprisingly he came along with me.

If he hadn't, I would have left him in the street.

*

We were in a street of tenements. It was almost deserted; I rapped on the nearest door. No answer, no sound inside. I rapped again, then tried the door. It was locked.

The next door—ancient and rickety as the first—was also locked, and no one answered. The third door, no one answered. By then it was raining hard; the knob turned under my fingers, and we stepped inside.

We left the door ajar, on the chance that a squad car or cab might pass, and for light. It was almost dark outside, apart from the light from the lightning flashes, but even so it was darker within. There was no light at all in the narrow, odorous hall; not even a light seeping under the apartment doors.

In the lightning flare, Hammond's face was pale. He was beginning to sober up, and his manner was uneasy.

We were there perhaps half an hour in that silent hall, watching the rain sleet down and the lightning flare and listening to the thunder. Two or three times, squad cars passed, nosing slowly down the drenched streets, but though Hammond looked longingly at them, I still didn't want to get wet.

Then the rain slowed and almost simultaneously a civilian cab appeared at the head of the block. "Come on," I said, tugging at his arm.

He balked. "Wait for a squad car," he mumbled.

"Why? Come on, Hammond, it may start to pour again in a minute."

"No!"

His behavior was exasperating me. Clearly it wasn't that he was too niggardly to pay for the cab; it was almost as if he were delaying going back to the branch office for some hidden reason. But that was ridiculous, of course.

I said, "Look, you can stay here if you want to, but I'm going." I jumped out of the doorway just in time to flag the cab; it rolled to a stop, and the driver backed to where I was standing. As I got in, I looked once more to the doorway where Hammond was standing, his face unreadable.

He made a gesture of some sort, but the lightning flashed again and I skipped into the cab. When I looked again he was invisible inside the doorway, and I told the driver to take me to the branch office of the Company.

Curious; but it was not an end to curious things that night. At the branch office, my car was waiting to take me back to Naples.

I surrendered my travel coupons to the cab driver and jumped from one vehicle to the other.

Before my driver could start, someone appeared at the window of the car and a sharp voice said, "Un momento, Signore 'Ammond!"

I stared at the man, a rather badly dressed Neapolitan. I said angrily, "Hammond isn't here!"

The man's expression changed. It had been belligerent; it now became astonished and apologetic. "A thousand times excuse me," he said. "The Signore 'Ammond, can you say where he is?"

I hesitated, but only for a moment. I didn't like the little man peering in my window, however humble and conciliatory he had become. I said abruptly, "No." And my driver took off, leaving the man standing there.

I turned to look back at him as we drove off.

It was ridiculous, but the way he was standing as we left, holding one hand in his pocket, eyes narrowed and thoughtful, made me think that he was carrying a gun. But, of course, that was impossible. The Company didn't permit lethal weapons, and who in all the world would challenge a rule of the Company?

*

When I showed up in the Naples office the next morning, Susan had my coffee ready and waiting for me. I said gratefully, "Bless you."

She chuckled. "That's not all," she said. "Here's something else you might like. Just remember though, if anyone asks, you got it out of the files yourself."

She slipped a folder under the piles of forms on my desk and disappeared. I peered at it curiously. It was labeled: "Policy BNT-3KT-890776, Blue Bolt Comprehensive. Insuree: Renata dell'Angela."

I could have been no more grateful had she given me the Company Mint.

But I had no chance to examine it. Gogarty was calling for me. I hastily swallowed my coffee and reported for orders.

They were simple enough. The appointment with Zorchi that I hadn't been able to keep the day before was set up for right then. I was already late and I had to leave without another glance at Rena's file.

The hospital Zorchi honored with his patronage was a marble-halled palace on the cliffs that rimmed the southern edge of the Bay of Naples. It was a luxurious, rich man's hospital, stuffy with its opulence; but the most opulent of all was the plush-lined three-room suite where Zorchi was.

SUPER PACK

A white-robed sister of some religious order led me into a silent elevator and along a statued hall. She tapped on a door, and left me in the care of a sharp-faced young man with glasses who introduced himself as Mr. Zorchi's secretary.

I explained my business. He contemptuously waved me to a brocaded chair, and left me alone for a good half hour.

By the time Zorchi was ready to see me, I was boiling. Nobody could treat a representative of the Company like an errand boy! I did my best to take into consideration the fact that he had just undergone major surgery—first under the wheels of the train, then under the knives of three of Naples' finest surgeons.

I said as pleasantly as I could, "I'm glad to see you at last."

The dark face on the pink embroidered pillow turned coldly toward me. "Che volete?" he demanded. The secretary opened his mouth to translate.

I said quickly, "Scusí; parlo un po' la lingua. Non bisogno un traduttore."

Zorchi said languidly in Italian, "In that case, Mario, you may go. What do you want with me, Weels?"

I explained my duties as a Claims Adjuster for the Company, pointing out that it was my task, indeed my privilege, to make settlement for injuries covered by Company policies. He listened condescendingly. I watched him carefully while I talked, trying to estimate the approach he might respond to if I was to win his confidence.

He was far from an attractive young man, I thought. No longer behind the shabby porter's uniform he had worn on the platform of the station, he still had an unkempt and slipshod appearance, despite the heavy silken dressing gown he wore and the manifest costliness of his room. The beard was still on his face; it, at least, had not been a disguise. It was not an attractive beard. It had been weeks, at the least, since any hand had trimmed it to shape and his hair was just as shaggy.

Zorchi was not impressed with my friendly words. When I had finished, he said coldly, "I have had claims against the Company before, Weels. Why is it that this time you make speeches at me?"

I said carefully, "Well, you must admit you are a rather unusual case."

"Case?" He frowned fiercely. "I am no case, Weels. I am Zorchi, if you please."

"Of course, of course. I only mean to say that—"

"That I am a statistic, eh?" He bobbed his head. "Surely. I comprehend. But I am not a statistic, you see. Or, at best, I am a statistic which will not fit into your electronic machines, am I not?"

I admitted, "As I say, you are a rather unusual ca—a rather unusual person, Mr. Zorchi."

He grinned coldly. "Good. We are agreed. Now that we have come to that understanding, are we finished with this interview?"

I coughed. "Mr. Zorchi, I'll be frank with you." He snorted, but I went on, "According to your records, this claim need not be paid. You see, you already have been paid for total disability, both a lump sum and a continuing settlement. There is no possibility of two claims for the loss of your legs, you must realize."

He looked at me with a touch of amusement. "I must?" he asked. "It is odd. I have discussed this, you understand, with many attorneys. The premiums were paid, were they not? The language of the policy is clear, is it not? My legs—would you like to observe the stumps yourself?"

He flung the silken covers off. I averted my eyes from the white-bandaged lower half of his torso, hairy and scrawny and horribly less than a man's legs should be.

I said desperately, "Perhaps I spoke too freely. I do not mean, Mr. Zorchi, that we will not pay your claim. The Company always lives up to the letter of its contracts."

He covered himself casually. "Very well. Give the check to my secretary, please. Are you concluded?"

"Not quite." I swallowed. I plunged right in. "Mr. Zorchi, what the hell are you up to? How do you do it? There isn't any fraud, I admit it. You really lost your legs— more than once. You grew new ones. But how? Don't you realize how important this is? If you can do it, why not others? If you are in some way pecu—that is, if the structure of your body is in some way different from that of others, won't you help us find out how so that we can learn from it? It isn't necessary for you to live as you do, you know."

He was looking at me with a hint of interest in his close-set, dull eyes. I continued, "Even if you can grow new legs, do you enjoy the pain of having them cut off? Have you ever stopped to think that someday, perhaps, you will miscalculate, and the wheels of the train, or the truck, or whatever you use, may miss your legs and kill you? That's no way for a man to live, Mr. Zorchi. Why not talk freely to me, let me help you? Why not take the Company into your confidence, instead of living by fraud and deceit and—"

I had gone too far. Livid, he snarled, "Ass! That will cost your Company, I promise. Is it fraud for me to suffer like this? Do I enjoy it, do you think? Look, ass!" He flung the covers aside again, ripped at the white bandages with his hands— Blood spurted. He uncovered the raw stumps and jerked them at me.

I do not believe any sight of my life shocked me as much as that; it was worse than the Caserta hemp fields, worse than the terrible gone moment when Marianna died, worse than anything I could imagine.

He raved, "See this fraud, look at it closely! Truly, I grow new legs, but does that make it easier to lose the old? It is the pain of being born, Weels, a pain you will never know! I grow legs, I grow arms, I grow eyes. I will never die! I will live on like a reptile or a fish."

His eyes were staring. Ignoring the blood spurting from his stumps, ignoring my attempts to say something, he pounded his abdomen. "Twelve times I have been cut—do you see even a scar? My appendix, it is bad; it traps filth, and the filth makes me sick. And I have it cut out—and it grows again; and I have it cut out again, and it grows back. And the pain, Weels, the pain never stops!" He flung the robe open, slapped his narrow, hairy chest.

I gasped. Under the scraggly hair was a rubble of boils and wens, breaking and matting the hair as he struck himself in frenzy. "Envy me, Weels!" he shouted. "Envy the man whose body defends itself against everything! I will live forever, I promise it, and I will always be in pain, and someone will pay for every horrible moment of it! Now get out, get out!"

I left under the hating eyes of the sharp-faced secretary who silently led me to the door.

*

I had put Zorchi through a tantrum and subjected myself to as disagreeable a time as I'd ever had. And I hadn't accomplished a thing. I knew that well enough. And if I hadn't known it by myself, I would have found out.

Gogarty pointed it out to me, in detail. "You're a big disappointment to me," he moaned sourly. "Ah, the hell with it. What were you trying to accomplish, anyway?" I said defensively, "I thought I might appeal to his altruism. After all, you didn't give me very explicit instructions."

"I didn't tell you to remember to wipe your nose either," he said bitterly. He shook his head, the anger disappearing. "Well," he said disconsolately, "I don't suppose we're any worse off than we were. I guess I'd better try this myself." He must have caught a hopeful anticipatory gleam in my eye, because he said quickly, "Not right now, Wills. You've made that impossible. I'll just have to wait until he cools off."

I said nothing; just stood there waiting for him to let me go. I was sorry things hadn't worked out but, after all, he had very little to complain about. Besides, I wanted to get back to my desk and the folder about Rena dell'Angela. It wasn't so much that I was interested in her as a person, I reminded myself. I was just curious...

SUPER PACK

Once again, I had to stay curious for a while. Gogarty had other plans for me. Before I knew what was happening, I was on my way out of the office again, this time to visit another Neapolitan hospital, where some of the severely injured in the recent war were waiting final settlement of their claims. It was a hurry-up matter, which had been postponed too many times already; some of the injured urgently required major medical treatment, and the hospital was howling for approval of their claims before they'd begin treatment.

This one was far from a marble palace. It had the appearance of a stucco tenement, and all of the patients were in wards. I was a little surprised to see expediters guarding the entrance.

I asked one of them, "Anything wrong?"

He looked at me with a flicker of astonishment, recognizing the double-breasted Claim Adjuster uniform, surprised, I think, at my asking him a question. "Not as long as we're here, sir," he said.

"I mean, I was wondering what you were doing here."

The surprise became overt. "Vaults," he said succinctly.

I prodded no further. I knew what he meant by vaults, of course. It was part of the Company's beneficent plan for ameliorating the effects of even such tiny wars as the Naples-Sicily affair that those who suffered radiation burns got the best treatment possible. And the best treatment, of course, was suspended animation. The deadly danger of radiation burns lay in their cumulative effect; the first symptoms were nothing, the man was well and able to walk about. Degeneration of the system followed soon, the marrow of the bone gave up on its task of producing white corpuscles, the blood count dropped, the tiny radiant poisons in his blood spread and worked their havoc. If he could be gotten through the degenerative period he might live. But, if he lived, he would still die. That is, if his life processes continued, the radiation sickness would kill him. The answer was to stop the life process, temporarily, by means of the injections and deep-freeze in the vaults. It was used for more than radiation, of course. Marianna, for instance—

Well, anyway, that was what the vaults were. These were undoubtedly just a sort of distribution point, where local cases were received and kept until they could be sent to the main Company vaults up the coast at Anzio.

I wasn't questioning the presence of vaults there; I was only curious why the Company felt they needed guarding.

I found myself so busy, though, that I had no time to think about it. A good many of the cases in this shabby hospital really needed the Company's help. But a great many of them were obvious attempts at fraud.

There was a woman, for instance, in the maternity ward. During the war, she'd had to hide out after the Capodichino bombing and hadn't been able to reach medical service. So her third child was going to be a girl, and she was asking indemnity under the gender-guarantee clause. But she had only Class-C coverage and her first two had been boys; a daughter was permissive in any of the first four pregnancies. She began swearing at me before I finished explaining these simple facts to her.

I walked out of the ward, hot under the collar. Didn't these people realize we were trying to help them? They didn't appear to be aware of it. Only the terribly injured, the radiation cases, the amputees, the ones under anesthetic—only these gave me no arguments, mainly because they couldn't talk.

Most of them were on their way to the vaults, I found. My main job was revision of their policies to provide for immobilization. Inevitably, there are some people who will try to take advantage of anything.

The retirement clause in the basic contract was the joker here. Considering that the legal retirement age under the universal Blue Heaven policy was seventy-five years—calendar years, not metabolic years—there were plenty of invalids who wanted a few years in the vaults for reasons that had nothing to do with health. If they could sleep away two or three decades, they could, they thought, emerge at a physical age of forty or so and live idly off the Company the rest of their lives.

They naturally didn't stop to think that if any such practice became common the Company would simply be unable to pay claims. And they certainly didn't think, or care that, if the Company went bankrupt, the world as we knew it would end.

It was a delicate problem; we couldn't deny them medical care, but we couldn't permit them the vaults unless they were either in clearly urgent need, or were willing to sign an extension waiver to their policies...

I saw plenty of that, that afternoon. The radiation cases were the worst, in that way, because they still could talk and argue. Even while they were being loaded with drugs, even while they could see with their own eyes the blood-count graph dipping lower and lower, they still complained at being asked to sign the waiver.

There was even some fear of the vaults themselves—though every living human had surely seen the Company's indoctrination films that showed how the injected drugs slowed life processes and inhibited the body's own destructive enzymes; how the apparently lifeless body, down to ambient air temperature, would be slipped into its hermetic plastic sack and stacked away, row on row, far underground, to sleep away the months or years or, if necessary, the centuries. Time meant nothing to the suspendees. It was hard to imagine being afraid of as simple and natural a process as that!

Although I had to admit that the vaults looked a lot like morgues...

I didn't enjoy it. I kept thinking of Marianna. She had feared the vaults too, in the childish, unreasoning, feminine way that was her characteristic. When the Blue Blanket technicians had turned up the diagnosis of leukemia, they had proposed the sure-thing course of putting her under suspension while the slow-acting drugs—specially treated to operate even under those conditions—worked their cure, but she had refused. There had been, they admitted, a ninety-nine and nine-tenths percent prospect of a cure without suspension...

It just happened that Marianna was in the forlorn one-tenth that died.

I couldn't get her out of my mind. The cases who protested or whined or pleaded or shrieked that they were being tortured and embalmed alive didn't help. I was glad when the afternoon was over and I could get back to the office.

*

As I came in the door, Gogarty was coming in, too, from the barbershop downstairs. He was freshly shaved and beaming.

"Quitting time, Tom," he said amiably, though his eyes were memorizing the pile of incomplete forms on my desk. "All work and no play, you know." He nudged me. "Not that you need reminding, eh? Still, you ought to tell your girl that she shouldn't call you on office time, Tom."

"Call me? Rena called me?"

He nodded absently, intent on the desk. "Against Company rules, you know. Say, I don't like to push you, but aren't you running a little behind here?"

I said with some irritation, "I don't have much chance to catch up, the way I've been racing around the country, you know. And there's plenty to be done."

He said soothingly, "Now, take it easy, Tom. I was only trying to say that there might be some easier way to handle these things." He speared a form, glanced over it casually. He frowned. "Take this, for instance. The claim is for catching cold as a result of exposure during the evacuation of Cerignola. What would you do with that one?"

"Why—pay it, I suppose."

"And put in the paper work? Suppose it's a phony, Tom? Not one case of coryza in fifty is genuine."

"What would you do?" I asked resentfully.

He said without hesitation, "Send it back with Form CBB-23A192. Ask for laboratory smear-test reports."

I looked over the form. A long letter was attached; it said in more detail than was necessary that there had been no laboratory service during the brief war, at least where the policyholder happened to be, and therefore he could submit only the affidavits of three registered physicians. It looked like a fair claim to me. If it was up to me, I would have paid it automatically.

I temporized. "Suppose it's legitimate?"

"Suppose it is? Look at it this way, Tom. If it's phony, this will scare him off, and you'd be saving the Company the expense and embarrassment of paying off a fraudulent claim. If it's legitimate, he'll resubmit it—at a time when, perhaps, we won't be so busy. Meanwhile that's one more claim handled and disposed of, for our progress reports to the Home Office."

I stared at him unbelievingly. But he looked back in perfect calm, until my eyes dropped. After all, I thought, he was right in a way. The mountain of work on my desk was certainly a logjam, and it had to be broken somehow. Maybe rejecting this claim would work some small hardship in an individual case, but what about the hundreds and thousands of others waiting for attention? Wasn't it true that no small hardship to an individual was as serious as delaying all those others?

It was, after all, that very solicitude for the people at large that the Company relied on for its reputation—that, and the ironclad guarantee of prompt and full settlement.

I said, "I suppose you're right."

He nodded, and turned away. Then he paused. "I didn't mean to bawl you out for that phone call, Tom," he said. "Just tell her about the rule, will you?"

"Sure. Oh, one thing." He waited. I coughed. "This girl, Rena. I don't know much about her, you know. Is she, well, someone you know?"

He said, "Heavens, no. She was making a pest out of herself around here, frankly. She has a claim, but not a very good one. I don't know all the details, because it's encoded, but the machines turned it down automatically. I do know that she, uh—" he sort of half winked—"wants a favor. Her old man is in trouble. I'll look it up for you some time, if you want, and get the details. I think he's in the cooler—that is, the clinic—up at Anzio."

He scratched his plump jowls. "I didn't think it was fair to you for me to have a girl at dinner and none for you; Susan promised to bring someone along, and this one was right here, getting in the way. She said she liked Americans, so I told her you would be assigned to her case." This time he did wink. "No harm, of course. You certainly wouldn't be influenced by any, well, personal relationship, if you happened to get into one. Oh, a funny thing. She seemed to recognize your name."

That was a jolt. "She what?"

Gogarty shrugged. "Well, she reacted to it. 'Thomas Wills,' I said. She'd been acting pretty stand-offish, but she warmed up quick. Maybe she just likes the name, but right then is when she told me she liked Americans."

I cleared my throat. "Mr. Gogarty," I said determinedly, "please get me straight on something. You say this girl's father is in some kind of trouble, and you imply she knows me. I want to know if you've ever had any kind of report, or even heard any kind of rumor, that would make you think that I was in the least sympathetic to any anti-Company groups? I'm aware that there were stories—"

He stopped me. "I never heard any, Tom," he said definitely.

I hesitated. It seemed like a good time to open up to Gogarty; I opened my mouth to start, but I was too late. Susan called him off for what she claimed was an urgent phone call and, feeling let-down, I watched him waddle away.

Because it was, after all, time that I took down my back hair with my boss.

*

46

SUPER PACK

Well, I hadn't done anything too terribly bad—anyway, I hadn't meant to do anything bad. And the circumstances sort of explained it, in a way. And it was all in the past, and—

And nothing. I faced the facts. I had spent three solid weeks getting blind drunk, ranting and raving and staggering up to every passerby who would listen and whining to him that the Company was evil, the Company was murderous, the Company had killed my wife.

There was no denying it. And I had capped it all off one bleary midnight, with a brick through the window of the Company branch office that served my home. It was only a drunken piece of idiocy, I kept telling myself. But it was a drunken piece of idiocy that landed me in jail, that had been permanently indorsed on every one of my policies, that was in the confidential pages of my Company service record. It was a piece of idiocy that anyone might have done. But it would have meant deep trouble for me, if it hadn't been for the intercession of my wife's remote relative, Chief Underwriter Defoe.

It was he who had bailed me out. He had never told me how he had found out that I was in jail. He appeared, read the riot-act to me and got me out. He put me over the coals later, yes, but he'd bailed me out. He'd told me I was acting like a child—and convinced me of it, which was harder. And when he was convinced I had snapped out of it, he personally backed me for an appointment to the Company's school as a cadet Claims Adjuster.

I owed a considerable debt of gratitude to my ex-remote-in-law, Chief Underwriter Defoe.

*

While I still was brooding, Gogarty came back. He looked unhappy. "Hammond," he said bitterly. "He's missing. Look, was he drunk when you left him last night?" I nodded. "Thought so. Never showed up for work. Not at his quarters. The daily ledger's still open at his office, because there's no responsible person to sign it. So naturally I've got to run out to Caserta now, and what Susan will say—" He muttered away.

I remembered the file that was buried under the papers on my desk, when he mentioned Susan's name.

As soon as he was out of the office, I had it open.

And as soon as I had it open, I stared at it in shock.

The title page of the sheaf inside was headed: Signorina Renata dell'Angela. Age 22; daughter of Benedetto dell'Angela; accepted to general Class-AA; no employment. There were more details.

But across all, in big red letters, was a rubber stamp: *Policy Canceled. Reassigned Class-E.*

It meant that the sad-eyed Rena was completely uninsurable.

CHAPTER FOUR

Phone or no phone, I still had her address.

It was still daylight when I got out of the cab, and I had a chance for a good look at the house. It was a handsome place by day; the size of the huge white stucco wall didn't fit the *uninsurable* notation on Rena's claim. That wall enclosed a garden; the garden could hardly hold less than an AA house. And Class-Es were ordinarily either sent to public hostels—at the Company's expense, to be sure—or existed on the charity of friends or relatives. And Class-Es seldom had friends in Class-AA houses.

I knocked at the gate. A fat woman, age uncertain but extreme, opened a little panel and peered at me. I asked politely, "Miss dell'Angela?"

The woman scowled. "Che dice?"

I repeated: "May I see Miss dell'Angela? I'm a Claims Adjuster for the Company. I have some business with her in connection with her policies."

"Ha!" said the woman. She left it at that for a moment, pursing her lips and regarding me thoughtfully. Then she shrugged apathetically. "Momento," she said wearily, and left me standing outside the gate.

From inside there was a muttering of unfamiliar voices. I thought I heard a door open, and the sound of steps, but when the fat woman came back she was alone.

Silently she opened the door and nodded me in. I started automatically up the courtyard toward the enclosed house, but she caught my arm and motioned me toward another path. It led down a flowered lane through a grape arbor to what might, at one time, have been a caretaker's hut.

I knocked on the door of the hut, comprehending where Rena dell'Angela lived as a Class-E uninsurable.

Rena herself opened it, her face flushed, her expression surprised— apprehensive, almost, I thought at first. It was the first time I had seen her by daylight. She was—oh, there was no other word. She was lovely. She said quickly, "Mr. Wills! I didn't expect you."

I said, "You phoned me. I came as soon as I could."

She hesitated. "I did," she admitted. "It was—I'm sorry, Mr. Wills. It was an impulse. I shouldn't have done it."

"What was it, Rena?"

She shook her head. "I am sorry. It doesn't matter. But I am a bad hostess; won't you come in?"

The room behind the door was long and narrow, with worn furniture and a door that led, perhaps, to another room behind. It seemed dusty and, hating myself as a snooping fool, I took careful note that there was a faint aroma of tobacco. I had been quite sure that she didn't smoke, that evening we had met.

She gestured at a chair—there only were two, both pulled up to a crude wooden table, on which were two poured cups of coffee. "Please sit down," she invited. I reminded myself that it was, after all, none of my business if she chose to entertain friends—even friends who smoked particularly rancid tobacco. And if they preferred not to be around when I came to the door, why, that was their business, not mine. I said cautiously, "I didn't mean to interrupt you."

"Interrupt me?" She saw my eyes on the cups. "Oh—oh, no, Mr. Wills. That other cup is for you, you see. I poured it when Luisa told me you were at the gate. It isn't very good, I'm afraid," she said apologetically.

I made an effort to sip the coffee; it was terrible. I set it down. "Rena, I just found out about your policies. Believe me, I'm sorry. I hadn't known about it, when we had dinner together; I would have— Well, I don't know what I would have done. There isn't much I can do, truthfully; I don't want you thinking I have any great power. But I wish I had known—I might not have made you cry, at any rate."

She smiled an odd sort of smile. "That wasn't the reason, Mr. Wills."

"Please call me Tom. Well, then, why did you cry?"

50

"It is of no importance. Please."

I coughed and tried a different tack. "You understand that I do have some authority. And I would like to help you if I can—if you'll let me."

"Let you? How could I prevent it?"

Her eyes were deep and dark. I shook myself and pulled the notes I'd made on her policies from my pocket. In the most official voice I could manage, I said, "You see, there may be some leeway in interpreting the facts. As it stands, frankly, there isn't much hope. But if you'll give me some information—"

"Certainly."

"All right. Now, your father—Benedetto dell'Angela. He was a casualty of the war with Sicily; he got a dose of radiation, and he is at present in a low-metabolism state in the clinic at Anzio, waiting for the radiogens to clear out of his system. Is that correct?"

"It is what the Company's report said," she answered.

Her tone was odd. Surely she wasn't doubting a Company report!

"As his dependent, Rena, you applied for subsistence benefits on his Blue Blanket policies, as well as war-risk benefits under the Blue Bolt. Both applications were refused; the Blue Blanket because your father is technically not hospitalized; the Blue Bolt, as well as all your other personal policies, was cancelled, because of—" I stuttered over it—"of activities against the best interest of the Company. Specifically, giving aid and comfort to a known troublemaker whose name is given here as Slovetski." I showed her the cancellation sheet I had stolen from the files.

She shrugged. "This much I know, Tom," she said.

"Why?" I demanded. "This man is believed to have been instrumental in inciting the war with Sicily!"

She flared, "Tom, that's a lie! Slovetski is an old friend of my father's—they studied together in Berlin, many years ago. He is utterly, completely against war—any war!"

FREDERIK POHL

I hesitated. "Well, let's put that aside. But you realize that, in view of this, the Company can maintain—quite properly in a technical sense—that you contributed to the war, and therefore you can't collect Blue Bolt compensation for a war you helped bring about. You were warned, you see. You can't even say that you didn't know what you were doing."

"Tom," Rena's voice was infinitely patient and sad. "I knew what I was doing."

"In that case, Rena, you have to admit that it seems fair enough. Still, perhaps we can get something for you—even if only a refund of your premiums. The Company doesn't always follow the letter of the law, there are always exceptions, so—"

Her expression stopped me. She was smiling, but it was the tortured smile of Prometheus contemplating the cosmic jest that was ripping out his vitals.

I asked uncertainly, "Don't you believe me?"

"Believe you, Tom? Indeed I do." She laughed out loud that time. "After what happened to my father, I assure you, Tom, I am certain that the Company doesn't always follow the law."

I shook my head quickly. "No, you don't understand. I—"

"I understand quite well." She studied me for a moment, then patted my hand. "Let us talk of something else."

"Won't you tell me why your policy was cancelled?"

She said evenly, "It's in the file. Because I was a bad girl."

"But why? Why—"

"Because, Tom. Please, no more. I know you are trying to be just as helpful as you can, but there is no help you can give."

"You don't make it easy, Rena."

"It can't be easy! You see, I admit everything. I was warned. I helped an old friend whom the Company wanted to—shall we say—treat for radiation sickness? So there is no question that my policy can be cancelled. All legal. It is not the only one of its kind, you know. So why discuss it?"

52

"Why shouldn't we?"

Her expression softened. "Because—because we do not agree. And never shall." I stared at her blankly. She was being very difficult. Really, I shouldn't be bothering with her, someone I barely knew, someone I hadn't even heard of until—

That reminded me. I said, "Rena, how did you know my name?"

Her eyes went opaque. "Know your name, Tom? Why, Mr. Gogarty introduced us."

"No. You knew of me before that. Come clean, Rena. Please."

She said flatly, "I don't know what you mean." She was beginning to act agitated.

I had seen her covertly glancing at her watch several times; now she held it up openly—ostentatiously, in fact. "I am sorry, but you'd better go," she said with a hint of anxiety in her voice. "Please excuse me."

Well, there seemed no good reason to stay. So I went—not happily; not with any sense of accomplishment; and fully conscious of the figure I cut to the unseen watcher in the other room, the man whose coffee I had usurped.

Because there was no longer a conjecture about whether there had been such a person or not. I had heard him sneeze three times.

*

Back at my hotel, a red light was flashing on the phone as I let myself in. I unlocked the playback with my room key and got a recorded message that Gogarty wanted me to phone him at once.

He answered the phone on the first ring, looking like the wrath of God. It took me a moment to recognize the symptoms; then it struck home.

The lined gray face, the jittery twitching of the head, the slow, tortured movements; here was a man with a classic textbook case of his ailment. The evidence was medically conclusive. He had been building up to a fancy drinking party, and something made him stop in the middle.

There were few tortures worse than a grade-A hangover, but one of those that qualified was the feeling of having the drink die slowly, going through the process of sobering up without the anesthetic of sleep.

He winced as the scanning lights from the phone hit him. "Wills," he said sourly. "About time. Listen, you've got to go up to Anzio. We've got a distinguished visitor, and he wants to talk to you."

"Me?"

"You! He knows you—his name is Defoe."

The name crashed over me; I hadn't expected that, of all things. He was a member of the Council of Underwriters! I thought they never ventured far from the Home Office. In fact, I thought they never had a moment to spare from the awesome duties of running the Company.

Gogarty explained. "He appeared out of nowhere at Carmody Field. I was still in Caserta! Just settling down to a couple of drinks with Susan, and they phoned me to say Chief Underwriter Defoe is on my doorstep!"

I cut in, "What does he want?"

Gogarty puffed his plump cheeks. "How do I know? He doesn't like the way things are going, I guess. Well, I don't like them either! But I've been twenty-six years with the Company, and if he thinks... Snooping and prying. There are going to be some changes in the office, I can tell you. Somebody's been passing on all kinds of lying gossip and—" He broke off and stared at me calculatingly as an idea hit him.

Then he shook his head. "No. Couldn't be you, Wills, could it? You only got here, and Defoe's obviously been getting this stuff for weeks. Maybe months. Still— Say, how did you come to know him?"

It was none of his business. I said coldly, "At the Home Office. I guess I'll take the morning plane up to Anzio, then."

"The hell you will. You'll take the night train. It gets you there an hour earlier." Gogarty jerked his head righteously—then winced and clutched his temple. He said miserably, "Oh, damn. Tom, I don't like all of this. I think something happened to Hammond."

I repeated, "Happened? What could happen to him?"

"I don't know. But I found out a few things. He's been seen with some mighty peculiar people in Caserta. What's this about somebody with a gun waiting at the office for him when you were there?"

It took a moment for me to figure out what he was talking about. "Oh," I said, "you mean the man at the car? I didn't know he had a gun, for certain."

"I do," Gogarty said shortly. "The expediters tried to pick him up today, to question him about Hammond. He shot his way out."

I told Gogarty what I knew, although it wasn't much. He listened abstractedly and, when I had finished, he sighed. "Well, that's no help," he grumbled. "Better get ready to catch your train."

I nodded and reached to cut off the connection. He waved half-heartedly. "Oh, yes," he added, "give my regards to Susan if you see her."

"Isn't she here?"

He grimaced. "Your friend Defoe said he needed a secretary. He requisitioned her."

*

I boarded the Anzio train from the same platform where I had seen Zorchi dive under the wheels. But this was no sleek express; it was an ancient three-car string that could not have been less than fifty years out of date. The cars were not even air-conditioned.

Sleep was next to impossible, so I struck up a conversation with an expediter officer. He was stand-offish at first but, when he found out I was a Claims Adjuster, he mellowed and produced some interesting information.

It was reasonable that Defoe would put aside his other duties and make a quick visit to Anzio, because Anzio seemed to need someone to do something about it pretty badly. My officer was part of a new levy being sent up there; the garrison was being doubled; there had been trouble. He was vague about what kind of "trouble" it had been, but it sounded like mob violence. I mentioned Caserta and the near-riot I had been in; the officer's eyes hooded over, and about five minutes after that he pointedly leaned back and pulled his hat over his eyes. Evidently it was not good form to discuss actual riots.

I accepted the rebuke, but I was puzzled in my mind as I tried to get some sleep for myself.

What kind of a place was this Naples, where mobs rioted against the Company and even intelligent-seeming persons like Renata dell'Angela appeared to have some reservations about it?

CHAPTER FIVE

I slept, more or less, for an hour or so in that cramped coach seat. I was half asleep when the train-expediter nudged my elbow and said, "Anzio."

It was early—barely past daybreak. It was much too early to find a cab. I got directions from a drowsing stationmaster and walked toward the vaults.

The "clinic," as the official term went, was buried in the feet of the hills just beyond the beaches. I was astonished at the size of it. Not because it was so large; on the contrary. It was, as far as I could see, only a broad, low shed.

Then it occurred to me that the vaults were necessarily almost entirely underground, for the sake of economy in keeping them down to the optimum suspendee temperature. It was safe enough and simple enough to put a man in suspended animation but, as I understood it, it was necessary to be sure that the suspendees never got much above fifty degrees temperature for any length of time. Above that, they had an unwelcome tendency to decay.

This was, I realized, the first full-scale "clinic" I had ever seen. I had known that the Company had hundreds, perhaps thousands, of them scattered all over the world.

I had heard that the Company had enough of them, mostly in out-of-the-way locations, to deep-freeze the entire human race at once, though that seemed hardly reasonable.

I had even heard some ugly, never-quite-made-clear stories about why the Company had so many clinics...but when people began hinting at such ridiculous unpleasantness, I felt it was my duty to make it clear that I wanted to hear no subversive talk. So I had never got the details—and certainly would never have believed them for a moment if I had.

*

It was very early in the morning, as I say, but it seemed that I was not the first to arrive at the clinic. On the sparse grass before the main entrance, half a dozen knots of men and women were standing around apathetically. Some of them glared at me as I came near them, for reasons I did not understand; others merely stared.

I heard a hoarse whisper as I passed one group of middle-aged women. One of them was saying, "Benedetto non é morte." She seemed to be directing it to me; but it meant nothing. The only comment that came to my somewhat weary mind was, "So what if Benedetto isn't dead?"

A huge armed expediter, yawning and scratching, let me in to the executive office. I explained that I had been sent for by Mr. Defoe. I had to wait until Mr. Defoe was ready to receive me and was finally conducted to a suite of rooms.

This might have once been an authentic clinic; it had the aseptic appearance of a depressing hospital room. One for, say, Class-Cs with terminal myasthenia. Now, though, it had been refitted as a private guest suite, with an attempt at luxurious drapes and deep stuffed armchairs superimposed on the basic adjustable beds and stainless steel plumbing.

I hadn't seen Defoe in some time, but he hadn't changed at all. He was, as always, the perfect model of a Company executive of general-officer rank. He was formal, but not unyielding. He was tall, distinguished-gray at the temples, spare, immaculately outfitted in the traditional vest and bow tie.

I recalled our first meeting. He was from the side of Marianna's family that she talked about, and she fluttered around for three whole days, checking our Blue Plate policies for every last exotic dish we could squeeze out to offer him, planning the television programs allowed under our entertainment policies, selecting the most respectable of our friends—"acquaintances" would be a better description; Marianna didn't make friends easily—to make up a dinner party. He'd arrived at the stroke of the hour he was due, and had brought with him what was undoubtedly his idea of a princely gift for newlyweds—a paid-up extra-coverage maternity benefit rider on our Blue Blanket policies.

We thanked him effusively. And, for my part, sincerely. That was before I had known Marianna's views on children; she had no intentions of raising a family.

*

As I walked in on Defoe in his private suite at the clinic, he was standing with his back to me, at a small washstand, peering at his reflection in a mirror. He appeared to have finished shaving. I rubbed my own bristled chin uneasily.

He said over his shoulder, "Good morning, Thomas. Sit down."

I sat on the edge of an enormous wing chair. He pursed his lips, stretched the skin under his chin and, when he seemed perfectly satisfied the job was complete, he said as though he were continuing a conversation, "Fill me in on your interview with Zorchi, Thomas."

It was the first I'd known he'd ever *heard* of Zorchi. I hesitantly began to tell him about the meeting in the hospital. It did not, I knew, do me very much credit, but it simply didn't occur to me to try to make my own part look better. I suppose that if I thought of the matter at all, I simply thought that Defoe would instantly detect any attempt to gloss things over. He hardly seemed to be paying attention to me, though; he was preoccupied with the remainder of his morning ritual—carefully massaging his face with something fragrant, brushing his teeth with a maddening, old-fashioned insistence on careful strokes, combing his hair almost strand by strand.

Then he took a small bottle with a daub attached to the stopper and touched it to the distinguished gray at his temples.

I spluttered in the middle of a word; I had never thought of the possibility that the handsomely grayed temples of the Company's senior executives, as inevitable as the vest or the watch chain, were equally a part of the uniform! Defoe gave me a long inquiring look in the mirror; I coughed and went on with a careful description of Zorchi's temper tantrum.

Defoe turned to me and nodded gravely. There was neither approval nor disapproval. He had asked for information and the information had been received.

He pressed a communicator button and ordered breakfast. The microphone must have been there, but it was invisible. He sat down at a small, surgical-looking table, leaned back and folded his hands.

"Now," he said, "tell me what happened in Caserta just before Hammond disappeared."

Talking to Defoe had something of the quality of shouting down a well. I collected my thoughts and told him all I knew on the riot at the branch office.

While I was talking, Defoe's breakfast arrived. He didn't know I hadn't eaten anything, of course—I say "of course" because I know he couldn't have known, he didn't ask. I looked at it longingly, but all my looking didn't alter the fact that there was only one plate, one cup, one set of silverware.

He ate his breakfast as methodically as he'd brushed his teeth. I doubt if it took him five minutes. Since I finished the Caserta story in about three, the last couple of minutes were in dead silence, Defoe eating, me sitting mute as a disconnected jukebox.

Then he pushed the little table away, lit a cigarette and said, "You may smoke if you wish, Thomas. Come in, Susan."

He didn't raise his voice; and when, fifteen seconds later, Susan Manchester walked in, he didn't look at all impressed with the efficiency of his secretary, his intercom system, or himself. The concealed microphone, it occurred to me, had heard him order breakfast and request his secretary to walk in. It had undoubtedly heard—and most probably recorded—every word I had said.

How well they did things on the upper echelon of the Company!

Susan looked—different. She was as blonde and pretty as ever. But she wasn't bubbly. She smiled at me in passing and handed Defoe a typed script, which he scanned carefully.

He asked, "Nothing new on Hammond?"

"No, sir," she said.

"All right. You may leave this." She nodded and left. Defoe turned back to me. "I have some news for you, Thomas. Hammond has been located."

"That's good," I said. "Not too badly hung over, I hope."

He gave me an arctic smile. "Hardly. He was found by a couple of peasants who were picking grapes. He's dead."

CHAPTER SIX

Hammond dead! He had had his faults, but he was an officer of the Company and a man I had met. Dead!

I asked, "How? What happened?"

"Perhaps you can tell me that, Thomas," said Defoe.

I sat startledly erect, shocked by the significance of the words. I said hotly, "Damn it, Mr. Defoe, you know I had nothing to do with this! I've been all over the whole thing with you and I thought you were on my side! Just because I said a lot of crazy things after Marianna died doesn't mean I'm anti-Company—and it certainly doesn't mean I'd commit murder. If you think that, then why the devil did you put me in cadet school?"

Defoe merely raised his hand by bending the wrist slightly; it was enough to stop me, though. "Gently, Thomas. I don't think you did it—that much should be obvious. And I put you in cadet school because I had work for you."

"But you said I knew something I was holding back."

Defoe waggled the hand reprovingly. "I said you might be able to tell me who killed Hammond. And so you might—but not yet. I count heavily on you for help in this area, Thomas. There are two urgent tasks to be done. Hammond's death—" he paused and shrugged, and the shrug was all of Hammond's epitaph—"is only an incident in a larger pattern; we need to work out the pattern itself."

He glanced again at the typed list Susan had handed him. "I find that I can stay in the Naples area for only a short time; the two tasks must be done before I leave. I shall handle one myself. The other I intend to delegate to you.

"First we have the unfortunate situation in regard to the state of public morale. Unfortunate? Perhaps I should say disgraceful. There is quite obviously a nucleus of troublemakers at work, Thomas, and Gogarty has not had the wit to find them and take the appropriate steps. Someone else must. Second, this Zorchi is an unnecessary annoyance. I do not propose to let the Company be annoyed, Thomas. Which assignment would you prefer?"

I said hesitantly, "I don't know if Mr. Gogarty would like me to—"

"Gogarty is an ass! If he had not blundered incessantly since he took over the district, I should not have had to drop important work to come here."

I thought for a second. Digging out an undercover ring of troublemakers didn't sound particularly easy. On the other hand, I had already tried my luck with Zorchi.

"Perhaps you'd better try Zorchi," I said.

"Try?" Defoe allowed himself to look surprised. "As you wish. I think you will learn something from watching me handle it, Thomas. Shall we join Signore Zorchi now?"

"He's here?"

Defoe said impatiently, "Of course, Thomas. Come along."

*

Zorchi's secretary was there, too. He was in a small anteroom, sitting on a hard wooden chair; as we passed him, I saw the hostility in his eyes. He didn't say a word.

Beyond him, in an examination room, was Zorchi, slim, naked and hideous, sitting on the edge of a surgical cot and trying not to look ill at ease. He had been shaved from head to knee stumps. Esthetically, at least, it had been a mistake. I never saw such a collection of skin eruptions on a human.

He burst out, faster than my language-school Italian could follow, in a stream of argument and abuse. Defoe listened icily for a moment, then shut him up in Italian as good as his own, "Answer questions; otherwise keep quiet. I will not warn you again."

I don't know if even Defoe could have stopped Zorchi under normal conditions. But there is something about being naked in the presence of fully dressed opponents that saps the will; and I guessed, too, that the shaving had made Zorchi feel nakeder than ever before in his life. I could see why he'd worn a beard and I wished he still had it.

"Dr. Lawton," said Defoe, "have you completed your examination of the insured?"

A youngish medical officer of the Company said, "Yes, sir. I have the slides and reports right here; they just came up from the laboratory." He handed a stapled collection of photographic prints and papers to Defoe, who took his own good time to examine them while the rest of us stood and waited.

Defoe finally put the papers down and nodded. "In a word, this bears out our previous discussion."

Lawton nodded. "If you will observe his legs, you will see that the skin healing is complete; already a blastema has formed and—"

"I know," Defoe said impatiently. "Signore Zorchi, I regret to say that I have bad news for you."

Zorchi waved his hand defiantly. "You are the bad news."

Defoe ignored him. "You have a grave systemic imbalance. There is great danger of serious ill effects."

"To what?" snarled Zorchi. "The Company's bank account?"

"No, Zorchi. To your life." Defoe shook his head. "There are indications of malignancy."

"Malignancy?" Zorchi looked startled. "What kind? Do you mean cancer?"

"Exactly." Defoe patted his papers. "You see, Zorchi, healthy human flesh does not grow like a salamander's tail."

The phone rang; impeccable in everything, Defoe waited while Dr. Lawton nervously answered it. Lawton said a few short words, listened for a moment and hung up, looking worried.

He said: "The crowd outside is getting rather large. That was the expeditercaptain from the main gate. He says—"

"I presume he has standing orders," Defoe said. "We need not concern ourselves with that, need we?"

"Well—" The doctor looked unhappy.

"Now, Zorchi," Defoe went on, dismissing Lawton utterly, "do you enjoy life?" "I despise it!" Zorchi spat to emphasize how much.

"But you cling to it. You would not like to die, would you? Worse still, you would not care to live indefinitely with carcinoma eating you piece by piece." Zorchi just glowered suspiciously.

"Perhaps we can cure you, however," Defoe went on reflectively. "It is by no means certain. I don't want to raise false hopes. But there is the possibility—"

"The possibility that you will cure me of collecting on my policies, eh?" Zorchi demanded belligerently. "You are crazy, Defoe. Never!"

Defoe looked at him for a thoughtful moment. To Lawton, he said: "Have you this man's claim warranty? It has the usual application for medical treatment, I presume?" He nodded as Lawton confirmed it. "You see, Mr. Zorchi? As a matter of routine, no claim can be paid unless the policyholder submits to our medical care. You signed the usual form, so—"

"One moment! You people never put me through this before! Did you change the contract on me?"

"No, Signore Zorchi. The same contract, but this time we will enforce it. I think I should warn you of something, though."

He riffled through the papers and found a photographic print to show Zorchi. "This picture isn't you, Signore. It is a picture of a newt. The doctor will explain it to you."

The print was an eight-by-ten glossy of a little lizard with something odd about its legs. Puzzled, Zorchi held it as though the lizard were alive and venomous. But as the doctor spoke, the puzzlement turned into horror and fury.

"What Mr. Defoe means," said Lawton, "is that totipotency—that is, the ability to regenerate lost tissues, as you can, even when entire members are involved—is full of unanswered riddles. We have found, for instance, that X-ray treatment on your leg helps a new leg to form rapidly, just as it does on the leg of the salamanders. The radiation appears to stimulate the formation of the blastema, which—well, never mind the technical part. It speeds things up."

His eyes gleamed with scientific interest. "But we tried the experiment of irradiating limbs that had not been severed. It worked the same way, oddly enough. New limbs were generated even though the old ones were still there. That's why the salamander in the photo has four hands on one of its limbs—nine legs altogether, counting that half-formed one just beside the tail. Curious-looking little beast, isn't it?"

Defoe cleared his throat. "I only mention, Signore, that the standard treatment for malignancy is X-radiation."

Zorchi's eyes flamed—rage battling it out with terror. He said shrilly, "But you can't make a laboratory animal out of me! I'm a policyholder!"

"Nature did it, Signore Zorchi, not us," Defoe said.

Zorchi's eyes rolled up in his head and closed; for a moment, I thought he had fainted and leaped forward to catch him rather than let his legless body crash to the floor. But he hadn't fainted. He was muttering, half aloud, sick with fear, "For the love of Mary, Defoe! Please, please, I beg you! Please!"

It was too much for me. I said, shaking with rage, "Mr. Defoe, you can't force this man to undergo experimental radiation that might make a monster out of him! I insist that you reconsider!"

Defoe threw his head back. "What, Thomas?" he snapped.

I said firmly, "He has no one here to advise him—I'll take the job. Zorchi, listen to me! You've signed the treatment application and he's right enough about that— you can't get out of it. But you don't have to take this treatment! Every policyholder has the right to refuse any new and unguaranteed course of treatment, no matter what the circumstances. All you've got to do is agree to go into suspension in the va—in the clinic here, pending such time as your condition can be infallibly cured. Do it, man! Don't let them make you a freak—demand suspension! What have you got to lose?"

SUPER PACK

I never saw a man go so to pieces as Zorchi, when he realized how nearly Defoe had trapped him into becoming a guinea pig. Whimpering thanks to me, he hastily signed the optional agreement for suspended animation and, as quickly as I could, I left him there.

Defoe followed me. We passed the secretary in the anteroom while Dr. Lawton was explaining the circumstances to him; the man was stricken with astonishment, almost too paralyzed to sign the witnessing form Defoe had insisted on. I knew the form well—I had been about to sign one for Marianna when, at the last moment, she decided against the vaults in favor of the experimental therapy that hadn't worked.

Outside in the hall, Defoe stopped and confronted me. I braced myself for the blast to end all blasts.

I could hardly believe my eyes. The great stone face was smiling!

"Thomas," he said inexplicably, "that was masterful. I couldn't have done better myself."

CHAPTER SEVEN

We walked silently through the huge central waiting room of the clinic.

There should have been scores of relatives of suspendees milling around, seeking information—there was, I knew, still a steady shipment of suspendees coming in from the local hospitals; I had seen it myself. But there were hardly more than a dozen or so persons in sight, with a single clerk checking their forms and answering their questions.

It was too quiet. Defoe thought so, too; I saw his frown.

Now that I had had a few moments to catch my breath, I realized that I had seen a master judoist at work. It was all out of the textbooks—as a fledgling Claims Adjuster, I had had the basic courses in handling difficult cases—but not one man in a million could apply textbook rules as skillfully and successfully as Defoe did with Zorchi.

Push a man hard and he will lunge back; push him hard enough and persistently enough, and he will lunge back farther than his vision carries him, right to the position you planned for him in the first place. And I, of course, had been only a tool in Defoe's hand; by interceding for Zorchi, I had tricked the man into the surrender Defoe wanted.

And he had complimented me for it!

I couldn't help wondering, though, whether the compliment Defoe gave me was part of some still subtler scheme...

Defoe nodded curtly to the expediter-captain at the door, who saluted and pressed the teleswitch that summoned Defoe's limousine.

Defoe turned to me. "I have business in Rome and must leave at once. You will have to certify Zorchi's suspension this afternoon; since I won't be here, you'll have to come back to the clinic for it. After that, Thomas, you can begin your assignment."

I said uncertainly, "What—where shall I begin?"

One eyebrow lifted a trifle. "Where? Wherever you think proper, Thomas. Or must I handle this myself?"

The proper answer, and the one I longed to make, was "Yes." Instead I said, "Not at all, Mr. Defoe. It's only that I didn't even know there was an undercover group until you told me about it a few moments ago; I don't know exactly where to start. Gogarty never mentioned—"

"Gogarty," he cut in, "is very likely to be relieved as District Administrator before long. I should like to replace him with someone already on the scene—" he glanced at me to be sure I understood—"provided, that is, that I can find someone of proven competence. Someone who has the ability to handle this situation without the necessity of my personal intervention."

The limousine arrived then, with an armed expediter riding beside the chauffeur. Defoe allowed me to open the door for him and follow him in.

"Do you understand me?" he asked as the driver started off.

"I think so," I said.

"Good. I do not suppose that Gogarty has given you any information about the malcontents in this area."

"No."

"It may be for the best; his information is clearly not good." Defoe stared broodingly out the window at the silent groups of men and women on the grass before the clinic. "Your information is there," he said as they passed out of sight. "Learn what you can. Act when you know enough. And, Thomas—"

"Yes?"

"Have you given thought to your future?"

I shifted uncomfortably. "Well, I've only been a Claims Adjuster a little while, you know. I suppose that perhaps I might eventually get promoted, even become a District Administrator—"

He looked at me impersonally. "Dream higher," he advised.

*

FREDERIK POHL

I stood watching after Defoe's limousine, from the marquee of the hotel where he had left me to take a room and freshen up. Dream higher. He had the gift of intoxication.

Higher than a District Administrator! It could mean only—the Home Office. Well, it was not impossible, after all. The Home Office jobs had to go to someone; the supermen who held them now—the Defoes and the Carmodys and the dozen or more others who headed up departments or filled seats on the Council of Underwriters—couldn't live forever. And the jobs had to be filled by someone. Why not me? Only one reason, really. I was not a career man. I hadn't had the early academy training from adolescence on; I had come to the service of the Company itself relatively late in life. The calendar legislated against me.

Of course, I thought to myself, I was in a pretty good position, in a way, because of Defoe's evident interest in me. With him helping and counseling me, it might be easier.

I thought that and then I stopped myself, shocked. I was thinking in terms of personal preferment. That was not the Company way! If I had learned anything in my training, I had learned that Advancement was on merit alone.

Advancement had to be on merit alone...else the Company became an oligarchy, deadly and self-perpetuating.

Shaken, I sat in the dingy little hotel room that was the best the town of Anzio had for me and opened my little Black Book. I thumbed through the fine-printed pages of actuarial tables and turned to the words of Millen Carmody, Chief Underwriter, in the preface. They were the words that had been read to me and the others at our graduation at the Home Office, according to the tradition:

Remember always that the Company serves humanity, not the reverse. The Company's work is the world's work. The Company can end, forever, the menace of war and devastation; but it must not substitute a tyranny of its own. Corruption breeds tyrants. Corruption has no place in the Company.

SUPER PACK

They were glorious words. I read them over again, and stared at the portrait of Underwriter Carmody that was the frontispiece of the handbook. It was a face to inspire trust—wise and human, grave, but with warmth in the wide-spaced eyes.

Millen Carmody was not a man you could doubt. As long as men like him ran the Company—and he was the boss of them all, the Chief Underwriter, the highest position the Company had to offer—there could be no question of favoritism or corruption.

*

After eating, I shaved, cleaned up a little and went back to the clinic.

There was trouble in the air, no question of it. More expediters were in view, scattered around the entrance, a dozen, cautious yards away from the nearest knots of civilians. Cars with no official company markings, but with armor-glass so thick that it seemed yellow, were parked at the corners. And people were everywhere.

People who were quiet. Too quiet. There were some women—but not enough to make the proportion right. And there were no children.

I could almost feel the thrust of their eyes as I entered the clinic.

Inside, the aura of strain was even denser. If anything, the place looked more normal than it had earlier; there were more people. The huge waiting room was packed and a dozen sweating clerks were interviewing long lines of persons. But here, as outside, the feeling was wrong; the crowds weren't noisy enough; they lacked the nervous boisterousness they should have had.

Dr. Lawton looked worried. He greeted me and showed me to a small room near the elevators. There was a cocoon of milky plastic on a wheeled table; I looked closer, and inside the cocoon, recognizable through the clear plastic over the face, was the waxlike body of Luigi Zorchi. The eyes were closed and he was completely still. I would have thought him dead if I had not known he was under the influence of the drugs used in the suspension of life in the vaults.

I said: "Am I supposed to identify him or something?"

"We know who he is," Lawton snorted. "Sign the commitment, that's all."

I signed the form he handed me, attesting that Luigi Zorchi, serial number such-and-such, had requested and was being granted immobilization and suspension in lieu of cash medical benefits. They rolled the stretcher-cart away, with its thick foam-plastic sack containing the inanimate Zorchi.

"Anything else?" I asked. Lawton shook his head moodily. "Nothing you can help with. I told Defoe this was going to happen!"

"What?"

He glared at me. "Man, didn't you just come in through the main entrance? Didn't you see that mob?"

"Well, I wouldn't call it a mob," I began.

"You wouldn't now," he broke in. "But you will soon enough. They're working themselves up. Or maybe they're waiting for something. But it means trouble, I promise, and I warned Defoe about it. And he just stared at me as if I was some kind of degenerate."

I said sharply, "What are you afraid of? Right outside, you've got enough expediters to fight a war."

"Afraid? Me?" He looked insulted. "Do you think I'm worried about my own skin, Wills? No, sir. But do you realize that we have suspendees here who need protection? Eighty thousand of them. A mob like that—"

"Eighty thousand?" I stared at him. The war had lasted only a few weeks!

"Eighty thousand. A little more, if anything. And every one of them is a ward of the Company as long as he's suspended. Just think of the damage suits, Wills."

I said, still marveling at the enormous number of casualties out of that little war, "Surely the suspendees are safe here, aren't they?"

"Not against mobs. The vaults can handle anything that might happen in the way of disaster. I don't think an H-bomb right smack on top of them would disturb more than the top two or three decks at most. But you never know what mobs will do. If they once get in here— And Defoe wouldn't listen to me!" \ As I went back into the hall, passing the main entrance, the explosion burst. I stared out over the heads of the dreadfully silent throng in the entrance hall, looking toward the glass doors, as was everyone else inside. Beyond the doors, an arc of expediters was retreating toward us; they paused, fired a round of gas-shells over the heads of the mob outside, and retreated again.

Then the mob was on them, in a burst of screaming fury. Hidden gas guns appeared, and clubs, and curious things that looked like slingshots. The crowd broke for the entrance. The line of expediters wavered but held. There was a tangle of hand-to-hand fights, each one a vicious struggle. But the expediters were professionals; outnumbered forty to one, they savagely chopped down their attackers with their hands, their feet and the stocks of their guns. The crowd hesitated. No shot had yet been fired, except toward the sky.

The air whined and shook. From low on the horizon, a needle-nosed jet thundered in. A plane! Aircraft never flew in the restricted area over the Company's major installations. Aircraft didn't barrel in at treetop height, fast and low, without a hint of the recognition numbers every aircraft had to carry.

From its belly sluiced a silvery milt of explosives as it came in over the heads of the mob, peeled off and up and away, then circled out toward the sea for another approach. A hail of tiny blasts rattled in the clear space between the line of expediters and the entrance. The big doors shook and cracked.

*

The expediters stared white-faced at the ship. And the crowd began firing. An illegal hard-pellet gun peppered the glass of the doors with pockmarks. The guarding line of expediters was simply overrun.

Inside the waiting room, where I stood frozen, hell broke out. The detachment of expediters, supervising the hundreds inside leaped for the doors to fight back the surging mob. But the mob inside the doors, the long orderly lines before the interviewing clerks, now split into a hundred screaming, milling centers of panic. Some rushed toward the doors; some broke for the halls of the vaults themselves. I couldn't see what was going on outside any more. I was swamped in a rush of women panicked out of their senses.

Panic was like a plague. I saw doctors and orderlies struggling against the tide, a few scattered expediters battling to turn back the terrified rush. But I was swept along ahead of them all, barely able to keep my feet. An expediter fell a yard from me. I caught up his gun and began striking out. For this was what Lawton had feared—the mob loose in the vaults!

I raced down a side corridor, around a corner, to the banked elevators that led to the deeps of the clinic. There was fighting there, but the elevator doors were closed. Someone had had the wit to lock them against the mob. But there were stairs; I saw an emergency door only a few yards away. I hesitated only long enough to convince myself, through the fear, that my duty was to the Company and to the protection of its helpless wards below. I bolted through the door and slammed it behind me, spun the levers over and locked it. In a moment, I was running down a long ramp toward the cool immensities of the vaults.

If Lawton had not mentioned the possible consequences of violence to the suspendees, I suppose I would have worried only about my own skin. But here I was. I stared around, trying to get my bearings. I was in a sort of plexus of hallways, an open area with doors on all sides leading off to the vaults. I was alone; the noise from above and outside was cut off completely.

No, I was not alone! I heard running footsteps, light and quick, from another ramp. I turned in time to see a figure speed down it, pause only a second at its base, and disappear into one of the vaults. It was a woman, but not a woman in nurse's uniform. Her back had been to me, yet I could see that one hand held a gas gun, the other something glittering and small.

I followed, not quite believing what I had seen. For I had caught only a glimpse of her face, far off and from a bad angle—but I was as sure as ever I could be that it was Rena dell'Angela!

She didn't look back. She was hurrying against time, hurrying toward a destination that obsessed her thoughts. I followed quietly enough, but I think I might have thundered like an elephant herd and still been unheard.

We passed a strange double-walled door with a warning of some sort lettered on it in red; then she swung into a side corridor where the passage was just wide enough for one. On either side were empty tiers of shelves waiting for suspendees. I speeded up to reach the corner before she could disappear.

But she wasn't hurrying now. She had come to a bay of shelves where a hundred or so bodies lay wrapped in their plastic sacks, each to his own shelf. Dropping to her knees, she began checking the tags on the cocoons at the lowest level.

She whispered something sharp and imploring. Then, straightening abruptly, she dropped the gas gun and took up the glittering thing in her other hand. Now I could see that it was a hypodermic kit in a crystal case. From it she took a little flask of purplish liquid and, fingers shaking, shoved the needle of the hypodermic into the plastic stopper of the vial.

Moving closer, I said: "It won't work, Rena."

She jumped and swung to face me, holding the hypodermic like a stiletto. Seeing my face, she gasped and wavered.

I stepped by her and looked down at the tag on the cocooned figure. *Benedetto dell'Angela, Napoli*, it said, and then the long string of serial numbers that identified him.

It was what I had guessed.

"It won't work," I repeated. "Be smart about this, Rena. You can't revive him without killing him."

Rena half-closed her eyes. She whispered, "Would death be worse than this?" I hadn't expected this sort of superstitious nonsense from her. I started to answer, but she had me off guard. In a flash, she raked the glittering needle toward my face and, as I stumbled back involuntarily, her other hand lunged for the gas gun I had thrust into my belt.

Only luck saved me. Not being in a holster, the gun's front sight caught and I had the moment I needed to cuff her away. She gasped and spun up against the tiers of shelves. The filled hypodermic shattered against the floor, spilling the contents into a purple, gleaming pool of fluorescence.

Rena took a deep breath and stood erect. There were tears in her eyes again. She said in a detached voice: "Well done, Mr. Wills."

"Are you crazy?" I crackled. "This is your father. Do you want to kill him? It takes a doctor to revive him. You're an educated woman, Rena, not a witch-ridden peasant! You know better than this!"

She laughed—a cold laugh. "Educated! A peasant woman would have kicked you to death and succeeded. I'm educated, all right! Two hundred men, a plane, twenty women risking themselves up there to get me through the door. All our plans—and I can't remember a way to kill you in time. I'm too educated to hate you, Claims Adjuster Wills!" She choked on the words. Then she shook her head dully. "Go ahead, turn me in and get it over with."

I took a deep breath. Turn her in? I hadn't thought that far ahead. True, that was the obvious thing to do; she had confessed that the whole riot outside was a diversion to get her down in the vaults, and anyone who could summon up that sort of organized anti-Company violence was someone who automatically became my natural enemy.

But perhaps I was too educated and too soft as well. There had been tears on her face, over her father's body. I could not remember having heard that conspirators cried.

And I sympathized a little. I had known what it was like to weep over the body of someone I loved. Despite our difficulties, despite everything, I would have done anything in the world to bring Marianna back to life. I couldn't. Rena—she believed—could revive her father.

I didn't want to turn her in.

I *shouldn't* turn her in. It was my duty not to turn her in, for hadn't Defoe himself ordered me to investigate the dissident movement of which she was clearly a part? Wouldn't it be easier for me to win her confidence, and trick her into revealing its secrets, than to have her arrested?

The answer, in all truth, was No. She was not a trickable girl, I was sure. But it was, at least, a rationale, and I clung to it.

I coughed and said: "Rena, will you make a bargain?"

She stared drearily. "Bargain?"

"I have a room at the Umberto. If I get you out of here, will you go to my room and wait for me there?"

Her eyes narrowed sharply for a second. She parted her lips to say something, but only nodded.

"Your word, Rena? I don't want to turn you in."

She looked helplessly at the purple spilled pool on the floor, and wistfully at the sack that held her father. Then she said, "My word on it. But you're a fool, Tom!"

"I know it!" I admitted.

I hurried her back up the ramp, back toward the violence upstairs. If it was over, I would have to talk her out of the clinic, somehow cover up the fact that she had been in the vaults. If it was still going on, though—

It was.

We blended ourselves with the shouting, rioting knots. I dragged her into the main waiting room, saw her thrust through the doors. Things were quieting even then. And I saw two women hastening toward her through the fight, and I do not think it was a coincidence that the steam went out of the rioters almost at once.

I stayed at the clinic until everything was peaceful again, though it was hours.

I wasn't fooling myself. I didn't have a shred of real reason for not having her arrested. If she had information to give, I was not the type to trick it out of her—even if she really was waiting at the Umberto, which was, in itself, not likely. If I had turned her in, Defoe would have had the information out of her in moments; but not I.

She was an enemy of the Company.

And I was unable to betray her.

CHAPTER EIGHT

Dr. Lawton, who seemed to be Chief Medical Officer for Anzio Clinic, said grimly: "This wasn't an accident. It was planned. The question is, why?"

The expediters had finished driving the rioters out of the clinic itself, and gas guns were rapidly dispersing the few left outside the entrance. At least thirty unconscious forms were scattered around—and one or two that were worse than unconscious.

I said, "Maybe they were hoping to loot the clinic." It wasn't a very good lie. But then, I hadn't had much practice in telling lies to an officer of the Company.

Lawton pursed his lips and ignored the suggestion. "Tell me something, Wills. What were you doing down below?"

I said quickly, "Below? You mean a half an hour ago?"

"That's what I mean." He was gentle, but—well, not exactly suspicious. Curious. I improvised: "I—I thought I saw someone running down there. One of the rioters. So I chased after her—after *him*." I corrected, swallowing the word just barely in time.

He nodded. "Find anything?"

It was a tough question. Had I been seen going in or coming out? If it was coming out—Rena had been with me.

I took what we called a "calculated risk"—that is, I got a firm grip on my courage and told a big fat and possibly detectable lie. I said, "Nobody that I could find. But I still think I heard something. The trouble is, I don't know the vaults very well. I was afraid I'd get lost."

Apparently it was on the way in that I had been spotted, for Lawton said thoughtfully, "Let's take a look."

We took a couple of battered expediters with us—I didn't regard them as exactly necessary, but I couldn't see how I could tell Lawton that. The elevators were working again, so we came out in a slightly different part of the vaults than I had seen before; it was not entirely acting on my part when I peered around.

Lawton accepted my statement that I wasn't quite sure where I had heard the noises, without argument. He accepted it all too easily; he sent the expediters scouring the corridors at random.

And, of course, one of them found the pool of spilled fluorescence from the hypodermic needle I had knocked out of Rena's hand.

We stood there peering at the smear of purplish color, the shattered hypodermic, Rena's gas gun.

Lawton mused, "Looks like someone's trying to wake up some of our sleepers. That's our standard antilytic, if I'm not mistaken." He scanned the shelves. "Nobody missing around here. Take a look in the next few sections of the tiers."

The expediters saluted and left.

"They won't find anyone missing," Lawton predicted, "And that means we have to take a physical inventory of the whole damn clinic. Over eighty thousand suspendees to check." He made a disgusted noise.

I said, "Maybe they were scared off before they finished."

"Maybe. Maybe not. We'll have to check, that's all."

"Are you sure that stuff is to revive the suspendees?" I persisted. "Couldn't it just have been someone wandering down here by mistake during the commotion and—"

"And carrying a hypodermic needle by mistake, and armed with a gas gun by mistake. Sure, Wills."

The expediters returned and Lawton looked at them sourly.

They shook their heads. He shrugged. "Tell you what, Wills," he said. "Let's go back to the office and—"

He stopped, peering down the corridor. The last of our expediters was coming toward us—not alone.

"Well, what do you know!" said Lawton. "Wills, it looks like he's got your fugitive!"

The expediter was dragging a small writhing figure behind him; we could hear whines and pleading. For a heart-stopping second, I thought it was Rena, against all logic.

But it wasn't. It was a quavery ancient, a bleary-eyed wreck of a man, long past retirement age, shabbily dressed and obviously the sort who cut his pension policies to the barest minimum—and then whined when his old age was poverty-stricken.

Lawton asked me: "This the man?"

"I—I couldn't recognize him," I said.

Lawton turned to the weeping old man. "Who were you after?" he demanded. All he got was sobbing pleas to let him go; all he was likely to get was more of the same. The man was in pure panic.

We got him up to one of the receiving offices on the upper level, half carried by the expediters. Lawton questioned him mercilessly for half an hour before giving up. The man was by then incapable of speech.

He had said, as nearly as we could figure it out, only that he was sorry he had gone into the forbidden place, he didn't mean to go into the forbidden place, he had been sleeping in the shadow of the forbidden place when fighting began and he fled inside.

It was perfectly apparent to me that he was telling the truth—and, more, that any diversionary riot designed to get him inside with a hypodermic and gas gun would have been planned by maniacs, for I doubted he could have found the trigger of the gun. But Lawton seemed to think he was lying.

It was growing late. Lawton offered to drive me to my hotel, leaving the man in the custody of the expediters. On the way, out of curiosity, I asked: "Suppose he had succeeded? Can you revive a suspendee as easily as that, just by sticking a needle in his arm?"

Lawton grunted. "Pretty near, that and artificial respiration. One case in a hundred might need something else—heart massage or an incubator, for instance. But most of the time an antilytic shot is enough."

Then Rena had not been as mad as I thought.

I said: "And do you think that old man could have accomplished anything?"

Lawton looked at me curiously. "Maybe."

"Who do you suppose he was after?"

Lawton said off-handedly. "He was right near Bay 100, wasn't he?"

"Bay 100?" Something struck a chord; I remembered following Rena down the corridor, passing a door that was odd in some way. Was the number 100 on that door? "Is that the one that's locked off, with the sign on it that says anybody who goes in is asking for trouble?"

"That's the one. Though," he added, "nobody is going to get in. That door is triple-plate armor; the lock opens only to the personal fingerprint pattern of Defoe and two or three others."

"What's inside it that's so important?"

He said coldly, "How would I know? I can't open the door." And that was the end of the conversation. I knew *he* was lying.

*

I had changed my bet with myself on the way. I won it. Rena was in the room waiting for me. She was sound asleep, stretched out on the bed. She looked as sober-faced and intent in her sleep as a little girl—a look I had noticed in Marianna's sleeping face once.

It was astonishing how little I thought about Marianna anymore.

I considered very carefully before I rang for a bellboy, but it seemed wisest to let her sleep and take my chances with the house detective, if any. There was none, it turned out. In fact, the bellboy hardly noticed her—whether out of indifference or because he was well aware that I had signed for the room with an official travelcredit card of the Company, it didn't much matter. He succeeded in conveying, without saying a word, that the Blue Sky was the limit.

I ordered dinner, waving away the menu and telling him to let the chef decide. The chef decided well. Among other things, there was a bottle of champagne in a bucket of ice.

Rena woke up slowly at first, and then popped to a sitting position, eyes wide. I said quickly, "Everything's all right. No one saw you at the clinic."

She blinked once. In a soft voice, she said, "Thank you." She sighed a very small sigh and slipped off the bed.

I realized as Rena was washing up, comparisons were always odious, but— Well, if a strange man had found Marianna with her dress hitched halfway up her thigh, asleep on his bed, he'd have been in for something. What the "something" would be might depend on circumstances; it might be a raging order to knock before he came in, it might only be a storm of blushes and a couple of hours of meticulously prissy behavior. But she wouldn't just let it slide. And Rena, by simply disregarding it, was as modest as any girl could be.

After all, I told myself, warming to the subject, it wasn't as if I were some excitable adolescent. I could see a lovely girl's legs without getting all stirred up. For that matter, I hardly even noticed them, come to think of it. And if I did notice them, it was certainly nothing of any importance; I had dismissed it casually, practically forgotten it, in fact.

She came back and said cheerfully, "I'm hungry!" And so, I realized, was I.

We started to eat without much discussion, except for the necessary talk of the table. I felt very much at ease sitting across from her, in spite of the fact that she had placed herself in opposition to the Company. I felt relaxed and comfortable; nothing bothered me. Certainly, I went on in my mind, I was as free and easy with her as with any man; it didn't matter that she was an attractive girl at all. I wasn't thinking of her in that way, only as someone who needed some help.

I came to. She was looking at me with friendly curiosity. She said, "Is that an American idiom, Tom, when you said, 'Please pass the legs'?"

*

We didn't open the champagne: it didn't seem quite appropriate. We had not discussed anything of importance while we were eating, except that I had told her about the old man; she evidently knew nothing about him. She was concerned, but I assured her he was safe with the Company—what did she think they were, barbarians? She didn't answer.

But after dinner, with our coffee, I said: "Now let's get down to business. What were you doing in the clinic?"

"I was trying to rescue my father," she said.

"Rescue, Rena? Rescue from what?"

"Tom, please. You believe in the Company, do you not?"

"Of course!"

"And I do not. We shall never agree. I am grateful to you for not turning me in, and I think perhaps I know what it cost you to do it. But that is all, Tom."

"But the Company—"

"When you speak of the Company, what is it you see? Something shining and wonderful? It is not that way with me; what I see is—rows of my friends, frozen in the vaults or the expediters and that poor old man you caught."

There was no reasoning with her. She had fixed in her mind that all the suspendees were the victims of some sinister brutality. Of course, it wasn't like that at all.

Suspension wasn't death; everyone knew that. In fact, it was the antithesis of death. It saved lives by taking the maimed and sick and putting them mercifully to sleep, until they could be repaired.

True, their bodies grew cold, the lungs stopped pumping, the heart stopped throbbing; true, no doctor could tell, on sight, whether a suspendee was "alive" or "dead." The life processes were not entirely halted, but they were slowed enormously—enough so that chemical diffusion in the jellylike blood carried all the oxygen the body needed. But there was a difference: The dead were dead, whereas the suspendees could be brought back to life at any moment the Company chose.

But I couldn't make her see that. I couldn't even console her by reminding her that the old man was a mere Class E. For so was she.

I urged reasonably: "Rena, you think something is going on under the surface. Tell me about it. Why do you think your father was put in suspension?"

"To keep him out of the way. Because the Company is afraid of him."

I played a trump card: "Suppose I told you the real reason he's in the vaults."

She was hit by that, I could tell. She was staring at me with wonder in her eyes.

"You don't have to speculate about it, Rena. I looked up his record, you see."

"You—you—"

I nodded. "It's right there in black and white. They're trying to save his life. He has radiation poisoning. He was a war casualty. It's standard medical practice in cases like his to put them in suspension for a while, until the level of radioactivity dies down and they can safely be revived. Now what do you say?"

She merely stared at me.

I pressed on persuasively: "Rena, I don't mean to call your beliefs superstitions or anything like that. Please understand me. You have your own cultural heritage and—well, I know that it looks as though he is some kind of 'undead,' or however you put it, in your folk stories. I know there are legends of vampires and zombies and so on, but—"

She was actually laughing. "You're thinking of Central Europe, Tom, not Naples. And anyway—" she was laughing only with her eyes now—"I do not believe that the legends say that vampires are produced by intravenous injections of chlorpromazine and pethidine in a lytic solution—which is, I believe, the current technique at the clinics."

I flared peevishly: "Damn it, don't you want him saved?"

The laughter was gone. She gently touched my hand. "I'm sorry. I don't mean to be a shrew and that remark wasn't kind. Must we discuss it?"

"Yes!"

"Very well." She faced me, chin out and fierce. "My father does not have radiation poisoning, Tom."

"He does."

"He does not! He is a prisoner, not a patient. He loved Naples. That's why he was put to sleep—for fifty years, or a hundred, until everything he knew and loved grows away from him and nobody cares what he has to say anymore. They won't kill him—they don't have to! They just want him out of the way, because he sees the Company for what it is."

"And what is that?"

"Tyranny, Tom," she said quietly.

I burst out, "Rena, that's silly! The Company is the hope of the world. If you talk like that, you'll be in trouble. That's dangerous thinking, young lady. It attacks the foundations of our whole society!"

"Good! I was hoping it would!"

We were shouting at each other like children. I took time to remember one of the priceless rules out of the *Adjusters' Handbook*: *Never lose your temper; think before you speak.* We glared at each other in furious silence for a moment before I forced myself to simmer down.

Only then did I remember that I needed to know something she might be able to tell me. Organization, Defoe had said—an organization that opposed the Company, that was behind Hammond's death and the riot at the clinic and more, much more.

"Rena, why did your friends kill Hammond?"

Her poise was shaken. "Who?" she asked.

"Hammond. In Caserta. By a gang of anti-Company hoodlums."

Her eyes flashed, but she only said: "I know nothing of any killings."

"Yet you admit you belong to a subversive group?"

"I admit nothing," she said shortly.

"But you do. I know you do. You said as much to me, when you were prevented from reviving your father."

She shrugged.

I went on: "Why did you call me at the office, Rena? Was it to get me to help you work against the Company?"

She looked at me for a long moment. Then she said: "It was. And would you like to know why I picked you?"

"Well, I suppose—"

"Don't suppose, Tom." Her nostrils were white. She said coldly: "You seemed like a very good bet, as far as we could tell. I will tell you something you don't know. There is a memorandum regarding you in the office of the Chief of Expediters in Naples. I do not choose to tell you how I know of it, but even your Mr. Gogarty doesn't know it exists. It is private and secret, and it says of you, 'Loyalty doubtful. Believed in contact with underground movement. Keep under close but secret surveillance'."

That one rocked me, I admit. "But that's all wrong!" I finally burst out. "I admit I went through a bad time after Marianna died, but—"

She was smiling, though still angry. "Are you apologizing to me?"

"No, but—" I stopped. That was a matter to be taken up with Defoe, I told myself, and I was beginning to feel a little angry, too.

"All right," I said. "There's been a mistake; I'll see that it's straightened out. But even if it was true, did you think I was the kind of man to join a bunch of murderers?"

"We are not murderers!"

"Hammond's body says different."

"We had nothing to do with that, Tom!"

"Your friend Slovetski did." It was a shot in the dark. It missed by a mile.

She said loftily: "If he is such a killer, how did you escape? When I had my interview with you, and it became apparent that the expediters werc less than accurate, the information came a little late. You could easily have given us trouble—Slovetski was in the next room. Why didn't he shoot you dead?"

"Maybe he didn't want to be bothered with my body."

"And maybe you are all wrong about us!"

"No! If you're against the Company, I can't be wrong. The Company is the greatest blessing the world has ever known—it's made the world a paradise!"

"It has?" She made a snorting sound. "How?"

"By bringing countless blessings to all of us. *Countless!*"

She was shaking with the effort of controlling her temper. "Name one!" I swore in exasperation. "All right," I said. "It ended war."

She nodded—not a nod of agreement, but because she had expected that answer. "Right out of the textbooks and propaganda pieces, Tom. Tell me, why is my father in the vaults?"

"Because he has radiation poisoning!"

"And how did he get this radiation poisoning?"

"How?" I blinked at her. "You know how, Rena. In the war between Naples and— the war—"

Rena said remorselessly, "That's right, Tom, the war. The war that couldn't have existed, because the Company ended war—everybody knows that. Ah, Tom! For God, tell me, why is the world blind? Everyone believes, no one questions. The Company ended war—it says so itself. And the blind world never sees the little wars that rage, all the time, one upon the heels of another. The Company has ended disease. But how many deaths are there? The Company has abolished poverty. But am I living in riches, Tom? Was the old man who ran into the vaults?"

I stammered, "But—but, Rena, the statistical charts show very clearly—"

"No, Tom," she said, gentle again. "The statistical charts show less war, not no war. They show *less* disease."

She rubbed her eyes wearily—and even then I thought: Marianna wouldn't have dared; it would have smeared her mascara.

"The trouble with you, Tom, is that you're an American. You don't know how it is in the world, only in America. You don't know what it was like after the Short War, when America won and the flying squads of Senators came over and the governments that were left agreed to defederate. You're used to a big and united country, not little city-states. You don't have thousands of years of intrigue and tyranny and plot behind you, so you close your eyes and plunge ahead, and if the charts show things are getting a *little* better, you think they are perfect."

She shook her head. "But not us, Tom. We can't afford that. We walk with eyes that dart about, seeking danger. Sometimes we see ghosts, but sometimes we see real menace. You look at the charts and you see that there are fewer wars than before. We—we look at the charts and we see our fathers and brothers dead in a little war that hardly makes a ripple on the graph. You don't even see them, Tom. You don't even see the disease cases that don't get cured—because the techniques are 'still experimental,' they say. You don't—Tom! What is it?"

I suppose I showed the pain of remembrance. I said with an effort, "Sorry, Rena. You made me think of something. Please go on."

"That's all of it, Tom. You in America can't be blamed. The big lie—the lie so preposterous that it cannot be questioned, the thing that proves itself because it is so unbelievable that no one would say it if it weren't true—is not an American invention. It is European, Tom. You aren't inoculated against it. We are."

I took a deep breath. "What about your father, Rena? Do you really think the Company is out to get him?"

She looked at me searchingly, then looked hopelessly away. "Not as you mean it, Tom," she said at last. "No, I am no paranoid. I think he is—inconvenient. I think the Company finds him less trouble in the deepfreeze than he would be walking around."

"But don't you agree that he needs treatment?"

"For what? For the radiation poisoning that he got from the atomic explosion he was nowhere near, Tom? Remember, he is my father! I was with him in the war— and he never stirred a kilometer from our home. You've been there, the big house where my aunt Luisa now lives. Did you see bomb craters there?"

"That's a lie!" I had to confess it to myself: Rena was beginning to mean something to me. But there were emotional buttons that even she couldn't push. If she had been a man, any man, I would have had my fist in her face before she had said that much; treason against the Company was more than I could take. "You can't convince me that the Company deliberately falsifies records. Don't forget, Rena, I'm an executive of the Company! Nothing like that could go on!" Her eyes flared, but her lips were rebelliously silent.

I said furiously: "I'll hear no more of that. Theoretical discussions are all right; I'm as broadminded as the next man. But when you accuse the Company of outright fraud, you—well, you're mistaken."

We glowered at each other for a long moment. My eyes fell first.

I said sourly, "I'm sorry if I called you a liar. I—I didn't mean to be offensive." "Nor I, Tom." she hesitated. "Will you remember that I asked you not to make me discuss it?"

She stood up. "Thank you very much for a dinner. And for listening. And most of all, for giving me another chance to rescue my father."

I looked at my watch automatically—and incredulously. "It's late, Rena. Have you a place to stay?"

She shrugged. "N—yes, of course, Tom. Don't worry about me; I'll be all right"

"Are you sure?"

"Very sure."

Her manner was completely confident—so much so that I knew it for an act. I said: "Please, Rena, you've been through a tough time and I don't want you wandering around. You can't get back to Naples tonight."

"I know."

"Well?"

"Well what, Tom?" she said. "I won't lie to you—I haven't a place to go to here. I would have had, this afternoon, if I had succeeded. But by now, everything has changed. They—that is, my friends will assume that I have been captured by the Company. They won't be where I could find them, Tom. Say they are silly if you wish. But they will fear that the Company might—request me to give their names."

I said crisply, "Stay here, Rena. No—listen to me. You stay here. I'll get another room."

"Thank you, Tom, but you can't. There isn't a room in Anzio; there are families of suspendees sleeping in the grass tonight."

"I can sleep in the grass if I have to."

She shook her head. "Thank you," she repeated.

I stood between her and the door. "Then we'll both stay here. I'll sleep on the couch. You can have the bed." I hesitated, then added, "You can trust me, Rena."

She looked at me gravely for a moment. Then she smiled. "I'm sure I can, Tom. I appreciate your offer. I accept."

*

I am built too long for a hotel-room couch, particularly a room in a Mediterranean coastal fleabag. I lay staring into the white Italian night; the Moon brightened the clouds outside the window, and the room was clearly enough illuminated to show me the bed and the slight, motionless form in it. Rena was not a restless sleeper, I thought. Nor did she snore.

Rena was a most self-possessed girl, in fact. She had overruled me when I tried to keep the bellboy from clearing away the dinner service. "Do you think no other Company man ever had a girl in his room?" she innocently asked. She borrowed a pair of the new pajamas Defoe's thoughtful expediters had bought and put in the bureau. But I hadn't expected that, while the bellboy was clearing away, she would be softly singing to herself in the bath.

He had seemed not even to hear.

He had also leaped to conclusions—not that it was much of a leap, I suppose.

But he had conspicuously not removed the bottle of champagne and its silver bucket of melting ice.

It felt good, being in the same room with Rena.

I shifted again, hunching up my torso to give my legs a chance to stretch out. I looked anxiously to see if the movement had disturbed her.

There is a story about an animal experimenter who left a chimpanzee in an empty room. He closed the door on the ape and bent to look through the keyhole, to see what the animal would do. But all he saw was an eye—because the chimp was just as curious about the experimenter.

In the half-light, I saw a sparkle of moonlight in Rena's eye; she was watching me. She half-giggled, a smothered sound.

"You ought to be asleep," I accused.

"And you, Tom."

I obediently closed my eyes, but I didn't stop seeing her.

If only she weren't a fanatic.

And if she had to be a fanatic, why did she have to be the one kind that was my natural enemy, a member of the group of irresponsible troublemakers that Defoe had ordered me to "handle"?

What, I wondered, did he mean by "handle"? Did it include chlorpromazine in a lytic solution and a plastic cocoon?

I put that thought out of my mind; there was no chance whatever that her crazy belief, that the Company was using suspension as a retaliatory measure, was correct. But thinking of Defoe made me think of my work. After all, I told myself, Rena was more than a person. She was a key that could unlock the whole riddle. She had the answers—if there was a movement of any size, she would know its structure.

I thought for a moment and withdrew the "if." She had admitted the riot of that afternoon was planned. It had to be a tightly organized group.

And she had to have the key.

*

At last, I had been getting slightly drowsy, but suddenly I was wide awake.

There were two possibilities. I faced the first of them shakily—she might be right. Everything within me revolted against the notion, but I accepted it as a theoretical possibility. If so, I would, of course, have to revise some basic notions.

On the other hand, she might be wrong. I was certain she was wrong. But I was equally certain she was no raddled malcontent and if she was wrong, and I could prove it to her, she herself might make some revisions.

Propped on one elbow, I peered at her. "Rena?" I whispered questioningly.

She stirred. "Yes, Tom?"

"If you're not asleep, can we take a couple more minutes to talk?"

"Of course." I sat up and reached for the light switch, but she said, "Must we have the lights? The Moon is very bright."

"Sure." I sat on the edge of the couch and reached for a cigarette. "Can I offer you a deal, Rena?"

"What sort of deal?"

"A horse trade. You think the Company is corrupt and your father is not a casualty, right?"

"Correct, Tom."

"And I think the Company is not corrupt and your father has radiation poisoning. One of us has to be wrong, right?"

"Correct, Tom."

93

"Let's find out. There are ways of testing for radiation sickness. I'll go into the clinic in the morning and get the answer."

She also lifted up on one elbow, peering at me, her long hair braided down her back. "Will you?"

"Sure. And we'll make bets on it, Rena. If you are wrong—if your father has radiation poisoning—I want you to tell me everything there is to tell about the riot today and the people behind it. If I'm wrong—" I swallowed—"if I'm wrong, I'll get your father out of there for you. Somehow. I promise it, Rena."

There was absolute silence for a long time. Then she swung out of the bed and hurried over to me, her hands on mine. She looked at me and again I saw tears. "Will you do that, Tom?" she asked, hardly audible.

"Why, sure," I said awkwardly. "But you have to promise—"

"I promise!"

She was staring at me, at arm's length. And then something happened. She wasn't staring and she wasn't at arm's length.

Kissing her was like tasting candied violets; and the Moon made her lovelier than anything human; and the bellboy had not been so presumptuous, after all, when he left us the champagne.

CHAPTER NINE

Dr. Lawton was "away from his desk" the next morning. That was all to the good. I was not a hardened enough conspirator to seek out chances to make mistakes, and although I had a perfectly good excuse for wanting to go down into the vaults again, I wasn't anxious to have to use it. The expediter-officer in charge, though, didn't even ask for reasons. He furnished me with what I wanted—a map of the vaults and a radiation-counter—and turned me loose.

Looking at the map, I was astonished at the size of this subterranean pyramid. Lawton had said we had eighty-odd thousand sleepers filed away and that had surprised me, but by the chart I held in my hand, there was space for perhaps ten times that many. It was beyond belief that so much space was really needed, I thought—unless there was some truth to Rena's belief that the Company used the clinics for prisons...

I applied myself to the map. And, naturally, I read it wrong. It was very simple; I merely went to the wrong level, that was all.

It looked wrong as soon as I stepped out of the elevator. An elderly, officious civilian with a British accent barred my way. "You aren't one of us, are you?"

I said, "I doubt it."

"Then would you mind?" he asked politely, and indicated a spot on the side of the hall. Perhaps I was suggestible, but I obeyed his request without question. It was just as well, because a sort of procession rounded a bend and came down the corridor. There was a wheeled stretcher, with three elderly civilians puttering around it, and a bored medic following with a jar of something held aloft, feeding through a thin plastic tube into the arm of the man on the stretcher, as well as half a dozen others of more nondescript types.

The man who had stopped me nearly ran to meet the stretcher. He stared into the waxy face and whispered, "It's he! Oh, absolutely, it is he!"

I looked and the face was oddly familiar. It reminded me of my childhood; it had a link with school days and the excitement of turning twelve. By the way the four old men were carrying on, however, it meant more than that to them. It meant, if not the Second Coming, at least something close to it.

By then I had figured out that this was that rare event in the day of a clinic—a revival. I had never seen one. I suppose I could have got out of the way and gone about my conspiratorial business, and it is no credit to me as a conspirator that I did not. But I was fascinated.

Too fascinated to wonder why revivals were so rare...

*

The medic looked at his watch and, with careless efficiency, plucked the tube out of the waxy man's arm.

"Two minutes," he said to one of the civilians. "Then he'll be as good as he ever was. You've got his clothes and release papers?"

"Oh, definitely," said the civilian, beaming.

"Okay. And you understand that the Company takes no responsibility beyond the policy covering? After all, he was one of the first men suspended. We think we can give him another year or so—which is a year more than he would have had, at that—but he's not what you'd call a Grade A risk."

"Certainly," agreed the civilian. "Can we talk to him now?"

"As soon as he opens his eyes."

The civilian bent over the man, who no longer looked waxy. His face was now a mottled gray and his eyelids were flickering. He had begun to breathe heavily and irregularly, and he was mumbling something I couldn't understand. The civilian whispered in his ear and the revived man opened his eyes and looked at him.

It was like seeing the dead come to life. It was exactly that, in fact; twenty minutes before, no chemical test, no stethoscope or probing thumb in the eye socket could have detected the faint living glow in the almost-dead cells. And yet—now he looked, he breathed, he spoke.

"I made it," were his first understandable words.

"Indeed you did!" crowed the civilian in charge, while all of the others murmured happily to each other. "Sir, it is my pleasure to welcome you back to us. You are in Anzio, Italy. And I am Thomas Welbourne, at your service."

The faint eyes sparkled. Dead, near-dead or merely decrepit, this was a man who wanted to enjoy life. Minutes out of the tomb, he said: "No! Not young Tommy Welbourne!"

"His grandson, sir," said the civilian.

I had it just then—that face had watched me through a whole year of school. It had been in a frame at the front of the room, with half a dozen other faces. It had a name under it, which, try as I might, I couldn't recall; but the face was there all the same. It was an easy one to keep in mind—strong though sunken, ancient but very much alive.

He was saying, in a voice as confident as any youth's, "Ah, Tommy, I've lived to see it! Tell me, have you been to Mars? What is on the other side of the Moon? And the Russians—what are the Russians up to these days?"

The civilian coughed and tried to interrupt, but the figure on the stretcher went on heedlessly: "All those years gone—what wonders must we have. A tunnel under the Atlantic, I'll wager! And ships that fly a hundred times the speed of sound. Tell me, Tommy Welbourne! Don't keep an old man waiting!"

The civilian said reluctantly, but patiently, "Perhaps it will take a little explaining, sir. You see, there have been changes—"

"I know it, boy! That's what I'm asking you!"

"Well, not that sort of changes, sir. We've learned new virtues since your time— patience and stability, things of that sort. You see—"

The interesting part was over and the glances of the others in the party reminded me that I didn't belong here. I stole off, but not before the man on the stretcher noticed me and made a sort of clumsy two-fingered salute of hail and farewell as I left. It was exactly like the gesture in his picture on that schoolroom wall, up next to the presidents and the greatest of kings.

I found a staircase and climbed to another level of the boxlike clinic.

The local peasants called the vaults "coolers" or "ice cubes." I suppose the reason had something to do with the fact that they were cool and rectangular, on the whole—perhaps because, like icebergs, the great bulk of the vaults was below the surface. But whatever you called them, they were huge. And the clinic at Anzio was only one out of hundreds scattered all over the world.

It was all a matter of viewpoint. To me, the clinics were emblems of the Company's concern for the world. In any imaginable disaster—even if some fantastic plague struck the entire race at once—the affected population could be neatly and effectively preserved until medicine could catch up with their cures.

To Rena, they were prisons big enough to hold the human race.

It was time to find out which of us was right. I hurried through the corridors, between the tiers of sleepers, almost touching them on both sides. I saw the faint purplish gleam where Rena had spilled the fluid, and knelt beside the cocoon that held her father.

The UV sterilizers overhead made everything look ghastly violet, but in any light, the waxy face under the plastic would have looked dead as death itself. I couldn't blame Rena for weeping.

I took out the little radiation counter and looked at it awkwardly. There was nothing complicated about the device—fortunately, because I had had little experience with them. It was a cylinder with a flaring snout at one end, a calibrated gauge at the side, marked in micro-roentgens. The little needle flickered in the green area of the dial. I held it to myself and the reading didn't change. I pointed it up and pointed it down; it didn't change.

I held it to the radiation-seared body of Benedetto dell'Angela.

And it didn't change.

Radiation-seared? Not unless the instrument lied! If dell'Angela had ever in his life been within the disaster radius of an atomic explosion, it had been so long before that every trace of radioactive byproduct was gone!

Rena was right!

*

I worked like a machine, hardly thinking. I stood up and hurriedly touched the ion-tasting snout of the counter to the body on the shelf above Benedetto, the one above that, a dozen chosen at random up and down the aisle.

Two of them sent the needle surging clear off the scale; three were as untainted by radioactivity as Benedetto himself. A few others gave readings from "mild" to "lethal"—but all in the danger area.

Most were as untainted by radiation as Benedetto himself.

It was possible, I told myself frantically, that there were mysteries here I did not understand. Perhaps after a few months or a year, the radiation level would drop, so that the victim was still in deadly danger while the emitted radiation of his body was too slight to affect the counter. I didn't see how, but it was worth a thought. Anything was worth a thought that promised another explanation to this than the one Rena had given!

There had been, I remembered, a score or more of new suspendees in the main receiving vault at the juncture of the corridors. I hurried back to it. Here were fresh cases, bound to show on the gauge.

I leaned over the nearest one, first checking to make sure its identification tag was the cross-hatched red one that marked "radiation." I brought the counter close to the shriveled face—

But I didn't read the dial, not at first. I didn't have to. For I recognized that face. I had seen it, contorted in terror, mumbling frantic pleas for mercy, weeping and howling, on the old Class E uninsurable the expediters had found hiding in the vaults.

He had no radiation poisoning...unless a bomb had exploded in these very vaults in the past twelve hours.

It wasn't pleasant to stand there and stare around the vaults that were designed for the single purpose of saving human life—and to wonder how many of the eighty thousand souls it held were also prisoners.

And it wasn't even tolerable to think the thought that followed. If the Company was corrupt, and I had worked to do the Company's business, how much of this guilt was mine?

The Company, I had said and thought and tried to force others to agree, was the hope of humanity—the force that had permanently ended war (almost), driven out disease (nearly), destroyed the threat to any human of hunger or homelessness (in spite of the starving old man who slept in the shadow of the crypt, and others like him).

But I had to face the facts that controverted the Big Lie. If war was ended, what about Naples and Sicily, and Prague and Vienna, and all the squabbles in the Far East? *If there was no danger from disease, why had Marianna died?*

Rena had said that if there was no danger of disaster, no one would have paid their premiums. Obviously the Company could not have wanted that, but why had I never seen it before? Sample wars, sample deaths—the Company needed them. And no one, least of all me, fretted about how the samples felt about it.

Well, that was behind me. I'd made a bet with Rena, and I'd lost, and I had to pay off.

I opened the cased hypodermic kit Rena had given me and examined it uncomfortably. I had never used the old-fashioned sort of needle hypodermic; I knew a little something about the high-pressure spray type that forced its contents into the skin without leaving a mark, but I was very far from sure that I could manage this one without doing something wrong. Besides, there wasn't much of the fluid left, only the few drops left in the bottom of the bottle after Rena had loaded the needle that had been smashed.

I hurried back along the corridor toward Benedetto dell'Angela. I neared again the red-labeled door marked Bay 100, glanced at it in passing—and stopped.

This was the door that only a handful of people could open. It was labeled in five languages: "Entrance Strictly Prohibited. Experimental Section."

Why was it standing ajar?

And I heard a faint whisper of a moan: "*Aiutemi, aiutemi.*"

Someone inside was calling for help!

If I had been a hardened conspirator, I would never have stopped to investigate. But, of course, I wasn't. I pushed the door aside, against resistance, and peered in.

And that was my third major shock in the past quarter of an hour, because, writhing feebly just inside the door, staring up at me with an expression of pain and anger, was Luigi Zorchi.

He propped himself up on his hands, the rags of his plastic cocoon dangling from his shoulders.

"Oho," he said faintly. "The apprentice assassin again."

I found water for him at a bubble-fountain by the ramp; he drank at least a quart before I made him stop. Then he lay back, panting, staring at me. Except for the shreds of plastic and the bandages around the stumps of his legs, he was nude, like all the other suspendees inside their sacks. The luxuriant hair had already begun to grow back.

He licked his lips. More vigorous now, he snarled: "The plan fails, does it not?

You think you have Zorchi out of the way, but he will not stay there."

I said, "Zorchi, I'm sorry about all this. I—I know more now than I did yesterday."

He gaped. "Yesterday? Only *yesterday?*" He shook his head. "I would have thought a month, at the least. I have been crawling, assassin. Crawling for days, I thought." He tried to shrug—not easy, because he was leaning on his elbows.

"Very well, Weels. You may take me back to finish the job now. Sticking me with a needle and putting me on ice will not work. Perhaps you should kill me outright."

"Listen, Zorchi, I said I was sorry. Let's let it go at that for a moment. I—I admit you shouldn't be here. The question is, how do you come to be awake?"

"How not? I am Zorchi, Weels. Cut me and I heal; poison me and I cure myself." He spat furiously. "Starve me, however, and I no doubt will die, and it is true that you have come very near to starving me down here." He glowered at the shelves of cocooned bodies in the locked bay. "A pity, with all this pork and beef on the rack, waiting for me, but I find I am not a monster, Weels. It is a weakness; I do not suppose it would stop any Company man for a moment."

"Look, Zorchi," I begged, "take my word for it—I want to help you. You might as well believe me, you know. You can't be any worse off than you are."

He stared at me sullenly for a moment. Then, "True enough," he admitted.

"What then, Weels?"

I said hesitantly, "Well, I'd like to get you out of here..."

"Oh, yes. I would like that, too. How shall we do it?"

I rubbed the back of my neck thoughtfully, staring at him. I had had a sort of half-baked, partly worked out plan for rescuing Benedetto. Wake him up with the needle; find a medical orderly's whites somewhere; dress him; and walk him out.

It wasn't the best of all possible plans, but I had rank enough, particularly with Defoe off in Rome, to take a few liberties or stop questions if it became necessary.

And besides, I hadn't really thought I'd have to do it. I had fully expected—as recently as half an hour ago!—that I would find Benedetto raddled with gamma rays, a certainty for death if revived

SUPER PACK

before the half-life period of the radioelements in his body had brought the level down to safety.

That plan might work for Benedetto. But Zorchi, to mention only one possible obstacle, couldn't walk. And Benedetto, once I took off his beard with the razor Rena had insisted I bring for that purpose, would not be likely to be recognized by anyone.

Zorchi, on the other hand, was very nearly unforgettable.

I said honestly, "I don't know."

He nodded! "Nor do I, Weels. Take me then to your Defoe." His face wrinkled in an expression of fury and fear. "Die I can, if I must, but I do not wish to starve. It is good to be able to grow a leg, but do you understand that the leg must come from somewhere? I cannot make it out of air, Weels—I must eat. When I am in my home at Naples, I eat five, six, eight times a day; it is the way my body must have it. So if Defoe wishes to kill me, we will let him, but I must leave here now."

I shook my head. "Please understand me, Zorchi—I can't even do that for you. I can't have anybody asking me what I was doing down in this level." I hesitated only briefly; then, realizing that I was already in so deeply that secrecy no longer mattered, I told him about Benedetto dell'Angela, and the riot that failed, and my promise.

His reaction was incredulity. "You did not know, Weels? The arms and legs of the Company do not know what thoughts pass through its brain? Truly, the Company is a wonderful thing! Even the peasants know this much—the Company will do anything it must."

"I admit I never guessed. Now what?"

"That is up to you, Weels. If you try to take the two of us out, it endangers you. It is for you to decide."

So, of course, I could decide only one way.

I hid the hypodermic behind one of the bodies in Bay 100; it was no longer useful to me. I persuaded Zorchi to lie quietly in one of the tiers near Benedetto, slammed the heavy door to Bay 100, and heard the locks snap. That was the crossing of the Rubicon. You could open

103

that door easily enough from inside—that was to protect any personnel who might be caught in there. But only Defoe and a couple of others could open it from without, and the hypodermic was now as far out of reach as the Moon.

I opened Benedetto dell'Angela's face mask and shaved him, then sealed it again. I found another suspendee of about the same build, made sure the man was not radioactive, and transferred them. I switched tags: Benedetto dell'Angela was now Elio Barletteria. Then I walked unsteadily to the ramp, picked up the intercom and ordered the medical officer in charge to come down.

*

It was not Dr. Lawton who came, fortunately, but one of his helpers who had seen me before. I pointed to the pseudo-Barletteria. "I want this man revived." He sputtered, "You—you can't just take a suspendee out of his trance, Mr. Wills. It's a violation of medical ethics! These men are sick. They—"

"They'll be sicker still if we don't get some information from this one," I said grimly. "Are you going to obey Mr. Defoe's orders or not?"

He sputtered some more, but he gave in. His orderlies took Benedetto to the receiving station at the foot of the vault; one of them stood by while the doctor worriedly went through his routine. I sat and smoked, watching the procedure.

It was simple enough. One injection, a little chafing of the hands and feet by the bored orderly while the doctor glowered and I stonily refused to answer his questions, and a lot of waiting. And then the "casualty" stirred and moaned.

All the stand-by apparatus was there—the oxygen tent and the pulmotor and the heart stimulator and so on. But none of it was needed.

I said: "Fine, Doctor. Now send the orderly to have an ambulance standing by at the main entrance, and make out an exit pass for this casualty."

"No!" the doctor shouted. "This is against every rule, Mr. Wills. I insist on calling Dr. Lawton—"

"By all means," I said. "But there isn't much time. Make out the pass and get the ambulance, and we'll clear it with Dr. Lawton on the way out." He was all ready to say no again when I added: "This is by direct order of Mr. Defoe. Are you questioning his orders?"

He wasn't—not as long as I was going to clear it with Dr. Lawton. He did as I asked. One of the advantages of the Company's rigid regulations was that it was hard to enforce strict security on its personnel. If you didn't tell the staff that they were working for something needing covering up, you couldn't expect them to be constantly on guard.

When the orderly was gone and the doctor had scrawled out the pass, I said cordially, "Thank you, Doctor. Now would you like to know what all the fuss was about?"

"I certainly would," he snapped. "If you think—"

"I'm sorry," I apologized. "Come over here and take a look at this man."

I juggled the radiation counter in my hand as he stalked over. "Take a look at his eyes," I invited.

"Are you trying to tell me that this is a dangerously radioactive case? I warn you, Mr. Wills—"

"No, no," I said. "See for yourself. Look at the right eye, just beside the nose."

He bent over the awakening body, searchingly.

I clonked him with the radiation counter on the back of the head. They must have retired that particular counter from service after that; it wasn't likely to be very accurate any more.

The orderly found me bending over the doctor's body and calling for help. He bent, too, and he got the same treatment. Benedetto by then was awake; he listened to me and didn't ask questions. The blessings of dealing with conspirators—it was not necessary to explain things more than once.

And so, with a correctly uniformed orderly, who happened to be Benedetto dell'Angela, pushing the stretcher, and with myself displaying a properly made out pass to the expediter at the door, we rolled the sham-unconscious body of Luigi Zorchi out to a waiting ambulance.

I felt my pulse hammering as we passed the expediter at the door. I had thrown my coat over the place where legs should have been on "Barletteria," and Benedetto's old plastic cocoon, into which we had squeezed Zorchi, concealed most of him.

*

I needn't have worried. The expediter not only wasn't suspicious, he wasn't even interested.

Benedetto and I lifted Zorchi into the ambulance. Benedetto climbed in after him and closed the doors, and I went to the front. "You're dismissed," I told the driver. "I'll drive."

As soon as we were out of sight of the clinic, I found a phone, got Rena at the hotel, told her to meet me under the marquee. In five minutes, she was beside me and we were heading for the roads to the north.

"You win," I told her. "Your father's in back—along with somebody else. Now what? Do we just try to get lost in the hills somewhere?"

"No, Tom," she said breathlessly. "I—I have made arrangements." She giggled.

"I walked around the square and around, until someone came up to me. You do not know how many gentlemen came before that! But then one of my—friends showed up, to see if I was all right, and I arranged it. We go up the Rome highway two miles and there will be a truck."

"Fine," I said, stepping on the gas. "Now do you want to climb back and tell your father—"

I stopped in the middle of the word. Rena peered at me. "Tom," she asked anxiously, "is something wrong?"

SUPER PACK

I swallowed, staring after a disappearing limousine in the rearview mirror. "I— hope not," I said. "But your friends had better be there, because we don't have much time. I saw Defoe in the back of that limousine."

CHAPTER TEN

Rena craned her neck around the door and peered into the nave of the church. "He's kissing the Book," she reported. "It will be perhaps twenty minutes yet."

Her father said mildly, "I am in no hurry. It is good to rest here. Though truthfully, Mr. Wills, I thought I had been rested sufficiently by your Company."

I think we were all grateful for the rest. It had been a hectic drive up from Anzio. Even though Rena's "friends" were thoughtful people, they had not anticipated that we would have a legless man with us.

They had passports for Rena and myself and Benedetto; for Zorchi they had none. It had been necessary for him to hide under a dirty tarpaulin in the trunk of the ancient charcoal-burning car, while Rena charmed the Swiss Guards at the border. And it was risky. But the Guards charmed easily, and we got through.

Zorchi did not much appreciate it. He swore a ragged blue streak when we stopped in the shade of an olive grove and lugged him to the front seat again, and he didn't stop swearing until we hit the Appian Way. When the old gas-generator limped up a hill, he swore at its slowness; when it whizzed along the downgrades and level stretches, he swore at the way he was being bounced around.

I didn't regret rescuing Zorchi from the clinic—it was a matter of simple justice since I had helped trick him into it. But I did wish that it had been some more companionable personality that I had been obligated to.

Benedetto, on the other hand, shook my hand and said: "For God, I thank you," and I felt well repaid. But he was in the back seat being brought up to date by his daughter; I had the honor of Zorchi's company next to me...

There was a long Latin period from the church, a response from the altar boy, and then the final *Ite, missa est.* We heard the worshipers moving out of the church.

SUPER PACK

The priest came through the room we were waiting in, his robes swirling. He didn't look around, or give any sign that he knew we were there, though he almost stepped on Zorchi, sitting propped against a wall.

A moment later, another man in vaguely clerical robes entered and nodded to us. "Now we go below," he ordered.

Benedetto and I flanked Zorchi and carried him, an arm around each of our necks. We followed the sexton, or whatever he was, back into the church, before the altar—Benedetto automatically genuflected with the others, nearly making me spill Zorchi onto the floor—to a tapestry-hung door. He pushed aside the tapestry, and a cool, musty draft came up from darkness.

The sexton lit a taper with a pocket cigarette lighter and led us down winding, rickety steps. There was no one left in the church to notice us; if anyone had walked in, we were tourists, doing as countless millions of tourists had done before us over the centuries.

We were visiting the Catacombs.

Around us were the bones of the Christians of a very different Rome. Rena had told me about them: How they rambled under the modern city, the only entrances where churches had been built over them. How they had been nearly untouched for two thousand years. I even felt a little as though I really were a tourist as we descended, she had made me that curious to see them.

But I was disappointed. We lugged the muttering Zorchi through the narrow, musty corridors, with the bones of martyrs at our elbows, in the flickering light of the taper, and I had the curious feeling that I had been there before.

As, in a way, I had: I had been in the vaults of the Company's clinic at Anzio, in some ways very closely resembling these Catacombs—

Even to the bones of the martyrs.

I was almost expecting to see plastic sacks.

We picked our way through the warrens for several minutes, turning this way and that. I was lost in the first minute. Then the sexton stopped before a flat stone that had a crude, faded sketch of a fish on it; he leaned on it, and the stone discovered itself to be a door. We followed him through it into a metal-walled, high-ceilinged tunnel, utterly unlike the meandering Catacombs. I began to hear sounds; we went through another door, and light struck at our eyes.

I blinked and focused on a long room, half a dozen yards wide, almost as tall, at least fifty yards long. It appeared to be a section of an enormous tunnel; it appeared to be, and it was. Benedetto and I set Zorchi—still cursing—down on the floor and stared around.

There were people in the tunnel, dozens of them. There were desks and tables and file cabinets; it looked almost like any branch of the Company, with whirring mimeographs and clattering typewriters.

The sexton pinched out the taper and dropped it on the floor, as people came toward us.

"So now you are in our headquarters in Rome," said the man dressed as a sexton. "It is good to see you again, Benedetto."

"And it is much better to see you, Slovetski," the old man answered warmly.

*

This man Slovetski—I do not think I can say what he looked like.

He was, I found, the very leader of the "friends," the monarch of this underground headquarters. But he was a far cry from the image I had formed of a bearded agitator. There was a hint of something bright and fearful in his eyes, but his voice was warm and deep, his manner was reassuring, his face was friendly. Still— there was that cat-spark in his eyes.

Slovetski, that first day, gave me an hour of his time. He answered some of my questions—not all. The ones he smiled at, and shook his head, were about numbers and people. The ones he answered were about principles and things.

He would tell me, for instance, what he thought of the Company—endlessly. But he wouldn't say how many persons in the world were his followers. He wouldn't name any of the persons who were all around us. But he gladly told me about the place itself.

"History, Mr. Wills," he said politely. "History tells a man everything he needs to know. You look in the books, and you will learn of Mussolini, when this peninsula was all one state; he lived in Rome, and he started a subway. The archives even have maps. It is almost all abandoned now. Most of it was never finished. But the shafts are here, and the wiring that lights us still comes from the electric mains."

"And the only entrance is through the Catacombs?"

The spark gleamed bright in his eye for a second. Then he shrugged. "Why shouldn't I tell you? No. There are several others, but they are not all convenient." He chuckled. "For instance, one goes through a station on the part of the subway that is still in operation. But it would not have done for you, you see; Rena could not have used it. It goes through the gentlemen's washroom."

We chuckled, Slovetski and I. I liked him. He looked like what he once had been: a history teacher in a Company school, somewhere in Europe. We talked about History, and Civilization, and Mankind, and all the other capitalized subjects. He was very didactic and positive in what he said, just like a history teacher. But he was understanding. He made allowances for my background; he did not call me a fool. He was a patient monk instructing a novice in the mysteries of the order, and I was at ease with him.

But there was still that spark in his eye.

Rena disappeared almost as soon as we were safely in the tunnels. Benedetto was around, but he was as busy as Slovetski, and just as mysterious about what occupied him. So I had for company Zorchi.

We had lunch. "Food!" he said, and the word was an epithet. "They offer this to me for food! For pigs, Weels. Not for Zorchi!" He pushed the plate away from him and stared morosely at the table.

We were given a room to share, and one of Slovetski's men fixed up a rope-and-pulley affair so Zorchi could climb into his bed unaided. He was used to the help of a valet; the first time he tried it, he slipped and fell on the stumps of his legs. It must have hurt.

He shrieked, "Assassins! All of them! They put me in a kennel with the apprentice assassin, and the other assassins make a guillotine for me to kill myself on!" We had a long talk with Slovetski, on the ideals and principles of his movement. Zorchi stared mutinously at the wall. I found the whole thing very interesting— shocking, but interesting. But Zorchi was immune to shock—"Perhaps it is news to you, Weels, that the Company is a big beast?"—and he was interested in nothing in all the world but Zorchi.

By the end of the second day I stopped talking to him entirely. It wasn't kind. He disliked me, but he hated everyone else in the tunnel, so he had no one to talk to. But it was either that or hit him in the face, and—although many of my mores had changed overnight—I still did not think I could strike a man without legs.

And besides, the less I saw of Zorchi, the more time I had to think about Rena.

*

She returned on the third day, without a word of explanation to me of where she had been or what she had done. She greeted me and disappeared again, this time only for hours. Then she came back and said, "Now I am through, for a time. How have you liked our little hideaway?"

I said, "It gets lonesome."

"Lonesome?" Her brown eyes were wide and perfectly serious. "I had thought it would be otherwise, Tom. So many of us in this little space, how could you be lonesome?"

I took her hand. "I'm not lonesome now," I told her. We found a place to sit in a corner of the communal dining hall. Around us the life of the underground movement buzzed and swirled. It was much like a branch of the Company, as I have said; the work of this secret section seemed to be mostly a record-keeping depot for the activities that took place on the surface. But no one paid much attention to Rena and me.

What did we talk about? What couples have always talked about: Each other, and everything, and nothing. The only thing we did not talk about was my basic beliefs in regard to the Company. For I was too troubled in my mind to talk about them, and Rena sensitive enough not to bring them up.

For I had, with all honor, sworn an oath of allegiance to the Company; and I had not kept it.

I could not, even then, see any possibility of a world where the Company did not exist. For what the Company said of itself was true: Before the Company existed, men lived like beasts. There was always the instant danger of war and disease. No plan could be made, no hope could be held, that could not be wiped out by blind accident.

And yet, were men better off today? I could not doubt the truths I had been told. The Company permitted wars—I had seen it. The Company permitted disease—my own wife had died.

Somewhere there was an answer, but I couldn't find it. It was not, I was sure, in Slovetski's burning hatred of everything the Company stood for. But it could not be, either, in the unquestioning belief that I had once given.

But my views, it turned out, hardly mattered anymore; the die was cast. Benedetto appeared in the entrance to the dining hall, peering about. He saw us and came over, his face grave.

"I am sorry, Mr. Wills," he said. "I have been listening to Radio Napoli. It has just come over the air: A description of you, and an order for your arrest. The charge is—murder!"

I gaped at him, hardly believing. "Murder! But that's not true; I certainly never—"

Benedetto laid a hand on my shoulder. "Of course not, Mr. Wills. It is a fiction of the Company's, beyond doubt. But it is a fiction that may cause your death if you are discovered, do not doubt that."

I swallowed. "Who—whom did I murder?"

Benedetto shrugged. "I do not know who he is. The name they gave was Elio Barletteria."

That was the suspendee whose place Zorchi had usurped. I sat back, bewildered. It was true, at least, that I had had some connection with the man. But—kill him? Was it possible, I asked myself, that the mere act of taking him out of his plastic sack endangered his life? I doubted it, but still—

I asked Benedetto. He frowned. "It is—possible," he admitted at last. "We do not know much about the suspendees, Mr. Wills. The Company has seen to that. It is my opinion—only an opinion, I am afraid—that if this man Barletteria is dead, it had nothing to do with anything you did. Still—" he shrugged—"what difference does it make? If the Company calls you a murderer, you must be one, for the Company is always right. Is that not so?"

We left it at that, but I was far from easy in my mind. The dining hall filled, and we ate our evening meal, but I hardly noticed what I ate and I took no part in the conversation. Rena and her father considerately left me alone; Zorchi was, it seemed, sulking in our room, for he did not appear. But I was not concerned with him, for I had troubles of my own. I should have been...

After dinner was over, I excused myself and went to the tiny cubicle that had been assigned to Zorchi and myself. He wasn't there. Then I began to think: Would Zorchi miss a meal?

The answer was unquestionably no. With his metabolism, he needed many times the food of an ordinary person; his performance at table, in fact, was spectacular.

Something was wrong. I was shaken out of my self-absorption; I hurried to find Benedetto dell'Angela, and told him that Zorchi was gone.

It didn't take long for us to find the answer. The underground hideout was not large; it had only so many exits. It was only a matter of moments before one of the men Benedetto had ordered to search returned with an alarmed expression.

The exit that led through the subway station was ajar. Somehow Zorchi had hitched himself, on his stumps, down the long corridor and out the exit. It had to be while we were eating; he could never have made it except when everyone was in one room. How he had done it did not matter. The fact remained that Zorchi was gone and, with him, the secrecy of our hiding place.

CHAPTER ELEVEN

We had to move. There was no way out of it.

"Zorchi hates the Company," I protested. "I don't think he'll go to them and—"

"No, Wills." Slovetski patiently shook his head. "We can't take a chance. If we had been able to recapture him, then we could stay here. But he got clean away." There was admiration in his eyes. "What a conspirator he would have made! Such strength and determination! Think of it, Wills, a legless man in the city of Rome. He cannot avoid attracting attention. He can barely move by himself. And yet, our men track him into the subway station, to a telephone...and that is all. Someone picks him up. Who? A friend, one supposes—certainly not the Company, or they would have been here before this. But to act so quickly, Wills!"

Benedetto dell'Angela coughed. "Perhaps more to the point, Slovetski, is how quickly we ourselves shall now act."

Slovetski grinned. "All is ready," he promised. "See, evacuation already has begun!"

Groups of men were quickly placing file folders into cartons and carrying them off. They were not going far, I found later, only to a deserted section of the ancient Roman Catacombs, from which they could be retrieved and transported, little by little, at a later date.

By sundown, Rena and I were standing outside the little church which contained the entrance to the Catacombs. The two of us went together; only two. It would look quite normal, it was agreed, for a young man and a girl to travel together, particularly after my complexion had been suitably stained and my Company clothes discarded and replaced with a set of Rome's best ready-to-wears.

It did not occur to me at the time, but Rena must have known that her own safety was made precarious by being with me. Rena alone had nothing to fear, even if she had been caught and questioned by an agent of the Company. They would suspect her, because of her father, but suspicion would do her no harm. But Rena in the company of a wanted "murderer"—and one traveling in disguise—was far less safe...

We found an ancient piston-driven cab and threaded through almost all of Rome. We spun around the ancient stone hulk of the Colosseum, passed the balcony where a sign stated the dictator, Mussolini, used to harangue the crowds, and climbed a winding, expensive-looking street to the Borghese Gardens.

Rena consulted her watch. "We're early," she said. We had gelati in an open-air pavilion, listening to the wheezing of a sweating band; then, in the twilight, we wandered hand in hand under trees for half an hour.

Then Rena said, "Now it is time." We walked to the far end of the Gardens where a small copter-field served the Class-A residential area of Rome. A dozen copters were lined up at the end of the take-off hardstand. Rena led me to the nearest of them.

I looked at it casually, and stopped dead.

"Rena!" I whispered violently. "Watch out!" The copter was black and purple; it bore on its flank the marking of the Swiss Guard, the Roman police force.

She pressed my hand. "Poor Tom," she said. She walked boldly up to one of the officers lounging beside the copter and spoke briefly to him, too low for me to hear.

It was only when the big vanes overhead had sucked us a hundred yards into the air, and we were leveling off and heading south, that she said: "These are friends too, you see. Does it surprise you?"

I swallowed, staring at the hissing jets at the ends of the swirling vanes. "Well," I said, "I'm not exactly surprised, but I thought that your friends were, well, more likely to be—"

"To be rabble?" I started to protest, but she was not angry. She was looking at me with gentle amusement. "Still you believe, Tom. Deep inside you: An enemy of the Company must be, at the best, a silly zealot like my father and me—and at the worst, rabble." She laughed as I started to answer her. "No, Tom, if you are right, you should not deny it; and if you are wrong—you will see."

I sat back and stared, disgruntled, at the purple sunset over the Mediterranean. I never saw such a girl for taking the wind out of your sails.

*

Once across the border, the Guards had no status, and it was necessary for them to swing inland, threading through mountains and passes, remaining as inconspicuous as possible.

It was little more than an hour's flight until I found landmarks I could recognize. To our right was the bright bowl of Naples; far to our left, the eerie glow that marked bombed-out New Caserta. And ahead, barely visible, the faint glowing plume that hung over Mount Vesuvius.

Neither Rena nor the Guards spoke, but I could feel in their tense attitudes that this was the danger-point. We were in the lair of the enemy. Undoubtedly we were being followed in a hundred radars, and the frequency-pattern would reveal our copter for what it was—a Roman police plane that had no business in that area. Even if the Company let us pass, there was always the chance that some Neapolitan radarman, more efficient, or more anxious for a promotion, than his peers would alert an interceptor and order us down. Certainly, in the old days, interception would have been inevitable; for Naples had just completed a war, and only short weeks back an unidentified aircraft would have been blasted out of the sky.

But we were ignored.

And that, I thought to myself, was another facet to the paradox. For when, in all the world's years before these days of the Company, was there such complacency, such deep-rooted security, that a nation just out of a war should have soothed its combat-jangled nerves overnight? Perhaps the Company had not ended wars. But the fear of wars was utterly gone.

SUPER PACK

We fluttered once around the volcano, and dipped in to a landing on a gentle hump of earth halfway up its slope, facing Naples and the Bay. We were a few hundred yards from a cluster of buildings—perhaps a dozen, in all.

I jumped out, stumbling and recovering myself. Rena stepped lightly into my arms. And without a word, the Guards fed fuel to the jets, the rotor whirled, and the copter lifted away from us and was gone.

Rena peered about us, getting her bearings. There was a sliver of a moon in the eastern sky, enough light to make it possible to get about. She pointed to a dark hulk of a building far up the slope. "The Observatory. Come, Tom."

*

The volcanic soil was rich, but not very useful to farmers. It was not only the question of an eruption of the cone, for that sort of hazard was no different in kind than the risk of hailstorm or drought. But the mountain sides did not till easily, its volcanic slopes being perhaps steeper than those of most mountains.

The ground under our feet had never been in cultivation. It was pitted and rough, and grown up in a tangle of unfamiliar weeds. And it was also, I discovered with considerable shock, warm to the touch.

I saw a plume of vapor, faintly silver in the weak light, hovering over a hummock. Mist, I thought. Then it occurred to me that there was too much wind for mist. It was steam! I touched the soil. Blood heat, at least.

I said, with some difficulty, "Rena, look!"

She laughed. "Oh, it is an eruption, Tom. Of course it is. But not a new one. It is lava, you see, from the little blast the Sicilians touched off. Do not worry about it..."

We clambered over the slippery cogs of a funicular railway and circled the ancient stone base of the building she had pointed to. There was no light visible; but Rena found a small door, rapped on it and presently it opened.

119

Out of the darkness came Slovetski's voice: "Welcome."

Once this building had been the Royal Vulcanological Observatory of the Kingdom of Italy. Now it was a museum on the surface, and underneath another of the hideouts of Rena's "friends."

But this was a hideout somewhat more important than the one in the Roman Catacombs, I found. Slovetski made no bones about it.

He said, "Wills, you shouldn't be here. We don't know you. We can't trust you."

He held up a hand. "I know that you rescued dell'Angela. But that could all be an involved scheme of the Company. You could be a Company spy. You wouldn't be the first, Wills. And this particular installation is, shall I say, important. You may even find why, though I hope not. If we hadn't had to move so rapidly, you would never have been brought here. Now you're here, though, and we'll make the best of it." He looked at me carefully, then, and the glinting spark in the back of his eyes flared wickedly for a moment. "Don't try to leave. And don't go anywhere in this building where Rena or dell'Angela or I don't take you."

And that was that. I found myself assigned to the usual sort of sleeping accommodations I had come to expect in this group. Underground—cramped—and a bed harder than the Class-C Blue Heaven minimum.

*

The next morning, Rena breakfasted with me, just the two of us in a tower room looking down over the round slope of Vesuvius and the Bay beneath. She said: "The museum has been closed since the bomb landed near, so you can roam around the exhibits if you wish. There are a couple of caretakers, but they're with us. The rest of us will be in conference. I'll try to see you for lunch."

And she conducted me to an upper level of the Observatory and left me by myself. I had my orders—stay in the public area of the museum. I didn't like them. I wasn't used to being treated like a small boy, left by his mother in a Company day nursery while she busied herself with the important and incomprehensible affairs of adults.

Still, the museum was interesting enough, in a way. It had been taken over by the Company, it appeared, and although the legend frescoed around the main gallery indicated that it was supposed to be a historical museum of the Principality of Naples, it appeared by examination of the exhibits that the "history" involved was that of Naples vis-a-vis the Company.

Not, of course, that such an approach was entirely unfair. If it had not been for the intervention of the Company, after the Short War, it is more than possible that Naples as an independent state would never have existed.

It was the Company's insistence on the dismantling of power centers (as Millen Carmody himself had described it) that had created Naples and Sicily and Prague and Quebec and Baja California and all the others.

Only the United States had been left alone—and that, I think, only because nobody dared to operate on a wounded tiger. In the temper of the nation after the Short War, the Company would have survived less than a minute if it had proposed severing any of the fifty-one states...

The museum was interesting enough, for anyone with a taste for horrors. It showed the changes in Neapolitan life over the past century or so. There was a reconstruction of a typical Neapolitan home of the early Nineteen-forties: a squalid hovel, packed ten persons to the room, with an American G.I., precursor of the Company expediters, spraying DDT into the bedding. There was, by comparison, a typical Class-B Blue Heaven modern allotment—with a certain amount of poetic license; few Class-B homes really had polyscent showers and autocooks.

It was the section on warfare, however, that was most impressive. It was in the far back of the building, in a large chamber anchored to bedrock. It held a frightening display of weapons, from a Tiger Tank to a gas-gun. Bulking over everything else in the room, even the tank, was the thirty-foot height of a Hell-bomb in a four-story display. I looked at it a second time, vaguely disturbed by something I hadn't quite placed—an indigo gleam to the metal of the warhead, with a hint of evil under its lacquered sheen...

It was cobalt. I bent to read the legend: *This is the casing of the actual cobalt bomb that would have been used on Washington if the Short War had lasted one more day. It is calculated that, loaded with a Mark XII hydrogen-lithium bomb, sufficient radioactive Cobalt-60 would have been transmuted to end all life on Earth within thirty days.*

I looked at it again, shuddering.

Oh, it was safe enough now. Until the hydrogen reaction could turn the ordinary cobalt sheathing into the deadly isotope-60, it was just such stuff as was used to alloy magnets and make cobalt glass. It was even more valuable as a museum piece than as the highly purified metal.

Score one for the Company. They'd put a stop to that danger. Nobody would have a chance to arm it and send it off now. No small war would find it more useful than the bomb it would need—and no principality would risk the Company's wrath in using it. And while the conspiracy might have planes and helicopters, the fissionable material was too rigidly under Company control for them to have a chance. The Super Hell-bomb would never go off. And that was something that might mean more to the Company's credit than anything else.

Maybe it was possible that in this controversy both sides were right. And, of course, there was the obvious corollary.

I continued my wandering, looking at the exhibits, the rubble of the museum's previous history. The cast of the Pompeiian gladiator, caught by the cinder-fall in full flight, his straining body reproduced to every contorted line by the incandescent ashes that had encased him. The carefully chipped and labeled samples from the lava flows of the past two centuries. The awe-inspiring photographs of Vesuvius in eruption.

But something about the bomb casing kept bothering me. I wandered around a bit longer and then turned back to the main exhibit. The big casing stretched upward and downward, with narrow stairs leading down to the lower level at its base. It was on the staircase I'd noticed something before. Now I hesitated, trying to spot whatever it was. There was a hint of something down there. Finally, I shrugged and went down to inspect it more closely.

Lying at the base was a heavy radiation glove. A workman's glove, used and dirty with grease. And as my eyes darted up, I could see that the bolts on the lower servicing hatches were half-unscrewed.

Radiation gloves and tampering with the casing!

There were two doors to the pit for the bomb casing, but either one was better than risking the stairs again where someone might see me. Or so I figured. If they found I'd learned anything...

I grabbed for the nearer door, threw it open. I knew it was a mistake when the voice reached my ears.

"—after hitting the Home office with a Thousand-kiloton bomb. It's going to take fast work. Now the schedule I've figured out so far—God's damnation! How did you get in here, Wills?"

It was Slovetski, leaning across a table, staring at me. Around the table were Benedetto and four or five others I did not recognize. All of them looked at me as though I were the Antichrist, popped out of the marble at St. Peter's Basilica on Easter Sunday.

The spark was a raging flame in Slovetski's eyes. Benedetto dell'Angela said sharply, "Wait!" He strode over to me, half shielding me from Slovetski. "Explain this, Thomas," he demanded.

"I thought this was the hall door," I stammered, spilling the first words I could while I tried to find any excuse...

"Wills! I tell you, answer me!"

I said, "Look, did you expect me to carry a bell and cry unclean? I didn't mean to break in. I'll go at once..."

123

In a voice that shook, Slovetski said: "Wait one moment." He pressed a bell-button on the wall; we all stood there silent, the five of them staring at me, me wishing I was dead.

There was a patter of feet outside, and Rena peered in. She saw me and her hand went to her heart.

"Tom! But—"

Slovetski said commandingly, "Why did you permit him his liberty?"

Rena looked at him wide-eyed. "But, please, I asked you. You suggested letting him study the exhibits."

Benedetto nodded. "True, Slovetski," he said gravely. "You ordered her to attend until our—conference was over."

The flame surged wildly in Slovetski's eyes—not at me. But he got it under control. He said, "Take him away." He did not do me the courtesy of looking my way again. Rena took me by the hand and led me off, closing the door behind us.

As soon as we were outside, I heard a sharp babble of argument, but I could make out no words through the door. I didn't need to; I knew exactly what they were saying.

This was the proposition: *Resolved, that the easiest thing to do is put Wills out of the way permanently.* And with Slovetski's fiery eyes urging the positive, what eager debater would say him nay?

* * * *

Rena said: "I can't tell you, Tom. *Please* don't ask me!"

I said, "This is no kid's game, Rena! They're talking about bombing the Home Office!"

She shook her head. "Tom, Tom. You must have misunderstood."

"I heard them!"

"Tom, *please* don't ask me any more questions."

I slammed my hand down on the table and swore. It didn't do any good. She didn't even look up from the remains of her dinner.

It had been like that all afternoon. The Great Ones brooded in secret. Rena and I waited in her room, until the museum's public visiting hours were over and we could go up into the freer atmosphere of the reception lounge. And then we waited there.

I said mulishly: "Ever since I met you, Rena, I've been doing nothing but wait. I'm not built that way!"

No answer.

I said, with all of my patience: "Rena, I heard them talking about bombing the Home Office. Do you think I am going to forget that?"

Leadenly: "No, Tom."

"So what does it matter if you tell me more? If I cannot be trusted, I already know too much. If I can be trusted, what does it matter if I know the rest?"

Again tears. "Please don't ask me!"

I yelled: "At least you can tell me what we're waiting for!"

She dabbed at her eyes. "Please, Tom, I don't know much more than you do. Slovetski, he is like this sometimes. He gets, I suppose you would say, thoughtful. He concentrates so very much on one thing, you see, that he forgets everything around him. It is possible that he has forgotten that we are waiting. I don't know."

I snarled, "I'm tired of this. Go in and remind him!"

"No, Tom!" There was fright in her voice; and I found that she had told me one of the things I wanted to know. If it was not wise to remind Slovetski that I was waiting his pleasure, the probability was that it would not be pleasant for me when he remembered.

I said, "But you must know something, Rena. Don't you see that it could do no harm to tell me?"

She said miserably, "Tom, I know very little. I did not—did not know as much as you found out." I stared at her. She nodded. "I had perhaps a suspicion, it is true. Yes, I suspected. But I did not *really* think, Tom, that there was a question of bombing. It is not how we were taught. It is not what Slovetski promised, when we began."

"You mean you didn't know Slovetski was planning violence?"

She shook her head. "And even now, I think, perhaps you heard wrong, perhaps there was a mistake."

125

I stood up and leaned over her. "Rena, listen to me. There was no mistake. They're working on that casing. Tell me what you know!"

She shook her head, weeping freely.

I raged: "This is asinine! What can there be that you will not tell? The Company supply base that Slovetski hopes to raid to get a bomb? The officers he plans to bribe, to divert some other nation's quota of plutonium?"

She took a deep breath. "Not that, Tom."

"Then what? You don't mean to say that he has a complete underground separator plant—that he is making his own plutonium!"

She was silent for a long time, looking at me. Then she sighed. "I will tell you, Tom. No, he does not have a plant. He doesn't need one, you see. He already has a bomb."

I straightened. "That's impossible."

She was shaking her head. I protested, "But the—the quotas, Rena. The Company tracks every milligram of fissionable material from the moment it leaves the reactor! The inspections! Expediters with Geiger counters cover every city in the world!" "Not here, Tom. You remember that the Sicilians bombed Vesuvius? There is a high level of radioactivity all up and down the mountain. Not enough to be dangerous, but enough to mask a buried bomb." She closed her eyes. "And—well, you are right, Tom. I might as well tell you. In that same war, you see, there was a bomb that did not explode. You recall?"

"Yes, but—"

"But it couldn't explode, Tom. It was a dummy. Slovetski is a brilliant man. Before that bomb left the ground, he had diverted it. What went up was a hollow shell. What is left—the heart of the bomb—is buried forty feet beneath us."

I stared at her, the room reeling. I was clutching at straws. I whispered, "But that was only a fission bomb, Rena. Slovetski—I heard him—he said a Thousand-kiloton bomb. That means hydrogen, don't you see? Surely he hasn't tucked one of those away."

Rena's face was an agony of regret. "I do not understand all these things, so you must bear with me. I know this; there has been secret talk about the Milanese generators, and I know that the talk has to do with heavy water. And I am not stupid altogether, I know that from heavy water one can get what is used in a hydrogen bomb. And there is more, of course—lithium, perhaps? But he has that. You have seen it, I think. It is on a pedestal in this building."

I sat down hard. It was impossible. But it all fell into place. Given the fissionable core of the bomb—plus the deuterium, plus the lithium-bearing shell—it was no great feat to put the parts together and make a Hell-bomb.

The mind rejected it; it was too fantastic. It was frightful and terrifying, and worst of all was that something lurking at the threshold of memory, something about that bomb on display in the museum...

And, of course, I remembered.

"Rena!" I said, struggling for breath. I nearly could not go on, it was too dreadful to say. "Rena! Have you ever looked at that bomb? Have you read the placard on it? *That bomb is cobalt!*"

CHAPTER TWELVE

From the moment I had heard those piercing words from Slovetski's mouth, I had been obsessed with a vision. A Hell-bomb on the Home Office. America's eastern seaboard split open. New York a hole in the ocean, from Kingston to Sandy Hook; orange flames spreading across Connecticut and the Pennsylvania corner.

That was gone—and in its place was something worse.

Radiocobalt bombing wouldn't simply kill locally by a gout of flaring radiation. It would leave the atmosphere filled with colloidal particles of deadly, radioactive Cobalt-60. A little of that could be used to cure cancers and perform miracles. The amount released from the sheathing of cobalt—normal, "safe" cobalt—around a fissioning hydrogen bomb could kill a world. A single bomb of that kind could wipe out all life on Earth, as I remembered my schooling.

I'm no physicist; I didn't know what the quantities involved might mean, once the equations came off the drafting paper and settled like a ravening storm on the human race. But I had a glimpse of radioactive dust in every breeze, in every corner of every land. Perhaps a handful of persons in Cambodia or Vladivostok or Melbourne might live through it. But there was no question in my mind: If that bomb went off, it was the end of our civilization.

I saw it clearly.

And so, having betrayed the Company to Slovetski's gang, I came full circle.

Even Judas betrayed only One.

*

Getting away from the Observatory was simple enough, with Rena shocked and confused enough to look the other way. Finding a telephone near Mount Vesuvius was much harder.

I was two miles from the mountain before I found what I was looking for—a Blue Wing fully-automatic filling station. The electronic scanners clucked worriedly, as they searched for the car I should have been driving, and the policy-punching slot glowed red and receptive, waiting for my order. I ignored them.

What I wanted was inside the little unlocked building—a hushaphone-booth with vision attachment. The important thing was to talk direct to Defoe and only to Defoe. In the vision screen, impedance mismatch would make the picture waver if there was anyone uninvited listening in.

But I left the screen off while I put through my call. The office servo-operator (it was well after business hours) answered blandly, and I said: "Connect me with Defoe, crash priority."

It was set to handle priority matters on a priority basis; there was neither fuss nor argument, though a persistent buzzing in the innards of the phone showed that, even while the robot was locating Defoe for me, it was double-checking the connection to find out why there was no vision on the screen.

It said briskly, "Stand by, sir," and I was connected with Defoe's line—on a remote hookup with the hotel where he was staying, I guessed. I flicked the screen open.

But it wasn't Defoe on the other end of the line. It was Susan Manchester, with that uncharacteristic, oddly efficient look she had shown at the vaults.

She said crisply, and not at all surprised: "Tom Wills."

"That's right," I said, thinking quickly. Well, it didn't much matter. I should have realized that Defoe's secretary, howsoever temporary, would be taking his calls. I said rapidly: "Susan, I can't talk to you. It has to be Defoe. Take my word for it, it's important. Please put him on."

She gave me no more of an argument than the robot had.

In a second, Defoe was on the screen, and I put Susan out of my mind. She must have said something to him, because the big, handsome face was unsurprised, though the eyes were contracted. "Wills!" he snapped. "You fool! Where are you?"

I said, "Mr. Defoe, I have to talk to you. It's a very urgent matter."

"Come in and do it, Wills! Not over the telephone."

I shook my head. "No, sir. I can't. It's too, well, risky."

"Risky for you, you mean!" The words were icily disgusted. "Wills, you have betrayed me. No man ever got away with that. You're imposing on me, playing on my family loyalty to your dead wife, and I want to tell you that you won't get away with it. There's a murder charge against you, Wills! Come in and talk to me—or else the police will pick you up before noon."

I said with an effort, "I don't mean to impose on any loyalty, but, in common decency, you ought to hear—"

"Decency!" His face was cold. "You talk about decency! You and that dell'Angela traitor you joined. Decency! Wills, you're a disgrace to the memory of a decent and honest woman like Marianna. I can only say that I am glad—glad, do you hear me?—that she's dead and rid of you."

I said, "Wait a minute, Defoe! Leave Marianna out of this. I only—"

"Don't interrupt me! God, to think a man I trusted should turn out to be Judas himself! You animal, the Company has protected you from the day you were born, and you try to destroy it. Why, you pitiful idiot, you aren't fit to associate with the dogs in the kennel of a decent human being!"

There was more. Much, much more. It was a flow of abuse that paralyzed me, less because of what he said than because of who was saying it. Suave, competent Defoe, ranting at me like a wounded Gogarty! I couldn't have been more astonished if the portrait of Millen Carmody had whispered a bawdy joke from the frontispiece of the Handbook.

I stood there, too amazed to be furious, listening to the tirade from the midget image in the viewplate. It must have lasted for three or four minutes; then, almost in mid-breath, Defoe glanced at something outside my range of vision, and stopped his stream of abuse. I started to cut in while I could, but he held up one hand quickly.

He smiled gently. Very calmly, as though he had not been damning me a moment before, he said: "I shall be very interested to hear what you have to say."

That floored me. It took me a second to shake the cobwebs out of my brain before I said waspishly, "If you hadn't gone through all that jabber, you would have heard it long ago."

The midget in the scanner shrugged urbanely. "True," he conceded. "But then, Thomas, I wouldn't have had you."

And he reached forward and clicked off the phone. Tricked! Tricked and trapped! I cursed myself for stupidity. While he kept me on the line, the call was being traced—there was no other explanation. And I had fallen for it!

I slapped the door of the booth open and leaped out.

I got perhaps ten feet from the booth.

Then a rope dropped over my shoulders. Its noose yanked tight around my arms, and I was being dragged up, kicking futilely. I caught a glimpse of the broad Latin faces gaping at me from below, then two men on a rope ladder had me.

I was dragged in through the bottom hatch of a big helicopter with no markings. The hatch closed. Facing me was a lieutenant of expediters.

The two men tumbled in after me and reeled in the rope ladder, as the copter dipped and swerved away. I let myself go limp as the rope was loosened around me; when my hands were free I made my bid.

I leaped for the lieutenant; my fist caught him glancingly on the throat, sending him reeling and choking backward. I grabbed for the hard-pellet gun at his hip—he was pawing at it—and we tumbled across the floor.

It was, for one brief moment, a chance. I was no copter pilot, but the gun was all the pilot I'd need—if only I got it out.

But the expediters behind me were no amateurs. I ducked as the knotted end of the rope whipped savagely toward me. Then one of the other expediters was on my back; the gun came out, and flew free. And that was the end of that.

I had, I knew, been a fool to try it. But I wasn't sorry. They had too much rough-and-tumble training for me to handle. But that one blow had felt good. It didn't seem as worthwhile a few moments later. I was fastened to a seat, while the wheezing lieutenant gave orders in a strangled voice. "Not too many marks on him," he was saying. "Try it over the kidneys again..."

I never even thought of maintaining a heroic silence. They had had plenty of experience with the padded club, too, and I started to black out twice before finally I went all the way down.

*

I came to with a light shining in my eyes.

There was a doctor putting his equipment away. "He'll be all right, Mr. Defoe," he said, and snapped his bag shut and left the circle of light.

I felt terrible, but my head was clearing.

I managed to focus my eyes. Defoe was there, and a couple of other men. I recognized Gogarty, looking sick and dejected, and another face I knew—it was out of my Home Office training—an officer whose name I didn't recall, wearing the uniform of a lieutenant-general of expediters. That meant at least an expediter corps in Naples!

I said weakly, "Hi."

Defoe stood over me. He said, "I'm very glad to see you, Thomas. Coffee?"

He steadied my hands as I gulped it. When I had managed a few swallows, he took the cup away.

"I did not think you would resist arrest, Thomas," he said in a parental tone.

I said, "Damn it, you didn't have to arrest me! I came down here of my own free will!"

"Down?" His eyebrows rose. "Down from where do you mean, Thomas?"

"Down from Mount—" I hesitated, then finished. "All right. Down from Mount Vesuvius. The museum, where I was hiding out with the ringleaders of the anti-Company movement. Is that what you want to know?"

Defoe crackled: "Manning!" The lieutenant-general saluted and left the room. Defoe said, "That was the first thing I wanted, yes. But now I want much more. Please begin talking, Thomas. I will listen."

I talked. There was nothing to stop me. Even with my body a mass of aches and pains from the tender care of the Company's expediters, I still had to side with the Company in this. For the Cobalt-bomb ended all loyalties.

I left nothing important out, not even Rena. I admitted that I had taken Benedetto from the clinic, how we had escaped to Rome, how we had fled to Vesuvius...and what I had learned. I made it short, skipping a few unimportant things like Zorchi.

And Defoe sat sipping his coffee, listening, his warm eyes twinkling.

I stopped. He pursed his lips, considering.

"Silly," he said at last.

"Silly? What's silly!"

He said, "Thomas, I don't care about your casual affairs. And I would have excused your—precipitousness—since you have brought back certain useful information. Quite useful. I don't deny it. But I don't like being lied to, Thomas."

"I haven't lied!"

He said sharply, "There is no way to get fissionable material except through the Company!"

"Oh, hell!" I shook my head. "How about a dud bomb, Defoe?"

For the first time he looked puzzled. "Dud bomb?"

Gogarty looked sick. "There's—there's a report on your desk, Mr. Defoe," he said worriedly. "We—well—figured the half-masses just got close enough to boil instead of to explode. We—"

"I see." Defoe looked at him for a long moment. Then, disregarding Gogarty, he turned back to me, shoved the coffee at me. "All right, Thomas. They've got the warhead. Hydrogen? Cobalt? What about fuel?"

I told him what I knew. Gogarty, listening, licked his lips. I didn't envy him. I could see the worry in him, the fear of Defoe's later wrath. For in Defoe, as in Slovetski, there was that deadly fire. It blazed only when it was allowed to; but what it touched withered and died. I had not seen Defoe as tightly concentrated, as drivingly intent, before. I was sorry for Gogarty when at last, having drained me dry, Defoe left. But I was glad for me.

*

He was gone less than an hour—just time for me to eat a Class-C meal a silent expediter brought.

He thrust the door open and stared at me with whitely glaring eyes. "If I thought you were lying, Thomas..." His voice was cracking with suppressed emotion.

"What happened?" I demanded.

"Don't you know?" He stood trembling, staring at me. "You told the truth—or part of the truth. There was a hideout on Vesuvius. But an hour ago they got away—while you were wasting time. Was it a stall, Thomas? Did you know they would run?"

I said, "Defoe, don't you see, that's all to the good? If they had to run, they couldn't possibly take the bomb with them. That means—"

He was shaking his head. "Oh, but you're wrong, Thomas. According to the director of the albergo down the hill, three skyhook helicopters came over—big ones. They peeled the roof off, as easy as you please, and they lifted the bomb out and then flew away."

I said stupidly, "Where?"

He nodded. There was no emotion in his voice, only in his eyes. He might have been discussing the weather. "Where? That is a good question. I hope we will find it out, Thomas. We're checking the radar charts; they can't hide for long. But how did they get away at all? Why did you give them the time?"

He left me. Perversely, I was almost glad. It was part of the price of switching allegiance, I was learning, that shreds and tatters of loyalties cling to you and carry over. When I went against the Company to rescue Benedetto, I still carried with me my *Adjusters' Handbook*. And I confess that I never lost the habit of reading a page or two in it, even in the Catacombs, when things looked bad. And when I saw the murderous goal that Slovetski's men were marching toward, and I returned to Defoe, I still could feel glad that Benedetto, at least, had got away.

But not far.

It was only a few hours, but already broad daylight when Gogarty, looking shaken, came into the room. He said testily, "Damn it, Wills, I wish I'd never seen you! Come on! Defoe wants you with us."

"Come on where?" I got up as he gestured furiously for haste.

"Where do you think? Did you think your pals would be able to stay out of sight forever? We've got them pinpointed, bomb and all."

He was almost dragging me down the corridor, toward a courtyard. I limped out into the bright morning and blinked. The court was swarming with armed expediters, clambering into personnel-carrying copters marked with the vivid truce-team insignia of the Company. Gogarty hustled me into the nearest and the jets sizzled and we leaped into the air.

I shouted, over the screaming of the jets, "Where are we going?"

Gogarty spat and pointed down the long purple coastline. "To their hideout— Pompeii!"

CHAPTER THIRTEEN

No one discussed tactics with me, but it was clear that this operation was carefully planned. Our copter was second in a long string of at least a dozen that whirled down the coastline, past the foothills of Vesuvius, over the clusters of fishing villages and vineyards.

I had never seen Pompeii, but I caught a glimpse of something glittering and needle-nosed, upthrust in the middle of a cluster of stone buildings that might have been the ruins.

Then the first ten of the copters spun down to a landing, while two or three more flew a covering mission overhead.

The expediters, hard-pellet guns at the ready, leaped out and formed in a skirmish line. Gogarty and a pair of expediters stayed close by me, behind the line of attack; we followed the troops as they dog-trotted through a field of some sort of grain, around fresh excavations, down a defile into the shallow pit that held the ruins of first-century Pompeii.

I had no time for archeology, but I remember tripping over wide, shallow gutters in the stone-paved streets, and cutting through a tiny villa of some sort whose plaster walls still were decorated with faded frescoes.

Then we heard the spatter of gunfire and Gogarty, clutching at me, skidded to a halt. "This is specialist work," he panted. "Best thing we can do is stay out of it."

I peered around a column and saw a wide open stretch. Beyond it was a Roman arch and the ruined marble front of what once had been a temple of some sort; in the open ground lay the three gigantic copters Defoe had mentioned.

The vanes of one of them were spinning slowly, and it lurched and quivered as someone tried to get it off the ground under fire. But the big thing was in the middle of the area: The bomb, enormous and terrifying as its venomous nose thrust up into the sky. By its side was a tank truck, the side of it painted with the undoubtedly untrue legend that it contained crude olive oil. Hydrazine, more likely!

Hoses connected it with the base of the guided-missile bomb; and a knot of men were feverishly in action around it, some clawing desperately at the fittings of the bomb, some returning the skirmish fire of the expediters.

We had the advantage of surprise, but not very much of that. From the top of the ancient temple a rapid-fire pellet gun sprayed into the flank of the skirmish line, which immediately broke up as the expediters leaped for cover.

One man fell screaming out of the big skyhook copter, but someone remained inside, for it lurched and dipped and roared crazily across the field in as ragged a takeoff as I ever saw, until its pilot got it under control. It bobbed over the skirmish line under fire, but returning the fire as whatever few persons were inside it leaned out and strafed the expediters. Then the skyhook itself came under attack as the patrol copters swooped in.

The big ship staggered toward the nearest of them. It must have been intentional: We could see the faint flare of muzzle-blast as the two copters fired on each other; they closed, and there was a brutal rending noise as they collided. They were barely a hundred feet in the air; they crashed in a breath, and flames spread out from the wreckage.

And Slovetski's resources still had not run out. There was a roar and a screech of metal, and a one-man cobra tank slithered out of one of the buildings and came rapidly across the field toward the expediters.

Gogarty, beside me, was sobbing with fear; that little tank carried self-loading rockets. It blasted a tiny shrine into rubble, spun and came directly toward us. We ran. I didn't even see the second expediter aircraft come whirling in and put the cobra tank out of action with its heavy weapons. I heard the firing, but it was swallowed up in a louder screaming roar.

Gogarty stared at me from the drainage trench we had flung ourselves into. We both leaped up and ran back toward the open field.

There was an explosion as we got there—the fake "olive-oil" truck, now twenty yards from the bomb, had gone up in a violent blast. But we hardly noticed. For at the base of the bomb itself red-purple fire was billowing out. It screamed and howled and changed color to a blinding blue as the ugly squat shape danced and jiggled. The roar screamed up from a bull-bass to a shrieking coloratura and beyond as the bomb lifted and gained speed and, in the blink of an eye, was gone.

I hardly noticed that the sound of gunfire died raggedly away. We were not the only ones staring unbelievingly at the sky where that deadly shape had disappeared. Of the scores of men on both sides in that area, not a single eye was anywhere else.

The bomb had been fueled; we were too late. Its servitors, perhaps at the cost of their own lives, had torched it off. It was on its way.

The cobalt bomb—the single weapon that could poison the world and wipe out the human race—was on its way.

CHAPTER FOURTEEN

What can you do after the end? What becomes of any plot or plan, when an indigo-gleaming missile sprays murder into the sky and puts a period to planning? I do not think there ever was a battlefield as abruptly quiet as that square in old Pompeii. Once the bomb had gone, there was not a sound. The men who had been firing on each other were standing still, jaws hanging, eyes on the sky.

But it couldn't last. For one man was not surprised; one man knew what was happening and was ready for it.

A crouching figure at the top of the ruined temple gesticulated and shouted through a power-megaphone: "Give it up, Defoe! You've lost, you've lost!" It was Slovetski, and beside him a machine-gun crew sighted in on the nearest knot of expediters.

Pause, while the Universe waited. And then his answer came; it was a shot that screamed off a cracked capital, missing him by millimeters. He dropped from sight, and the battle was raging.

Human beings are odd. Now that the cause of the fight was meaningless, it doubled in violence. There were fewer than a hundred of Slovetski's men involved, and not much more than that many expediters. But for concentrated violence I think they must have overmatched anything in the Short War's ending.

I was a non-combatant; but the zinging of the hard-pellet fire swarmed all around me. Gogarty, in his storm sewer, was safe enough, but I was more exposed. While the rapid-fire weapons pattered all around me, I jumped up and zigzagged for the shelter of a low-roofed building.

The walls were little enough protection, but at least I had the illusion of safety. Most of all, I was out of sight.

I wormed my way through a gap in the wall to an inner chamber. It was as tiny a room as ever I have been in; less than six feet in its greatest dimension— length—and with most of its floor area taken up by what seemed to be a rude built-in bed. Claustrophobia hit me there; the wall on the other side was broken too, and I wriggled through.

The next room was larger; and it was occupied.

A man lay, panting heavily, in a corner. He pushed himself up on an elbow to look at me. In a ragged voice he said: "Thomas!" And he slumped back, exhausted by the effort, blood dripping from his shirt.

I leaped over to the side of Benedetto dell'Angela. The noise of the battle outside rose to a high pitch and dwindled raggedly away.

*

I suppose it was inertia that kept me going—certainly I could see with my mind's vision no reason to keep struggling. The world was at an end. There was no reason to try again to escape from the rubber hoses of the expediters—and, after I had seen the resistance end, and an expediter-officer appeared atop the temple where Slovetski had shouted his defiance, no possibility of rejoining the rebels. Without Slovetski, they were lost.

But I kept on.

Benedetto helped. He knew every snake-hole entrance and exit of all the hideouts of Slovetski's group. They had not survived against the strength of the Company without acquiring skill in escape routes; and here, too, they had a way out. It required a risky dash across open ground but, even with Benedetto on my back, I made it.

And then we were in old Pompeii's drainage sewer, the arched stone tunnel that once had carried sewage from the Roman town to the sea. It was a hiding place, and then a tunnel to freedom, for the two of us.

We waited there all of that day, Benedetto mumbling almost inaudibly beside me. In lucid moments, he told me the name of the hotel where Rena had gone when the Observatory was abandoned, but there seemed few lucid moments. Toward evening, he began to recover.

We found our way to the seashore just as darkness fell. There was a lateen-rigged fishing vessel of some sort left untended. I do not suppose the owner was far away, but he did not return in time to stop us.

Benedetto was very weak. He was muttering to himself, words that I could hardly understand. "Wasted, wasted, wasted," was the burden of his complaint. I did not know what he thought was wasted—except, perhaps, the world.

We slipped in to one of the deserted wharves under cover of darkness, and I left Benedetto to find a phone. It was risky, but what risk mattered when the world was at an end?

Rena was waiting at the hotel. She answered at once. I did not think the call had been intercepted—or that it would mean anything to anyone if it had. I went back to the boat to wait with Benedetto for Rena to arrive, in a rented car. We didn't dare chance a cab.

Benedetto was sitting up, propped rigidly against the mast, staring off across the water. Perhaps I startled him as I came to the boat; he turned awkwardly and cried out weakly.

Then he saw that it was I. He said something I could not understand and pointed out toward the west, where the Sun had gone down long before.

But there was still light there—though certainly not sunset.

Far off over the horizon was a faint glow! I couldn't understand at first, since I was sure the bomb had been zeroed-in on the Home Offices in New York; but something must have happened. From that glow, still showing in the darkness so many hours after the explosion as the dust particles gleamed bluely, it must have gone off over the Atlantic.

There was no doubt in my mind any longer. The most deadly weapon the world had ever known had gone off!

CHAPTER FIFTEEN

The hotel was not safe, of course, but what place was when the world was at an end? Rena and I, between us, got her father, Benedetto, upstairs into her room without attracting too much attention. We put him on the bed and peeled back his jacket.

The bullet had gone into his shoulder, a few inches above the heart. The bone was splintered, but the bleeding was not too much. Rena did what she could and, for the first time in what seemed like years, we had a moment's breathing space.

I said, "I'll phone for a doctor."

Benedetto said faintly, "No, Thomas! The Company!"

I protested, "What's the difference? We're all dead, now. You've seen—" I hesitated and changed it. "Slovetski has seen to that. There was cobalt in that bomb."

He peered curiously at me. "Slovetski? Did you suppose it was Slovetski who planned it so?" He shook his head—and winced at the pain. He whispered, "Thomas, you do not understand. It was my project, not Slovetski's. That one, he proposed to destroy the Company's Home Office; it was his thought that killing them would bring an end to evil. I persuaded him there was no need to kill—only to gamble."

I stared at him. "You're delirious!"

"Oh, no." He shook his head and succeeded in a tiny smile. "Do you not see it, Thomas? The great explosion goes off, the world is showered with particles of death. And then—what then?"

"We die!"

"Die? No! Have you forgotten the vaults of the clinics?"

It staggered me. I'd been reciting all the pat phrases from early schooling about the bomb! If it had gone off in the Short War, of course, it would have ended the human race! But I'd been a fool.

The vaults had been built to handle the extreme emergencies that couldn't be foreseen—even one that knocked out nearly the whole race. They hadn't expected that a cobalt-cased bomb would ever be used. Only the conspirators would have tried, and how could they get fissionables? But they were ready for even that. I'd been expecting universal doom.

"The clinics," Benedetto repeated as I stared at him.

It was the answer. Even radio-poisons of cobalt do not live forever. Five years, and nearly half of them would be gone; eleven years, and more than three-quarters would be dissipated. In fifty years, the residual activity would be down to a fraction of one per cent—and the human race could come back to the surface.

"But why?" I demanded. "Suppose the Company can handle the population of the whole world? Granted, they've space enough and one year is the same as fifty when you're on ice. But what's the use?"

He smiled faintly. "Bankruptcy, Thomas," he whispered. "So you see, we do not wish to fall into the Company's hands right now. For there is a chance that we will live...and perhaps the very faintest of chances that we will win!"

*

It wasn't even a faint chance—I kept telling myself that.

But, if anything could hurt the Company, the area in which it was vulnerable was money. Benedetto had been intelligent in that. Bombing the Home Office would have been an inconvenience, no more. But to disrupt the world's work with a fifty-year hiatus, while the air purged itself of the radioactive cobalt from the bomb, would mean fifty years while the Company lay dormant; fifty years while the policies ran their course and became due.

For that was the wonder of Benedetto's scheme: *The Company insured against everything.* If a man were to be exposed to radiation and needed to be put away, he automatically went on "disability" benefits, while his policy paid its own premiums! Multiply this single man by nearly four billion. The sum came out to a bankrupt Company.

It seemed a thin thread with which to strangle a monster. And yet, I thought of the picture of Millen Carmody in my Adjuster's Manual.

There was the embodiment of honor. Where a Defoe might cut through the legalities and flout the letter of the agreements, Carmody would be bound by his given word. The question, then, was whether Defoe would dare to act against Carmody.

Everything else made sense. Even exploding the bomb high over the Atlantic: It would be days before the first fall-out came wind-borne to the land, and in those days there would be time for the beginnings of the mass migration to the vaults.

Wait and see, I told myself. Wait and see. It was flimsy, but it was hope, and I had thought all hope was dead.

We could not stay in the hotel, and there was only one place for us to go. Slovetski captured, the Company after our scalps, the whole world about to be plunged into confusion—we had to get out of sight.

*

It took time. Zorchi's hospital gave me a clue; I tracked it down and located the secretary.

The secretary spat at me over the phone and hung up, but the second time I called him he grudgingly consented to give me another number to call. The new number was Zorchi's lawyer. The lawyer was opaque and uncommunicative, but proposed that I call him back in a quarter of an hour. In a quarter of an hour, I was on the phone. He said guardedly: "What was left in Bay 100?"

"A hypodermic and a bottle of fluid," I said promptly.

"That checks," he confirmed, and gave me a number.

And on the other end of that number I reached Zorchi.

"The junior assassin," he sneered. "And calling for help? How is that possible, Weels? Did my *avocatto* lie?"

I said stiffly, "If you don't want to help me, say so."

"Oh—" he shrugged. "I have not said that. What do you want?"

"Food, a doctor, and a place for three of us to hide for a while."

He pursed his lips. "To hide, is it?" He frowned. "That is very grave, Weels. Why should I hide you from what is undoubtedly your just punishment?"

"Because," I said steadily, "I have a telephone number. Which can be traced. Defoe doesn't know you've escaped, but that can be fixed!"

He laughed angrily. "Oh-ho. The assassin turns to blackmail, is that it?"

I said furiously, "Damn you, Zorchi, you know I won't turn you in. I only point out that I can—and that I will not. Now, will you help us or not?"

He said mildly, "Oh, of course. I only wished you to say 'please'—but it is not a trick you Company men are good at. Signore, believe me, I perish with loneliness for you and your two friends, whoever they may be. Listen to me, now." He gave me an address and directions for finding it. And he hung up.

Zorchi's house was far outside the city, along the road to New Caserta. It lay at the bend of the main highway, and I suppose I could have passed it a hundred thousand times without looking inside, it was so clearly the white-stuccoed, large but crumbling home of a mildly prosperous peasant. It was large enough to have a central court partly concealed from the road.

The secretary, spectacles and all, met us at the door—and that was a shock. "You must have roller skates," I told him.

He shrugged. "My employer is too forgiving," he said, with ice on his voice. "I had hoped to reach him before he made an error. As you see, I was too late." We lifted Benedetto off the seat; he was just barely conscious by now, and his face was ivory under the Mediterranean tan. I shook the secretary off and held Benedetto carefully in my arms as Rena held the door before me.

The secretary said, "A moment. I presume the car is stolen. You must dispose of it at once."

I snarled over my shoulder, "It isn't stolen, but the people that own it will be looking for it all right. You get rid of it."

He spluttered and squirmed, but I saw him climbing into the seat as I went inside. Zorchi was there waiting, in a fancy motorized wheelchair. He had legs! Apparently they were not fully developed as yet, but in the short few days since I had rescued him something had grown that looked like nearly normal limbs. He had also grown, in that short time, a heavy beard.

The sneer, however, was the same.

I made the error of saying, "Signore Zorchi, will you call a doctor for this man?" The thick lips writhed under the beard. "Signore it is now, is it? No longer the freak Zorchi, the case Zorchi, the half-man? God works many miracles, Weels. See the greatest of them all—it has transmuted the dog into a signore!"

I grated, "For God's sake, Zorchi, call a doctor!"

He said coldly, "You mentioned this over the phone, did you not? If you would merely walk on instead of bickering, you would find the doctor already here."

*

Plasma and antibiotics: They flowed into Benedetto from half a dozen plastic tubes like oil into the hold of a tanker. And I could see, in the moments when I watched, the color come back into his face, and the sunken eyes seem to come back to life.

The doctor gave him a sedative that made him sleep, and explained to us that Benedetto was an old man for such goings-on. But if he could be kept still for three or four weeks, the doctor said, counting the lire Zorchi's secretary paid him, there was no great danger.

If he could be kept still for three or four weeks. In scarcely ten days, the atmosphere of the planet would be death to breathe! Many things might happen to Benedetto in that time, but remaining still was not one of them.

Zorchi retired to his own quarters once the doctor was gone, and Rena and I left Benedetto to sleep.

We found a television set and turned it on, listening for word of the cobalt-bomb. We got recorded canzoni sung by a reedy tenor. We dialed, and found the Neapolitan equivalent of a soap opera, complete with the wise, fat old mother and the sobbing new daughter-in-law. It was like that on all the stations, while Rena and I stared at each other in disbelief.

Finally, at the regular hourly newscast, we got a flicker: "An unidentified explosion," the announcer was saying, "far out at sea, caused alarm to many persons last night. Although the origins are not known, it is thought that there is no danger. However, there has been temporary disturbance to all long-lines communications, and air travel is grounded while the explosion is being investigated."

We switched to the radio: it was true. Only the UHF television bands were on the air.

I said, "I can't figure that. If there's enough disturbance to ruin long-distance transmission, it ought to show up on the television."

Rena said doubtfully, "I do not remember for sure, Tom, but is there not something about television which limits its distance?"

"Well—I suppose so, yes. It's a line of sight transmission, on these frequencies at any rate. I don't suppose it has to be, except that all the television bands fall in VHF or UHF channels."

"Yes. And then, is it not possible that only the distance transmission is interrupted? On purpose, I mean?"

I slammed my hand on the arm of the chair. "On purpose! The Company—they are trying to keep this thing localized. But the idiots, don't they know that's impossible? Does Defoe think he can let the world burn up without doing anything to stop it—just by keeping the people from knowing what happened?"

She shrugged. "I don't know, Tom."

I didn't know either, but I suspected—and so did she. It was out of the question that the Company, with its infinite resources, its nerve-fibers running into every part of the world, should not know just what that bomb was, and what it would do. And what few days the world had—before the fallout became dangerous—were none too many.

Already the word should have been spread, and the first groups alerted for movement into the vaults, to wait out the day when the air would be pure again. If it was being delayed, there could be no good reason for it.

The only reason was Defoe. But what, I asked myself miserably, was Millen Carmody doing all this while? Was he going to sit back and placidly permit Defoe to pervert every ideal of the Company?

I could not believe it. It was not possible that the man who had written the inspiring words in the Handbook could be guilty of genocide.

Rena excused herself to look in on her father. Almost ashamed of myself, I took the battered book from my pocket and opened it to check on Millen Carmody's own preface.

It was hard to reconcile the immensely reassuring words with what I had seen. And, as I read them, I no longer felt safe and comforted.

*

There seemed to be no immediate danger, and Rena needed to get out of that house. There was nothing for Benedetto to do but wait, and Zorchi's servants could help him when it was necessary.

I took her by the arm and we strolled out into the garden, breathing deeply. That was a mistake. I had forgotten, in the inconspicuous air conditioning of Zorchi's home, that we were in the center of the hemp fields that had nearly cost me my dinner, so long ago, with Hammond. I wondered if I ever would know just why Hammond was killed. Playing both ends against the middle, it seemed—he had undoubtedly been in with Slovetski's group. Rena had admitted as much, and I was privately certain that he had been killed by them.

But of more importance was the stench in our nostrils. "Perhaps," said Rena, "across the road, in the walnut grove, it will not be as bad."

I hesitated, but it felt safe in the warm Italian night, and so we tried it. The sharp scent of the walnut trees helped a little; what helped even more was that the turbinates of the nostril can stand just so much, and when their tolerance is exceeded they surrender. So that it wasn't too long before, though the stench was as strong as ever, we hardly noticed it.

We sat against the thick trunk of a tree, and Rena's head fitted naturally against my shoulder. She was silent for a time, and so was I—it seemed good to have silence, after violent struggle and death.

Then she said: "Strange man."

"Me?"

"No. Oh, yes, Tom, if it comes to that, you, too. But I was thinking just now of Zorchi. Is it true, what you told me of his growing legs and arms so freely?"

"I thought everyone in Naples knew that. I thought he was a national hero."

"Of course, but I have never really known that the stories were true. How does it happen, Tom?"

I shrugged. "Heaven knows, I don't. I doubt if even Zorchi knows. His parents might have been involved in some sort of atomic business and got radiated, and so they produced a mutation. It's perfectly possible, you know."

"I have heard so, Tom."

"Or else it just happened. Something in his diet, in the way his glands responded to a sickness, some sort of medicine. No one knows."

"Cannot scientists hope to tell?"

"Well—" it was beginning to sound like the seeds of one of our old arguments— "well, I suppose so. Pure research isn't much encouraged these days."

"But it should be, you think?"

"Of course it should. The only hope of the world—" I trailed off. Through the trees was a bright, distant glare, and I had just remembered what it was.

"Is what, Tom?"

"There isn't any," I said, but only to myself. She didn't press me; she merely burrowed into my arm.

149

Perhaps the wind shifted, and the smell of the hemp fields grew stronger; perhaps it was only the foul thought that the glaring sky had triggered that contaminated my mood. But where I had been happy and relaxed—the C-bomb completely out of my mind for the moment—now I was too fully aware of what was ahead for all of us.

"Let's go back, Rena," I said. She didn't ask why. Perhaps she, too, was feeling the weight of our death sentence.

*

We caught the evening newscast; its story varied little from the early ones. Benedetto still slept, but Zorchi joined us as we watched it.

The announcer, face stamped with the careful blend of gravity and confidence that marks telecasters all over the world, was saying: "Late word on the bomb exploded over the North Atlantic indicates that there is some danger that radioactive ash may be carried to this area. The danger zones are now being mapped and surveyed, and residents of all such sections will be evacuated or placed in deep sleep until the danger is over.

"Blue Bolt policies give you complete protection against all hazards from this explosion. I repeat, Blue Bolt policies give you complete protection against all hazards from this explosion. Check your policies and be sure of your status. There is absolutely no risk for any person carrying the basic Blue Bolt minimum coverage or better."

I clicked off the set. "I wonder what the people in Shanghai are hearing tonight," I said.

Zorchi had only listened without comment, when I told him about the bomb that afternoon; he listened without comment now.

Rena said: "Tom, I've been wondering. You know, I—I don't have any insurance. Neither has my father, since we were canceled. And we're not the only ones without it, either."

I patted her hand. "We'll straighten this out," I promised. "You'll get your coverage back."

She gave me a skeptical look, but shook her head. "I don't mean just about father and me. What about all of the uninsurables, all over the world? The bomb goes off, and everybody with a policy files down into the vaults, but what about the others?"

I explained, "There are provisions for them. Some of them can be cared for under the dependency clauses in the policies of their next of kin. Others have various charitable arrangements—some localities, for instance, carry blanket floater policies for their paupers and prisoners and so on. And—well, I don't suppose it would ever come to that, but if someone turned up who had no coverage at all, he could be cared for out of the loss-pool that the Company carries for such contingencies. It wouldn't be luxurious, but he'd live. You see," I went on, warming to my subject, "the Company is set up so the actual premiums paid are meaningless. The whole objective of the Company is service; the premiums are only a way to that goal. The Company has no interest other than the good of the world, and—"

I stopped, feeling like a fool. Zorchi was laughing raucously.

I said resentfully, "I guess I asked for that, Zorchi. Well, perhaps what I said sounds funny. But, before God, Zorchi, that's the way the Company is set up. Here—" I picked the Handbook from the end table beside me and tossed it to him—"read what Millen Carmody says. I won't try to convince you. Just read it."

He caught it expertly and dropped it on the floor before him. "So much for your Chief Assassin," he remarked pleasantly. "The words are no doubt honied, Weels, but I am not at this moment interested to read them."

I shrugged. It was peculiar how even a reasonable man—I have always thought of myself as a reasonable man—could make a fool of himself. It was no sin that habit had betrayed me into exalting the Company; but it was, at the least, quite silly of me to take offense when my audience disagreed with me.

I said, in what must have been a surly tone, "I don't suppose you are—why should you? You hate the Company from the word go."

He shook his head mildly. "I? No, Weels. Believe me, I am the Company's most devoted friend. Without it, how would I feed my five-times-a-day appetite?"

I sneered at him. "If you're a friend to the Company, then my best buddy is a tapeworm."

"Meaning that Zorchi is a parasite?" His eyes were furious. "Weels, you impose on me too far! Be careful! Is it the act of a tapeworm that I bleed and die, over and over? Is it something I chose, did I pray to the saints, before my mother spawned me, that I should be born a monster? No, Weels! We are alike, you gentlemen of the Company and I—we live on blood money, it is true. But the blood I live on, man—it is my own!"

I said mollifyingly, "Zorchi, I've had a hard day. I didn't mean to be nasty. I apologize."

"Hah!"

"No, really."

He shrugged, abruptly quiet. "It is of no importance," he said. "If I wished to bear you a grudge, Weels, I would have more than that to give me cause." He sighed. "It all looked quite simple twenty-four hours ago, Weels. True, I had worked my little profession in this area as far as it might go—with your help, of course. But the world was before me—I had arranged to fly next week to the Parisian Anarch, to change my name and, perhaps within a month, with a new policy, suffer a severe accident that would provide me with francs for my hobbies. Why is it that you bring bad news always?"

I said, "Wasn't I of some little assistance to you at one time?"

"In helping me from the deepfreeze? Oh, yes, perhaps. But didn't you help me into it in the first place, as well? And surely you have already had sufficient credit for aiding my escape—I observe the young lady looking at you with the eyes of one who sees a hero."

I said in irritation, "You're infuriating, Zorchi. I suppose you know that. I never claimed any credit for helping you out of the clinic. As a matter of fact, I don't think I ever mentioned it. Everyone assumed that I had just happened to bring you along—no one questioned it."

He flared, "You let them assume, Weels? You let them assume that Zorchi was as helpless a side of pork as those other dead ones—you let them guess that you stuck me with a needle, so that it would seem how brave you were? Is it not true that I had revived by myself, Weels?"

I felt myself growing angry. "Of course! But I just didn't see any reason to—"

"To divide the credit, is that it, Weels? No, say no more; I have closed the subject. However, I point out that there is a difference between the rescue of a helpless hulk and the mere casual assistance one may be invited to give to a Zorchi."

I let it go at that. There was no point in arguing with that man, ever.

So I left the room—ostensibly to look in on Benedetto, actually to cool off a little. Benedetto seemed fine—that is, the dressings were still in place, he had not moved, his breath and pulse were slow and regular. I took my time before I went back to the room where Zorchi still sat waiting.

He had taken advantage of the time to improve his mind. The man's curiosity was insatiable; the more he denied it, the more it stuck out all over him. He had thrown the Handbook on the floor when I gave it to him, but as soon as I was out of sight he was leafing through it. He had it open on his lap, face down, as he faced me.

"Weels." There was, for once, no sardonic rasp to his voice. And his face, I saw, was bone-white. "Weels, permit me to be sure I understand you. It is your belief that this intelligent plan of seeding the world with poison to make it well will succeed, because you believe that a Signore Carmody will evict Defoe from power?"

I said, "Well, not exactly—"

"But almost exactly? That is, you require this Millen Carmody for your plan?" "It wasn't my plan. But you're right about the other."

"Very good." He extended the Handbook to me. "There is here a picture which calls itself Millen Carmody. Is that the man?"

I glanced at the familiar warm eyes on the frontispiece. "That's right. Have you seen him?"

"I have, indeed." The shaggy beard was twitching—I did not know whether with laughter or the coming of tears. "I saw him not long ago, Weels. It was in what they call Bay 100—you remember? He was in a little bag like the pasta one carries home from a store. He was quite sound asleep, Weels, in the shelf just below the one I woke up in."

CHAPTER SIXTEEN

So now at last I knew why Millen Carmody had permitted Defoe to turn the Company into a prison cell for the world. He couldn't forbid it, because the dead can forbid nothing, and Carmody was sleeping with the dead. No wonder Defoe was so concerned with the Naples sector!

How long? How long had Carmody been quietly out of the way, while Defoe made his plans and took his steps, and someone in a little room somewhere confected "statements" with Millen Carmody's signature on them and "interviews" that involved only one man?

It could not have been less than five or six years, I thought, counting back to the time when Defoe's name first began to register with me as an ordinary citizen, before I had married his cousin. Six years. That was the date of the Prague-Vienna war. And the year following, Hanoi clashed with Cebu. And the year after that, Auckland and Adelaide.

What in God's name was Defoe's plan? Nothing as simple as putting Carmody out of the way so that he could loot the Company. No man could wish to be that rich! It was meaningless...

Defoe could be playing for only one thing—power.

But it didn't matter; all that mattered was that now I knew that Carmody was an enemy to Defoe. He was therefore an ally to Rena and to me, and we needed allies. But how might we get Carmody out of Bay 100?

There weren't any good answers, though Rena and I, with the help of grumbling comments from Zorchi, debated it until the morning light began to shine. Frontal assault on the clinic was ridiculous. Even a diversionary raid such as Rena had staged to try to rescue her father—only ten days before!—would hardly get us in through the triple-locked door of Bay 100. Even if Slovetski's movement had still been able to muster the strength to do it, which was not likely.

It was maddening. I had hidden the hypodermic Rena had brought in Bay 100 to get it out of the way. Undoubtedly it was there still—perhaps only a few yards from Millen Carmody. If fifty cubic centimeters of a watery purplish liquid could have been plucked from the little glass bottle and moved the mere inches to the veins of his arms, the problem would be solved—for he could open the door from inside as easily as Zorchi had, and certainly once he was that far we could manage to get him out.

But the thing was impossible, no matter how we looked at it.

*

I suppose I fell asleep sitting in that chair, because I woke up in it. It was in the middle of a crazy nightmare about an avenging angel with cobalt-blue eyes burning at me out of heaven; and I wanted to run from him, but I was frozen by a little man with a hypodermic of ice. I woke up, and I was facing the television set.

Someone—Rena, I suppose—had covered me with a light spread. The set was blaring a strident tenor voice. Zorchi was hunched over, watching some opera; I might as well have been a thousand miles away.

I lay blearily watching the tiny figures flickering around the screen, not so much forgetting all the things that were on my mind as knowing what they were and that they existed, but lacking the strength to pick them up and look at them. The opera seemed to concern an Egyptian queen and a priest of some sort; I was not very interested in it, though it seemed odd that Zorchi should watch it so eagerly.

Perhaps, after all, there was something to his maudlin self-pity—perhaps I really did think of him as a monster or a dog, for I was as uneasy to see him watching an opera as I would have been to see an ape play the flute.

I heard trucks going by on the highway. By and by it began to penetrate through the haze that I was hearing a *lot* of trucks going by on the highway. I had no idea how heavily traveled the

Naples-Caserta road might be, but from the sound, they seemed nearly bumper to bumper, whizzing along at seventy or eighty miles an hour.

I got up stiffly and walked over to the window.

I had not been far wrong. There was a steady stream of traffic in both directions—not only trucks but buses and private cars, everything from late-model gyromaxions to ancient piston-driven farm trucks.

Zorchi heard me move, and turned toward me with a hooded expression. I pointed to the window.

"What's up?" I asked.

He said levelly, "The end of the world. It is now official; it has been on the television. Oh, they do not say it in just so many words, but it is there."

I turned to the television set and flicked off the tape-relay switch—apparently the opera had been recorded. Zorchi glared, but didn't try to stop me as I hunted on the broadcast bands for a news announcer.

I didn't have far to hunt. Every channel was the same: The Company was issuing orders and instructions. Every man, woman and child was to be ready within ten days for commitment to the clinic...

I tried to imagine the scenes of panic and turmoil that would be going on in downtown Naples at that moment.

*

The newscaster was saying: "Remember, if your Basic Blue Bolt policy number begins with the letters A, B or C—if it begins with the letters A, B or C—you are to report to the local first aid or emergency post at six hundred hours tomorrow. There is no danger. I repeat, there is no danger. This is merely a precaution taken by the Company for your protection." He didn't really look as though there were no danger, however. He looked like a man confronted by a ghost.

I switched to another channel. An equally harried-looking announcer: "—reported by a team of four physicists from the Royal

157

University to have produced a serious concentration of radioactive byproducts in the upper atmosphere. It is hoped that the cloud of dangerous gases will veer southward and pass harmlessly through the Eastern Mediterranean; however, strictly as a precautionary measure, it is essential that every person in this area be placed in a safety zone during the danger period, the peak of which is estimated to come within the next fourteen days. If there is any damage, it will be only local and confined to livestock—for which you will be reimbursed under your Blue Bolt coverage."

I switched to another channel. Local damage! Local to the face of the Earth! I tried all the channels; they were all the same.

The Company had evidently decided to lie to the human race. Keep them in the dark—make each little section believe that only it was affected—persuade them that they would be under for, at most, a few weeks or months.

Was that, I wondered, Defoe's scheme? Was he planning to try somehow to convince four billion people that fifty years were only a few weeks? It would never work—the first astronomer to look at a star, the first seaman to discover impossible errors in his tide table, would spot the lie.

More likely he was simply proceeding along what must always have been his basic assumption: The truth is wasted on the people.

Zorchi said with heavy irony, "If my guest is quite finished with the instrument, perhaps he will be gracious enough to permit me to resume Aïda."

*

I woke Rena and told her about the evacuation. She said, yawning, "But of course, Tom. What else could they do?" And she began discussing breakfast.

I went with her, but not to eat; in the dining hall was a small television set, and on it I could listen to the same repeat broadcasts over and over to my heart's content. It was—in a way—a thrilling sight. It is always impressive to see a giant machine in operation, and there was no machine bigger than the Company.

The idea of suspending a whole world, even piecemeal, was staggering. But if there had been panic at first in the offices of the Company, none of it showed. The announcers were harried and there was bustle and strain, but order presided.

Those long lines of vehicles outside the window; they were going somewhere; they were each one, I could see by the medallion slung across each radiator front, on the payroll of the Company.

Perhaps the trick of pretending to each section that only it would be affected was wise—I don't know. It was working, and I suppose that is the touchstone of wisdom. Naples knew that something was going on in Rome, of course, but was doubtful about the Milanese Republic. The Romans were in no doubt at all about Milan, but weren't sure about the Duchy of Monaco, down the Riviera shore. And the man on the street, if he gave it a thought at all, must have been sure that such faraway places as America and China were escaping entirely.

I suppose it was clever—there was no apparent panic. The trick took away the psychological horror of world catastrophe and replaced it with only a local terror, no different in kind than an earthquake or a flood. And there was always the sack of gold at the end of every catastrophe: Blue Bolt would pay for damage, with a free and uncounting hand.

Except that this time, of course, Blue Bolt would not, could not, pay at all.

*

By noon, Benedetto was out of bed.

He shouldn't have been, but he was conscious and we could not make him stay put—short of chains.

He watched the television and then listened as Rena and I brought him up to date. Like me, he was shocked and then encouraged to find that Millen Carmody was in the vaults—encouraged because it was at

159

least a handle for us to grasp the problem with; if we could get at Carmody, perhaps we could break Defoe's usurped power. Without him, Defoe would simply use the years while the world slept to forge a permanent dictatorship.

We got the old man to lie down, and left him. But not for long. Within the hour he came tottering to where we were sitting, staring at the television. He waved aside Rena's quick protest.

"There is no time for rest, my daughter," he said. "Do not scold me. I have a task."

Rena said worriedly, "Dear, you must stay in bed. The doctor said—"

"The doctor," Benedetto said formally, "is a fool. Shall I allow us to die here? Am I an ancient idiot, or am I Benedetto dell'Angela who with Slovetski led twenty thousand men?"

Rena said, "Please! You're sick!"

"Enough." Benedetto wavered, but stood erect. "I have telephoned. I have learned a great deal. The movement—" he leaned against the wall for support— "was not planned by fools. We knew there might be bad days; we do not collapse because a few of us are put out of service by the Company. I have certain emergency numbers to call; I call them. And I find—" he paused dramatically—"that there is news. Slovetski has escaped!"

I said, "That's impossible! Defoe wouldn't let him go!"

"Perhaps Slovetski did not consult him," Benedetto said with dignity. "At any rate, he is free and not far from here. And he is the answer we have sought, you understand."

"How?" I demanded. "What can he do that we can't?"

Benedetto smiled indulgently, though the smile was strained. His wound must have been giving him hell; it had had just enough time to stiffen up. He said, "Leave that to Slovetski, Thomas. It is his métier, not yours. I shall go to him now."

Well, I did what I could; but Benedetto was an iron-necked old man. I forbade him to leave and he laughed at me. I begged him to stay and he thanked me—and refused. Finally I abandoned him to Rena and Zorchi.

Zorchi gave up almost at once. "A majestic man!" he said admiringly, as he rolled into the room where I was waiting, on his little power cart. "One cannot reason with him."

And Rena, in time, gave up, too. But not easily. She was weeping when she rejoined me.

*

She had been unable even to get him to let her join him, or to consider taking someone else with him; he said it was his job alone. She didn't even know where he was going. He had said it was not permissible, in so critical a situation, for him to tell where Slovetski was.

Zorchi coughed. "As to that," he said, "I have already taken the liberty of instructing one of my associates to be ready. If the Signore has gone to meet Slovetski, my man is following him..."

So we waited, while the television announcers grew more and more grim-lipped and imperative.

I listened with only half my mind. Part of my thoughts were with Benedetto, who should have been in a hospital instead of wandering around on some dangerous mission. And partly I was still filled with the spectacle that was unfolding before us.

It was not merely a matter of preserving human lives. It was almost as important to provide the newly awakened men and women, fifty years from now, with food to eat and the homes and tools and other things that would be needed.

Factories and transportation gear—according to the telecasts—were being shut down and sealed to stand up under the time that would pass—"weeks," according to the telecast, but who needed to seal a tool in oil for a few weeks? Instructions were coming hourly over the air on what should be protected in each home, and how it was to be done. Probably even fifty years would not seriously damage most of the world's equipment—if the plans we heard on the air could be efficiently carried out.

But the farms were another matter. The preserving of seeds was routine, but I couldn't help wondering what these flat Italian fields would look like in fifty untended years. Would the radiocobalt sterilize even the weeds? I didn't think so, but I didn't know. If not, would the Italian peninsula once again find itself covered with the dense forests that Caesar had marched through, where Spartacus and his run-away slaves had lurked and struck out against the Senators?

And how many millions would die while the forests were being cleared off the face of the Earth again to make way for grain? Synthetic foods and food from the sea might solve that—the Company could find a way. But what about the mines— three, four and five thousand feet down—when the pumps were shut off and the underground water seeped in? What about the rails that the trains rode on? You could cosmoline the engines, perhaps, but how could you protect a million miles of track from the rains of fifty years?

So I sat there, watching the television and waiting. Rena was too nervous to stay in one place. Zorchi had mysterious occupations of his own. I sat and stared at the cathode screen.

Until the door opened behind me, and I turned to look.

Rena was standing there. Her face was an ivory mask. She clutched the door as her father had a few hours before; I think she looked weaker and sicker than he.

I said, for the first time, "Darling!" She stood silent, staring at me. I asked apprehensively, "What is it?"

The pale lips opened, but it was a moment before she could frame the words. Then her voice was hard to hear. "My father," she said. "He reached the place where he was meeting Slovetski, but the expediters were there before him. They shot him down in the street. And they are on their way here."

CHAPTER SEVENTEEN

It was quick and brutal. Somehow Benedetto had been betrayed; the expediters had known where he had come from. And that was the end of that.

They came swarming down on us in waves, at least a hundred of them, to capture a man, a girl and a cripple—Zorchi's servants had deserted us, melting into the hemp fields like roaches into a garbage dump. Zorchi had a little gun, a Beretta; he fired it once and wounded a man.

The rest was short and unpleasant.

They bound us and gagged us and flew us, trussed like game for the spit, to the clinic. I caught a glimpse of milling mobs outside the long, low walls as we came down. Then all I could see was the roof of the copter garage.

We were brought to a tiny room where Defoe sat at a desk. The Underwriter was smiling. "Hello, Thomas," he said, his eyes studying the bruise on my cheek. He turned toward Rena consideringly. "So this is your choice, eh, Thomas?" He studied Rena coolly. "Hardly my type. Still, by sticking with me, you could have had a harem."

Bound as I was, I started forward. Something hit me in the back at my first step, driving a hot rush of agony up from my kidneys. Defoe watched me catch my breath without a change of expression.

"My men are quite alert, Thomas. Please do not try that again. Once is amusing, but twice would annoy me." He sighed. "I seem to have been wrong about you, Thomas. Perhaps because I needed someone's help, I overestimated you. I thought long ago that beneath your conditioning you had brains. Manning is a machine, good for taking orders. Dr. Lawton is loyal, but not intelligent. And between loyalty and intelligence, I'll take brains. Loyalty I can provide for myself." He nodded gravely at the armed expediters.

Zorchi spat. "Kill us, butcher," he ordered. "It is enough I die without listening to your foolish babbling."

Defoe considered him. "You interest me, Signore. A surprise, finding you revived and with Wills. Before we're finished, you must tell me about that."

I saw Zorchi bristle and open his mouth, but a cold, suddenly calculating idea made me interrupt. "To get dell'Angela out as an attendant, I needed a patient for him to wheel. Zorchi had money, and I *expected* gratitude when I revived him later. It wasn't hard getting Lawton's assistant to stack his cocoon near Benedetto's."

"Lawton!" Defoe grimaced, but seemed to accept the story. He smiled at me suddenly. "I had hopes for you, then. That escape was well done—simple, direct. A little crude, but a good beginning. You could have been my number one assistant, Thomas. I thought of that when I heard of the things you were saying after Marianna died—I thought you might be awaking."

I licked my lips. "And when you picked me up after Marianna's death, and bailed me out of jail, you made sure the expediter corps had information that I was possibly not reliable. You made sure the information reached the underground, so they would approach me and I could spy for you. You wanted a patsy!"

The smile was gleaming this time. "Naturally, until you could prove yourself. And of course, I had you jailed for the things you said because I wanted it that way. A pity all my efforts were wasted on you, Thomas. I'm afraid you're not equipped to be a spy."

It took everything I had, but this time I managed to smile back. "On which side, Defoe? How many spies know you've got Millen Carmody down in Bay—"

That hit him. But I didn't have time to enjoy it. He made a sudden gesture, and the expediters moved. This time, when they dragged me down, it was very bad.

*

When I came to, I was in another room. Zorchi and Rena were with me, but not Defoe. It was a preparation chamber, racked with instruments, furnished with surgical benches.

SUPER PACK

A telescreen was flickering and blaring unheeded at one end of the room. I caught a glimpse of scenes of men, women and children standing in line, going in orderly queues through the medical inspections, filing into the clinic and its local branch stations for the sleep drug. The scenes were all in Naples; but they must have been, with local variations, on every telescreen on the globe.

Dr. Lawton appeared. He commanded coldly: "Take your clothes off."

I think that was the most humiliating moment of all.

It was, of course, only a medical formality. I knew that the suspendees had to be nude in their racks. But the very impersonality of the proceeding made it ugly. Reluctantly I began to undress, as did Rena, silent and withdrawn, and Zorchi, sputtering anger and threats. My whole body was a mass of redness; in a few hours the red would turn to purple and black, where the hoses of the expediters had caressed me.

Or did a suspendee bruise? Probably not. But it was small satisfaction.

Lawton was looking smug; no doubt he had insisted on the privilege of putting us under himself after I'd blamed him for Zorchi's escape. I couldn't blame him; I would have returned the favor with great joy.

Well, I had wanted to reach Millen Carmody, and Defoe was granting my wish. We might even lie on adjacent racks in Bay 100. After what I'd told Defoe, we should rate such reserved space!

Lawton approached with the hypospray, and a pair of expediters grabbed my arms. He said: "I want to leave one thought with you, Wills. Maybe it will give you some comfort." His smirk told me that it certainly would not. "Only Defoe and I can open Bay 100," he reminded me. "I don't think either of us will; and I expect you will stay there a long, long time."

He experimentally squirted a faint mist from the tip of the hypospray and nodded satisfaction. He went on: "The suspension is

165

effective for a long time—several hundred years, perhaps. But not forever. In time the enzymes of the body begin to digest the body itself." He pursed his lips thoughtfully. "I don't know if the sleeping brain knows it is pain or not. If it does, you'll know what it feels like to dissolve in your own gutwash..."

He smiled. "Good night," he crooned, and bent over my arm.

The spray from the end of the hypo felt chilly, but not at all painful. It was as though I had been touched with ice; the cold clung, and spread.

I was vaguely conscious of being dumped on one of the surgical tables, even more vaguely aware of seeing Rena slumping across another.

The light in the room yellowed, flickered and went out.

I thought I heard Rena's voice...

Then I heard nothing. And I saw nothing. And I felt nothing, except the penetrating cold, and then even the cold was gone.

CHAPTER EIGHTEEN

My nerves throbbed with the prickling of an infinity of needles. I was cold— colder than I had ever been. And over everything else came the insistent, blurred voice of Luigi Zorchi.

"Weels! Weels!"

At first it was an annoyance. Then, abruptly, full consciousness came rushing back, bringing some measure of triumph with it. It had worked! My needling of Defoe and my concealing of Zorchi's ability to revive himself had succeeded in getting us all put into Bay 100, where the precious hypodermic and fluid were hidden. After being pushed from pillar to post and back, even that much success was enough to shock me into awareness.

My heart was thumping like a rusty cargo steamer in a high sea. My lungs ached for air and burned when they got it. But I managed to open my eyes to see Zorchi bending over me. Beyond him, I saw the blue-lighted sterilizing lamps, the door that opened from inside, and the racked suspendees of Bay 100.

"It is time! But now finally you awake, you move!" Zorchi grumbled. "The body of Zorchi does not surrender to poisons; it throws them off. But then because of these small weak legs, I must wait for you! Come, Weels, no more dallying! We have still work to do to escape this abomination!"

I sat up clumsily, but the drugs seemed to have been neutralized. I was on the bottom tier, and I managed to locate the floor with my legs and stand up. "Thanks, Zorchi," I told him, trying to avoid looking at his ugly, naked body and the things that were almost his legs.

"Thanks are due," he admitted. "I am a modest man who expects no praise, but I have done much. I cannot deny it. It took greatness to crawl through this bay to find you. On my hands and these baby knees, Weels, I crawled. Almost, I am over-come with wonder at so heroic— But I digress. Weels, waste no more time in talking. We must revive the others who are above my reach. Then let us, for God, go and find food."

Somehow, though I was still weak, I managed to follow Zorchi and drag down the sacks containing Rena and Carmody. And while waiting for them to revive, I began to realize how little chance we would have to escape this time, naked and uncertain of what state affairs were in. I also realized what might happen if Lawton or Defoe decided to check up on Bay 100 now!

For the few minutes while Rena revived and recognized me, and while I explained how I'd figured it out, it was worth any risk. Then finally, Carmody stirred and sat up. Maybe we looked enough like devils in a blue hell to justify his first expression.

He wasn't much like my mental image of the great Millen Carmody. His face was like his picture, but it was an older face and haggard under the ugly light. Age was heavy on him, and he couldn't have been a noble figure at any time. Now he was a pot-bellied little man with scrawny legs and a faint tremble to his hands.

But there was no fat in his mind as he tried to absorb our explanations while he answered our questions in turn. He'd come to Naples, bringing his personal physician, Dr. Lawton. His last memory was of Lawton giving him a shot to relieve his indigestion.

It must have been rough to wake up here after that and find what a mess had been made of the world. But he took it, and his questions became sharper as he groped for the truth. Finally he sat back, nodding sickly. "Defoe!" he said bitterly. "Well, what do we do now, Mr. Wills?"

It shook me. I'd unconsciously expected him to take over at once. But the eyes of Rena and Zorchi also turned to me. Well, there wasn't much choice. We couldn't stay here and risk discovery. Nor could we hide anywhere in the clinic; when Defoe found us gone, no place would be safe.

"We pray," I decided. "And if prayers help, maybe we'll find some way out."

"I can help," Carmody offered. He grimaced. "I know this place and the combination to the private doors. Would it help if we reached the garage?"

I didn't know, but the garage was half a mile beyond the main entrance. If we could steal a car, we might make it. We had to try.

There were sounds of activity when we opened the door, but the section we were in seemed to be filled, and the storing of suspendees had moved elsewhere.

We shut and relocked the door and followed Carmody through the seemingly endless corridors, with Zorchi hobbling along, leaning on Rena and me and sweating in agony. We offered to carry him, but he would have none of that. We moved further and further back, while the sight of Carmody's round, bare bottom ahead ripped my feeling of awe for him into smaller and smaller shreds.

He stopped at a door I had almost missed and his fingers tapped out something on what looked like an ornamental pattern. The door opened to reveal stairs that led down two flights, winding around a small elevator shaft. At the bottom was a long corridor that must be the one leading underground to the garage. Opposite the elevator was another door, and Carmody worked its combination to reveal a storeroom, loaded with supplies the expediters might need.

He ripped a suit of the heavy gray coveralls off the wall and began donning them. "Radiation suits," he explained. They were ugly things, but better than nothing. Anyone seeing us in them might think we were on official business. Zorchi shook off our help and somehow got into a pair. Then he grunted and began pulling hard-pellet rifles and bandoliers of ammunition off the wall.

*

"Now, Weels, we are prepared. Let them come against us. Zorchi is ready!"

"Ready to kill yourself!" I said roughly. "Those things take practice!"

169

"And again I am the freak—the case who can do nothing that humans can do, eh, Weels?" He swore thickly, and there was something in his voice that abruptly roughened it. "Never Zorchi the man! There are Sicilians who would tell you different, could they open dead mouths to speak of their downed planes!"

"He was the best jet pilot Naples had," Rena said quietly.

It was my turn to curse. He was right; I hadn't thought of him as a man, or considered that he could do anything but regrow damaged tissues. "I'm sorry, Luigi!"

"No matter." He sighed, and then shrugged. "Come, take arms and ammunition and let us be out of this place. Even the nose of Zorchi can stand only so much of the smell of assassins!"

We moved down the passage, staggering along for what seemed to be hours, expecting every second to run into some official or expediter force. But apparently the passage wasn't being used much during the emergency. We finally reached stairs at the other end and headed up, afraid to attract attention by taking the waiting elevator.

At the top, Carmody frowned as he studied the side passages and doors. "Here, I guess," he decided. "This may still be a less used part of the garage." He reached for the door.

I stopped him. "Wait a minute. Is there any way back in, once we leave?"

"The combination will work—the master combination used by the Company heads. Otherwise, these doors are practically bomb-proof!" He pressed the combination and opened the door a crack.

Outside, I could see what seemed to be a small section of the Company car pool. There were sounds of trucks, but none were moving nearby. I saw a few men working on trucks a distance from us. Maybe luck was on our side.

I pointed to the nearest expediter patrol wagon—a small truck, really, enclosed except for the driver's seat. "That one, if there's fuel. We'll have to act as if we had a right to it, and hope for the best. Zorchi, can you manage it that far?"

"I shall walk like a born assassin," he assured me, but sweat began popping onto his forehead at what he was offering. Yet there was no sign of the agony he must have felt as he followed and managed to climb into the back with Rena and Carmody.

The fuel gauge was at the half mark and, as yet, there was no cry of alarm. I gunned the motor into life, watching the nearest workmen. They looked up casually, and then went back to their business. Ahead, I could see a clear lane toward the exit, with a few other trucks moving in and out. I headed for it, my hair prickling at the back of my neck.

We reached the entrance, passed through it, and were soon blending into the stream of cars that were passing the clinic on their way out for more suspension cases. The glass doors of the entrance were gone now, and workmen were putting up huge steel ones in their place, even while a steady stream of cases were hobbling or being carried into the clinic. Most of them were old or shabby, I noticed. The class-D type. The last ones to be admitted. We must have spent more time in the vault than I'd thought, and zero hour was drawing near.

Beyond the clinic, the whole of Anzio was a mass of abandoned cars that seemed to stretch for miles, and the few buildings not boarded up were obviously class-D dwellings, too poor to worry about. I cursed my way through a jam-up of trucks, and managed to find one of the side roads.

Then I pressed down on the throttle as far as I dared without attracting attention, until I could find a safe place to turn off with no other cars near to see me.

"Where to?" I asked. We couldn't go back to Zorchi's, since any expediter investigation would start there. Maybe we'd never be missed, but I couldn't risk it. If we had to, we could use some abandoned villa and hide out, but I was hoping for a better suggestion.

Zorchi looked blank, and Rena shrugged. "If we could only find Nikolas—" she suggested doubtfully.

I shook my head. I'd had a chance to think about that a little while the expediters took us to see Defoe, and I didn't like it. The leader of the revolution had apparently been captured by Defoe. According to Benedetto dell'Angela, he'd escaped. Yet Defoe hadn't tried to pump us about him. And when Benedetto set out to meet him, the expediters had descended at once.

It made an ugly picture. I had no wish to go looking for the man.

"There's my place," Carmody said finally. "I had places all over the world, kept ready for me and stocked. If Defoe let it be thought that I had retired, he must have kept them all up as I'd have done. Wait, let me orient myself. Up that road."

Places all over the world, with food that was wasted, and with servants who might never see their master! And I'd been brought up believing that the Underwriters were men of quiet, simple tastes! Carmody's clay feet were beginning to crumble up to the navel!

*

The villa was surrounded by trees, on a low hill that overlooked an artificial lake. It had been sealed off, but the combination lock yielded to Carmody's touch. There were beds made up and waiting, freezers stocked with food that sent Zorchi into ecstasy, and even a complete file of back issues of the Company paper. Carmody headed for those, with the look of a man hunting his lost past. He had a lot of catching up to do.

But it was the television set that interested me. It was still working, with taped material being broadcast. The appeal had been stepped up, asking for order and cooperation; I recognized the language as being pitched toward the lower classes now, though. And the clicking of a radiation-counter sounded as a constant background, with occasional shots of its meter, the needle well into the danger area.

Zorchi joined me and Rena, dribbling crumbs of meat down his beard. He snorted as he caught sight of the counter. "There is a real one in the other room, and it registers higher," he said. "It is interesting. For me, of no import. Doctors whom I trust have said Defoe is wrong; my body can resist damage from radiation—and perhaps even from old age. But for you and the young lady..."

He shut up at my expression, but the tape cut off and a live announcer came on before I could say anything. "A bulletin just in," he said, "shows that the government of Naples has unanimously passed a moratorium on all contracts, obligations and indebtedness for the duration of the emergency. The Company has just followed this with a declaration that it will extend the moratorium to include all crimes against the Company. During the emergency, the clinics will be available to all without prejudice, Director Defoe said today."

"A trap," Rena guessed. "We wouldn't have a chance, anyhow. But, Tom, does the other mean that—"

"It means your father was wrong," I answered. "As of right now—and probably in every government at the same time—the Company has been freed from any responsibility."

It didn't make any difference, of course. Benedetto had expected that everyone must secretly hate the Company as he did; he hadn't realized that men who have just been saved from the horrible danger of radiation death aren't going to turn against the agency that saved them. And damn it, the Company was saving them, after its opponents had risked annihilation of the race. Defoe would probably make sure the suspendees were awakened at a rate where he could keep absolute power, but not from any danger of bankruptcy.

*

Carmody had come out and listened, attracted by the broadcast radiation clicking, apparently. Now he asked enough questions to discover Benedetto's idea, and shook his head.

"It wouldn't work," he agreed with me. "Even if I still had control, I couldn't permit such a thing. What good would it do? Could money payments make food for a revived world, Miss dell'Angela? Would bankrupting the only agency capable of rebuilding the Earth be a thing of honor? Besides, even with what I've read, I can see no hope. There's nothing we can do."

"But if you can arouse the other Underwriters against Defoe," she insisted, "at least you can prevent *his* type of world!"

He shook his head. "How? All communications are in his hands. Even if I could fly to the Home Office, most of the ones I could trust—and there apparently are a few Defoe hasn't been able to retire—would be scattered, out of my reach. A week ago, there might have been a chance. Now, it's impossible. Impossible."

He shook his head sadly and wandered back toward the library. I could see that in his secret thoughts, he was wishing we'd left him safely in the vault. Maybe it would have been just as well.

"Cheer up," I told Rena. "Carmody's an old man—too old to think in terms of direct action, even when it's necessary. Defoe doesn't own the world yet!"

But later, when I located the books I wanted in the library and went out into the vine-covered bower in the formal garden, I wasn't as confident as I'd pretended.

Thinking wasn't a pleasant job, after all the years when I'd let others do my thinking for me. But now I had to do it for myself. Otherwise, the only alternative was to plan some means of quick death for us all before the radiation got too intense. And I couldn't accept that.

Rena had managed something Marianna couldn't have conceived—she'd quietly relinquished her fate into my hands, gambling on me with everything she had. Whether I wanted to or not, I'd taken the responsibility. Carmody was an old man; one who hadn't been able to keep Defoe from taking over in the first place. And Zorchi—well, he was Zorchi.

That night, the radiation detector suddenly took a sharp lift, its needle crossing over into the red. It was probably only a local rise. But it didn't make my thinking any more comfortable.

*

SUPER PACK

It was at breakfast that next morning when I finally took it up with Carmody. "Just what will the situation be at the clinic after they close down? How many will be kept awake? And what about their defenses?"

He frowned, trying to see my idea. Then he shrugged. "Too many, Tom. We had plotted out a course for such things as this a number of times in Planning. And our mob psychologists warned that there'd inevitably be a few who for one reason or another wouldn't come in in time, but who would then grow desperate and try to break in. Outlaws, looters, procrastinators, fanatics. That sort. So for some time, there should be at least twenty guards kept alert. And that's enough to defend a clinic. Atomic cannon at every entrance, of course, and the clinics are bombproof."

"Twenty, eh? And how about Defoe and Lawton? Will they sleep?" It seemed logical that they couldn't stay out of suspension for the whole fifty years or so. There'd be no profit to gaining a world after they were too old to use it.

"Not at first. There's a great deal of final administrative work to be done. There's a chamber equipped to keep a hundred or so men awake with radiation washed from the air, and containing adequate supplies, in cable contact with other clinics. They'll be there. Later, they'll take shifts, with only a couple of men awake at a time, I suppose. They may age a little that way, but not much."

He frowned again, and then slowly nodded. "It could be done, if we had some way to wait safely for six months. Getting back in is no problem for me."

"It's going to be done," I told him. "And a lot sooner. Are you willing to take the chance?"

"Have I any choice?" He shrugged again. "Do you think I haven't been sick at the idea of a man like Defoe in command of the Company for as long as he lives? Tom, my family started the Company. I've got an obligation to restore it to its right course. If there's any chance of keeping Defoe from being emperor of the world, I've got to take it. If you can put me in a position where I can get the honest Underwriters together again, where we can set up the Company as it was—"

"Why? So this will happen all over again?"

He looked shocked at Rena's question. "I don't blame you for being bitter, Miss dell'Angela. But with Defoe gone—"

"The Company made Defoe possible. In fact, it made him and Slovetski inevitable," I told him flatly. "That's its one great crime. Whenever you take power completely out of the hands of the many, it winds up in fewer and fewer hands. Those histories I was reading last night prove that. Carmody, what do you know about your own Company? Or the world? Leave the consolidation of power in Company hands out of it, and what has happened to progress?"

He frowned. "Well, we've leveled off a bit. We had to. We couldn't risk—"

"Exactly. You couldn't risk research that would lead to increased longevity—too many pensioners. You couldn't risk going to Mars—unpredictable dangers. You had to make the world fit actuarial charts. I remember seeing one of the first suspendees awakened. He expected things we could have done fifty years ago—and never will do. How many men today work their way out of their class? And why have classes so rigidly stratified? I've been reading your own speeches of nearly fifty years ago. I've got them here, together with some tables. Like to see them?"

He took the papers silently and began going through them, his shock giving way to a grudging realization. Maybe without the jolt of his awakening, he'd have laughed them off, but nothing was easy to dismiss with the hell brewing outside. At last he looked up.

"Tom, I'll admit the many times when I've been worried. I've considered starting research again countless times. I've been aware that dependence was growing too heavy on the Company. But we can't just toss it aside. It did bring an end to major war, when such a war would have ruined the Earth completely. It showed that nobody had to starve—that hardly anyone had to lack for any necessity, or die for lack of care. You can't throw that away."

"You can throw away its unrelated power." I knew I didn't have the answers. All this had been growing slowly in my mind since I'd first found Benedetto a political prisoner, but a lifetime wasn't enough to think it out, even with the books I'd found.

But I had to try. "In the middle ages, they had morality and politics tied into one bundle, Carmody. The church ruled. It wasn't good and they finally had to divorce church and state. Maybe the same applies to administrative politics and economics. The Company has shown what can be done economically. The church has survived as a great moral force outside material power. Now let's see if we can't put things in perspective.

"There's a precedent. The United States—the old government—was set up on the idea of balance of power: an elected Congress for the people to handle legislative tasks, a selected President to handle executive affairs, and a Judiciary mostly independent. On a world scale, as it can be done today—since the Company has really made it one world—the same can be done, with something like the Company to insure economics."

"I suppose every man who had any idealism has thought the same," Carmody said slowly. He sighed softly. "I remember trying to preach it to my father when I was just out of college. You're right. But can you set up such a perfect government? Can I? Tell me how, Tom, and I'll give you your chance, if I can."

Zorchi laughed cynically, but that was what I'd hoped Carmody might say.

"All right," I told him. "We can't do it. No one man is fit to rule, ever, or to establish rule. Oh, I had wish-dreams, a few days ago, I suppose, about what I'd do, if! But men have set out to establish new systems before, and done good jobs of it. Read the Constitution—a system put together artificially by expert political thinkers, and good for two hundred years, at least! And they didn't have our opportunities. For the first time, the world has to wait. Get the best minds you can, Carmody. Give them twenty-five years to work it out. They can come up with an answer. And then, when the world is awakened, you can start with it, fresh, without upsetting any old order. Is that your answer?"

"Most of it." There was a sudden light in his old eyes. "Yes, the sleep does make the chance possible. But how are you going to get the experts and assemble them?"

I pointed to Zorchi. "Hermes, the messenger of the gods. He's a jet pilot who can get all over the world. And he can move outside, without needing to worry about radiation."

"So?" Zorchi snorted again. "So, I am now your messenger, Weels! Do you think I would trouble myself so much for all of you, Weels?"

I grinned at him. "You defiantly speak of being a man. That makes you part of the human race. I'm simply taking you at your word."

"So?" he repeated, his face wooden. "Such a messenger would have much power, Weels. Suppose I choose to be Zorchi the ruler?"

"Not while Zorchi the man is also Zorchi the freak," I said with deliberate cruelty. "Go look at yourself."

And suddenly he smiled, his lips drawing back from his teeth. "Weels, for the first time you are honest. And for that as well as that I am a man, I will be Zorchi the messenger. But first, should we not decide on a plan of action? Or do we first rule and then conquer?"

"We wait first," I told him.

On the wall, the radiation indicator clicked steadily, its needle moving further into the red.

CHAPTER NINETEEN

The second day, the television went off the air with the final curt announcement that anyone not inside the clinics at noon would be left outside permanently. Then the set went dead, leaving only the clucking and beeping of our own radiation indicator. I'd thrown it out twice and brought it back both times.

Civilization had ended on the third day, though all the conveniences in the villa went on smoothly, except for the meter reading that told us nothing could be smooth. It was higher than the predictions I had heard, though I still hoped that was only a sporadic local phenomenon that would level out later. In the face of that, it was hard to believe that even a few men would remain outside the clinics, though I was counting on it.

We waited another twenty-four hours, forcing ourselves to sit in the villa, discussing plans, when our nerves were yelling for action. We had only an estimate to go on. If we got there too soon, there would be more awake than we could handle. Too late and we'd be radiation cases, good for nothing but the vaults.

It was a relief to leave at last, taking our weapons in the truck. We were wearing the radiation suits, hoping they'd protect us, and Zorchi spent the last two days devising pads and straps to cushion and strengthen his developing legs.

The world was dead. Cars had been abandoned in the middle of the road, making driving difficult.

The towns and villas were deserted, boarded up or simply abandoned. We might have been the last men on Earth, and we felt that we were as we headed for Anzio. This wasn't just a road, or Naples—or all of Italy. It was the world.

Then Rena pointed. Ahead, a boy was walking beside a dog, the animal's left rear leg bound and splintered as if it had been broken. I started to slow, then forced myself to drive on. As we passed, I saw that the boy was about fourteen, and his face was dirty and tear-streaked. He shook one fist at us, and came trudging on.

"If we win, we'll have the door open when he gets there," Rena said. "For him and his dog! If not, it won't matter how long it takes him. You couldn't stop, Tom." It didn't make me feel any better. But now dusk was falling, and we slowed, waiting until it was dark to park quietly near the garage. In front of the entrance, I could see a small ring of fires, and by their light a few figures moving about. They were madmen, of course—and yet, probably less mad than others who must be prowling through the towns, looting for things they could never use.

It seemed incredible that anyone could be outside, but the psychologists had apparently been right. These were determined men, willing to wait for the forlorn chance that some miracle might give them a futile, even more forlorn chance to try battering down the great doors. Maybe somewhere in the world, such a group might succeed. But not here. As I watched, there was a crackle of automatic gunfire from the entrance. The guards were awake, all right, and not taking chances on any poor devil getting too close.

*

There were no guards in the vault garage. We were prepared in case someone might be stationed inside the private entrance, as much prepared as we could be; since Carmody had been listed as still living, an ordinary guard who recognized him would probably let us in first and then try to report—giving us time to handle him. But we were lucky. The door opened to Carmody's top-secret combination.

"We designed such combinations into a few doors in case of internal revolution locally while no Underwriters were around. We never considered having an Underwriter lead a revolution from outside," he whispered to us.

The underground passage was deserted, and this time Carmody led through another corridor, to a stairs that seemed to wind up forever. Zorchi groaned, then caught himself.

"It leads to the main reception room," Carmody said.

With the men outside, most of the guards who still remained awake might be there. But we had to chance it. We stopped when we reached the top, catching our breath while Zorchi sank to the floor, writhing silently.

Then Rena threw back the door, Zorchi's rifle poked through, and I was leaping for the main door controls, hoping the memory I had was accurate. I was nearly to them when the two guards standing beside them turned.

They yelled, just as my rifle spat. At that range, I couldn't miss. And behind, I heard Zorchi's gun spit. The second guard slumped sickly to the floor, holding his stomach. I grabbed for the controls, while other yells sounded, and feet began pounding toward me.

There was no time to look back. The doors were slowly moving apart and Carmody was beside me, smashing a maul from the storeroom onto the electronic controls of the atomic cannon. I twisted between the opening doors.

"We've seized the vaults," I shouted. "We need help. Any man who joins us will be saved!"

I couldn't wait to watch, but I heard a hoarse, answering shout, and the sound of feet.

Carmody's maul had ruined the door controls. But the other guards were nearly on us. I saw two more sprawled on the floor. Zorchi hadn't missed. Then Carmody's fingers had found another of the private doors that looked like simple panels here. Rena and Carmody were through, and I yanked Zorchi after me, just as a bullet whined over his head. Behind us, I heard uncontrolled yelling as men from outside began pouring in.

It was our only hope. They had to take care of the guards, who were still probably shocked at finding us inside. We headed for the private quarters where Defoe would be, praying that there would be only a few there.

*

181

This passage was useless to us, though. It led from office to office for the doctors who superintended here. We came out into an office, watching our chance for the hall we had to take. I could see the men who had been outside in action now. A few had guns of some kind, but the clubs in the hands of the others were just as deadly in such a desperation attack; men who had seen themselves already dead weren't afraid of chances. About a score of the expediter guards were trying to hold off at least twice their number.

Then the hall seemed clear and we leaped into it. Suddenly gongs began ringing everywhere. Some guard had finally reached or remembered the alarm system. Carmody cursed, and tried to move faster.

The small private vault for the executives lay through the administration quarters and down several levels, before it was entered through a short passageway. Carmody had mapped it for me often enough. But he knew it by physical memory, which was better than my training. He'd also taught me the combination, but I left the door to his practiced fingers when we came to it. \ The elevator wasn't up. We couldn't wait. We raced down the stairs that circled it. Here Carmody's age told against him, and he fell behind. Rena and I were going down neck and neck with Zorchi throwing himself along with us. He had dropped his rifle and picked up a submachine gun from one of the fallen guards, and he clung to it now, using only one hand on the rail.

It was a reflection on a gun-barrel that saved us. The picked expediters were hidden in the dark mouth of the passageway, waiting for us to turn the stairs. But I caught a gleam of metal, and threw up my gun. Instantly, Zorchi was beside me, the submachine spitting as quickly as I could fire the first shot. "Aim for the wall. Ricochet!"

The ambushers had counted too much on surprise. They weren't ready to have the tables turned, nor for the trick Zorchi had suggested. Here we couldn't fire directly, but the bouncing shots worked almost as well. There were screams of men being hit, and the crazed pandemonium of others suddenly afraid.

Shots came toward us, but the wall that protected them—or was supposed to— ruined their shooting.

Zorchi abruptly dropped, landing with a thud on his side. I grunted sickly, thinking he was hit.

Then I saw the submachine gun point squarely into the passageway. It began spitting out death. By the time we could reach him, the expediters were dead or dying. There had been seven of them.

Zorchi staggered into the passage, through the bodies, crying something. I jumped after him, blinking my eyes to make out what he had seen. Then I caught sight of a door at the back being silently closed. It was a thick, massive slab, like the door to a bank vault.

Zorchi made a final leap that brought a sob of anguish as he landed on his weak legs, but his gun barrel slapped into the slit of opening. The door ground against it, strained and stopped. Zorchi pulled the trigger briefly.

For a second, then, there was silence. A second later, Defoe's voice came out through the thin slit. "You win. Dr. Lawton and I are alone and unarmed. We're coming out."

The door began opening again, somewhat jerkily this time. I watched it, expecting a trick, but there was none.

Inside the vault, the first room was obviously for guards and for the control of the equipment needed to wash all contamination out of the air and to provide the place with security for a century, even if all the rest of the Earth turned into a radioactive hell.

Lawton was slumped beside the controls, his head cradled in his arms. But at the sight of us, he stood up groggily, his mouth open, and shock on his face.

Defoe's eyes widened a trifle, but he stood quietly, and the bleak smile never faltered. "Congratulations, Thomas," he said. "My one fault again—I underrated the opposition. I wasn't expecting miracles. Hello, Millen. Fancy meeting you here."

"Search the place," I ordered.

Carmody went past the two without looking at them, with Rena close behind. A minute later, I heard a triumphant shout. They came back with a cringing man who seemed totally unlike the genial Sam Gogarty who had first introduced me to fine food and to Rena. His eyes were on Carmody, and his skin was gray white. He started to babble incoherently.

Carmody grinned at him. "You've got things twisted, Gogarty. Tom Wills is in charge of this affair." He turned toward one of the smaller offices. "As I remember it, there should be a transmitting setup in here. I want to make sure it works. If it does, some of the Underwriters are going to get a surprise, unless they're suspended."

Gogarty watched him go, and then sank slowly to a chair, shaking his head as he looked up at me. His lips twisted into bitter resignation. "You wouldn't understand, Tom. All my life, worked for things. Class-C, digging in a mine, eating Class-D, getting no fun, so I could buy Class-B employment. Then Class-A. Not many can do it, but I sweated it out. Thirty years living like a dog and killing myself with work and study. Not even a real woman until I met Susan, and she went to Defoe. But I wanted it easier for the young men. I wanted everybody to have a good life. No harm to anyone. Pull together, and forget the tough times. Then you had to come and blow the roof off..."

*

I felt sick. It was probably all true, and few men could make it. But if that's what it took to advance under the Company rules, it was justification enough for our fight.

"You'll be all right, Sam," I told him. "You'll go to sleep with the others. And when you wake up, you may have to work like hell again, but it'll be to rebuild the Earth, not to ruin it. Maybe there'll even be a chance with Susan again."

Defoe laughed sardonically. "Very nice, Thomas. And I suppose you mean it. What's in the future for me?"

"Suspension until the new government gets organized and can decide your case. I'd like to vote now for permanent suspension."

His face lost some of his amusement. Then he shrugged. "All right, I suppose I knew that. But now will you satisfy my curiosity? Just how did you work the business with Bay 100?"

"What happened to Slovetski?" I asked. I couldn't be sure about some of my suspicions over Benedetto's death, but I couldn't take chances that the man might still be loose somewhere, or else hiding out here until we were off guard.

He shook his head. "I can answer, but I'm waiting for a better offer."

"Sam?" I asked.

Gogarty nodded slowly. "All right, Tom. I guess you're the boss now. And I think I'm even glad of it. I always liked you. I'll answer about Slovetski."

Defoe snarled and swung, then saw my rifle coming up, and straightened again. "You win once more, Thomas. Your great international rebel cooperated with us very nicely after we caught him. We arranged for him to receive all calls to his most secret hideout right here in this room. It netted us his fellow conspirators— including your father, Miss dell'Angela!"

She gasped faintly, but her head came up at once. "Nikolas was no traitor. You're lying!"

"Why should I lie?" he asked. "With the right use of certain drugs, any man can become a traitor. And Dr. Lawton is an expert on drugs."

"Where is he?" I asked.

He shrugged. "How should I know? He wanted a radioactive world, so I let him enjoy it. We put him outside just before we closed the doors permanently."

Gogarty nodded confirmation. I turned it over. He might even have been one of the men waiting outside. But it wouldn't matter.

Without his organization and with a world where life outside was impossible, Slovetski's power was finished.

I turned to Zorchi. "The men who broke in will be going crazy soon," I told him. "While Rena finds the paging system and reassures them they'll all be treated in the reception room, how about getting Lawton to locate and revive a couple of the doctors you know and trust?"

*

Rena came back from the paging system, and Zorchi prodded Lawton with the gun, heading him toward the files that would show the location of the doctors. Gogarty stood up doubtfully, but I shook my head. Zorchi was able to handle a man of Lawton's type, even without full use of his legs, and I couldn't trust Gogarty yet.

"You can give me a hand with Defoe, Sam," I suggested. "We'd better strap him down first."

Gogarty nodded, and then suddenly let out a shocked cry, and was cringing back!

In the split second when both Rena and I had looked away, Defoe had whipped out an automatic and was now covering us, his teeth exposed in a taut smile. "Never underestimate an opponent, Thomas," he said. "And never believe what he says. You should have searched me, you know."

The gun was centered on Rena, and he waited, as if expecting me to make some move. All I could do was stand there, cursing myself. I'd thought of everything— except the obvious!

Defoe backed toward the door and slipped around it, drawing its heavy weight slowly shut until only a crack showed. Then he laughed. "Give my love to Millen," he said, and laughed softly.

I jumped for the door, but his feet were already moving out of the passage. The door began opening again, but I knew it was too late. Then, it was open. And amazingly, Defoe stood not ten feet away.

At the other end of the passage, a ragged bloody figure was standing, swaying slowly from side to side, holding a rifle. I took a second look to recognize Nikolas Slovetski. He was moving slowly toward Defoe. And now Defoe jerked back and began frantically digging for the automatic he must have pocketed.

Slovetski leaped, tossing the gun aside in a way that indicated it must have been empty. A bullet from Defoe's automatic caught his shoulder in mid-leap, but it couldn't stop him. He crashed squarely on Defoe, swinging a knife as the other went down. It missed, ringing against the hard floor.

I'd come unfrozen by then. I kicked the knife aside and grabbed the gun from Defoe's hands. Slovetski lay limp on him, and I rolled the smaller man aside.

Defoe was out cold from the blow of his head hitting the floor. Gogarty had come out behind me and now began binding him up. He opened his eyes slowly, blinked, and tried to grin as he stared at the bonds. He swung his head to the figure on the floor beside him. "Shall we go quietly, Nikolas?" he asked, as Gogarty picked him up and carried him back to the private vault.

But his sarcasm was wasted on Slovetski. The man must have been dying as he stumbled and groped his way toward the place where he knew Defoe must be. And the bullet in the shoulder had finished him. Rena bent over him, a faint sob on her lips.

Surprisingly, he fought his way back to consciousness, staring up at her. "Rena," he said weakly. "Benedetto! I loved him. I—" Then his head rolled toward me. "At least, I lived to die in a revolution, Thomas. Dirty business, revolution. When in the course of human events, it becomes—" He died before he could finish. I went looking for Lawton, to make sure Defoe was suspended at once. He'd be the last political suspendee, if I had anything to do with it, but there would be a certain pleasure in watching Lawton do the job.

CHAPTER TWENTY

The doors of the reception hall were closed again, but there was no lock now. One of the two doctors whom Zorchi had trusted was there now, waiting for the stragglers who came in slowly as a result of our broadcast. We couldn't reach them all, of course, but some could be saved. The men who had fought with us were treated and suspended. Even the boy and his dog had finally reached us and been put away.

In the main room of the executive vault, Carmody was waiting for Rena and me as we came in, haggard from lack of sleep, but somehow younger-looking than he had been since we had first revived him.

He stood up, managing a tired smile. "The first work's done, Tom," he said. "It wasn't too hard, once they learned Defoe was suspended; a lot of the others were afraid of him, I guess. So far, I've only contacted the ones I can trust, but it's a beginning. I've gotten tapes of their delegation of authority to you as acting assistant Chief Underwriter. I guess the factor that influenced them most was your willingness to give up all hopes of suspension for the emergency. And having Zorchi was a help, too—one man like him is worth an army now. I'll introduce you tomorrow."

He stumbled out, heading toward the sleeping quarters.

Well, I had the chance I'd wanted. And I had his promise to put off suspension until things were running properly. With time to develop a small staff, and with a chance to begin the work of locating the men to study the problems that had to be solved, I couldn't ask for much more.

Zorchi grinned at me. "Emperor Weels!" he mocked.

I grinned back. "If you ever say that seriously, Luigi, I want you to say it with a bullet through my brain. I've seen enough cases of power corrupting."

For a second, he studied me. "If that day should come, then there shall be the bullet. But now, even I must sleep," he said.

Then he glanced at Rena. "I have left orders that a priest should be wakened." She colored faintly.

SUPER PACK

"You'll be best man, I suppose?" I asked.

This time, even his beard couldn't conceal his amusement. "Is Zorchi not always the best man?" he asked as he left us alone.

I stared at the vault that would be my home for the next twenty-five or fifty years—until I was an old man, and the rest of the world was ready to be awakened.

"It's a lousy place to spend a honeymoon," I told Rena.

She leaned against me. "But perhaps a good place to bring up children," she said. "A place to teach them that their children will have a good world, Tom. That's all a woman ever wants, I guess."

I drew her to me. It was a good way to think of the future, whatever happened.

And it would be a better world, where the virtues of the Company could be used. Probably it wouldn't be perfect.

Even the best form of government all the experts could devise couldn't offer a permanent solution. But it could give men a chance to fight their way to a still better world.

THE DAY OF THE BOOMER DUKES

TABLE OF CONTENTS

FORAMINIFERA 9

Paptaste udderly, semped sempsemp dezhavoo, qued schmerz—Excuse me. I mean to say that it was like an endless diet of days, boring, tedious....

No, it loses too much in the translation. Explete my reasons, I say. Do my reasons matter? No, not to you, for you are troglodytes, knowing nothing of causes, understanding only acts. Acts and facts, I will give you acts and facts.

First you must know how I am called. My "name" is Foraminifera 9-Hart Bailey's Beam, and I am of adequate age and size. (If you doubt this, I am prepared to fight.) Once the—the tediety of life, as you might say, had made itself clear to me, there were, of course, only two alternatives. I do not like to die, so that possibility was out; and the remaining alternative was flight.

Naturally, the necessary machinery was available to me. I arrogated a small viewing machine, and scanned the centuries of the past in the hope that a sanctuary might reveal itself to my aching eyes. Kwel tediety that was! Back, back I went through the ages. Back to the Century of the Dog, back to the Age of the Crippled Men. I found no time better than my own. Back and back I peered, back as far as the Numbered Years. The Twenty-Eighth Century was boredom unendurable, the Twenty-Sixth a morass of dullness. Twenty-Fifth, Twenty-Fourth—wherever I looked, tediety was what I found.

*

I snapped off the machine and considered. Put the problem thus: Was there in all of the pages of history no age in which a 9-Hart Bailey's Beam might find adventure and excitement? There had to be! It was not possible, I told myself, despairing, that from the dawn of the dreaming primates until my own time there was no era at all in which I could be—happy? Yes, I suppose happiness is what I was looking for. But where was it? In my viewer, I had fifty centuries or more to look back upon. And that was, I decreed, the trouble; I could spend my life staring into the viewer, and yet never discover the time that was right for me. There were simply too many eras to choose from. It was like an enormous library in which there must, there had to be, contained the one fact I was looking for—that, lacking an index, I might wear my life away and never find.

"*Index!*"

I said the word aloud! For, to be sure, it was the answer. I had the freedom of the Learning Lodge, and the index in the reading room could easily find for me just what I wanted.

Splendid, splendid! I almost felt cheerful. I quickly returned the viewer I had been using to the keeper, and received my deposit back. I hurried to the Learning Lodge and fed my specifications into the index, as follows, that is to say: Find me a time in recent past where there is adventure and excitement, where there is a secret, colorful band of desperadoes with whom I can ally myself. I then added two specifications—second, that it should be before the time of the high radiation levels; and first, that it should be after the discovery of anesthesia, in case of accident—and retired to a desk in the reading room to await results.

It took only a few moments, which I occupied in making a list of the gear I wished to take with me. Then there was a hiss and a crackle, and in the receiver of the desk a book appeared. I unzipped the case, took it out, and opened it to the pages marked on the attached reading tape.

I had found my wonderland of adventure!

*

Ah, hours and days of exciting preparation! What a round of packing and buying; what a filling out of forms and a stamping of visas; what an orgy of injections and inoculations and preventive therapy! Merely getting ready for the trip made my pulse race faster and my adrenalin balance rise to the very point of paranoia; it was like being given a true blue new chance to live.

SUPER PACK

At last I was ready. I stepped into the transmission capsule; set the dials; unlocked the door, stepped out; collapsed the capsule and stored it away in my carry-all; and looked about at my new home.

Pyew! Kwel smell of staleness, of sourness, above all of coldness! It was a close matter then if I would be able to keep from a violent eructative stenosis, as you say. I closed my eyes and remembered warm violets for a moment, and then it was all right.

The coldness was not merely a smell; it was a physical fact. There was a damp grayish substance underfoot which I recognized as snow; and in a hard-surfaced roadway there were a number of wheeled vehicles moving, which caused the liquefying snow to splash about me. I adjusted my coat controls for warmth and deflection, but that was the best I could do. The reek of stale decay remained. Then there were also the buildings, painfully almost vertical. I believe it would not have disturbed me if they had been truly vertical; but many of them were minutes of arc from a true perpendicular, all of them covered with a carbonaceous material which I instantly perceived was an inadvertent deposit from the air. It was a bad beginning!

However, I was not *bored*.

*

I made my way down the "street," as you say, toward where a group of young men were walking toward me, five abreast. As I came near, they looked at me with interest and kwel respect, conversing with each other in whispers.

I addressed them: "Sirs, please direct me to the nearest recruiting office, as you call it, for the dread Camorra."

They stopped and pressed about me, looking at me intently. They were handsomely, though crudely dressed in coats of a striking orange color, and long trousers of an extremely dark material.

I decreed that I might not have made them understand me—it is always probable, it is understood, that a quicknik course in dialects of the past may not give one instant command of spoken communication in the field. I spoke again: "I wish to encounter a representative of the Camorra, in other words the Black Hand, in other words the cruel and sinister Sicilian terrorists named the Mafia. Do you know where these can be found?"

One of them said, "Nay. What's that jive?"

I puzzled over what he had said for a moment, but in the end decreed that his message was sensefree. As I was about to speak, however, he said suddenly: "Let's rove, man." And all five of them walked quickly away a few "yards." It was quite disappointing. I observed them conferring among themselves, glancing at me, and for a time proposed terminating my venture, for I then believed that it would be better to return "home," as you say, in order to more adequately research the matter.

*

However, the five young men came toward me again. The one who had spoken before, who I now detected was somewhat taller and fatter than the others, spoke as follows: "You're wanting the Mafia?" I agreed. He looked at me for a moment. "Are you holding?"

He was inordinately hard to understand. I said, slowly and with patience, "Keska that 'holding' say?"

"Money, man. You going to slip us something to help you find these cats?"

"Certainly, money. I have a great quantity of money instantly available," I rejoined him. This appeared to relieve his mind.

There was a short pause, directly after which this first of the young men spoke: "You're on, man. Yeah, come with us. What's to call you?" I queried this last statement, and he expanded: "The name. What's the name?"

"You may call me Foraminifera 9," I directed, since I wished to be incognito, as you put it, and we proceeded along the "street." All five of the young men indicated a desire to serve me, offering indeed to take my carry-all. I rejected this, politely.

I looked about me with lively interest, as you may well believe. Kwel dirt, kwel dinginess, kwel cold! And yet there was a certain charm which I can determine no way of expressing in this language. Acts and facts, of course. I shall not attempt to capture the subjectivity which is the charm, only to transcribe the physical datum—perhaps even data, who knows? My companions, for example: They were in appearance overwrought, looking about them continually, stopping entirely and drawing me with them into the shelter of a "door" when another man, this one wearing blue clothing and a visored hat appeared. Yet they were clearly devoted to me, at that moment, since they had put aside their own projects in order to escort me without delay to the Mafia.

*

Mafia! Fortunate that I had found them to lead me to the Mafia! For it had been clear in the historical work I had consulted that it was not ultimately easy to gain access to the Mafia. Indeed, so secret were they that I had detected no trace of their existence in other histories of the period. Had I relied only on the conventional work, I might never have known of their great underground struggle against what you term society. It was only in the actual contemporary volume itself, the curiosity titled U.S.A. Confidential by one Lait and one Mortimer, that I had descried that, throughout the world, this great revolutionary organization flexed its tentacles, the plexus within a short distance of where I now stood, battling courageously. With me to help them, what heights might we not attain! Kwel dramatic delight!

My meditations were interrupted. "Boomers!" asserted one of my five escorts in a loud, frightened tone. "Let's cut, man!" he continued, leading me with them into another entrance. It appeared, as well as I could decree, that the cause of his ejaculative outcry was the discovery of perhaps three, perhaps four, other young men, in coats of the same shiny material as my escorts. The difference was that they were of a different color, being blue.

*

We hastened along a lengthy chamber which was quite dark, immediately after which the large, heavy one opened a way to a serrated incline leading downward. It was extremely dark, I should say. There was also an extreme smell, quite like that of the outer air, but enormously intensified; one would suspect that there was an incomplete combustion of, perhaps, wood or coal, as well as a certain quantity of general decay. At any rate, we reached the bottom of the incline, and my escort behaved quite badly. One of them said to the other four, in these words: "Them jumpers follow us sure. Yeah, there's much trouble. What's to prime this guy now and split?"

Instantly they fell upon me with violence. I had fortunately become rather alarmed at their visible emotion of fear, and already had taken from my carry-all a Stollgratz 16, so that I quickly turned it on them. I started to replace the Stollgratz 16 as they fell to the floor, yet I realized that there might be an additional element of danger. Instead of putting the Stollgratz 16 in with the other trade goods, which I had brought to assist me in negotiating with the Mafia, I transferred it to my jacket. It had become clear to me that the five young men of my escort had intended to abduct and rob me—indeed had intended it all along, perhaps having never intended to convoy me to the office of the Mafia. And the other young men, those who wore the blue jackets in place of the orange, were already descending the incline toward me, quite rapidly.

"Stop," I directed them. "I shall not entrust myself to you until you have given me evidence that you entirely deserve such trust."

*

They all halted, regarding me and the Stollgratz 16. I detected that one of them said to another: "That cat's got a zip."

The other denied this, saying: "That no zip, man. Yeah, look at them Leopards. Say, you bust them flunkies with that thing?"

I perceived his meaning quite quickly. "You are 'correct'," I rejoined. "Are you associated in friendship with them flunkies?"

"Hell, no. Yeah, they're Leopards and we're Boomer Dukes. You cool them, you do us much good." I received this information as indicating that the two socio-economic units were inimical, and unfortunately lapsed into an example of the Bivalent Error. Since p implied not-q, I sloppily assumed that not-q implied r (with, you understand, r being taken as the class of phenomena pertinently favorable to me). This was a very poor construction, and of course resulted in certain difficulties. Qued, after all. I stated:

"Them flunkies offered to conduct me to a recruiting office, as you say, of the Mafia, but instead tried to take from me the much money I am holding." I then went on to describe to them my desire to attain contact with the said Mafia; meanwhile they descended further and grouped about me in the very little light, examining curiously the motionless figures of the Leopards.

They seemed to be greatly impressed; and at the same time, very much puzzled. Naturally. They looked at the Leopards, and then at me.

They gave every evidence of wishing to help me; but of course if I had not forgotten that one cannot assume from the statements "not-Leopard implies Boomer Duke" and "not-Leopard implies Foraminifera 9" that, qued, "Boomer Duke implies Foraminifera 9" ... if I had not forgotten this, I say, I should not have been "deceived." For in practice they were as little favorable to me as the Leopards. A certain member of their party reached a position behind me.

I quickly perceived that his intention was not favorable, and attempted to turn around in order to discharge at him with the Stollgratz 16, but he was very rapid. He had a metallic cylinder, and with it struck my head, knocking "me" unconscious.

SHIELD 8805

This candy store is called Chris's. There must be ten thousand like it in the city. A marble counter with perhaps five stools, a display case of cigars and a bigger one of candy, a few dozen girlie magazines hanging by clothespin-sort-of things from wire ropes along the wall. It has a couple of very small glass-topped tables under the magazines. And a juke—I can't imagine a place like Chris's without a juke.

I had been sitting around Chris's for a couple of hours, and I was beginning to get edgy. The reason I was sitting around Chris's was not that I liked Cokes particularly, but that it was one of the hanging-out places of a juvenile gang called The Leopards, with whom I had been trying to work for nearly a year; and the reason I was becoming edgy was that I didn't see any of them there.

The boy behind the counter—he had the same first name as I, Walter in both cases, though my last name is Hutner and his is, I believe, something Puerto Rican—the boy behind the counter was dummying up, too. I tried to talk to him, on and off, when he wasn't busy. He wasn't busy most of the time; it was too cold for sodas. But he just didn't want to talk. Now, these kids love to talk. A lot of what they say doesn't make sense—either bullying, or bragging, or purposeless swearing—but talk is their normal state; when they quiet down it means trouble. For instance, if you ever find yourself walking down Thirty-Fifth Street and a couple of kids pass you, talking, you don't have to bother looking around; but if they stop talking, turn quickly. You're about to be mugged. Not that Walt was a mugger—as far as I know; but that's the pattern of the enclave.

*

So his being quiet was a bad sign. It might mean that a rumble was brewing—and that meant that my work so far had been pretty nearly a failure. Even worse, it might mean that somehow the Leopards had discovered that I had at last passed my examinations and been appointed to the New York City Police Force as a rookie patrolman, Shield 8805.

Trying to work with these kids is hard enough at best. They don't like outsiders. But they particularly hate cops, and I had been trying for some weeks to decide how I could break the news to them.

The door opened. Hawk stood there. He didn't look at me, which was a bad sign. Hawk was one of the youngest in the Leopards, a skinny, very dark kid who had been reasonably friendly to me. He stood in the open door, with snow blowing in past him. "Walt. Out here, man."

It wasn't me he meant—they call me "Champ," I suppose because I beat them all shooting eight-ball pool. Walt put down the comic he had been reading and walked out, also without looking at me. They closed the door.

*

Time passed. I saw them through the window, talking to each other, looking at me. It was something, all right. They were scared. That's bad, because these kids are like wild animals; if you scare them, they hit first—it's the only way they know to defend themselves. But on the other hand, a rumble wouldn't scare them—not where they would show it; and finding out about the shield in my pocket wouldn't scare them, either. They hated cops, as I say; but cops were a part of their environment. It was strange, and baffling.

Walt came back in, and Hawk walked rapidly away. Walt went behind the counter, lit a cigaret, wiped at the marble top, picked up his comic, put it down again and finally looked at me. He said: "Some punk busted Fayo and a couple of the boys. It's real trouble."

I didn't say anything.

He took a puff on his cigaret. "They're chilled, Champ. Five of them."

"Chilled? Dead?" It sounded bad; there hadn't been a real rumble in months, not with a killing.

He shook his head. "Not dead. You're wanting to see, you go down Gomez's cellar. Yeah, they're all stiff but they're breathing. I be along soon as the old man comes back in the store."

He looked pretty sick. I left it at that and hurried down the block to the tenement where the Gomez family lived, and then I found out why.

*

They were sprawled on the filthy floor of the cellar like winoes in an alley. Fayo, who ran the gang; Jap; Baker; two others I didn't know as well. They were breathing, as Walt had said, but you just couldn't wake them up.

Hawk and his twin brother, Yogi, were there with them, looking scared. I couldn't blame them. The kids looked perfectly all right, but it was obvious that they weren't. I bent down and smelled, but there was no trace of liquor or anything else on their breath.

I stood up. "We'd better get a doctor."

"Nay. You call the meat wagon, and a cop comes right with it, man," Yogi said, and his brother nodded.

I laid off that for a moment. "What happened?"

Hawk said, "You know that witch Gloria, goes with one of the Boomer Dukes? She opened her big mouth to my girl. Yeah, opened her mouth and much bad talk came out. Said Fayo primed some jumper with a zip and the punk cooled him, and then a couple of the Boomers moved in real cool. Now they got the punk with the zip and much other stuff, real stuff."

"What kind of stuff?"

Hawk looked worried. He finally admitted that he didn't know what kind of stuff, but it was something dangerous in the way of weapons. It had been the "zip" that had knocked out the five Leopards.

I sent Hawk out to the drug-store for smelling salts and containers of hot black coffee—not that I knew what I was doing, of course, but they were dead set against calling an ambulance. And the boys didn't seem to be in any particular danger, only sleep.

*

However, even then I knew that this kind of trouble was something I couldn't handle alone. It was a tossup what to do—the smart thing was to call the precinct right then and there; but I couldn't help feeling that that would make the Leopards clam up hopelessly. The six months I had spent trying to work with them had not been too successful—a lot of the other neighborhood workers had made a lot more progress than I—but at least they were willing to talk to me; and they wouldn't talk to uniformed police.

Besides, as soon as I had been sworn in, the day before, I had begun the practice of carrying my .38 at all times, as the regulations say. It was in my coat. There was no reason for me to feel I needed it. But I did. If there was any truth to the story of a "zip" knocking out the boys—and I had all five of them right there for evidence—I had the unpleasant conviction that there was real trouble circulating around East Harlem that afternoon.

"Champ. They all waking up!"

I turned around, and Hawk was right. The five Leopards, all of a sudden, were stirring and opening their eyes. Maybe the smelling salts had something to do with it, but I rather think not.

We fed them some of the black coffee, still reasonably hot. They were scared; they were more scared than anything I had ever seen in those kids before. They could hardly talk at first, and when finally they came around enough to tell me what had happened I could hardly believe them. This man had been small and peculiar, and he had been looking for, of all things, the "Mafia," which he had read about in history books—*old* history books.

Well, it didn't make sense, unless you were prepared to make a certain assumption that I refused to make. Man from Mars? Nonsense. Or from the future? Equally ridiculous....

*

201

Then the five Leopards, reviving, began to walk around. The cellar was dark and dirty, and packed with the accumulation of generations in the way of old furniture and rat-inhabited mattresses and piles of newspapers; it wasn't surprising that we hadn't noticed the little gleaming thing that had apparently rolled under an abandoned potbelly stove.

Jap picked it up, squalled, dropped it and yelled for me.

I touched it cautiously, and it tingled. It wasn't painful, but it was an odd, unexpected feeling—perhaps you've come across the "buzzers" that novelty stores sell which, concealed in the palm, give a sudden, surprising tingle when the owner shakes hands with an unsuspecting friend. It was like that, like a mild electric shock. I picked it up and held it. It gleamed brightly, with a light of its own; it was round; it made a faint droning sound; I turned it over, and it spoke to me. It said in a friendly, feminine whisper: *Warning, this portatron attuned only to Bailey's Beam percepts. Remain quiescent until the Adjuster comes.*

That settled it. Any time a lit-up cue ball talks to me, I refer the matter to higher authority. I decided on the spot that I was heading for the precinct house, no matter what the Leopards thought.

But when I turned and headed for the stairs, I couldn't move. My feet simply would not lift off the ground. I twisted, and stumbled, and fell in a heap; I yelled for help, but it didn't do any good. The Leopards couldn't move either.

We were stuck there in Gomez's cellar, as though we had been nailed to the filthy floor.

COW

When I see what this flunky has done to them Leopards, I call him a cool cat right away. But then we jump him and he ain't so cool. Angel and Tiny grab him under the arms and I'm grabbing the stuff he's carrying. Yeah, we get out of there.

There's bulls on the street, so we cut through the back and over the fences. Tiny don't like that. He tells me, "Cow. What's to leave this cat here? He must weigh eighteen tons." "You're bringing him," I tell him, so he shuts up. That's how it is in the Boomer Dukes. When Cow talks, them other flunkies shut up fast.

We get him in the loft over the R. and I. Social Club. Damn, but it's cold up there. I can hear the pool balls clicking down below so I pass the word to keep quiet. Then I give this guy the foot and pretty soon he wakes up.

As soon as I talk to him a little bit I figure we had luck riding with us when we see them Leopards. This cat's got real bad stuff. Yeah, I never hear of anything like it. But what it takes to make a fight he's got. I take my old pistol and give it to Tiny. Hell, it makes him happy and what's it cost me? Because what this cat's got makes that pistol look like something for babies.

*

First he don't want to talk. "Stomp him," I tell Angel, but he's scared. He says, "Nay. This is a real weird cat, Cow. I'm for cutting out of here."

"Stomp him," I tell him again, pretty quiet, but he does it. He don't have to tell me this cat's weird, but when the cat gets the foot a couple of times he's willing to talk. Yeah, he talks real funny, but that don't matter to me. We take all the loot out of his bag, and I make this cat tell me what it's to do. Damn, I don't know what he's talking about one time out of six, but I know enough. Even Tiny catches on after a while, because I see him put down that funky old pistol I gave him that he's been loving up.

I'm feeling pretty good. I wish a couple of them chicken Leopards would turn up so I could show them what they missed out on. Yeah, I'll take on them, and the Black Dogs, and all the cops in the world all at once—that's how good I'm feeling. I feel so good that I don't even like it when Angel lets out a yell and comes up with a wad of loot. It's like I want to prime the U.S. Mint for chickenfeed, I don't want it to come so easy.

But money's on hand, so I take it off Angel and count it. This cat was really loaded; there must be a thousand dollars here.

I take a handful of it and hand it over to Angel real cool. "Get us some charge," I tell him. "There's much to do and I'm feeling ready for some charge to do it with."

"How many sticks you want me to get?" he asks, holding on to that money like he never saw any before.

I tell him: "Sticks? Nay. I'm for real stuff tonight. You find Four-Eye and get us some horse." Yeah, he digs me then. He looks like he's pretty scared and I know he is, because this punk hasn't had anything bigger than reefers in his life. But I'm for busting a couple of caps of H, and what I do he's going to do. He takes off to find Four-Eye and the rest of us get busy on this cat with the funny artillery until he gets back.

*

It's like I'm a million miles down Dream Street. Hell, I don't want to wake up.

But the H is wearing off and I'm feeling mean. Damn, I'll stomp my mother if she talks big to me right then.

I'm the first one on my feet and I'm looking for trouble. The whole place is full now. Angel must have passed the word to everybody in the Dukes, but I don't even remember them coming in. There's eight or ten cats lying around on the floor now, not even moving. This won't do, I decide.

If I'm on my feet, they're all going to be on their feet. I start to give them the foot and they begin to move. Even the weirdie must've had some H. I'm guessing that somebody slipped him some to see what would happen, because he's off on Cloud Number Nine. Yeah, they're feeling real mean when they wake up, but I handle them cool. Even that little flunky Sailor starts to go up against me but I look at him cool and he chickens. Angel and Pete are real sick, with the shakes and the heaves, but I ain't waiting for them to feel good. "Give me that loot," I tell Tiny, and he hands over the stuff we took off the weirdie. I start to pass out the stuff.

"What's to do with this stuff?" Tiny asks me, looking at what I'm giving him.

I tell him, "Point it and shoot it." He isn't listening when the weirdie's telling me what the stuff is. He wants to know what it does, but I don't know that. I just tell him, "Point it and shoot it, man." I've sent one of the cats out for drinks and smokes and he's back by then, and we're all beginning to feel a little better, only still pretty mean. They begin to dig me.

"Yeah, it sounds like a rumble," one of them says, after a while.

I give him the nod, cool. "You're calling it," I tell him. "There's much fighting tonight. The Boomer Dukes is taking on the world!"

SANDY VAN PELT

The front office thought the radio car would give us a break in spot news coverage, and I guessed as wrong as they did. I had been covering City Hall long enough, and that's no place to build a career—the Press Association is very tight there, there's not much chance of getting any kind of exclusive story because of the sharing agreements. So I put in for the radio car. It meant taking the night shift, but I got it.

I suppose the front office got their money's worth, because they played up every lousy auto smash the radio car covered as though it were the story of the Second Coming, and maybe it helped circulation. But I had been on it for four months and, wouldn't you know it, there wasn't a decent murder, or sewer explosion, or running gun fight between six P.M. and six A.M. any night I was on duty in those whole four months. What made it worse, the kid they gave me as photographer—Sol Detweiler, his name was—couldn't drive worth a damn, so I was stuck with chauffeuring us around.

We had just been out to LaGuardia to see if it was true that Marilyn Monroe was sneaking into town with Aly Khan on a night plane—it wasn't—and we were coming across the Triborough Bridge, heading south toward the East River Drive, when the office called. I pulled over and parked and answered the radiophone.

*

It was Harrison, the night City Editor. "Listen, Sandy, there's a gang fight in East Harlem. Where are you now?"

It didn't sound like much to me, I admit. "There's always a gang fight in East Harlem, Harrison. I'm cold and I'm on my way down to Night Court, where there may or may not be a story; but at least I can get my feet warm."

"Where are you now?" Harrison wasn't fooling. I looked at Sol, on the seat next to me; I thought I had heard him snicker. He began to fiddle with his camera without looking at me. I pushed the "talk" button and told Harrison where I was. It pleased him very much; I

wasn't more than six blocks from where this big rumble was going on, he told me, and he made it very clear that I was to get on over there immediately.

I pulled away from the curb, wondering why I had ever wanted to be a newspaperman; I could have made five times as much money for half as much work in an ad agency. To make it worse, I heard Sol chuckle again. The reason he was so amused was that when we first teamed up I made the mistake of telling him what a hot reporter I was, and I had been visibly cooling off before his eyes for a better than four straight months.

Believe me, I was at the very bottom of my career that night. For five cents cash I would have parked the car, thrown the keys in the East River, and taken the first bus out of town. I was absolutely positive that the story would be a bust and all I would get out of it would be a bad cold from walking around in the snow.

And if that doesn't show you what a hot newspaperman I really am, nothing will.

*

Sol began to act interested as we reached the corner Harrison had told us to go to. "That's Chris's," he said, pointing at a little candy store. "And that must be the pool hall where the Leopards hang out."

"You know this place?"

He nodded. "I know a man named Walter Hutner. He and I went to school together, until he dropped out, couple weeks ago. He quit college to go to the Police Academy. He wanted to be a cop."

I looked at him. "You're going to college?"

"Sure, Mr. Van Pelt. Wally Hutner was a sociology major—I'm journalism—but we had a couple of classes together. He had a part-time job with a neighborhood council up here, acting as a sort of adult adviser for one of the gangs."

"They need advice on how to be gangs?"

"No, that's not it, Mr. Van Pelt. The councils try to get their workers accepted enough to bring the kids in to the social centers, that's all. They try to get them off the streets. Wally was working with a bunch called the Leopards."

I shut him up. "Tell me about it later!" I stopped the car and rolled down a window, listening.

*

Yes, there was something going on all right. Not at the corner Harrison had mentioned—there wasn't a soul in sight in any direction. But I could hear what sounded like gunfire and yelling, and, my God, even bombs going off! And it wasn't too far away. There were sirens, too—squad cars, no doubt.

"It's over that way!" Sol yelled, pointing. He looked as though he was having the time of his life, all keyed up and delighted. He didn't have to tell me where the noise was coming from, I could hear for myself. It sounded like D-Day at Normandy, and I didn't like the sound of it.

I made a quick decision and slammed on the brakes, then backed the car back the way we had come. Sol looked at me. "What—"

"Local color," I explained quickly. "This the place you were talking about? Chris's? Let's go in and see if we can find some of these hoodlums."

"But, Mr. Van Pelt, all the pictures are over where the fight's going on!"

"Pictures, shmictures! Come on!" I got out in front of the candy store, and the only thing he could do was follow me.

Whatever they were doing, they were making the devil's own racket about it. Now that I looked a little more closely I could see that they must have come this way; the candy store's windows were broken; every other street light was smashed; and what had at first looked like a flight of steps in front of a tenement across the street wasn't anything of the kind—it was a pile of bricks and stone from the false-front cornice on the roof! How in the world they had managed to knock that down I had no idea; but it sort of convinced me that, after all, Harrison had been right about this being a *big* fight.

Over where the noise was coming from there were queer flashing lights in the clouds overhead—reflecting exploding flares, I thought.

*

No, I didn't want to go over where the pictures were. I like living. If it had been a normal Harlem rumble with broken bottles and knives, or maybe even home-made zip guns—I might have taken a chance on it, but this was for real.

"Come on," I yelled to Sol, and we pushed the door open to the candy store.

At first there didn't seem to be anyone in, but after we called a couple times a kid of about sixteen, coffee-colored and scared-looking, stuck his head up above the counter.

"You. What's going on here?" I demanded. He looked at me as if I was some kind of a two-headed monster. "Come on, kid. Tell us what happened."

"Excuse me, Mr. Van Pelt." Sol cut in ahead of me and began talking to the kid in Spanish. It got a rise out of him; at least Sol got an answer. My Spanish is only a little bit better than my Swahili, so I missed what was going on, except for an occasional word. But Sol was getting it all. He reported: "He knows Walt; that's what's bothering him. He says Walt and some of the Leopards are in a basement down the street, and there's something wrong with them. I can't exactly figure out what, but—"

"The hell with them. What about *that?*"

"You mean the fight? Oh, it's a big one all right, Mr. Van Pelt. It's a gang called the Boomer Dukes. They've got hold of some real guns somewhere—I can't exactly understand what kind of guns he means, but it sounds like something serious. He says they shot that parapet down across the street. Gosh, Mr. Van Pelt, you'd think it'd take a cannon for something like that. But it has something to do with Walt Hutner and all the Leopards, too."

I said enthusiastically, "Very good, Sol. That's fine. Find out where the cellar is, and we'll go interview Hutner."

"But Mr. Van Pelt, the pictures—"

"Sorry. I have to call the office." I turned my back on him and headed for the car.

*

The noise was louder, and the flashes in the sky brighter—it looked as though they were moving this way. Well, I didn't have any money tied up in the car, so I wasn't worried about leaving it in the street. And somebody's cellar seemed like a very good place to be. I called the office and started to tell Harrison what we'd found out; but he stopped me short. "Sandy, where've you been? I've been trying to call you for—Listen, we got a call from Fordham. They've detected radiation coming from the East Side—it's got to be what's going on up there! Radiation, do you hear me? That means atomic weapons! Now, you get th—"

Silence.

"Hello?" I cried, and then remembered to push the talk button. "Hello? Harrison, you there?"

Silence. The two-way radio was dead.

I got out of the car; and maybe I understood what had happened to the radio and maybe I didn't. Anyway, there was something new shining in the sky. It hung below the clouds in parts, and I could see it through the bottom of the clouds in the middle; it was a silvery teacup upside down, a hemisphere over everything.

It hadn't been there two minutes before.

*

I heard firing coming closer and closer. Around a corner a bunch of cops came, running, turning, firing; running, turning and firing again. It was like the retreat from Caporetto in miniature. And what was chasing them? In a minute I saw. Coming around the corner was a kid with a lightning-blue satin jacket and two funny-looking guns in his hand; there was a silvery aura around him, the same color as the lights in the sky; and I swear I saw those cops' guns hit him twenty times in twenty seconds, but he didn't seem to notice.

SUPER PACK

Sol and the kid from the candy store were right beside me. We took another look at the one-man army that was coming down the street toward us, laughing and prancing and firing those odd-looking guns. And then the three of us got out of there, heading for the cellar. Any cellar.

PRIAM'S MAW

My occupation was "short-order cook", as it is called. I practiced it in a locus entitled "The White Heaven," established at Fifth Avenue, Newyork, between 1949 and 1962 C.E. I had created rapport with several of the aboriginals, who addressed me as Bessie, and presumed to approve the manner in which I heated specimens of minced ruminant quadruped flesh (deceased to be sure). It was a satisfactory guise, although tiring.

Using approved techniques, I was compiling anthropometric data while "I" was, as they say, "brewing coffee." I deem the probability nearly conclusive that it was the double duty, plus the datum that, as stated, "I" was physically tired, which caused me to overlook the first signal from my portatron. Indeed, I might have overlooked the second as well except that the aboriginal named Lester stated: "Hey, Bessie. Ya got an alarm clock in ya pocketbook?" He had related the annunciator signal of the portatron to the only significant datum in his own experience which it resembled, the ringing of a bell.

I annotated his dossier to provide for his removal in case it eventuated that he had made an undesirable intuit (this proved unnecessary) and retired to the back of the "store" with my carry-all. On identifying myself to the portatron, I received information that it was attuned to a Bailey's Beam, identified as Foraminifera 9-Hart, who had refused treatment for systemic weltschmerz and instead sought to relieve his boredom by adventuring into this era.

I thereupon compiled two recommendations which are attached: 2, a proposal for reprimand to the Keeper of the Learning Lodge for failure to properly annotate a volume entitled *U.S.A. Confidential* and, 1, a proposal for reprimand to the Transport Executive, for permitting Bailey's Beam-class personnel access to temporal transport. Meanwhile, I left the "store" by a rear exit and directed myself toward the locus of the transmitting portatron.

*

SUPER PACK

I had proximately left when I received an additional information, namely that developed weapons were being employed in the area toward which I was directing. This provoked that I abandon guise entirely. I went transparent and quickly examined all aboriginals within view, to determine if any required removal; but none had observed this. I rose to perhaps seventy-five meters and sped at full atmospheric driving speed toward the source of the alarm. As I crossed a "park" I detected the drive of another Adjuster, whom I determined to be Alephplex Priam's Maw—that is, my father. He bespoke me as follows: "Hurry, Besplex Priam's Maw. That crazy Foraminifera has been captured by aboriginals and they have taken his weapons away from him." "Weapons?" I inquired. "Yes, weapons," he stated, "for Foraminifera 9-Hart brought with him more than forty-three kilograms of weapons, ranging up to and including electronic."

I recorded this datum and we landed, went opaque in the shelter of a doorway and examined our percepts. "Quarantine?" asked my father, and I had to agree. "Quarantine," I voted, and he opened his carry-all and set-up a quarantine shield on the console. At once appeared the silvery quarantine dome, and the first step of our adjustment was completed. Now to isolate, remove, replace.

Queried Alephplex: "An Adjuster?" I observed the phenomenon to which he was referring. A young, dark aboriginal was coming toward us on the "street," driving a group of police aboriginals before him. He was armed, it appeared, with a fission-throwing weapon in one hand and some sort of tranquilizer—I deem it to have been a Stollgratz 16—in the other; moreover, he wore an invulnerability belt. The police aboriginals were attempting to strike him with missile weapons, which the belt deflected. I neutralized his shield, collapsed him and stored him in my carry-all. "Not an Adjuster," I asserted my father, but he had already perceived that this was so. I left him to neutralize and collapse the police aboriginals while I zeroed in on the portatron. I did not envy him his job with the police

213

aboriginals, for many of them were "dead," as they say. It required the most delicate adjustments.

*

The portatron developed to be in a "cellar" and with it were some nine or eleven aboriginals which it had immobilized pending my arrival. One spoke to me thus: "Young lady, please call the cops! We're stuck here, and—" I did not wait to hear what he wished to say further, but neutralized and collapsed him with the other aboriginals. The portatron apologized for having caused me inconvenience; but of course it was not its fault, so I did not neutralize it. Using it for d-f, I quickly located the culprit, Foraminifera 9-Hart Bailey's Beam, nearby. He spoke despairingly in the dialect of the locus, "Besplex Priam's Maw, for God's sake get me out of this!" "Out!" I spoke to him, "you'll wish you never were 'born,' as they say!" I neutralized but did not collapse him, pending instructions from the Central Authority. The aboriginals who were with him, however, I did collapse.

Presently arrived Alephplex, along with four other Adjusters who had arrived before the quarantine shield made it not possible for anyone else to enter the disturbed area. Each one of us had had to abandon guise, so that this locus of Newyork 1939-1986 must require new Adjusters to replace us—a matter to be charged against the guilt of Foraminifera 9-Hart Bailey's Beam, I deem.

*

This concluded Steps 3 and 2 of our Adjustment, the removal and the isolation of the disturbed specimens. We are transmitting same disturbed specimens to you under separate cover herewith, in neutralized and collapsed state, for the manufacture of simulacra thereof. One regrets to say that they number three thousand eight hundred forty-six, comprising all aboriginals within the quarantined area who had first-hand knowledge of the anachronisms caused by Foraminifera's importation of contemporary weapons into this locus.

Alephplex and the four other Adjusters are at present reconstructing such physical damage as was caused by the use of said weapons. Simultaneously, while I am preparing this report, "I" am maintaining the quarantine shield which cuts off this locus, both physically and temporally, from the remainder of its environment. I deem that if replacements for the attached aboriginals can be fabricated quickly enough, there will be no significant outside percept of the shield itself, or of the happenings within it—that is, by maintaining a quasi-stasis of time while the repairs are being made, an outside aboriginal observer will see, at most, a mere flicker of silver in the sky. All Adjusters here present are working as rapidly as we can to make sure the shield can be withdrawn, before so many aboriginals have observed it as to make it necessary to replace the entire city with simulacra. We do not wish a repetition of the California incident, after all.

THE TUNNEL UNDER THE WORLD

TABLE OF CONTENTS

I

On the morning of June 15th, Guy Burckhardt woke up screaming out of a dream.

It was more real than any dream he had ever had in his life. He could still hear and feel the sharp, ripping-metal explosion, the violent heave that had tossed him furiously out of bed, the searing wave of heat.

He sat up convulsively and stared, not believing what he saw, at the quiet room and the bright sunlight coming in the window.

He croaked, "Mary?"

His wife was not in the bed next to him. The covers were tumbled and awry, as though she had just left it, and the memory of the dream was so strong that instinctively he found himself searching the floor to see if the dream explosion had thrown her down.

But she wasn't there. Of course she wasn't, he told himself, looking at the familiar vanity and slipper chair, the uncracked window, the unbuckled wall. It had only been a dream.

"Guy?" His wife was calling him querulously from the foot of the stairs. "Guy, dear, are you all right?"

He called weakly, "Sure."

There was a pause. Then Mary said doubtfully, "Breakfast is ready. Are you sure you're all right? I thought I heard you yelling—"

Burckhardt said more confidently, "I had a bad dream, honey. Be right down."

*

In the shower, punching the lukewarm-and-cologne he favored, he told himself that it had been a beaut of a dream. Still, bad dreams weren't unusual, especially bad dreams about explosions. In the past thirty years of H-bomb jitters, who had not dreamed of explosions?

Even Mary had dreamed of them, it turned out, for he started to tell her about the dream, but she cut him off. "You *did?*" Her voice was astonished. "Why, dear, I dreamed the same thing! Well, almost the same thing. I didn't actually *hear* anything. I dreamed that something woke me up, and then there was a sort of quick bang, and then something hit me on the head. And that was all. Was yours like that?"

Burckhardt coughed. "Well, no," he said. Mary was not one of these strong-as-a-man, brave-as-a-tiger women. It was not necessary, he thought, to tell her all the little details of the dream that made it seem so real. No need to mention the splintered ribs, and the salt bubble in his throat, and the agonized knowledge that this was death. He said, "Maybe there really was some kind of explosion downtown. Maybe we heard it and it started us dreaming."

Mary reached over and patted his hand absently. "Maybe," she agreed. "It's almost half-past eight, dear. Shouldn't you hurry? You don't want to be late to the office."

He gulped his food, kissed her and rushed out—not so much to be on time as to see if his guess had been right.

But downtown Tylerton looked as it always had. Coming in on the bus, Burckhardt watched critically out the window, seeking evidence of an explosion. There wasn't any. If anything, Tylerton looked better than it ever had before: It was a beautiful crisp day, the sky was cloudless, the buildings were clean and inviting. They had, he observed, steam-blasted the Power & Light Building, the town's only skyscraper—that was the penalty of having Contro Chemical's main plant on the outskirts of town; the fumes from the cascade stills left their mark on stone buildings.

None of the usual crowd were on the bus, so there wasn't anyone Burckhardt could ask about the explosion. And by the time he got out at the corner of Fifth and Lehigh and the bus rolled away with a muted diesel moan, he had pretty well convinced himself that it was all imagination.

He stopped at the cigar stand in the lobby of his office building, but Ralph wasn't behind the counter. The man who sold him his pack of cigarettes was a stranger.

"Where's Mr. Stebbins?" Burckhardt asked.

The man said politely, "Sick, sir. He'll be in tomorrow. A pack of Marlins today?"

"Chesterfields," Burckhardt corrected.

"Certainly, sir," the man said. But what he took from the rack and slid across the counter was an unfamiliar green-and-yellow pack.

"Do try these, sir," he suggested. "They contain an anti-cough factor. Ever notice how ordinary cigarettes make you choke every once in a while?"

*

Burckhardt said suspiciously, "I never heard of this brand."

"Of course not. They're something new." Burckhardt hesitated, and the man said persuasively, "Look, try them out at my risk. If you don't like them, bring back the empty pack and I'll refund your money. Fair enough?"

Burckhardt shrugged. "How can I lose? But give me a pack of Chesterfields, too, will you?"

He opened the pack and lit one while he waited for the elevator. They weren't bad, he decided, though he was suspicious of cigarettes that had the tobacco chemically treated in any way. But he didn't think much of Ralph's stand-in; it would raise hell with the trade at the cigar stand if the man tried to give every customer the same high-pressure sales talk.

The elevator door opened with a low-pitched sound of music. Burckhardt and two or three others got in and he nodded to them as the door closed. The thread of music switched off and the speaker in the ceiling of the cab began its usual commercials.

No, not the *usual* commercials, Burckhardt realized. He had been exposed to the captive-audience commercials so long that they hardly registered on the outer ear any more, but what was coming from the recorded program in the basement of the building caught his attention. It wasn't merely that the brands were mostly unfamiliar; it was a difference in pattern.

There were jingles with an insistent, bouncy rhythm, about soft drinks he had never tasted. There was a rapid patter dialogue between what sounded like two ten-year-old boys about a candy bar, followed by an authoritative bass rumble: "Go right out and get a DELICIOUS Choco-Bite and eat your TANGY Choco-Bite *all up*. That's *Choco-Bite!*" There was a sobbing female whine: "I *wish* I had a Feckle Freezer! I'd do *anything* for a Feckle Freezer!" Burckhardt reached his floor and left the elevator in the middle of the last one. It left him a little uneasy. The commercials were not for familiar brands; there was no feeling of use and custom to them.

But the office was happily normal—except that Mr. Barth wasn't in. Miss Mitkin, yawning at the reception desk, didn't know exactly why. "His home phoned, that's all. He'll be in tomorrow."

"Maybe he went to the plant. It's right near his house."

She looked indifferent. "Yeah."

A thought struck Burckhardt. "But today is June 15th! It's quarterly tax return day—he has to sign the return!"

Miss Mitkin shrugged to indicate that that was Burckhardt's problem, not hers. She returned to her nails.

Thoroughly exasperated, Burckhardt went to his desk. It wasn't that he couldn't sign the tax returns as well as Barth, he thought resentfully. It simply wasn't his job, that was all; it was a responsibility that Barth, as office manager for Contro Chemicals' downtown office, should have taken.

*

He thought briefly of calling Barth at his home or trying to reach him at the factory, but he gave up the idea quickly enough. He didn't really care much for the people at the factory and the less contact he had with them, the better. He had been to the factory once, with Barth; it had been a confusing and, in a way, a frightening experience. Barring a handful of executives and engineers, there wasn't a soul in the factory—that is, Burckhardt corrected himself, remembering what Barth had told him, not a *living* soul—just the machines.

According to Barth, each machine was controlled by a sort of computer which reproduced, in its electronic snarl, the actual memory and mind of a human being. It was an unpleasant thought. Barth, laughing, had assured him that there was no Frankenstein business of robbing graveyards and implanting brains in machines. It was only a matter, he said, of transferring a man's habit patterns from brain cells to vacuum-tube cells. It didn't hurt the man and it didn't make the machine into a monster.

But they made Burckhardt uncomfortable all the same.

He put Barth and the factory and all his other little irritations out of his mind and tackled the tax returns. It took him until noon to verify the figures—which Barth could have done out of his memory and his private ledger in ten minutes, Burckhardt resentfully reminded himself.

He sealed them in an envelope and walked out to Miss Mitkin. "Since Mr. Barth isn't here, we'd better go to lunch in shifts," he said. "You can go first."

"Thanks." Miss Mitkin languidly took her bag out of the desk drawer and began to apply makeup.

Burckhardt offered her the envelope. "Drop this in the mail for me, will you? Uh—wait a minute. I wonder if I ought to phone Mr. Barth to make sure. Did his wife say whether he was able to take phone calls?"

"Didn't say." Miss Mitkin blotted her lips carefully with a Kleenex. "Wasn't his wife, anyway. It was his daughter who called and left the message."

"The kid?" Burckhardt frowned. "I thought she was away at school."

"She called, that's all I know."

Burckhardt went back to his own office and stared distastefully at the unopened mail on his desk. He didn't like nightmares; they spoiled his whole day. He should have stayed in bed, like Barth.

*

A funny thing happened on his way home. There was a disturbance at the corner where he usually caught his bus—someone was screaming something about a new kind of deep-freeze—so he walked an extra block. He saw the bus coming and started to trot. But behind him, someone was calling his name. He looked over his shoulder; a small harried-looking man was hurrying toward him.

Burckhardt hesitated, and then recognized him. It was a casual acquaintance named Swanson. Burckhardt sourly observed that he had already missed the bus.

He said, "Hello."

Swanson's face was desperately eager. "Burckhardt?" he asked inquiringly, with an odd intensity. And then he just stood there silently, watching Burckhardt's face, with a burning eagerness that dwindled to a faint hope and died to a regret. He was searching for something, waiting for something, Burckhardt thought. But whatever it was he wanted, Burckhardt didn't know how to supply it.

Burckhardt coughed and said again, "Hello, Swanson."

Swanson didn't even acknowledge the greeting. He merely sighed a very deep sigh.

"Nothing doing," he mumbled, apparently to himself. He nodded abstractedly to Burckhardt and turned away.

Burckhardt watched the slumped shoulders disappear in the crowd. It was an *odd* sort of day, he thought, and one he didn't much like. Things weren't going right.

Riding home on the next bus, he brooded about it. It wasn't anything terrible or disastrous; it was something out of his experience entirely. You live your life, like any man, and you form a network of impressions and reactions. You *expect* things. When you open your medicine chest, your razor is expected to be on the second shelf; when you lock your front door, you expect to have to give it a slight extra tug to make it latch.

It isn't the things that are right and perfect in your life that make it familiar. It is the things that are just a little bit wrong—the sticking latch, the light switch at the head of the stairs that needs an extra push because the spring is old and weak, the rug that unfailingly skids underfoot.

It wasn't just that things were wrong with the pattern of Burckhardt's life; it was that the *wrong* things were wrong. For instance, Barth hadn't come into the office, yet Barth *always* came in.

Burckhardt brooded about it through dinner. He brooded about it, despite his wife's attempt to interest him in a game of bridge with the neighbors, all through the evening. The neighbors were people he liked—Anne and Farley Dennerman. He had known them all their lives. But they were odd and brooding, too, this night and he barely listened to Dennerman's complaints about not being able to get good phone service or his wife's comments on the disgusting variety of television commercials they had these days.

Burckhardt was well on the way to setting an all-time record for continuous abstraction when, around midnight, with a suddenness that surprised him—he was strangely *aware* of it happening—he turned over in his bed and, quickly and completely, fell asleep.

SUPER PACK

II

On the morning of June 15th, Burckhardt woke up screaming.

It was more real than any dream he had ever had in his life. He could still hear the explosion, feel the blast that crushed him against a wall. It did not seem right that he should be sitting bolt upright in bed in an undisturbed room.

His wife came pattering up the stairs. "Darling!" she cried. "What's the matter?"

He mumbled, "Nothing. Bad dream."

She relaxed, hand on heart. In an angry tone, she started to say: "You gave me such a shock—"

But a noise from outside interrupted her. There was a wail of sirens and a clang of bells; it was loud and shocking.

The Burckhardts stared at each other for a heartbeat, then hurried fearfully to the window.

There were no rumbling fire engines in the street, only a small panel truck, cruising slowly along. Flaring loudspeaker horns crowned its top. From them issued the screaming sound of sirens, growing in intensity, mixed with the rumble of heavy-duty engines and the sound of bells. It was a perfect record of fire engines arriving at a four-alarm blaze.

Burckhardt said in amazement, "Mary, that's against the law! Do you know what they're doing? They're playing records of a fire. What are they up to?"

"Maybe it's a practical joke," his wife offered.

"Joke? Waking up the whole neighborhood at six o'clock in the morning?" He shook his head. "The police will be here in ten minutes," he predicted. "Wait and see."

But the police weren't—not in ten minutes, or at all. Whoever the pranksters in the car were, they apparently had a police permit for their games.

223

The car took a position in the middle of the block and stood silent for a few minutes. Then there was a crackle from the speaker, and a giant voice chanted:

"Feckle Freezers! Feckle Freezers! Gotta have a Feckle Freezer! Feckle, Feckle, Feckle, Feckle, Feckle, Feckle—"

It went on and on. Every house on the block had faces staring out of windows by then. The voice was not merely loud; it was nearly deafening.

Burckhardt shouted to his wife, over the uproar, "What the hell is a Feckle Freezer?"

"Some kind of a freezer, I guess, dear," she shrieked back unhelpfully.

*

Abruptly the noise stopped and the truck stood silent. It was still misty morning; the Sun's rays came horizontally across the rooftops. It was impossible to believe that, a moment ago, the silent block had been bellowing the name of a freezer.

"A crazy advertising trick," Burckhardt said bitterly. He yawned and turned away from the window. "Might as well get dressed. I guess that's the end of—"

The bellow caught him from behind; it was almost like a hard slap on the ears. A harsh, sneering voice, louder than the arch-angel's trumpet, howled:

"Have you got a freezer? *It stinks!* If it isn't a Feckle Freezer, *it stinks!* If it's a last year's Feckle Freezer, *it stinks!* Only this year's Feckle Freezer is any good at all! You know who owns an Ajax Freezer? Fairies own Ajax Freezers! You know who owns a Triplecold Freezer? Commies own Triplecold Freezers! Every freezer but a brand-new Feckle Freezer *stinks!*"

The voice screamed inarticulately with rage. "I'm warning you! Get out and buy a Feckle Freezer right away! Hurry up! Hurry for Feckle! Hurry for Feckle! Hurry, hurry, hurry, Feckle, Feckle, Feckle, Feckle, Feckle, Feckle...."

SUPER PACK

It stopped eventually. Burckhardt licked his lips. He started to say to his wife, "Maybe we ought to call the police about—" when the speakers erupted again. It caught him off guard; it was intended to catch him off guard. It screamed:

"Feckle, Feckle, Feckle, Feckle, Feckle, Feckle, Feckle, Feckle. Cheap freezers ruin your food. You'll get sick and throw up. You'll get sick and die. Buy a Feckle, Feckle, Feckle, Feckle! Ever take a piece of meat out of the freezer you've got and see how rotten and moldy it is? Buy a Feckle, Feckle, Feckle, Feckle, Feckle. Do you want to eat rotten, stinking food? Or do you want to wise up and buy a Feckle, Feckle, Feckle—"

That did it. With fingers that kept stabbing the wrong holes, Burckhardt finally managed to dial the local police station. He got a busy signal—it was apparent that he was not the only one with the same idea—and while he was shakingly dialing again, the noise outside stopped.

He looked out the window. The truck was gone.

*

Burckhardt loosened his tie and ordered another Frosty-Flip from the waiter. If only they wouldn't keep the Crystal Cafe so *hot*! The new paint job—searing reds and blinding yellows—was bad enough, but someone seemed to have the delusion that this was January instead of June; the place was a good ten degrees warmer than outside.

He swallowed the Frosty-Flip in two gulps. It had a kind of peculiar flavor, he thought, but not bad. It certainly cooled you off, just as the waiter had promised. He reminded himself to pick up a carton of them on the way home; Mary might like them. She was always interested in something new.

He stood up awkwardly as the girl came across the restaurant toward him. She was the most beautiful thing he had ever seen in Tylerton. Chin-height, honey-blonde hair and a figure that—well, it was all hers. There was no doubt in the world that the dress that clung to her was the only thing she wore. He felt as if he were blushing as she greeted him.

"Mr. Burckhardt." The voice was like distant tomtoms. "It's wonderful of you to let me see you, after this morning."

He cleared his throat. "Not at all. Won't you sit down, Miss—"

"April Horn," she murmured, sitting down—beside him, not where he had pointed on the other side of the table. "Call me April, won't you?"

She was wearing some kind of perfume, Burckhardt noted with what little of his mind was functioning at all. It didn't seem fair that she should be using perfume as well as everything else. He came to with a start and realized that the waiter was leaving with an order for *filets mignon* for two.

"Hey!" he objected.

"Please, Mr. Burckhardt." Her shoulder was against his, her face was turned to him, her breath was warm, her expression was tender and solicitous. "This is all on the Feckle Corporation. Please let them—it's the *least* they can do."

He felt her hand burrowing into his pocket.

"I put the price of the meal into your pocket," she whispered conspiratorially. "Please do that for me, won't you? I mean I'd appreciate it if you'd pay the waiter—I'm old-fashioned about things like that."

She smiled meltingly, then became mock-businesslike. "But you must take the money," she insisted. "Why, you're letting Feckle off lightly if you do! You could sue them for every nickel they've got, disturbing your sleep like that."

*

With a dizzy feeling, as though he had just seen someone make a rabbit disappear into a top hat, he said, "Why, it really wasn't so bad, uh, April. A little noisy, maybe, but—"

"Oh, Mr. Burckhardt!" The blue eyes were wide and admiring. "I knew you'd understand. It's just that—well, it's such a *wonderful* freezer that some of the outside men get carried away, so to speak. As soon as the main office found out about what happened, they sent representatives around to every house on the block to apologize. Your wife told us where we could phone you—and I'm so very pleased that you were willing to let me have lunch with you, so that I could apologize, too. Because truly, Mr. Burckhardt, it is a *fine* freezer.

"I shouldn't tell you this, but—" the blue eyes were shyly lowered—"I'd do almost anything for Feckle Freezers. It's more than a job to me." She looked up. She was enchanting. "I bet you think I'm silly, don't you?"

Burckhardt coughed. "Well, I—"

"Oh, you don't want to be unkind!" She shook her head. "No, don't pretend. You think it's silly. But really, Mr. Burckhardt, you wouldn't think so if you knew more about the Feckle. Let me show you this little booklet—"

Burckhardt got back from lunch a full hour late. It wasn't only the girl who delayed him. There had been a curious interview with a little man named Swanson, whom he barely knew, who had stopped him with desperate urgency on the street—and then left him cold.

But it didn't matter much. Mr. Barth, for the first time since Burckhardt had worked there, was out for the day—leaving Burckhardt stuck with the quarterly tax returns.

What did matter, though, was that somehow he had signed a purchase order for a twelve-cubic-foot Feckle Freezer, upright model, self-defrosting, list price $625, with a ten per cent "courtesy" discount—"Because of that *horrid* affair this morning, Mr. Burckhardt," she had said.

And he wasn't sure how he could explain it to his wife.

*

He needn't have worried. As he walked in the front door, his wife said almost immediately, "I wonder if we can't afford a new freezer, dear. There was a man here to apologize about that noise and—well, we got to talking and—"

She had signed a purchase order, too.

It had been the damnedest day, Burckhardt thought later, on his way up to bed. But the day wasn't done with him yet. At the head of the stairs, the weakened spring in the electric light switch refused to click at all. He snapped it back and forth angrily and, of course, succeeded in jarring the tumbler out of its pins. The wires shorted and every light in the house went out.

"Damn!" said Guy Burckhardt.

"Fuse?" His wife shrugged sleepily. "Let it go till the morning, dear."

Burckhardt shook his head. "You go back to bed. I'll be right along."

It wasn't so much that he cared about fixing the fuse, but he was too restless for sleep. He disconnected the bad switch with a screwdriver, stumbled down into the black kitchen, found the flashlight and climbed gingerly down the cellar stairs. He located a spare fuse, pushed an empty trunk over to the fuse box to stand on and twisted out the old fuse.

When the new one was in, he heard the starting click and steady drone of the refrigerator in the kitchen overhead.

He headed back to the steps, and stopped.

Where the old trunk had been, the cellar floor gleamed oddly bright. He inspected it in the flashlight beam. It was metal!

"Son of a gun," said Guy Burckhardt. He shook his head unbelievingly. He peered closer, rubbed the edges of the metallic patch with his thumb and acquired an annoying cut—the edges were *sharp*.

The stained cement floor of the cellar was a thin shell. He found a hammer and cracked it off in a dozen spots—everywhere was metal.

The whole cellar was a copper box. Even the cement-brick walls were false fronts over a metal sheath!

*

Baffled, he attacked one of the foundation beams. That, at least, was real wood. The glass in the cellar windows was real glass.

He sucked his bleeding thumb and tried the base of the cellar stairs. Real wood. He chipped at the bricks under the oil burner. Real bricks. The retaining walls, the floor—they were faked.

It was as though someone had shored up the house with a frame of metal and then laboriously concealed the evidence.

The biggest surprise was the upside-down boat hull that blocked the rear half of the cellar, relic of a brief home workshop period that Burckhardt had gone through a couple of years before. From above, it looked perfectly normal. Inside, though, where there should have been thwarts and seats and lockers, there was a mere tangle of braces, rough and unfinished.

"But I *built* that!" Burckhardt exclaimed, forgetting his thumb. He leaned against the hull dizzily, trying to think this thing through. For reasons beyond his comprehension, someone had taken his boat and his cellar away, maybe his whole house, and replaced them with a clever mock-up of the real thing.

"That's crazy," he said to the empty cellar. He stared around in the light of the flash. He whispered, "What in the name of Heaven would anybody do that for?"

Reason refused an answer; there wasn't any reasonable answer. For long minutes, Burckhardt contemplated the uncertain picture of his own sanity.

He peered under the boat again, hoping to reassure himself that it was a mistake, just his imagination. But the sloppy, unfinished bracing was unchanged. He crawled under for a better look, feeling the rough wood incredulously. Utterly impossible!

He switched off the flashlight and started to wriggle out. But he didn't make it. In the moment between the command to his legs to move and the crawling out, he felt a sudden draining weariness flooding through him.

Consciousness went—not easily, but as though it were being taken away, and Guy Burckhardt was asleep.

III

On the morning of June 16th, Guy Burckhardt woke up in a cramped position huddled under the hull of the boat in his basement—and raced upstairs to find it was June 15th.

The first thing he had done was to make a frantic, hasty inspection of the boat hull, the faked cellar floor, the imitation stone. They were all as he had remembered them—all completely unbelievable.

The kitchen was its placid, unexciting self. The electric clock was purring soberly around the dial. Almost six o'clock, it said. His wife would be waking at any moment.

Burckhardt flung open the front door and stared out into the quiet street. The morning paper was tossed carelessly against the steps—and as he retrieved it, he noticed that this was the 15th day of June.

But that was impossible. *Yesterday* was the 15th of June. It was not a date one would forget—it was quarterly tax-return day.

He went back into the hall and picked up the telephone; he dialed for Weather Information, and got a well-modulated chant: "—and cooler, some showers. Barometric pressure thirty point zero four, rising ... United States Weather Bureau forecast for June 15th. Warm and sunny, with high around—"

He hung the phone up. June 15th.

"Holy heaven!" Burckhardt said prayerfully. Things were very odd indeed. He heard the ring of his wife's alarm and bounded up the stairs.

Mary Burckhardt was sitting upright in bed with the terrified, uncomprehending stare of someone just waking out of a nightmare.

"Oh!" she gasped, as her husband came in the room. "Darling, I just had the most *terrible* dream! It was like an explosion and—"

"Again?" Burckhardt asked, not very sympathetically. "Mary, something's funny! I *knew* there was something wrong all day yesterday and—"

He went on to tell her about the copper box that was the cellar, and the odd mock-up someone had made of his boat. Mary looked astonished, then alarmed, then placatory and uneasy.

She said, "Dear, are you *sure*? Because I was cleaning that old trunk out just last week and I didn't notice anything."

"Positive!" said Guy Burckhardt. "I dragged it over to the wall to step on it to put a new fuse in after we blew the lights out and—"

"After we what?" Mary was looking more than merely alarmed.

"After we blew the lights out. You know, when the switch at the head of the stairs stuck. I went down to the cellar and—"

Mary sat up in bed. "Guy, the switch didn't stick. I turned out the lights myself last night."

Burckhardt glared at his wife. "Now I *know* you didn't! Come here and take a look!"

He stalked out to the landing and dramatically pointed to the bad switch, the one that he had unscrewed and left hanging the night before....

Only it wasn't. It was as it had always been. Unbelieving, Burckhardt pressed it and the lights sprang up in both halls.

*

Mary, looking pale and worried, left him to go down to the kitchen and start breakfast. Burckhardt stood staring at the switch for a long time. His mental processes were gone beyond the point of disbelief and shock; they simply were not functioning.

He shaved and dressed and ate his breakfast in a state of numb introspection. Mary didn't disturb him; she was apprehensive and soothing. She kissed him good-by as he hurried out to the bus without another word.

Miss Mitkin, at the reception desk, greeted him with a yawn. "Morning," she said drowsily. "Mr. Barth won't be in today."

Burckhardt started to say something, but checked himself. She would not know that Barth hadn't been in yesterday, either, because she was tearing a June 14th pad off her calendar to make way for the "new" June 15th sheet.

He staggered to his own desk and stared unseeingly at the morning's mail. It had not even been opened yet, but he knew that the Factory Distributors envelope contained an order for twenty thousand feet of the new acoustic tile, and the one from Finebeck & Sons was a complaint.

After a long while, he forced himself to open them. They were.

By lunchtime, driven by a desperate sense of urgency, Burckhardt made Miss Mitkin take her lunch hour first—the June-fifteenth-that-was-yesterday, *he* had gone first. She went, looking vaguely worried about his strained insistence, but it made no difference to Burckhardt's mood.

The phone rang and Burckhardt picked it up abstractedly. "Contro Chemicals Downtown, Burckhardt speaking."

The voice said, "This is Swanson," and stopped.

Burckhardt waited expectantly, but that was all. He said, "Hello?"

Again the pause. Then Swanson asked in sad resignation, "Still nothing, eh?"

"Nothing what? Swanson, is there something you want? You came up to me yesterday and went through this routine. You—"

The voice crackled: "Burckhardt! Oh, my good heavens, *you remember*! Stay right there—I'll be down in half an hour!"

"What's this all about?"

"Never mind," the little man said exultantly. "Tell you about it when I see you. Don't say any more over the phone—somebody may be listening. Just wait there. Say, hold on a minute. Will you be alone in the office?"

"Well, no. Miss Mitkin will probably—"

"Hell. Look, Burckhardt, where do you eat lunch? Is it good and noisy?"

"Why, I suppose so. The Crystal Cafe. It's just about a block—"

"I know where it is. Meet you in half an hour!" And the receiver clicked.

*

The Crystal Cafe was no longer painted red, but the temperature was still up. And they had added piped-in music interspersed with commercials. The advertisements were for Frosty-Flip, Marlin Cigarettes—"They're sanitized," the announcer purred—and something called Choco-Bite candy bars that Burckhardt couldn't remember ever having heard of before. But he heard more about them quickly enough.

While he was waiting for Swanson to show up, a girl in the cellophane skirt of a nightclub cigarette vendor came through the restaurant with a tray of tiny scarlet-wrapped candies.

"Choco-Bites are *tangy*," she was murmuring as she came close to his table. "Choco-Bites are *tangier* than tangy!"

Burckhardt, intent on watching for the strange little man who had phoned him, paid little attention. But as she scattered a handful of the confections over the table next to his, smiling at the occupants, he caught a glimpse of her and turned to stare.

"Why, Miss Horn!" he said.

The girl dropped her tray of candies.

Burckhardt rose, concerned over the girl. "Is something wrong?"

But she fled.

The manager of the restaurant was staring suspiciously at Burckhardt, who sank back in his seat and tried to look inconspicuous. He hadn't insulted the girl! Maybe she was just a very strictly reared young lady, he thought—in spite of the long bare legs under the cellophane skirt—and when he addressed her, she thought he was a masher.

Ridiculous idea. Burckhardt scowled uneasily and picked up his menu.

"Burckhardt!" It was a shrill whisper.

Burckhardt looked up over the top of his menu, startled. In the seat across from him, the little man named Swanson was sitting, tensely poised.

"Burckhardt!" the little man whispered again. "Let's get out of here! They're on to you now. If you want to stay alive, come on!"

There was no arguing with the man. Burckhardt gave the hovering manager a sick, apologetic smile and followed Swanson out. The little man seemed to know where he was going. In the street, he clutched Burckhardt by the elbow and hurried him off down the block.

"Did you see her?" he demanded. "That Horn woman, in the phone booth? She'll have them here in five minutes, believe me, so hurry it up!"

*

Although the street was full of people and cars, nobody was paying any attention to Burckhardt and Swanson. The air had a nip in it—more like October than June, Burckhardt thought, in spite of the weather bureau. And he felt like a fool, following this mad little man down the street, running away from some "them" toward—toward what? The little man might be crazy, but he was afraid. And the fear was infectious.

"In here!" panted the little man.

It was another restaurant—more of a bar, really, and a sort of second-rate place that Burckhardt had never patronized.

"Right straight through," Swanson whispered; and Burckhardt, like a biddable boy, side-stepped through the mass of tables to the far end of the restaurant.

It was "L"-shaped, with a front on two streets at right angles to each other. They came out on the side street, Swanson staring coldly back at the question-looking cashier, and crossed to the opposite sidewalk.

They were under the marquee of a movie theater. Swanson's expression began to relax.

"Lost them!" he crowed softly. "We're almost there."

He stepped up to the window and bought two tickets. Burckhardt trailed him in to the theater. It was a weekday matinee and the place was almost empty. From the screen came sounds of gunfire and horse's hoofs. A solitary usher, leaning against a bright brass rail, looked briefly at them and went back to staring boredly at the picture as Swanson led Burckhardt down a flight of carpeted marble steps.

They were in the lounge and it was empty. There was a door for men and one for ladies; and there was a third door, marked "MANAGER" in gold letters. Swanson listened at the door, and gently opened it and peered inside.

"Okay," he said, gesturing.

Burckhardt followed him through an empty office, to another door—a closet, probably, because it was unmarked.

But it was no closet. Swanson opened it warily, looked inside, then motioned Burckhardt to follow.

It was a tunnel, metal-walled, brightly lit. Empty, it stretched vacantly away in both directions from them.

Burckhardt looked wondering around. One thing he knew and knew full well:

No such tunnel belonged under Tylerton.

*

There was a room off the tunnel with chairs and a desk and what looked like television screens. Swanson slumped in a chair, panting.

"We're all right for a while here," he wheezed. "They don't come here much any more. If they do, we'll hear them and we can hide."

"Who?" demanded Burckhardt.

The little man said, "Martians!" His voice cracked on the word and the life seemed to go out of him. In morose tones, he went on: "Well, I think they're Martians. Although you could be right, you know; I've had plenty of time to think it over these last few weeks, after they got you, and it's possible they're Russians after all. Still—"

"Start from the beginning. Who got me when?"

235

Swanson sighed. "So we have to go through the whole thing again. All right. It was about two months ago that you banged on my door, late at night. You were all beat up—scared silly. You begged me to help you—"

"*I* did?"

"Naturally you don't remember any of this. Listen and you'll understand. You were talking a blue streak about being captured and threatened, and your wife being dead and coming back to life, and all kinds of mixed-up nonsense. I thought you were crazy. But—well, I've always had a lot of respect for you. And you begged me to hide you and I have this darkroom, you know. It locks from the inside only. I put the lock on myself. So we went in there—just to humor you—and along about midnight, which was only fifteen or twenty minutes after, we passed out."

"Passed out?"

Swanson nodded. "Both of us. It was like being hit with a sandbag. Look, didn't that happen to you again last night?"

"I guess it did," Burckhardt shook his head uncertainly.

"Sure. And then all of a sudden we were awake again, and you said you were going to show me something funny, and we went out and bought a paper. And the date on it was June 15th."

"June 15th? But that's today! I mean—"

"You got it, friend. It's *always* today!"

It took time to penetrate.

Burckhardt said wonderingly, "You've hidden out in that darkroom for how many weeks?"

"How can I tell? Four or five, maybe. I lost count. And every day the same—always the 15th of June, always my landlady, Mrs. Keefer, is sweeping the front steps, always the same headline in the papers at the corner. It gets monotonous, friend."

236

It was Burckhardt's idea and Swanson despised it, but he went along. He was the type who always went along.

"It's dangerous," he grumbled worriedly. "Suppose somebody comes by? They'll spot us and—"

"What have we got to lose?"

Swanson shrugged. "It's dangerous," he said again. But he went along.

Burckhardt's idea was very simple. He was sure of only one thing—the tunnel went somewhere. Martians or Russians, fantastic plot or crazy hallucination, whatever was wrong with Tylerton had an explanation, and the place to look for it was at the end of the tunnel.

They jogged along. It was more than a mile before they began to see an end. They were in luck—at least no one came through the tunnel to spot them. But Swanson had said that it was only at certain hours that the tunnel seemed to be in use.

Always the fifteenth of June. Why? Burckhardt asked himself. Never mind the how. *Why?*

And falling asleep, completely involuntarily—everyone at the same time, it seemed. And not remembering, never remembering anything—Swanson had said how eagerly he saw Burckhardt again, the morning after Burckhardt had incautiously waited five minutes too many before retreating into the darkroom. When Swanson had come to, Burckhardt was gone. Swanson had seen him in the street that afternoon, but Burckhardt had remembered nothing.

And Swanson had lived his mouse's existence for weeks, hiding in the woodwork at night, stealing out by day to search for Burckhardt in pitiful hope, scurrying around the fringe of life, trying to keep from the deadly eyes of *them*.

Them. One of "them" was the girl named April Horn. It was by seeing her walk carelessly into a telephone booth and never come out that Swanson had found the tunnel. Another was the man at the cigar stand in Burckhardt's office building. There were more, at least a dozen that Swanson knew of or suspected.

They were easy enough to spot, once you knew where to look—for they, alone in Tylerton, changed their roles from day to day. Burckhardt was on that 8:51 bus, every morning of every day-that-was-June-15th, never different by a hair or a moment. But April Horn was sometimes gaudy in the cellophane skirt, giving away candy or cigarettes; sometimes plainly dressed; sometimes not seen by Swanson at all.

Russians? Martians? Whatever they were, what could they be hoping to gain from this mad masquerade?

Burckhardt didn't know the answer—but perhaps it lay beyond the door at the end of the tunnel. They listened carefully and heard distant sounds that could not quite be made out, but nothing that seemed dangerous. They slipped through.

And, through a wide chamber and up a flight of steps, they found they were in what Burckhardt recognized as the Contro Chemicals plant.

*

Nobody was in sight. By itself, that was not so very odd—the automatized factory had never had very many persons in it. But Burckhardt remembered, from his single visit, the endless, ceaseless busyness of the plant, the valves that opened and closed, the vats that emptied themselves and filled themselves and stirred and cooked and chemically tasted the bubbling liquids they held inside themselves. The plant was never populated, but it was never still.

Only—now it *was* still. Except for the distant sounds, there was no breath of life in it. The captive electronic minds were sending out no commands; the coils and relays were at rest.

Burckhardt said, "Come on." Swanson reluctantly followed him through the tangled aisles of stainless steel columns and tanks.

They walked as though they were in the presence of the dead. In a way, they were, for what were the automatons that once had run the factory, if not corpses? The machines were controlled by computers that were really not computers at all, but the electronic analogues of living brains. And if they were turned off, were they not dead? For each had once been a human mind.

Take a master petroleum chemist, infinitely skilled in the separation of crude oil into its fractions. Strap him down, probe into his brain with searching electronic needles. The machine scans the patterns of the mind, translates what it sees into charts and sine waves. Impress these same waves on a robot computer and you have your chemist. Or a thousand copies of your chemist, if you wish, with all of his knowledge and skill, and no human limitations at all.

Put a dozen copies of him into a plant and they will run it all, twenty-four hours a day, seven days of every week, never tiring, never overlooking anything, never forgetting....

Swanson stepped up closer to Burckhardt. "I'm scared," he said.

They were across the room now and the sounds were louder. They were not machine sounds, but voices; Burckhardt moved cautiously up to a door and dared to peer around it.

It was a smaller room, lined with television screens, each one—a dozen or more, at least—with a man or woman sitting before it, staring into the screen and dictating notes into a recorder. The viewers dialed from scene to scene; no two screens ever showed the same picture.

The pictures seemed to have little in common. One was a store, where a girl dressed like April Horn was demonstrating home freezers. One was a series of shots of kitchens. Burckhardt caught a glimpse of what looked like the cigar stand in his office building.

It was baffling and Burckhardt would have loved to stand there and puzzle it out, but it was too busy a place. There was the chance that someone would look their way or walk out and find them.

*

They found another room. This one was empty. It was an office, large and sumptuous. It had a desk, littered with papers. Burckhardt stared at them, briefly at first—then, as the words on one of them caught his attention, with incredulous fascination.

He snatched up the topmost sheet, scanned it, and another, while Swanson was frenziedly searching through the drawers.

Burckhardt swore unbelievingly and dropped the papers to the desk.

Swanson, hardly noticing, yelped with delight: "Look!" He dragged a gun from the desk. "And it's loaded, too!"

Burckhardt stared at him blankly, trying to assimilate what he had read. Then, as he realized what Swanson had said, Burckhardt's eyes sparked. "Good man!" he cried. "We'll take it. We're getting out of here with that gun, Swanson. And we're going to the police! Not the cops in Tylerton, but the F.B.I., maybe. Take a look at this!"

The sheaf he handed Swanson was headed: "Test Area Progress Report. Subject: Marlin Cigarettes Campaign." It was mostly tabulated figures that made little sense to Burckhardt and Swanson, but at the end was a summary that said:

Although Test 47-K3 pulled nearly double the number of new users of any of the other tests conducted, it probably cannot be used in the field because of local sound-truck control ordinances.

The tests in the 47-K12 group were second best and our recommendation is that retests be conducted in this appeal, testing each of the three best campaigns with and without the addition of sampling techniques.

An alternative suggestion might be to proceed directly with the top appeal in the K12 series, if the client is unwilling to go to the expense of additional tests.

All of these forecast expectations have an 80% probability of being within one-half of one per cent of results forecast, and more than 99% probability of coming within 5%.

Swanson looked up from the paper into Burckhardt's eyes. "I don't get it," he complained.

Burckhardt said, "I don't blame you. It's crazy, but it fits the facts, Swanson, *it fits the facts*. They aren't Russians and they aren't

Martians. These people are advertising men! Somehow—heaven knows how they did it—they've taken Tylerton over. They've got us, all of us, you and me and twenty or thirty thousand other people, right under their thumbs.

"Maybe they hypnotize us and maybe it's something else; but however they do it, what happens is that they let us live a day at a time. They pour advertising into us the whole damned day long. And at the end of the day, they see what happened—and then they wash the day out of our minds and start again the next day with different advertising."

*

Swanson's jaw was hanging. He managed to close it and swallow. "Nuts!" he said flatly.

Burckhardt shook his head. "Sure, it sounds crazy—but this whole thing is crazy. How else would you explain it? You can't deny that most of Tylerton lives the same day over and over again. You've *seen* it! And that's the crazy part and we have to admit that that's true—unless we are the crazy ones. And once you admit that somebody, somehow, knows how to accomplish that, the rest of it makes all kinds of sense.

"Think of it, Swanson! They test every last detail before they spend a nickel on advertising! Do you have any idea what that means? Lord knows how much money is involved, but I know for a fact that some companies spend twenty or thirty million dollars a year on advertising. Multiply it, say, by a hundred companies. Say that every one of them learns how to cut its advertising cost by only ten per cent. And that's peanuts, believe me!

"If they know in advance what's going to work, they can cut their costs in half—maybe to less than half, I don't know. But that's saving two or three hundred million dollars a year—and if they pay only ten or twenty per cent of that for the use of Tylerton, it's still dirt cheap for them and a fortune for whoever took over Tylerton."

Swanson licked his lips. "You mean," he offered hesitantly, "that we're a—well, a kind of captive audience?"

Burckhardt frowned. "Not exactly." He thought for a minute. "You know how a doctor tests something like penicillin? He sets up a series of little colonies of germs on gelatine disks and he tries the stuff on one after another, changing it a little each time. Well, that's us—we're the germs, Swanson. Only it's even more efficient than that. They don't have to test more than one colony, because they can use it over and over again."

It was too hard for Swanson to take in. He only said: "What do we do about it?"

"We go to the police. They can't use human beings for guinea pigs!"

"How do we get to the police?"

Burckhardt hesitated. "I think—" he began slowly. "Sure. This place is the office of somebody important. We've got a gun. We'll stay right here until he comes along. And he'll get us out of here."

Simple and direct. Swanson subsided and found a place to sit, against the wall, out of sight of the door. Burckhardt took up a position behind the door itself—

And waited.

*

The wait was not as long as it might have been. Half an hour, perhaps. Then Burckhardt heard approaching voices and had time for a swift whisper to Swanson before he flattened himself against the wall.

It was a man's voice, and a girl's. The man was saying, "—reason why you couldn't report on the phone? You're ruining your whole day's test! What the devil's the matter with you, Janet?"

"I'm sorry, Mr. Dorchin," she said in a sweet, clear tone. "I thought it was important."

The man grumbled, "Important! One lousy unit out of twenty-one thousand."

"But it's the Burckhardt one, Mr. Dorchin. Again. And the way he got out of sight, he must have had some help."

"All right, all right. It doesn't matter, Janet; the Choco-Bite program is ahead of schedule anyhow. As long as you're this far, come on in the office and make out your worksheet. And don't worry about the Burckhardt business. He's probably just wandering around. We'll pick him up tonight and—"

They were inside the door. Burckhardt kicked it shut and pointed the gun.

"That's what you think," he said triumphantly.

It was worth the terrified hours, the bewildered sense of insanity, the confusion and fear. It was the most satisfying sensation Burckhardt had ever had in his life. The expression on the man's face was one he had read about but never actually seen: Dorchin's mouth fell open and his eyes went wide, and though he managed to make a sound that might have been a question, it was not in words.

The girl was almost as surprised. And Burckhardt, looking at her, knew why her voice had been so familiar. The girl was the one who had introduced herself to him as April Horn.

Dorchin recovered himself quickly. "Is this the one?" he asked sharply.

The girl said, "Yes."

Dorchin nodded. "I take it back. You were right. Uh, you—Burckhardt. What do you want?"

*

Swanson piped up, "Watch him! He might have another gun."

"Search him then," Burckhardt said. "I'll tell you what we want, Dorchin. We want you to come along with us to the FBI and explain to them how you can get away with kidnapping twenty thousand people."

"Kidnapping?" Dorchin snorted. "That's ridiculous, man! Put that gun away—you can't get away with this!"

Burckhardt hefted the gun grimly. "I think I can."

Dorchin looked furious and sick—but, oddly, not afraid. "Damn it—" he started to bellow, then closed his mouth and swallowed. "Listen," he said persuasively, "you're making a big mistake. I haven't kidnapped anybody, believe me!"

"I don't believe you," said Burckhardt bluntly. "Why should I?"

"But it's true! Take my word for it!"

Burckhardt shook his head. "The FBI can take your word if they like. We'll find out. Now how do we get out of here?"

Dorchin opened his mouth to argue.

Burckhardt blazed: "Don't get in my way! I'm willing to kill you if I have to. Don't you understand that? I've gone through two days of hell and every second of it I blame on you. Kill you? It would be a pleasure and I don't have a thing in the world to lose! Get us out of here!"

Dorchin's face went suddenly opaque. He seemed about to move; but the blonde girl he had called Janet slipped between him and the gun.

"Please!" she begged Burckhardt. "You don't understand. You mustn't shoot!"

"*Get out of my way!*"

"But, Mr. Burckhardt—"

She never finished. Dorchin, his face unreadable, headed for the door. Burckhardt had been pushed one degree too far. He swung the gun, bellowing. The girl called out sharply. He pulled the trigger. Closing on him with pity and pleading in her eyes, she came again between the gun and the man.

Burckhardt aimed low instinctively, to cripple, not to kill. But his aim was not good.

The pistol bullet caught her in the pit of the stomach.

*

Dorchin was out and away, the door slamming behind him, his footsteps racing into the distance.

Burckhardt hurled the gun across the room and jumped to the girl.

Swanson was moaning. "That finishes us, Burckhardt. Oh, why did you do it? We could have got away. We could have gone to the police. We were practically out of here! We—"

Burckhardt wasn't listening. He was kneeling beside the girl. She lay flat on her back, arms helter-skelter. There was no blood, hardly any sign of the wound; but the position in which she lay was one that no living human being could have held.

Yet she wasn't dead.

She wasn't dead—and Burckhardt, frozen beside her, thought: *She isn't alive, either.*

There was no pulse, but there was a rhythmic ticking of the outstretched fingers of one hand.

There was no sound of breathing, but there was a hissing, sizzling noise.

The eyes were open and they were looking at Burckhardt. There was neither fear nor pain in them, only a pity deeper than the Pit.

She said, through lips that writhed erratically, "Don't—worry, Mr. Burckhardt. I'm—all right."

Burckhardt rocked back on his haunches, staring. Where there should have been blood, there was a clean break of a substance that was not flesh; and a curl of thin golden-copper wire.

Burckhardt moistened his lips.

"You're a robot," he said.

The girl tried to nod. The twitching lips said, "I am. And so are you."

V

Swanson, after a single inarticulate sound, walked over to the desk and sat staring at the wall. Burckhardt rocked back and forth beside the shattered puppet on the floor. He had no words.

The girl managed to say, "I'm—sorry all this happened." The lovely lips twisted into a rictus sneer, frightening on that smooth young face, until she got them under control. "Sorry," she said again. "The—nerve center was right about where the bullet hit. Makes it difficult to—control this body."

Burckhardt nodded automatically, accepting the apology. Robots. It was obvious, now that he knew it. In hindsight, it was inevitable. He thought of his mystic notions of hypnosis or Martians or something stranger still—idiotic, for the simple fact of created robots fitted the facts better and more economically.

All the evidence had been before him. The automatized factory, with its transplanted minds—why not transplant a mind into a humanoid robot, give it its original owner's features and form?

Could it know that it was a robot?

"All of us," Burckhardt said, hardly aware that he spoke out loud. "My wife and my secretary and you and the neighbors. All of us the same."

"No." The voice was stronger. "Not exactly the same, all of us. I chose it, you see. I—" this time the convulsed lips were not a random contortion of the nerves—" I was an ugly woman, Mr. Burckhardt, and nearly sixty years old. Life had passed me. And when Mr. Dorchin offered me the chance to live again as a beautiful girl, I jumped at the opportunity. Believe me, I *jumped*, in spite of its disadvantages. My flesh body is still alive—it is sleeping, while I am here. I could go back to it. But I never do."

"And the rest of us?"

"Different, Mr. Burckhardt. I work here. I'm carrying out Mr. Dorchin's orders, mapping the results of the advertising tests, watching you and the others live as he makes you live. I do it by choice, but you have no choice. Because, you see, you are dead."

"Dead?" cried Burckhardt; it was almost a scream.

The blue eyes looked at him unwinkingly and he knew that it was no lie. He swallowed, marveling at the intricate mechanisms that let him swallow, and sweat, and eat.

He said: "Oh. The explosion in my dream."

"It was no dream. You are right—the explosion. That was real and this plant was the cause of it. The storage tanks let go and what the blast didn't get, the fumes killed a little later. But almost everyone died in the blast, twenty-one thousand persons. You died with them and that was Dorchin's chance."

"The damned ghoul!" said Burckhardt.

*

The twisted shoulders shrugged with an odd grace. "Why? You were gone. And you and all the others were what Dorchin wanted—a whole town, a perfect slice of America. It's as easy to transfer a pattern from a dead brain as a living one. Easier—the dead can't say no. Oh, it took work and money—the town was a wreck—but it was possible to rebuild it entirely, especially because it wasn't necessary to have all the details exact.

"There were the homes where even the brains had been utterly destroyed, and those are empty inside, and the cellars that needn't be too perfect, and the streets that hardly matter. And anyway, it only has to last for one day. The same day—June 15th—over and over again; and if someone finds something a little wrong, somehow, the discovery won't have time to snowball, wreck the validity of the tests, because all errors are canceled out at midnight."

The face tried to smile. "That's the dream, Mr. Burckhardt, that day of June 15th, because you never really lived it. It's a present from Mr. Dorchin, a dream that he gives you and then takes back at the end of the day, when he has all his figures on how many of you responded to what variation of which appeal, and the maintenance crews go down the tunnel to go through the whole city, washing out the new dream with their little electronic drains, and then the dream starts all over again. On June 15th.

"Always June 15th, because June 14th is the last day any of you can remember alive. Sometimes the crews miss someone—as they missed you, because you were under your boat. But it doesn't matter. The ones who are missed give themselves away if they show it—and if

247

they don't, it doesn't affect the test. But they don't drain us, the ones of us who work for Dorchin. We sleep when the power is turned off, just as you do. When we wake up, though, we remember." The face contorted wildly. "If I could only forget!"

Burckhardt said unbelievingly, "All this to sell merchandise! It must have cost millions!"

The robot called April Horn said, "It did. But it has made millions for Dorchin, too. And that's not the end of it. Once he finds the master words that make people act, do you suppose he will stop with that? Do you suppose—"

The door opened, interrupting her. Burckhardt whirled. Belatedly remembering Dorchin's flight, he raised the gun.

"Don't shoot," ordered the voice calmly. It was not Dorchin; it was another robot, this one not disguised with the clever plastics and cosmetics, but shining plain. It said metallically: "Forget it, Burckhardt. You're not accomplishing anything. Give me that gun before you do any more damage. Give it to me *now*."

*

Burckhardt bellowed angrily. The gleam on this robot torso was steel; Burckhardt was not at all sure that his bullets would pierce it, or do much harm if they did. He would have put it to the test—

But from behind him came a whimpering, scurrying whirlwind; its name was Swanson, hysterical with fear. He catapulted into Burckhardt and sent him sprawling, the gun flying free.

"Please!" begged Swanson incoherently, prostrate before the steel robot. "He would have shot you—please don't hurt me! Let me work for you, like that girl. I'll do anything, anything you tell me—"

The robot voice said. "We don't need your help." It took two precise steps and stood over the gun—and spurned it, left it lying on the floor.

The wrecked blonde robot said, without emotion, "I doubt that I can hold out much longer, Mr. Dorchin."

"Disconnect if you have to," replied the steel robot.

Burckhardt blinked. "But you're not Dorchin!"

The steel robot turned deep eyes on him. "I am," it said. "Not in the flesh—but this is the body I am using at the moment. I doubt that you can damage this one with the gun. The other robot body was more vulnerable. Now will you stop this nonsense? I don't want to have to damage you; you're too expensive for that. Will you just sit down and let the maintenance crews adjust you?"

Swanson groveled. "You—you won't punish us?"

The steel robot had no expression, but its voice was almost surprised. "Punish you?" it repeated on a rising note. "How?"

Swanson quivered as though the word had been a whip; but Burckhardt flared: "Adjust *him*, if he'll let you—but not me! You're going to have to do me a lot of damage, Dorchin. I don't care what I cost or how much trouble it's going to be to put me back together again. But I'm going out of that door! If you want to stop me, you'll have to kill me. You won't stop me any other way!"

The steel robot took a half-step toward him, and Burckhardt involuntarily checked his stride. He stood poised and shaking, ready for death, ready for attack, ready for anything that might happen.

Ready for anything except what did happen. For Dorchin's steel body merely stepped aside, between Burckhardt and the gun, but leaving the door free.

"Go ahead," invited the steel robot. "Nobody's stopping you."

*

Outside the door, Burckhardt brought up sharp. It was insane of Dorchin to let him go! Robot or flesh, victim or beneficiary, there was nothing to stop him from going to the FBI or whatever law he could find away from Dorchin's synthetic empire, and telling his story. Surely the corporations who paid Dorchin for test results had no notion of the ghoul's technique he used; Dorchin would have to keep it from them, for the breath of publicity would put a stop to it. Walking out meant death, perhaps—but at that moment in his pseudo-life, death was no terror for Burckhardt.

There was no one in the corridor. He found a window and stared out of it. There was Tylerton—an ersatz city, but looking so real and familiar that Burckhardt almost imagined the whole episode a dream. It was no dream, though. He was certain of that in his heart and equally certain that nothing in Tylerton could help him now.

It had to be the other direction.

It took him a quarter of an hour to find a way, but he found it—skulking through the corridors, dodging the suspicion of footsteps, knowing for certain that his hiding was in vain, for Dorchin was undoubtedly aware of every move he made. But no one stopped him, and he found another door.

It was a simple enough door from the inside. But when he opened it and stepped out, it was like nothing he had ever seen.

First there was light—brilliant, incredible, blinding light. Burckhardt blinked upward, unbelieving and afraid.

He was standing on a ledge of smooth, finished metal. Not a dozen yards from his feet, the ledge dropped sharply away; he hardly dared approach the brink, but even from where he stood he could see no bottom to the chasm before him. And the gulf extended out of sight into the glare on either side of him.

*

No wonder Dorchin could so easily give him his freedom! From the factory, there was nowhere to go—but how incredible this fantastic gulf, how impossible the hundred white and blinding suns that hung above!

A voice by his side said inquiringly, "Burckhardt?" And thunder rolled the name, mutteringly soft, back and forth in the abyss before him.

Burckhardt wet his lips. "Y-yes?" he croaked.

"This is Dorchin. Not a robot this time, but Dorchin in the flesh, talking to you on a hand mike. Now you have seen, Burckhardt. Now will you be reasonable and let the maintenance crews take over?"

Burckhardt stood paralyzed. One of the moving mountains in the blinding glare came toward him.

It towered hundreds of feet over his head; he stared up at its top, squinting helplessly into the light.

It looked like—

Impossible!

The voice in the loudspeaker at the door said, "Burckhardt?" But he was unable to answer.

A heavy rumbling sigh. "I see," said the voice. "You finally understand. There's no place to go. You know it now. I could have told you, but you might not have believed me, so it was better for you to see it yourself. And after all, Burckhardt, why would I reconstruct a city just the way it was before? I'm a businessman; I count costs. If a thing has to be full-scale, I build it that way. But there wasn't any need to in this case."

From the mountain before him, Burckhardt helplessly saw a lesser cliff descend carefully toward him. It was long and dark, and at the end of it was whiteness, five-fingered whiteness....

"Poor little Burckhardt," crooned the loudspeaker, while the echoes rumbled through the enormous chasm that was only a workshop. "It must have been quite a shock for you to find out you were living in a town built on a table top."

VI

It was the morning of June 15th, and Guy Burckhardt woke up screaming out of a dream.

It had been a monstrous and incomprehensible dream, of explosions and shadowy figures that were not men and terror beyond words.

He shuddered and opened his eyes.

Outside his bedroom window, a hugely amplified voice was howling.

Burckhardt stumbled over to the window and stared outside. There was an out-of-season chill to the air, more like October than June;

but the scent was normal enough—except for the sound-truck that squatted at curbside halfway down the block. Its speaker horns blared:

"Are you a coward? Are you a fool? Are you going to let crooked politicians steal the country from you? NO! Are you going to put up with four more years of graft and crime? NO! Are you going to vote straight Federal Party all up and down the ballot? YES! *You just bet you are!*"

Sometimes he screams, sometimes he wheedles, threatens, begs, cajoles ... but his voice goes on and on through one June 15th after another.

THE HATED

The bar didn't have a name. No name of any kind. Not even an indication that it had ever had one. All it said on the outside was:

Cafe EAT *Cocktails*

which doesn't make a lot of sense. But it was a bar. It had a big TV set going ya-ta-ta ya-ta-ta in three glorious colors, and a jukebox that tried to drown out the TV with that lousy music they play. Anyway, it wasn't a kid hangout. I kind of like it. But I wasn't supposed to be there at all; it's in the contract. I was supposed to stay in New York and the New England states.

Cafe-EAT-*Cocktails* was right across the river. I think the name of the place was Hoboken, but I'm not sure. It all had a kind of dreamy feeling to it. I was—

Well, I couldn't even remember going there. I remembered one minute I was downtown New York, looking across the river. I did that a lot. And then I was there. I don't remember crossing the river at all.

I was drunk, you know.

*

You know how it is? Double bourbons and keep them coming. And after a while the bartender stops bringing me the ginger ale because gradually I forget to mix them. I got pretty loaded long before I left New York. I realize that. I guess I had to get pretty loaded to risk the pension and all.

Used to be I didn't drink much, but now, I don't know, when I have one drink, I get to thinking about Sam and Wally and Chowderhead and Gilvey and the captain. If I don't drink, I think about them, too, and then I take a drink. And that leads to another drink, and it all comes out to the same thing. Well, I guess I said it already, I drink a pretty good amount, but you can't blame me.

There was a girl.

I always get a girl someplace. Usually they aren't much and this one wasn't either. I mean she was probably somebody's mother. She was around thirty-five and not so bad, though she had a long scar under her ear down along her throat to the little round spot where her larynx was. It wasn't ugly. She smelled nice—while I could still smell, you know—and she didn't talk much. I liked that. Only—

Well, did you ever meet somebody with a nervous cough? Like when you say something funny—a little funny, not a big yock—they don't laugh and they don't stop with just smiling, but they sort of cough? She did that. I began to itch. I couldn't help it. I asked her to stop it.

She spilled her drink and looked at me almost as though she was scared—and I had tried to say it quietly, too.

"Sorry," she said, a little angry, a little scared. "*Sorry*. But you don't have to—"

"Forget it."

"Sure. But you asked me to sit down here with you, remember? If you're going to—"

"*Forget it!*" I nodded at the bartender and held up two fingers. "You need another drink," I said. "The thing is," I said, "Gilvey used to do that."

"What?"

"That cough."

She looked puzzled. "You mean like this?"

"*Goddam it, stop it!*" Even the bartender looked over at me that time. Now she was really mad, but I didn't want her to go away. I said, "Gilvey was a fellow who went to Mars with me. Pat Gilvey."

"*Oh.*" She sat down again and leaned across the table, low. "*Mars.*"

*

The bartender brought our drinks and looked at me suspiciously. I said, "Say, Mac, would you turn down the air-conditioning?"

"My name isn't Mac. No."

"Have a heart. It's too cold in here."

"Sorry." He didn't sound sorry.

I was cold. I mean that kind of weather, it's always cold in those places. You know around New York in August? It hits eighty,

eighty-five, ninety. All the places have air-conditioning and what they really want is for you to wear a shirt and tie.

But I like to walk a lot. You would, too, you know. And you can't walk around much in long pants and a suit coat and all that stuff. Not around there. Not in August. And so then, when I went into a bar, it'd have one of those built-in freezers for the used-car salesmen with their dates, or maybe their wives, all dressed up. For what? But I froze.

"*Mars*," the girl breathed. "*Mars*."

I began to itch again. "Want to dance?"

"They don't have a license," she said. "Byron, I didn't know you'd been to *Mars*! Please *tell* me about it."

"It was all right," I said.

That was a lie.

She was interested. She forgot to smile. It made her look nicer. She said, "I knew a man—my brother-in-law—he was my husband's brother—I mean my ex-husband—"

"I get the idea."

"He worked for General Atomic. In Rockford, Illinois. You know where that is?"

"Sure." I couldn't go there, but I knew where Illinois was.

"He worked on the first Mars ship. Oh, fifteen years ago, wasn't it? He always wanted to go himself, but he couldn't pass the tests." She stopped and looked at me.

I knew what she was thinking. But I didn't always look this way, you know. Not that there's anything wrong with me now, I mean, but I couldn't pass the tests any more. Nobody can. That's why we're all one-trippers.

I said, "The only reason I'm shaking like this is because I'm cold."

It wasn't true, of course. It was that cough of Gilvey's. I didn't like to think about Gilvey, or Sam or Chowderhead or Wally or the captain. I didn't like to think about any of them. It made me shake.

You see, we couldn't kill each other. They wouldn't let us do that. Before we took off, they did something to our minds to make sure. What they did, it doesn't last forever. It lasts for two years and then it wears off. That's long enough, you see, because that gets you to Mars and back; and it's plenty long enough, in another way, because it's like a strait-jacket.

You know how to make a baby cry? Hold his hands. It's the most basic thing there is. What they did to us so we couldn't kill each other, it was like being tied up, like having our hands held so we couldn't get free. Well. But two years was long enough. Too long.

The bartender came over and said, "Pal, I'm sorry. See, I turned the air-conditioning down. You all right? You look so—"

I said, "Sure, I'm all right."

He sounded worried. I hadn't even heard him come back. The girl was looking worried, too, I guess because I was shaking so hard I was spilling my drink. I put some money on the table without even counting it.

"It's all right," I said. "We were just going."

"We were?" She looked confused. But she came along with me. They always do, once they find out you've been to Mars.

*

In the next place, she said, between trips to the powder room, "It must take a lot of courage to sign up for something like that. Were you scientifically inclined in school? Don't you have to know an awful lot to be a space-flyer? Did you ever see any of those little monkey characters they say live on Mars? I read an article about how they lived in little cities of pup-tents or something like that—only they didn't make them, they grew them. Funny! Ever see those? That trip must have been a real drag, I bet. What is it, nine months? You couldn't have a baby! Excuse me— Say, tell me. All that time, how'd you—well, manage things? I mean didn't you ever have to go to the you-know or anything?"

"We managed," I said.

She giggled, and that reminded her, so she went to the powder room again. I thought about getting up and leaving while she was gone, but what was the use of that? I'd only pick up somebody else.

It was nearly midnight. A couple of minutes wouldn't hurt. I reached in my pocket for the little box of pills they give us—it isn't refillable, but we get a new prescription in the mail every month, along with the pension check. The label on the box said:

CAUTION

Use only as directed by physician. Not to be taken by persons suffering heart condition, digestive upset or circulatory disease. Not to be used in conjunction with alcoholic beverages.

I took three of them. I don't like to start them before midnight, but anyway I stopped shaking.

I closed my eyes, and then I was on the ship again. The noise in the bar became the noise of the rockets and the air washers and the sludge sluicers. I began to sweat, although this place was air-conditioned, too.

I could hear Wally whistling to himself the way he did, the sound muffled by his oxygen mask and drowned in the rocket noise, but still perfectly audible. The tune was *Sophisticated Lady*. Sometimes it was *Easy to Love* and sometimes *Chasing Shadows*, but mostly *Sophisticated Lady*. He was from Juilliard.

Somebody sneezed, and it sounded just like Chowderhead sneezing. You know how everybody sneezes according to his own individual style? Chowderhead had a ladylike little sneeze; it went *hutta*, real quick, all through the mouth, no nose involved. The captain went *Hrasssh*; Wally was Ashoo, ashoo, *ashoo*. Gilvey was *Hutch*-uh. Sam didn't sneeze much, but he sort of coughed and sprayed, and that was worse.

Sometimes I used to think about killing Sam by tying him down and having Wally and the captain sneeze him to death. But that was a kind of a joke, naturally, when I was feeling good. Or pretty good. Usually I thought about a knife for Sam. For Chowderhead it was a gun, right in the belly, one shot. For Wally it was a tommy gun—just stitching him up and down, you know, back and forth. The captain I would put in a cage with hungry lions, and Gilvey I'd strangle with my bare hands. That was probably because of the cough, I guess.

*

She was back. "Please tell me about it," she begged. "I'm *so* curious."

I opened my eyes. "You want me to tell you about it?"

"Oh, please!"

"About what it's like to fly to Mars on a rocket?"

"Yes!"

"All right," I said.

It's wonderful what three little white pills will do. I wasn't even shaking.

"There's six men, see? In a space the size of a Buick, and that's all the room there is. Two of us in the bunks all the time, four of us on watch. Maybe you want to stay in the sack an extra ten minutes—because it's the only place on the ship where you can stretch out, you know, the only place where you can rest without somebody's elbow in your side. But you can't. Because by then it's the next man's turn.

"And maybe you don't have elbows in your side while it's your turn off watch, but in the starboard bunk there's the air-regenerator master valve—I bet I could still show you the bruises right around my kidneys—and in the port bunk there's the emergency-escape-hatch handle. That gets you right in the temple, if you turn your head too fast.

"And you can't really sleep, I mean not soundly, because of the noise. That is, when the rockets are going. When they aren't going, then you're in free-fall, and that's bad, too, because you dream about falling. But when they're going, I don't know, I think it's worse. It's pretty loud.

"And even if it weren't for the noise, if you sleep too soundly you might roll over on your oxygen line. Then you dream about drowning. Ever do that? You're strangling and choking and you can't get any air? It isn't dangerous, I guess. Anyway, it always woke me up in time. Though I heard about a fellow in a flight six years ago—

"Well. So you've always got this oxygen mask on, all the time, except if you take it off for a second to talk to somebody. You don't do that very often, because what is there to say? Oh, maybe the first couple of weeks, sure—everybody's friends then. You don't even need the mask, for that matter. Or not very much. Everybody's still pretty clean. The place smells—oh, let's see—about like the locker room in a gym. You know? You can stand it. That's if nobody's got space sickness, of course. We were lucky that way.

"But that's about how it's going to get anyway, you know. Outside the masks, it's soup. It isn't that you smell it so much. You kind of *taste* it, in the back of your mouth, and your eyes sting. That's after the first two or three months. Later on, it gets worse.

"And with the mask on, of course, the oxygen mixture is coming in under pressure. That's funny if you're not used to it. Your lungs have to work a little bit harder to get rid of it, especially when you're asleep, so after a while the muscles get sore. And then they get sorer. And then—

"Well.

"Before we take off, the psych people give us a long doo-da that keeps us from killing each other. But they can't stop us from thinking about it. And afterward, after we're back on Earth—this is what you won't read about in the articles—they keep us apart. You know how they work it? We get a pension, naturally. I mean there's got to be a pension, otherwise there isn't enough money in the world to make anybody go. But in the contract, it says to get the pension we have to stay in our own area.

"The whole country's marked off. Six sections. Each has at least one big city in it. I was lucky, I got a lot of them. They try to keep it so every man's home town is in his own section, but—well, like with us, Chowderhead and the captain both happened to come from Santa Monica. I think it was Chowderhead that got California, Nevada, all that Southwest area. It was the luck of the draw. God knows what the captain got.

"Maybe New Jersey," I said, and took another white pill.

*

We went on to another place and she said suddenly, "I figured something out. The way you keep looking around."

"What did you figure out?"

"Well, part of it was what you said about the other fellow getting New Jersey. This is New Jersey. You don't belong in this section, right?"

"Right," I said after a minute.

"So why are you here? I know why. You're here because you're looking for somebody."

"That's right."

She said triumphantly, "You want to find that other fellow from your crew! You want to fight him!"

I couldn't help shaking, white pills or no white pills. But I had to correct her.

"No. I want to kill him."

"How do you know he's here? He's got a lot of states to roam around in, too, doesn't he?"

"Six. New Jersey, Pennsylvania, Delaware, Maryland—all the way down to Washington."

"Then how do you know—"

"He'll be here." I didn't have to tell her how I knew. But I knew.

I wasn't the only one who spent his time at the border of his assigned area, looking across the river or staring across a state line, knowing that somebody was on the other side. I knew. You fight a war and you don't have to guess that the enemy might have his troops a thousand miles away from the battle line. You know where his troops will be. You know he wants to fight, too.

Hutta. Hutta.

I spilled my drink.

I looked at her. "You—you didn't—"

She looked frightened. "What's the matter?"

"*Did you just sneeze?*"

"Sneeze? Me? Did I—"

I said something quick and nasty, I don't know what. No! It hadn't been her. I knew it.

It was Chowderhead's sneeze.

*

Chowderhead. Marvin T. Roebuck, his name was. Five feet eight inches tall. Dark-complected, with a cast in one eye. Spoke with a Midwest kind of accent, even though he came from California—"shrick" for "shriek," "hawror" for "horror," like that. It drove me crazy after a while. Maybe that gives you an idea what he talked about mostly. A skunk. A thoroughgoing, deep-rooted, mother-murdering skunk.

I kicked over my chair and roared, "Roebuck! Where are you, damn you?"

The bar was all at once silent. Only the jukebox kept going.

"I know you're here!" I screamed. "Come out and get it! You louse, I told you I'd get you for calling me a liar the day Wally sneaked a smoke!"

Silence, everybody looking at me.

Then the door of the men's room opened.

He came out.

He looked *lousy.* Eyes all red-rimmed and his hair falling out—the poor crumb couldn't have been over twenty-nine. He shrieked, "You!" He called me a million names. He said, "You thieving rat, I'll teach you to try to cheat me out of my candy ration!"

He had a knife.

261

I didn't care. I didn't have anything and that was stupid, but it didn't matter. I got a bottle of beer from the next table and smashed it against the back of a chair. It made a good weapon, you know; I'd take that against a knife any time.

I ran toward him, and he came all staggering and lurching toward me, looking crazy and desperate, mumbling and raving—I could hardly hear him, because I was talking, too. Nobody tried to stop us. Somebody went out the door and I figured it was to call the cops, but that was all right. Once I took care of Chowderhead, I didn't care what the cops did.

I went for the face.

He cut me first. I felt the knife slide up along my left arm but, you know, it didn't even hurt, only kind of stung a little. I didn't care about that. I got him in the face, and the bottle came away, and it was all like gray and white jelly, and then blood began to spring out. He screamed. Oh, that scream! I never heard anything like that scream. It was what I had been waiting all my life for.

I kicked him as he staggered back, and he fell. And I was on top of him, with the bottle, and I was careful to stay away from the heart or the throat, because that was too quick, but I worked over the face, and I felt his knife get me a couple times more, and—

And—

*

And I woke up, you know. And there was Dr. Santly over me with a hypodermic needle that he'd just taken out of my arm, and four male nurses in fatigues holding me down. And I was drenched with sweat.

For a minute, I didn't know where I was. It was a horrible queasy falling sensation, as though the bar and the fight and the world were all dissolving into smoke around me.

Then I knew where I was.

It was almost worse.

I stopped yelling and just lay there, looking up at them.

Dr. Santly said, trying to keep his face friendly and noncommittal, "You're doing much better, Byron, boy. *Much* better."

I didn't say anything.

He said, "You worked through the whole thing in two hours and eight minutes. Remember the first time? You were sixteen hours killing him. Captain Van Wyck it was that time, remember? Who was it this time?"

"Chowderhead." I looked at the male nurses. Doubtfully, they let go of my arms and legs.

"Chowderhead," said Dr. Santly. "Oh—Roebuck. That boy," he said mournfully, his expression saddened, "he's not coming along nearly as well as you. *Nearly*. He can't run through a cycle in less than five hours. And, that's peculiar, it's usually you he— Well, I better not say that, shall I? No sense setting up a counter-impression when your pores are all open, so to speak?" He smiled at me, but he was a little worried in back of the smile.

I sat up. "Anybody got a cigarette?"

"Give him a cigarette, Johnson," the doctor ordered the male nurse standing alongside my right foot.

Johnson did. I fired up.

"You're coming along *splendidly*," Dr. Santly said. He was one of these psych guys that thinks if you say it's so, it makes it so. You know that kind? "We'll have you down under an hour before the end of the week. That's *marvelous* progress. Then we can work on the conscious level! You're doing extremely well, whether you know it or not. Why, in six months—say in eight months, because I like to be conservative—" he twinkled at me—"we'll have you out of here! You'll be the first of your crew to be discharged, you know that?"

"That's nice," I said. "The others aren't doing so well?"

"No. Not at all well, most of them. Particularly Dr. Gilvey. The run-throughs leave him in terrible shape. I don't mind admitting I'm worried about him."

"That's nice," I said, and this time I meant it.

*

He looked at me thoughtfully, but all he did was say to the male nurses, "He's all right now. Help him off the table."

It was hard standing up. I had to hold onto the rail around the table for a minute. I said my set little speech: "Dr. Santly, I want to tell you again how grateful I am for this. I was reconciled to living the rest of my life confined to one part of the country, the way the other crews always did. But this is much better. I appreciate it. I'm sure the others do, too."

"Of course, boy. Of course." He took out a fountain pen and made a note on my chart; I couldn't see what it was, but he looked gratified. "It's no more than you have coming to you, Byron," he said. "I'm grateful that I could be the one to make it come to pass."

He glanced conspiratorially at the male nurses. "You know how important this is to me. It's the triumph of a whole new approach to psychic rehabilitation. I mean to say our heroes of space travel are entitled to freedom when they come back home to Earth, aren't they?"

"Definitely," I said, scrubbing some of the sweat off my face onto my sleeve.

"So we've got to end this system of designated areas. We can't avoid the tensions that accompany space travel, no. But if we can help you eliminate harmful tensions with a few run-throughs, why, it's not too high a price to pay, is it?"

"Not a bit."

"I mean to say," he said, warming up, "you can look forward to the time when you'll be able to mingle with your old friends from the rocket, free and easy, without any need for restraint. That's a lot to look forward to, isn't it?"

"It is," I said. "I look forward to it very much," I said. "And I know exactly what I'm going to do the first time I meet one—I mean without any restraints, as you say," I said. And it was true; I did. Only it wouldn't be a broken beer bottle that I would do it with.

SUPER PACK

I had much more elaborate ideas than that.

PYTHIAS

Sure, Larry Connaught saved my life—but it was how he did it that forced me to murder him!

I am sitting on the edge of what passes for a bed. It is made of loosely woven strips of steel, and there is no mattress, only an extra blanket of thin olive-drab. It isn't comfortable; but of course they expect to make me still more uncomfortable.

They expect to take me out of this precinct jail to the District prison and eventually to the death house.

Sure, there will be a trial first, but that is only a formality. Not only did they catch me with the smoking gun in my hand and Connaught bubbling to death through the hole in his throat, but I admitted it.

I—knowing what I was doing, with, as they say, malice aforethought—deliberately shot to death Laurence Connaught. They execute murderers. So they mean to execute me.

Especially because Laurence Connaught had saved my life.

Well, there are extenuating circumstances. I do not think they would convince a jury.

Connaught and I were close friends for years. We lost touch during the war. We met again in Washington, a few years after the war was over. We had, to some extent, grown apart; he had become a man with a mission. He was working very hard on something and he did not choose to discuss his work and there was nothing else in his life on which to form a basis for communication. And—well, I had my own life, too. It wasn't scientific research in my case—I flunked out of med school, while he went on. I'm not ashamed of it; it is nothing to be ashamed of. I simply was not able to cope with the messy business of carving corpses. I didn't like it, I didn't want to do it, and when I was forced to do it, I did it badly. So—I left.

Thus I have no string of degrees, but you don't need them in order to be a Senate guard.

*

Does that sound like a terribly impressive career to you? Of course not; but I liked it. The Senators are relaxed and friendly when the guards are around, and you learn wonderful things about what goes on behind the scenes of government. And a Senate guard is in a position to do favors—for newspapermen, who find a lead to a story useful; for government officials, who sometimes base a whole campaign on one careless, repeated remark; and for just about anyone who would like to be in the visitors' gallery during a hot debate.

Larry Connaught, for instance. I ran into him on the street one day, and we chatted for a moment, and he asked if it was possible to get him in to see the upcoming foreign relations debate. It was; I called him the next day and told him I had arranged for a pass. And he was there, watching eagerly with his moist little eyes, when the Secretary got up to speak and there was that sudden unexpected yell, and the handful of Central American fanatics dragged out their weapons and began trying to change American policy with gunpowder.

You remember the story, I suppose. There were only three of them, two with guns, one with a hand grenade. The pistol men managed to wound two Senators and a guard. I was right there, talking to Connaught. I spotted the little fellow with the hand grenade and tackled him. I knocked him down, but the grenade went flying, pin pulled, seconds ticking away. I lunged for it. Larry Connaught was ahead of me.

The newspaper stories made heroes out of both of us. They said it was miraculous that Larry, who had fallen right on top of the grenade, had managed to get it away from himself and so placed that when it exploded no one was hurt.

For it did go off—and the flying steel touched nobody. The papers mentioned that Larry had been knocked unconscious by the blast. He was unconscious, all right.

He didn't come to for six hours and when he woke up, he spent the next whole day in a stupor.

I called on him the next night. He was glad to see me.

"That was a close one, Dick," he said. "Take me back to Tarawa."

I said, "I guess you saved my life, Larry."

"Nonsense, Dick! I just jumped. Lucky, that's all."

"The papers said you were terrific. They said you moved so fast, nobody could see exactly what happened."

He made a deprecating gesture, but his wet little eyes were wary. "Nobody was really watching, I suppose."

"I was watching," I told him flatly.

He looked at me silently for a moment.

"I was between you and the grenade," I said. "You didn't go past me, over me, or through me. But you were on top of the grenade."

He started to shake his head.

I said, "Also, Larry, you fell *on* the grenade. It exploded underneath you. I know, because I was almost on top of you, and it blew you clear off the floor of the gallery. Did you have a bulletproof vest on?"

*

He cleared his throat. "Well, as a matter of—"

"Cut it out, Larry! What's the answer?"

He took off his glasses and rubbed his watery eyes. He grumbled, "Don't you read the papers? It went off a yard away."

"Larry," I said gently, "I was there."

He slumped back in his chair, staring at me. Larry Connaught was a small man, but he never looked smaller than he did in that big chair, looking at me as though I were Mr. Nemesis himself.

Then he laughed. He surprised me; he sounded almost happy. He said, "Well, hell, Dick—I had to tell somebody about it sooner or later. Why not you?"

I can't tell you all of what he said. I'll tell most of it—but not the part that matters.

I'll never tell *that* part to *anybody*.

Larry said, "I should have known you'd remember." He smiled at me ruefully, affectionately. "Those bull sessions in the cafeterias, eh? Talking all night about everything. But you remembered."

268

"You claimed that the human mind possessed powers of psychokinesis," I said. "You argued that just by the mind, without moving a finger or using a machine, a man could move his body anywhere, instantly. You said that nothing was impossible to the mind."

I felt like an absolute fool saying those things; they were ridiculous notions. Imagine a man *thinking* himself from one place to another! But—I had been on that gallery.

I licked my lips and looked to Larry Connaught for confirmation.

"I was all wet," Larry laughed. "Imagine!"

I suppose I showed surprise, because he patted my shoulder.

He said, becoming sober, "Sure, Dick, you're wrong, but you're right all the same. The mind alone can't do anything of the sort—that was just a silly kid notion. But," he went on, "*but* there are—well, techniques—linking the mind to physical forces—simple physical forces that we all use every day—that can do it all. Everything! Everything I ever thought of and things I haven't found out yet.

"Fly across the ocean? In a second, Dick! Wall off an exploding bomb? Easily! You saw me do it. Oh, it's work. It takes energy—you can't escape natural law. That was what knocked me out for a whole day. But that was a hard one; it's a lot easier, for instance, to make a bullet miss its target. It's even easier to lift the cartridge out of the chamber and put it in my pocket, so that the bullet can't even be fired. Want the Crown Jewels of England? I could get them, Dick!"

I asked, "Can you see the future?"

He frowned. "That's silly. This isn't supersti—"

"How about reading minds?"

*

Larry's expression cleared. "Oh, you're remembering some of the things I said years ago. No, I can't do that either, Dick. Maybe, some day, if I keep working at this thing— Well, I can't right now. There are things I can do, though, that are just as good."

"Show me something you can do," I asked.

He smiled. Larry was enjoying himself; I didn't begrudge it to him. He had hugged this to himself for years, from the day he found his first clue, through the decade of proving and experimenting, almost always being wrong, but always getting closer.... He *needed* to talk about it. I think he was really glad that, at last, someone had found him out.

He said, "Show you something? Why, let's see, Dick." He looked around the room, then winked. "See that window?"

I looked. It opened with a slither of wood and a rumble of sash weights. It closed again.

"The radio," said Larry. There was a *click* and his little set turned itself on. "Watch it."

It disappeared and reappeared.

"It was on top of Mount Everest," Larry said, panting a little.

The plug on the radio's electric cord picked itself up and stretched toward the baseboard socket, then dropped to the floor again.

"No," said Larry, and his voice was trembling, "I'll show you a hard one. Watch the radio, Dick. I'll run it without plugging it in! The electrons themselves—"

He was staring intently at the little set. I saw the dial light go on, flicker, and hold steady; the speaker began to make scratching noises. I stood up, right behind Larry, right over him.

I used the telephone on the table beside him. I caught him right beside the ear and he folded over without a murmur. Methodically, I hit him twice more, and then I was sure he wouldn't wake up for at least an hour. I rolled him over and put the telephone back in its cradle.

I ransacked his apartment. I found it in his desk: All his notes. All the information. The secret of how to do the things he could do.

I picked up the telephone and called the Washington police. When I heard the siren outside, I took out my service revolver and shot him in the throat. He was dead before they came in.

*

For, you see, I knew Laurence Connaught. We were friends. I would have trusted him with my life. But this was more than just a life.

Twenty-three words told how to do the things that Laurence Connaught did. Anyone who could read could do them. Criminals, traitors, lunatics—the formula would work for anyone.

Laurence Connaught was an honest man and an idealist, I think. But what would happen to any man when he became God? Suppose you were told twenty-three words that would let you reach into any bank vault, peer inside any closed room, walk through any wall? Suppose pistols could not kill you?

They say power corrupts; and absolute power corrupts absolutely. And there can be no more absolute power than the twenty-three words that can free a man of any jail or give him anything he wants. Larry was my friend. But I killed him in cold blood, knowing what I did, because he could not be trusted with the secret that could make him king of the world.

But I can.

The Knights of Arthur

Table of Contents

I

There was three of us—I mean if you count Arthur. We split up to avoid attracting attention. Engdahl just came in over the big bridge, but I had Arthur with me so I had to come the long way around.

When I registered at the desk, I said I was from Chicago. You know how it is. If you say you're from Philadelphia, it's like saying you're from St. Louis or Detroit—I mean *nobody* lives in Philadelphia any more. Shows how things change. A couple years ago, Philadelphia was all the fashion. But not now, and I wanted to make a good impression.

I even tipped the bellboy a hundred and fifty dollars. I said: "Do me a favor. I've got my baggage booby-trapped—"

"Natch," he said, only mildly impressed by the bill and a half, even less impressed by me.

"I mean *really* booby-trapped. Not just a burglar alarm. Besides the alarm, there's a little surprise on a short fuse. So what I want you to do, if you hear the alarm go off, is come running. Right?"

"And get my head blown off?" He slammed my bags onto the floor. "Mister, you can take your damn money and—"

"Wait a minute, friend." I passed over another hundred. "Please? It's only a shaped charge. It won't hurt anything except anybody who messes around, see? But I don't want it to go off. So you come running when you hear the alarm and scare him away and—"

"No!" But he was less positive. I gave him two hundred more and he said grudgingly: "All right. If I hear it. Say, what's in there that's worth all that trouble?"

"Papers," I lied.

He leered. "Sure."

"No fooling, it's just personal stuff. Not worth a penny to anybody but me, understand? So don't get any ideas—"

He said in an injured tone: "Mister, naturally the *staff* won't bother your stuff. What kind of a hotel do you think this is?"

"Of course, of course," I said. But I knew he was lying, because I knew what kind of hotel it was. The staff was there only because being there gave them a chance to knock down more money than they could make any other way. What other kind of hotel was there?

Anyway, the way to keep the staff on my side was by bribery, and when he left I figured I had him at least temporarily bought. He promised to keep an eye on the room and he would be on duty for four more hours—which gave me plenty of time for my errands.

*

I made sure Arthur was plugged in and cleaned myself up. They had water running—New York's very good that way; they always have water running. It was even hot, or nearly hot. I let the shower splash over me for a while, because there was a lot of dust and dirt from the Bronx that I had to get off me. The way it looked, hardly anybody had been up that way since it happened.

I dried myself, got dressed and looked out the window. We were fairly high up—fifteenth floor. I could see the Hudson and the big bridge up north of us. There was a huge cloud of smoke coming from somewhere near the bridge on the other side of the river, but outside of that everything looked normal. You would have thought there were people in all those houses. Even the streets looked pretty good, until you noticed that hardly any of the cars were moving.

I opened the little bag and loaded my pockets with enough money to run my errands. At the door, I stopped and called over my shoulder to Arthur: "Don't worry if I'm gone an hour or so. I'll be back."

I didn't wait for an answer. That would have been pointless under the circumstances.

After Philadelphia, this place seemed to be bustling with activity. There were four or five people in the lobby and a couple of dozen more out in the street.

I tarried at the desk for several reasons. In the first place, I was expecting Vern Engdahl to try to contact me and I didn't want him messing with the luggage—not while Arthur might get nervous. So I told the desk clerk that in case anybody came inquiring for Mr. Schlaepfer, which was the name I was using—my real name being Sam Dunlap—he was to be told that on no account was he to go to my room but to wait in the lobby; and in any case I would be back in an hour.

"Sure," said the desk clerk, holding out his hand.

I crossed it with paper. "One other thing," I said. "I need to buy an electric typewriter and some other stuff. Where can I get them?"

"PX," he said promptly.

"PX?"

"What used to be Macy's," he explained. "You go out that door and turn right. It's only about a block. You'll see the sign."

"Thanks." That cost me a hundred more, but it was worth it. After all, money wasn't a problem—not when we had just come from Philadelphia.

*

The big sign read "PX," but it wasn't big enough to hide an older sign underneath that said "Macy's." I looked it over from across the street.

Somebody had organized it pretty well. I had to admire them. I mean I don't like New York—wouldn't live there if you gave me the place—but it showed a sort of go-getting spirit. It was no easy job getting a full staff together to run a department store operation, when any city the size of New York must have a couple thousand stores. You know what I mean? It's like running a hotel or anything else—how are you going to get people to work for you when they can just as easily walk down the street, find a vacant store and set up their own operation?

But Macy's was fully manned. There was a guard at every door and a walking patrol along the block-front between the entrances to make sure nobody broke in through the windows. They all wore green armbands and uniforms—well, lots of people wore uniforms.

I walked over.

"Afternoon," I said affably to the guard. "I want to pick up some stuff. Typewriter, maybe a gun, you know. How do you work it here? Flat rate for all you can carry, prices marked on everything, or what is it?"

He stared at me suspiciously. He was a monster; six inches taller than I, he must have weighed two hundred and fifty pounds. He didn't look very smart, which might explain why he was working for somebody else these days. But he was smart enough for what he had to do.

He demanded: "You new in town?"

I nodded.

He thought for a minute. "All right, buddy. Go on in. You pick out what you want, see? We'll straighten out the price when you come out."

"Fair enough." I started past him.

He grabbed me by the arm. "No tricks," he ordered. "You come out the same door you went in, understand?"

"Sure," I said, "if that's the way you want it."

That figured—one way or another: either they got a commission, or, like everybody else, they lived on what they could knock down. I filed that for further consideration.

Inside, the store smelled pretty bad. It wasn't just rot, though there was plenty of that; it was musty and stale and old. It was dark, or nearly. About one light in twenty was turned on, in order to conserve power. Naturally the escalators and so on weren't running at all.

*

I passed a counter with pencils and ball-point pens in a case. Most of them were gone—somebody hadn't bothered to go around in back and had simply knocked the glass out—but I found one that worked and an old order pad to write on. Over by the elevators there was a store directory, so I went over and checked it, making a list of the departments worth visiting.

SUPER PACK

Office Supplies would be the typewriter. Garden & Home was a good bet—maybe I could find a little wheelbarrow to save carrying the typewriter in my arms. What I wanted was one of the big ones where all the keys are solenoid-operated instead of the cam-and-roller arrangement—that was all Arthur could operate. And those things were heavy, as I knew. That was why we had ditched the old one in the Bronx.

Sporting Goods—that would be for a gun, if there were any left. Naturally, they were about the first to go after it happened, when *everybody* wanted a gun. I mean everybody who lived through it. I thought about clothes—it was pretty hot in New York—and decided I might as well take a look.

Typewriter, clothes, gun, wheelbarrow. I made one more note on the pad—try the tobacco counter, but I didn't have much hope for that. They had used cigarettes for currency around this area for a while, until they got enough bank vaults open to supply big bills. It made cigarettes scarce.

I turned away and noticed for the first time that one of the elevators was stopped on the main floor. The doors were closed, but they were glass doors, and although there wasn't any light inside, I could see the elevator was full. There must have been thirty or forty people in the car when it happened.

I'd been thinking that, if nothing else, these New Yorkers were pretty neat—I mean if you don't count the Bronx. But here were thirty or forty skeletons that nobody had even bothered to clear away.

You call that neat? Right in plain view on the ground floor, where everybody who came into the place would be sure to go—I mean if it had been on one of the upper floors, what difference would it have made?

I began to wish we were out of the city. But naturally that would have to wait until we finished what we came here to do—otherwise, what was the point of coming all the way here in the first place?

*

277

The tobacco counter was bare. I got the wheelbarrow easily enough—there were plenty of those, all sizes; I picked out a nice light red-and-yellow one with rubber-tired wheel. I rolled it over to Sporting Goods on the same floor, but that didn't work out too well. I found a 30-30 with telescopic sights, only there weren't any cartridges to fit it—or anything else. I took the gun anyway; Engdahl would probably have some extra ammunition.

Men's Clothing was a waste of time, too—I guess these New Yorkers were too lazy to do laundry. But I found the typewriter I wanted.

I put the whole load into the wheelbarrow, along with a couple of odds and ends that caught my eye as I passed through Housewares, and I bumped as gently as I could down the shallow steps of the motionless escalator to the ground floor.

I came down the back way, and that was a mistake. It led me right past the food department. Well, I don't have to tell you what *that* was like, with all the exploded cans and the rats as big as poodles. But I found some cologne and soaked a handkerchief in it, and with that over my nose, and some fast footwork for the rats, I managed to get to one of the doors.

It wasn't the one I had come in, but that was all right. I sized up the guard. He looked smart enough for a little bargaining, but not too smart; and if I didn't like his price, I could always remember that I was supposed to go out the other door.

I said: "Psst!"

When he turned around, I said rapidly: "Listen, this isn't the way I came in, but if you want to do business, it'll be the way I come out."

He thought for a second, and then he smiled craftily and said: "All right, come on."

Well, we haggled. The gun was the big thing—he wanted five thousand for that and he wouldn't come down. The wheelbarrow he was willing to let go for five hundred. And the typewriter—he scowled at the typewriter as though it were contagious.

"What you want that for?" he asked suspiciously. I shrugged.

"Well—" he scratched his head—"a thousand?"

I shook my head.

"Five hundred?"

I kept on shaking.

"All right, all right," he grumbled. "Look, you take the other things for six thousand—including what you got in your pockets that you don't think I know about, see? And I'll throw this in. How about it?"

That was fine as far as I was concerned, but just on principle I pushed him a little further. "Forget it," I said. "I'll give you fifty bills for the lot, take it or leave it. Otherwise I'll walk right down the street to Gimbel's and—"

He guffawed.

"Whats the matter?" I demanded.

"Pal," he said, "you kill me. Stranger in town, hey? You can't go anyplace but here."

"Why not?"

"Account of there *ain't* anyplace else. See, the chief here don't like competition. So we don't have to worry about anybody taking their trade elsewhere, like—we burned all the other places down."

That explained a couple of things. I counted out the money, loaded the stuff back in the wheelbarrow and headed for the Statler; but all the time I was counting and loading, I was talking to Big Brainless; and by the time I was actually on the way, I knew a little more about this "chief."

And that was kind of important, because he was the man we were going to have to know very well.

II

I locked the door of the hotel room. Arthur was peeping out of the suitcase at me.

I said: "I'm back. I got your typewriter." He waved his eye at me.

I took out the little kit of electricians' tools I carried, tipped the typewriter on its back and began sorting out leads. I cut them free from the keyboard, soldered on a ground wire, and began taping the leads to the strands of a yard of forty-ply multiplex cable.

It was a slow and dull job. I didn't have to worry about which solenoid lead went to which strand—Arthur could sort them out. But all the same it took an hour, pretty near, and I was getting hungry by the time I got the last connection taped. I shifted the typewriter so that both Arthur and I could see it, rolled in a sheet of paper and hooked the cable to Arthur's receptors.

Nothing happened.

"Oh," I said. "Excuse me, Arthur. I forgot to plug it in."

I found a wall socket. The typewriter began to hum and then it started to rattle and type:

DURA AUK UKOO RQK MWS AQB

It stopped.

"Come on, Arthur," I ordered impatiently. "Sort them out, will you?"

Laboriously it typed:

!!!

Then, for a time, there was a clacking and thumping as he typed random letters, peeping out of the suitcase to see what he had typed, until the sheet I had put in was used up.

I replaced it and waited, as patiently as I could, smoking one of the last of my cigarettes. After fifteen minutes or so, he had the hang of it pretty well. He typed:

YOU DAMQXXX DAMN FOOL WHUXXX WHY DID YOU LEAQNXXX LEAVE ME ALONE Q Q

"Aw, Arthur," I said. "Use your head, will you? I couldn't carry that old typewriter of yours all the way down through the Bronx. It was getting pretty beat-up. Anyway, I've only got two hands—"

YOU LOUSE, it rattled, ARE YOU TRYONXXX TRYING TO INSULT ME BECAUSE I DONT HAVE ANY Q Q

"Arthur!" I said, shocked. "You know better than that!"

The typewriter slammed its carriage back and forth ferociously a couple of times. Then he said: ALL RIGHT SAM YOU KNOW YOUVE GOT ME BY THE THROAT SO YOU CAN DO ANYTHING YOU WANT TO WITH ME WHO CARES ABOUT MY FEELINGS ANYHOW

"Please don't take that attitude," I coaxed.

WELL

"Please?"

He capitulated. ALL RIGHT SAY HEARD ANYTHING FROM ENGDAHL Q Q

"No."

ISNT THAT JUST LIKE HIM Q Q CANT DEPEND ON THAT MAN HE WAS THE LOUSIEST ELECTRICIANS MATE ON THE SEA SPRITE AND HE ISNT MUCH BETTER NOW SAY SAM REMEMBER WHEN WE HAD TO GET HIM OUT OF THE JUG IN NEWPORT NEWS BECAUSE

I settled back and relaxed. I might as well. That was the trouble with getting Arthur a new typewriter after a couple of days without one—he had so much garrulity stored up in his little brain, and the only person to spill it on was me.

*

Apparently I fell asleep. Well, I mean I must have, because I woke up. I had been dreaming I was on guard post outside the Yard at Portsmouth, and it was night, and I looked up and there was something up there, all silvery and bad. It was a missile—and that was silly, because you never see a missile. But this was a dream.

And the thing burst, like a Roman candle flaring out, all sorts of comet-trails of light, and then the whole sky was full of bright and colored snow. Little tiny flakes of light coming down, a mist of light, radiation dropping like dew; and it was so pretty, and I took a deep breath. And my lungs burned out like slow fire, and I coughed myself to death with the explosions of the missile banging against my flaming ears. . . .

Well, it was a dream. It probably wasn't like that at all—and if it had been, I wasn't there to see it, because I was tucked away safe under a hundred and twenty fathoms of Atlantic water. All of us were on the *Sea Sprite*.

But it was a bad dream and it bothered me, even when I woke up and found that the banging explosions of the missile were the noise of Arthur's typewriter carriage crashing furiously back and forth.

He peeped out of the suitcase and saw that I was awake. He demanded: HOW CAN YOU FALL ASLEEP WHEN WERE IN A PLACE LIKE THIS Q Q ANYTHING COULD HAPPEN SAM I KNOW YOU DONT CARE WHAT HAPPENS TO ME BUT FOR YOUR OWN SAKE YOU SHOULDNT

"Oh, dry up," I said.

Being awake, I remembered that I was hungry. There was still no sign of Engdahl or the others, but that wasn't too surprising—they hadn't known exactly when we would arrive. I wished I had thought to bring some food back to the room. It looked like long waiting and I wouldn't want to leave Arthur alone again—after all, he was partly right.

I thought of the telephone.

On the off-chance that it might work, I picked it up. Amazing, a voice from the desk answered.

I crossed my fingers and said: "Room service?"

And the voice answered amiably enough: "Hold on, buddy. I'll see if they answer."

Clicking and a good long wait. Then a new voice said: "Whaddya want?"

There was no sense pressing my luck by asking for anything like a complete meal. I would be lucky if I got a sandwich.

I said: "Please, may I have a Spam sandwich on Rye Krisp and some coffee for Room Fifteen Forty-one?"

"Please, you go to hell!" the voice snarled. "What do you think this is, some damn delicatessen? You want liquor, we'll get you liquor. That's what room service is for!"

*

I hung up. What was the use of arguing? Arthur was clacking peevishly:

WHATS THE MATTER SAM YOU THINKING OF YOUR BELLY AGAIN Q Q

"You would be if you—" I started, and then I stopped. Arthur's feelings were delicate enough already. I mean suppose that all you had left of what you were born with was a brain in a kind of sardine can, wouldn't you be sensitive? Well, Arthur was more sensitive than you would be, believe me. Of course, it was his own foolish fault—I mean you don't get a prosthetic tank unless you die by accident, or something like that, because if it's disease they usually can't save even the brain.

The phone rang again.

It was the desk clerk. "Say, did you get what you wanted?" he asked chummily.

"No."

"Oh. Too bad," he said, but cheerfully. "Listen, buddy, I forgot to tell you before. That Miss Engdahl you were expecting, she's on her way up."

I dropped the phone onto the cradle.

"Arthur!" I yelled. "Keep quiet for a while—trouble!"

283

He clacked once, and the typewriter shut itself off. I jumped for the door of the bathroom, cursing the fact that I didn't have cartridges for the gun. Still, empty or not, it would have to do.

I ducked behind the bathroom door, in the shadows, covering the hall door. Because there were two things wrong with what the desk clerk had told me. Vern Engdahl wasn't a "miss," to begin with; and whatever name he used when he came to call on me, it wouldn't be Vern Engdahl.

There was a knock on the door. I called: "Come in!"

The door opened and the girl who called herself Vern Engdahl came in slowly, looking around. I stayed quiet and out of sight until she was all the way in. She didn't seem to be armed; there wasn't anyone with her.

I stepped out, holding the gun on her. Her eyes opened wide and she seemed about to turn.

"Hold it! Come on in, you. Close the door!"

She did. She looked as though she were expecting me. I looked her over—medium pretty, not very tall, not very plump, not very old. I'd have guessed twenty or so, but that's not my line of work; she could have been almost any age from seventeen on.

The typewriter switched itself on and began to pound agitatedly. I crossed over toward her and paused to peer at what Arthur was yacking about: SEARCH HER YOU DAMN FOOL MAYBE SHES GOT A GUN

I ordered: "Shut up, Arthur. I'm *going* to search her. You! Turn around!"

*

She shrugged and turned around, her hands in the air. Over her shoulder, she said: "You're taking this all wrong, Sam. I came here to make a deal with you."

"Sure you did."

But her knowing my name was a blow, too. I mean what was the use of all that sneaking around if people in New York were going to know we were here?

I walked up close behind her and patted what there was to pat. There didn't seem to be a gun.

"You tickle," she complained.

I took her pocketbook away from her and went through it. No gun. A lot of money—an *awful* lot of money. I mean there must have been two or three hundred thousand dollars. There was nothing with a name on it in the pocketbook.

She said: "Can I put my hands down, Sam?"

"In a minute." I thought for a second and then decided to do it—you know, I just couldn't afford to take chances. I cleared my throat and ordered: "Take off your clothes."

Her head jerked around and she stared at me. "*What?*"

"Take them off. You heard me."

"Now wait a minute—" she began dangerously.

I said: "Do what I tell you, hear? How do I know you haven't got a knife tucked away?"

She clenched her teeth. "Why, you dirty little man! What do you think—" Then she shrugged. She looked at me with contempt and said: "All right. What's the difference?"

Well, there was a considerable difference. She began to unzip and unbutton and wriggle, and pretty soon she was standing there in her underwear, looking at me as though I were a two-headed worm. It was interesting, but kind of embarrassing. I could see Arthur's eye-stalk waving excitedly out of the opened suitcase.

I picked up her skirt and blouse and shook them. I could feel myself blushing, and there didn't seem to be anything in them.

I growled: "Okay, I guess that's enough. You can put your clothes back on now."

"Gee, thanks," she said.

She looked at me thoughtfully and then shook her head as if she'd never seen anything like me before and never hoped to again. Without another word, she began to get back into her clothes. I had to admire her poise. I mean she was perfectly calm about the whole thing. You'd have thought she was used to taking her clothes off in front of strange men.

Well, for that matter, maybe she was; but it wasn't any of my business.

*

Arthur was clacking distractedly, but I didn't pay any attention to him. I demanded: "All right, now who are you and what do you want?"

She pulled up a stocking and said: "You couldn't have asked me that in the first place, could you? I'm Vern Eng—"

"*Cut it out!*"

She stared at me. "I was only going to say I'm Vern Engdahl's partner. We've got a little business deal cooking and I wanted to talk to you about this proposition."

Arthur squawked: WHATS ENGDAHL UP TO NOW Q Q SAM IM WARNING YOU I DONT LIKE THE LOOK OF THIS THIS WOMAN AND ENGDAHL ARE PROBABLY DOUBLECROSSING US

I said: "All right, Arthur, relax. I'm taking care of things. Now start over, you. What's your name?"

She finished putting on her shoe and stood up. "Amy."

"Last name?"

She shrugged and fished in her purse for a cigarette. "What does it matter? Mind if I sit down?"

"Go ahead," I rumbled. "But don't stop talking!"

"Oh," she said, "we've got plenty of time to straighten things out." She lit the cigarette and walked over to the chair by the window. On the way, she gave the luggage a good long look.

Arthur's eyestalk cowered back into the suitcase as she came close. She winked at me, grinned, bent down and peered inside.

"My," she said, "he's a nice shiny one, isn't he?"

The typewriter began to clatter frantically. I didn't even bother to look; I told him: "Arthur, if you can't keep quiet, you have to expect people to know you're there."

She sat down and crossed her legs. "Now then," she said. "Frankly, he's what I came to see you about. Vern told me you had a pross. I want to buy it."

The typewriter thrashed its carriage back and forth furiously.

"Arthur isn't for sale."

"No?" She leaned back. "Vern's already sold me his interest, you know. And you don't really have any choice. You see, I'm in charge of materiel procurement for the Major. If you want to sell your share, fine. If you don't, why, we requisition it anyhow. Do you follow?"

I was getting irritated—at Vern Engdahl, for whatever the hell he thought he was doing; but at her because she was handy. I shook my head.

"Fifty thousand dollars? I mean for your interest?"

"No."

"Seventy-five?"

"No!"

"Oh, come on now. A hundred thousand?"

It wasn't going to make any impression on her, but I tried to explain: "Arthur's a friend of mine. He isn't for sale."

*

She shook her head. "What's the matter with you? Engdahl wasn't like this. He sold his interest for forty thousand and was glad to get it."

Clatter-clatter-clatter from Arthur. I didn't blame him for having hurt feelings that time.

Amy said in a discouraged tone: "Why can't people be reasonable? The Major doesn't like it when people aren't reasonable."

I lowered the gun and cleared my throat. "He doesn't?" I asked, cuing her. I wanted to hear more about this Major, who seemed to have the city pretty well under his thumb.

"No, he doesn't." She shook her head sorrowfully. She said in an accusing voice: "You out-of-towners don't know what it's like to try to run a city the size of New York. There are fifteen thousand people here, do you know that? It isn't one of your hick towns. And it's worry, worry, worry all the time, trying to keep things going."

"I bet," I said sympathetically. "You're, uh, pretty close to the Major?"

She said stiffly: "I'm not married to him, if that's what you mean. Though I've had my chances. . . . But you see how it is. Fifteen thousand people to run a place the size of New York! It's forty men to operate the power station, and twenty-five on the PX, and thirty on the hotel here. And then there are the local groceries, and the Army, and the Coast Guard, and the Air Force—though, really, that's only two men—and—Well, you get the picture."

"I certainly do. Look, what kind of a guy *is* the Major?"

She shrugged. "A guy."

"I mean what does he like?"

"Women, mostly," she said, her expression clouded. "Come on now. What about it?"

I stalled. "What do you want Arthur for?"

She gave me a disgusted look. "What do you think? To relieve the manpower shortage, naturally. There's more work than there are men. Now if the Major could just get hold of a couple of prosthetics, like this thing here, why, he could put them in the big installations. This one used to be an engineer or something, Vern said."

"Well . . . *like* an engineer."

*

Amy shrugged. "So why couldn't we connect him up with the power station? It's been done. The Major knows that—he was in the Pentagon when they switched all the aircraft warning net over from computer to prosthetic control. So why couldn't we do the same thing with our power station and release forty men for other assignments? This thing could work day, night, Sundays—what's the difference when you're just a brain in a sardine can?"

Clatter-rattle-*bang*.

She looked startled. "Oh. I forgot he was listening."

"No deal," I said.

She said: "A hundred and fifty thousand?"

A hundred and fifty thousand dollars. I considered that for a while. Arthur clattered warningly.

"Well," I temporized, "I'd have to be sure he was getting into good hands—"

The typewriter thrashed wildly. The sheet of paper fluttered out of the carriage. He'd used it up. Automatically I picked it up—it was covered with imprecations, self-pity and threats—and started to put a new one in.

"No," I said, bending over the typewriter, "I guess I couldn't sell him. It just wouldn't be right—"

That was my mistake; it was the wrong time for me to say that, because I had taken my eyes off her.

The room bent over and clouted me.

I half turned, not more than a fraction conscious, and I saw this Amy girl, behind me, with the shoe still in her hand, raised to give me another blackjacking on the skull.

The shoe came down, and it must have weighed more than it looked, and even the fractional bit of consciousness went crashing away.

III

I have to tell you about Vern Engdahl. We were all from the *Sea Sprite*, of course—me and Vern and even Arthur. The thing about Vern is that he was the lowest-ranking one of us all—only an electricians' mate third, I mean when anybody paid any attention to things like that—and yet he was pretty much doing the thinking for the rest of us. Coming to New York was his idea—he told us that was the only place we could get what we wanted.

Well, as long as we were carrying Arthur along with us, we pretty much needed Vern, because he was the one who knew how to keep the lash-up going. You've got no idea what kind of pumps and plumbing go into a prosthetic tank until you've seen one opened up. And, naturally, Arthur didn't want any breakdowns without somebody around to fix things up.

The *Sea Sprite*, maybe you know, was one of the old liquid-sodium-reactor subs—too slow for combat duty, but as big as a barn, so they made it a hospital ship. We were cruising deep when the missiles hit, and, of course, when we came up, there wasn't much for a hospital ship to do. I mean there isn't any sense fooling around with anybody who's taken a good deep breath of fallout.

So we went back to Newport News to see what had happened. And we found out what had happened. And there wasn't anything much to do except pay off the crew and let them go. But us three stuck together. Why not? It wasn't as if we had any families to go back to any more.

Vern just loved all this stuff—he'd been an Eagle Scout; maybe that had something to do with it—and he showed us how to boil drinking water and forage in the woods and all like that, because nobody in his right mind wanted to go near any kind of a town, until the cold weather set in, anyway. And it was always Vern, Vern, telling us what to do, ironing out our troubles.

It worked out, except that there was this one thing. Vern had bright ideas. But he didn't always tell us what they were.

So I wasn't so very surprised when I came to. I mean there I was, tied up, with this girl Amy standing over me, holding the gun like a club. Evidently she'd found out that there weren't any cartridges. And in a couple of minutes there was a knock on the door, and she yelled, "Come in," and in came Vern. And the man who was with him had to be somebody important, because there were eight or ten other men crowding in close behind.

I didn't need to look at the oak leaves on his shoulders to realize that here was the chief, the fellow who ran this town, the Major.

It was just the kind of thing Vern *would* do.

*

Vern said, with the look on his face that made strange officers wonder why this poor persecuted man had been forced to spend so much time in the brig: "Now, Major, I'm sure we can straighten all this out. Would you mind leaving me alone with my friend here for a moment?"

The Major teetered on his heels, thinking. He was a tall, youngish-bald type, with a long, worried, horselike face. He said: "Ah, do you think we should?"

"I guarantee there'll be no trouble, Major," Vern promised.

The Major pulled at his little mustache. "Very well," he said. "Amy, you come along."

"We'll be right here, Major," Vern said reassuringly, escorting him to the door.

"You bet you will," said the Major, and tittered. "Ah, bring that gun along with you, Amy. And be sure this man knows that we have bullets."

They closed the door. Arthur had been cowering in his suitcase, but now his eyestalk peeped out and the rattling and clattering from that typewriter sounded like the Battle of the Bulge.

I demanded: "Come on, Vern. What's this all about?"

Vern said: "How much did they offer you?"

Clatter-bang-BANG. I peeked, and Arthur was saying: WARNED YOU SAM THAT ENGDAHL WAS UP TO TRICKS PLEASE SAM PLEASE PLEASE PLEASE HIT HIM ON THE HEAD KNOCK HIM OUT HE MUST HAVE A GUN SO GET IT AND SHOOT OUR WAY OUT OF HERE

"A hundred and fifty thousand dollars," I said.

Vern looked outraged. "I only got forty!"

Arthur clattered: VERN I APPEAL TO YOUR COMMON DECENCY WERE OLD SHIPMATES VERN REMEMBER ALL THE TIMES I

"Still," Vern mused, "it's all common funds anyway, right? Arthur belongs to both of us."

I DONT DONT DONT REPEAT DONT BELONG TO ANYBODY BUT ME

"That's true," I said grudgingly. "But I carried him, remember."

SAM WHATS THE MATTER WITH YOU Q Q I DONT LIKE THE EXPRESSION ON YOUR FACE LISTEN SAM YOU ARENT

Vern said, "A hundred and fifty thousand, remember."

THINKING OF SELLING

"And of course we couldn't get out of here," Vern pointed out. "They've got us surrounded."

ME TO THESE RATS Q Q SAM VERN PLEASE DONT SCARE ME

*

I said, pointing to the fluttering paper in the rattling machine: "You're worrying our friend."

Vern shrugged impatiently.

I KNEW I SHOULDNT HAVE TRUSTED YOU, Arthur wept. THATS ALL I MEAN TO YOU EH

Vern said: "Well, Sam? Let's take the cash and get this thing over with. After all, he *will* have the best of treatment."

It was a little like selling your sister into white slavery, but what else was there to do? Besides, I kind of trusted Vern.

"All right," I said.

What Arthur said nearly scorched the paper.

Vern helped pack Arthur up for moving. I mean it was just a matter of pulling the plugs out and making sure he had a fresh battery, but Vern wanted to supervise it himself. Because one of the little things Vern had up his sleeve was that he had found a spot for himself on the Major's payroll. He was now the official Prosthetic (Human) Maintenance Department Chief.

The Major said to me: "Ah, Dunlap. What sort of experience have you had?"

"Experience?"

"In the Navy. Your friend Engdahl suggested you might want to join us here."

"Oh. I see what you mean." I shook my head. "Nothing that would do you any good, I'm afraid. I was a yeoman."

"Yeoman?"

"Like a company clerk," I explained. "I mean I kept records and cut orders and made out reports and all like that."

"Company clerk!" The eyes in the long horsy face gleamed. "Ah, you're mistaken, Dunlap! Why, that's *just* what we need. Our morning reports are in foul shape. Foul! Come over to HQ. Lieutenant Bankhead will give you a lift."

"Lieutenant Bankhead?"

I got an elbow in my ribs for that. It was that girl Amy, standing alongside me. "I," she said, "am Lieutenant Bankhead."

Well, I went along with her, leaving Engdahl and Arthur behind. But I must admit I wasn't sure of my reception.

Out in front of the hotel was a whole fleet of cars—three or four of them, at least. There was a big old Cadillac that looked like a gangsters' car—thick glass in the windows, tires that looked like they belonged on a truck. I was willing to bet it was bulletproof and also that it belonged to the Major. I was right both times. There was a little MG with the top down, and a couple of light trucks. Every one of them was painted bright orange, and every one of them had the star-and-bar of the good old United States Army on its side.

It took me back to old times—all but the unmilitary color. Amy led me to the MG and pointed.

"Sit," she said.

I sat. She got in the other side and we were off.

It was a little uncomfortable on account of I wasn't just sure whether I ought to apologize for making her take her clothes off. And then she tramped on the gas of that little car and I didn't think much about being embarrassed or about her black lace lingerie. I was only thinking about one thing—how to stay alive long enough to get out of that car.

IV

See, what we really wanted was an ocean liner.

The rest of us probably would have been happy enough to stay in Lehigh County, but Arthur was getting restless.

He was a terrible responsibility, in a way. I suppose there were a hundred thousand people or so left in the country, and not more than forty or fifty of them were like Arthur—I mean if you want to call a man in a prosthetic tank a "person." But we all did. We'd got pretty used to him. We'd shipped together in the war—and survived together, as a few of the actual fighters did, those who were lucky enough to be underwater or high in the air when the ICBMs landed—and as few civilians did.

I mean there wasn't much chance for surviving, for anybody who happened to be breathing the open air when it happened. I mean you can do just so much about making a "clean" H-bomb, and if you cut out the long-life fission products, the short-life ones get pretty deadly.

Anyway, there wasn't much damage, except of course that everybody was dead. All the surface vessels lost their crews. All the population of the cities were gone. And so then, when Arthur slipped on the gangplank coming into Newport News and broke his fool neck, why, we had the whole staff of the *Sea Sprite* to work on him. I mean what else did the surgeons have to do?

Of course, that was a long time ago.

But we'd stayed together. We headed for the farm country around Allentown, Pennsylvania, because Arthur and Vern Engdahl claimed to know it pretty well. I think maybe they had some hope of finding family or friends, but naturally there wasn't any of that. And when you got into the inland towns, there hadn't been much of an attempt to clean them up. At least the big cities and the ports had been gone over, in some spots anyway, by burial squads. Although when we finally decided to move out and went to Philadelphia—

Well, let's be fair; there had been fighting around there after the big fight. Anyway, that wasn't so very uncommon. That was one of the reasons that for a long time—four or five years, at any rate—we stayed away from big cities.

We holed up in a big farmhouse in Lehigh County. It had its own generator from a little stream, and that took care of Arthur's power needs; and the previous occupants had been just crazy about stashing away food. There was enough to last a century, and that took care of the two of us. We appreciated that. We even took the old folks out and gave them a decent burial. I mean they'd all been in the family car, so we just had to tow it to a gravel pit and push it in.

The place had its own well, with an electric pump and a hot-water system—oh, it was nice. I was sorry to leave but, frankly, Arthur was driving us nuts.

We never could make the television work—maybe there weren't any stations near enough. But we pulled in a couple of radio stations pretty well and Arthur got a big charge out of listening to them—see, he could hear four or five at a time and I suppose that made him feel better than the rest of us.

He heard that the big cities were cleaned up and every one of them seemed to want immigrants—they were pleading, pleading all the time, like the TV-set and vacuum-cleaner people used to in the old days; they guaranteed we'd like it if we only came to live in Philly, or Richmond, or Baltimore, or wherever. And I guess Arthur kind of hoped we might find another pross. And then—well, Engdahl came up with this idea of an ocean liner.

It figured. I mean you get out in the middle of the ocean and what's the difference what it's like on land? And it especially appealed to Arthur because he wanted to do some surface sailing. He never had when he was real—I mean when he had arms and legs like anybody else. He'd gone right into the undersea service the minute he got out of school.

And—well, sailing was what Arthur knew something about and I suppose even a prosthetic man wants to feel useful. It was like Amy said: He could be hooked up to an automated factory—

SUPER PACK

Or to a ship.

*

HQ for the Major's Temporary Military Government—that's what the sign said—was on the 91st floor of the Empire State Building, and right there that tells you something about the man. I mean you know how much power it takes to run those elevators all the way up to the top? But the Major must have liked being able to look down on everybody else.

Amy Bankhead conducted me to his office and sat me down to wait for His Military Excellency to arrive. She filled me in on him, to some degree. He'd been an absolute nothing before the war; but he had a reserve commission in the Air Force, and when things began to look sticky, they'd called him up and put him in a Missile Master control point, underground somewhere up around Ossining.

He was the duty officer when it happened, and naturally he hadn't noticed anything like an enemy aircraft, and naturally the anti-missile missiles were still rusting in their racks all around the city; but since the place had been operating on sealed ventilation, the duty complement could stay there until the short half-life radioisotopes wore themselves out.

And then the Major found out that he was not only in charge of the fourteen men and women of his division at the center—he was ranking United States Military Establishment officer farther than the eye could see. So he beat it, fast as he could, for New York, because what Army officer doesn't dream about being stationed in New York? And he set up his Temporary Military Government—and that was nine years ago.

If there hadn't been plenty to go around, I don't suppose he would have lasted a week—none of these city chiefs would have. But as things were, he was in on the ground floor, and as newcomers trickled into the city, his boys already had things nicely organized.

It was a soft touch.

*

Well, we were about a week getting settled in New York and things were looking pretty good. Vern calmed me down by pointing out that, after all, we had to sell Arthur, and hadn't we come out of it plenty okay?

And we had. There was no doubt about it. Not only did we have a fat price for Arthur, which was useful because there were a lot of things we would have to buy, but we both had jobs working for the Major.

Vern was his specialist in the care and feeding of Arthur and I was his chief of office routine—and, as such, I delighted his fussy little soul, because by adding what I remembered of Navy protocol to what he was able to teach me of Army routine, we came up with as snarled a mass of red tape as any field-grade officer in the whole history of all armed forces had been able to accumulate. Oh, I tell you, nobody sneezed in New York without a report being made out in triplicate, with eight endorsements.

Of course there wasn't anybody to send them to, but that didn't stop the Major. He said with determination: "Nobody's ever going to chew *me* out for non-compliance with regulations—even if I have to invent the regulations myself!"

We set up in a bachelor apartment on Central Park South—the Major had the penthouse; the whole building had been converted to barracks—and the first chance we got, Vern snaffled some transportation and we set out to find an ocean liner.

See, the thing was that an ocean liner isn't easy to steal. I mean we'd scouted out the lay of the land before we ever entered the city itself, and there were plenty of liners, but there wasn't one that looked like we could just jump in and sail it away. For that we needed an organization. Since we didn't have one, the best thing to do was borrow the Major's.

Vern turned up with Amy Bankhead's MG, and he also turned up with Amy. I can't say I was displeased, because I was beginning to like the girl; but did you ever try to ride three people in the seats of an MG? Well, the way to do it is by having one passenger sit in the other passenger's lap, which would have been all right except that Amy insisted on driving.

We headed downtown and over to the West Side. The Major's Topographical Section—one former billboard artist—had prepared road maps with little red-ink Xs marking the streets that were blocked, which was most of the streets; but we charted a course that would take us where we wanted to go. Thirty-fourth Street was open, and so was Fifth Avenue all of its length, so we scooted down Fifth, crossed over, got under the Elevated Highway and whined along uptown toward the Fifties.

"There's one," cried Amy, pointing.

I was on Vern's lap, so I was making the notes. It was a Fruit Company combination freighter-passenger vessel. I looked at Vern, and Vern shrugged as best he could, so I wrote it down; but it wasn't exactly what we wanted. No, not by a long shot.

*

Still, the thing to do was to survey our resources, and then we could pick the one we liked best. We went all the way up to the end of the big-ship docks, and then turned and came back down, all the way to the Battery. It wasn't pleasure driving, exactly—half a dozen times we had to get out the map and detour around impenetrable jams of stalled and empty cars—or anyway, if they weren't exactly empty, the people in them were no longer in shape to get out of our way. But we made it.

We counted sixteen ships in dock that looked as though they might do for our purposes. We had to rule out the newer ones and the reconverted jobs. I mean, after all, U-235 just lasts so long, and you can steam around the world on a walnut-shell of it, or whatever it is, but you can't store it. So we had to stick with the ships that were powered with conventional fuel—and, on consideration, only oil at that.

But that left sixteen, as I say. Some of them, though, had suffered visibly from being left untended for nearly a decade, so that for our purposes they might as well have been abandoned in the middle of the Atlantic; we didn't have the equipment or ambition to do any great amount of salvage work.

The *Empress of Britain* would have been a pretty good bet, for instance, except that it was lying at pretty nearly a forty-five-degree angle in its berth. So was the *United States*, and so was the *Caronia*. The *Stockholm* was straight enough, but I took a good look, and only one tier of portholes was showing above the water—evidently it had settled nice and even, but it was on the bottom all the same. Well, that mud sucks with a fine tight grip, and we weren't going to try to loosen it.

All in all, eleven of the sixteen ships were out of commission just from what we could see driving by.

Vern and I looked at each other. We stood by the MG, while Amy sprawled her legs over the side and waited for us to make up our minds.

"Not good, Sam," said Vern, looking worried.

I said: "Well, that still leaves five. There's the *Vulcania*, the *Cristobal*—"

"Too small."

"All right. The *Manhattan*, the *Liberté* and the *Queen Elizabeth*."

Amy looked up, her eyes gleaming. "Where's the question?" she demanded. "Naturally, it's the *Queen*."

I tried to explain. "Please, Amy. Leave these things to us, will you?"

"But the Major won't settle for anything but the best!"

"The *Major*?"

*

I glanced at Vern, who wouldn't meet my eyes. "Well," I said, "look at the problems, Amy. First we have to check it over. Maybe it's been burned out—how do we know? Maybe the channel isn't even deep enough to float it any more—how do we know? Where are we going to get the oil for it?"

"We'll get the oil," Amy said cheerfully.

"And what if the channel isn't deep enough?"

"She'll float," Amy promised. "At high tide, anyway. Even if the channel hasn't been dredged in ten years."

I shrugged and gave up. What was the use of arguing?

We drove back to the *Queen Elizabeth* and I had to admit that there was a certain attraction about that big old dowager. We all got out and strolled down the pier, looking over as much as we could see.

The pier had never been cleaned out. It bothered me a little—I mean I don't like skeletons much—but Amy didn't seem to mind. The *Queen* must have just docked when it happened, because you could still see bony queues, as though they were waiting for customs inspection.

Some of the bags had been opened and the contents scattered around—naturally, somebody was bound to think of looting the *Queen*. But there were as many that hadn't been touched as that had been opened, and the whole thing had the look of an amateur attempt. And that was all to the good, because the fewer persons who had boarded the *Queen* in the decade since it happened, the more chance of our finding it in usable shape.

Amy saw a gangplank still up, and with cries of girlish glee ran aboard.

I plucked at Vern's sleeve. "You," I said. "What's this about what the *Major* won't settle for less than?"

He said: "Aw, Sam, I had to tell her something, didn't I?"

"But what about the Major—"

He said patiently: "You don't understand. It's all part of my plan, see? The Major is the big thing here and he's got a birthday coming up next month. Well, the way I put it to Amy, we'll fix him up with a yacht as a birthday present, see? And, of course, when it's all fixed up and ready to lift anchor—"

I said doubtfully: "That's the hard way, Vern. Why couldn't we just sort of get steam up and take off?"

He shook his head. "*That* is the hard way. This way we get all the help and supplies we need, understand?"

I shrugged. That was the way it was, so what was the use of arguing?

But there was one thing more on my mind. I said: "How come Amy's so interested in making the Major happy?"

Vern chortled. "Jealous, eh?"

"I asked a question!"

"Calm down, boy. It's just that he's in charge of things here so naturally she wants to keep in good with him."

I scowled. "I keep hearing stories about how the Major's chief interest in life is women. You sure she isn't ambitious to be one of them?"

He said: "The reason she wants to keep him happy is so she *won't* be one of them."

V

The name of the place was Bayonne.

Vern said: "One of them's *got* to have oil, Sam. It *has* to."

"Sure," I said.

"There's no question about it. Look, this is where the tankers came to discharge oil. They'd come in here, pump the oil into the refinery tanks and—"

"Vern," I said. "Let's look, shall we?"

He shrugged, and we hopped off the little outboard motorboat onto a landing stage. The tankers towered over us, rusty and screeching as the waves rubbed them against each other.

There were fifty of them there at least, and we poked around them for hours. The hatches were rusted shut and unmanageable, but you could tell a lot by sniffing. Gasoline odor was out; smell of seaweed and dead fish was out; but the heavy, rank smell of fuel oil, that was what we were sniffing for. Crews had been aboard these ships when the missiles came, and crews were still aboard.

Beyond the two-part superstructures of the tankers, the skyline of New York was visible. I looked up, sweating, and saw the Empire State Building and imagined Amy up there, looking out toward us.

She knew we were here. It was her idea. She had scrounged up a naval engineer, or what she called a naval engineer—he had once been a stoker on a ferryboat. But he claimed he knew what he was talking about when he said the only thing the *Queen* needed to make 'er go was oil. And so we left him aboard to tinker and polish, with a couple of helpers Amy detached from the police force, and we tackled the oil problem.

Which meant Bayonne. Which was where we were.

It had to be a tanker with at least a fair portion of its cargo intact, because the *Queen* was a thirsty creature, drinking fuel not by the shot or gallon but by the ton.

"Saaam! Sam *Dunlap*!"

FREDERIK POHL

I looked up, startled. Five ships away, across the U of the mooring, Vern Engdahl was bellowing at me through cupped hands.

"I found it!" he shouted. "Oil, lots of oil! Come look!"

I clasped my hands over my head and looked around. It was a long way around to the tanker Vern was on, hopping from deck to deck, detouring around open stretches.

I shouted: "I'll get the boat!"

He waved and climbed up on the rail of the ship, his feet dangling over, looking supremely happy and pleased with himself. He lit a cigarette, leaned back against the upward sweep of the rail and waited.

It took me a little time to get back to the boat and a little more time than that to get the damn motor started. Vern! "Let's not take that lousy little twelve horse-power, Sam," he'd said reasonably. "The twenty-five's more what we need!" And maybe it was, but none of the motors had been started in most of a decade, and the twenty-five was just that much harder to start now.

I struggled over it, swearing, for twenty minutes or more.

The tanker by whose side we had tied up began to swing toward me as the tide changed to outgoing.

*

For a moment there, I was counting seconds, expecting to have to make a jump for it before the big red steel flank squeezed the little outboard flat against the piles.

But I got it started—just about in time. I squeezed out of the trap with not much more than a yard to spare and threaded my way into open water.

There was a large, threatening sound, like an enormous slow cough.

I rounded the stern of the last tanker between me and open water, and looked into the eye of a fire-breathing dragon.

Vern and his cigarettes! The tanker was loose and ablaze, bearing down on me with the slow drift of the ebbing tide. From the hatches on the forward deck, two fountains of fire spurted up and out, like enormous nostrils spouting flame. The hawsers had been burned through, the ship was adrift, I was in its path—

And so was the frantically splashing figure of Vern Engdahl, trying desperately to swim out of the way in the water before it.

What kept it from blowing up in our faces I will never know, unless it was the pressure in the tanks forcing the flame out; but it didn't. Not just then. Not until I had Engdahl aboard and we were out in the middle of the Hudson, staring back; and then it went up all right, all at once, like a missile or a volcano; and there had been fifty tankers in that one mooring, but there weren't any any more, or not in shape for us to use.

I looked at Engdahl.

He said defensively: "Honest, Sam, I thought it was oil. It *smelled* like oil. How was I to know—"

"Shut up," I said.

He shrugged, injured. "But it's all right, Sam. No fooling. There are plenty of other tankers around. Plenty. Down toward the Amboys, maybe moored out in the channel. There must be. We'll find them."

"No," I said. "*You* will."

And that was all I said, because I am forgiving by nature; but I thought a great deal more.

Surprisingly, though, he did find a tanker with a full load, the very next day.

It became a question of getting the tanker to the *Queen*. I left that part up to Vern, since he claimed to be able to handle it.

It took him two weeks. First it was finding the tanker, then it was locating a tug in shape to move, then it was finding someone to pilot the tug. Then it was waiting for a clear and windless day—because the pilot he found had got all his experience sailing Star boats on Long Island Sound—and then it was easing the tanker out of Newark Bay, into the channel, down to the pier in the North River—

Oh, it was work and no fooling. I enjoyed it very much, because I didn't have to do it.

*

But I had enough to keep me busy at that. I found a man who claimed he used to be a radio engineer. And if he was an engineer, I was Albert Einstein's mother, but at least he knew which end of a soldering iron was hot. There was no need for any great skill, since there weren't going to be very many vessels to communicate with.

Things began to move.

The advantage of a ship like the *Queen,* for our purposes, was that the thing was pretty well automated to start out with. I mean never mind what the seafaring unions required in the way of flesh-and-blood personnel. What it came down to was that one man in the bridge or wheelhouse could pretty well make any part of the ship go or not go.

The engine-room telegraph wasn't hooked up to control the engines, no. But the wiring diagram needed only a few little changes to get the same effect, because where in the original concept a human being would take a look at the repeater down in the engine room, nod wisely, and push a button that would make the engines stop, start, or whatever—why, all we had to do was cut out the middleman, so to speak.

Our genius of the soldering iron replaced flesh and blood with some wiring and, presto, we had centralized engine control.

The steering was even easier. Steering was a matter of electronic control and servomotors to begin with. Windjammers in the old movies might have a man lashed to the wheel whose muscle power turned the rudder, but, believe me, a big superliner doesn't. The rudders weigh as much as any old windjammer ever did from stem to stern; you have to have motors to turn them; and it was only a matter of getting out the old soldering iron again.

By the time we were through, we had every operational facility of the *Queen* hooked up to a single panel on the bridge.

Engdahl showed up with the oil tanker just about the time we got the wiring complete. We rigged up a pump and filled the bunkers till they were topped off full. We guessed, out of hope and ignorance, that there was enough in there to take us half a dozen times around the world at normal cruising speed, and maybe there was. Anyway, it didn't matter, for surely we had enough to take us anywhere we wanted to go, and then there would be more.

We crossed our fingers, turned our ex-ferry-stoker loose, pushed a button—

Smoke came out of the stacks.

The antique screws began to turn over. Astern, a sort of hump of muddy water appeared. The *Queen* quivered underfoot. The mooring hawsers creaked and sang.

"Turn her off!" screamed Engdahl. "She's headed for Times Square!"

Well, that was an exaggeration, but not much of one; and there wasn't any sense in stirring up the bottom mud. I pushed buttons and the screws stopped. I pushed another button, and the big engines quietly shut themselves off, and in a few moments the stacks stopped puffing their black smoke.

The ship was alive.

Solemnly Engdahl and I shook hands. We had the thing licked. All, that is, except for the one small problem of Arthur.

*

The thing about Arthur was they had put him to work.

It was in the power station, just as Amy had said, and Arthur didn't like it. The fact that he didn't like it was a splendid reason for staying away from there, but I let my kind heart overrule my good sense and paid him a visit.

It was way over on the East Side, miles and miles from any civilized area. I borrowed Amy's MG, and borrowed Amy to go with it, and the two of us packed a picnic lunch and set out. There were reports of deer on Avenue A, so I brought a rifle, but we never saw one; and if you want my opinion, those reports were nothing but wishful thinking. I mean if people couldn't survive, how could deer?

We finally threaded our way through the clogged streets and parked in front of the power station.

"There's supposed to be a guard," Amy said doubtfully.

I looked. I looked pretty carefully, because if there was a guard, I wanted to see him. The Major's orders were that vital defense installations—such as the power station, the PX and his own barracks building—were to be guarded against trespassers on a shoot-on-sight basis and I wanted to make sure that the guard knew we were privileged persons, with passes signed by the Major's own hand. But we couldn't find him. So we walked in through the big door, peered around, listened for the sounds of machinery and walked in that direction.

And then we found him; he was sound asleep. Amy, looking indignant, shook him awake.

"Is that how you guard military property?" she scolded. "Don't you know the penalty for sleeping at your post?"

The guard said something irritable and unhappy. I got her off his back with some difficulty, and we located Arthur.

Picture a shiny four-gallon tomato can, with the label stripped off, hanging by wire from the flashing-light panels of an electric computer. That was Arthur. The shiny metal cylinder was his prosthetic tank; the wires were the leads that served him for fingers, ears and mouth; the glittering panel was the control center for the Consolidated Edison Eastside Power Plant No. 1.

"Hi, Arthur," I said, and a sudden ear-splitting thunderous hiss was his way of telling me that he knew I was there.

I didn't know exactly what it was he was trying to say and I didn't want to; fortune spares me few painful moments, and I accept with gratitude the ones it does. The Major's boys hadn't bothered to bring Arthur's typewriter along—I mean who cares what a generator-governor had to offer in the way of conversation?—so all he could do was blow off steam from the distant boilers.

*

Well, not quite all. Light flashed; a bucket conveyor began crashingly to dump loads of coal; and an alarm gong began to pound.

"Please, Arthur," I begged. "Shut up a minute and listen, will you?"

More lights. The gong rapped half a dozen times sharply, and stopped.

I said: "Arthur, you've got to trust Vern and me. We have this thing figured out now. We've got the *Queen Elizabeth*—"

A shattering hiss of steam—meaning delight this time, I thought. Or anyway hoped.

"—and its only a question of time until we can carry out the plan. Vern says to apologize for not looking in on you—" *hiss*—"but he's been busy. And after all, you know it's more important to get everything ready so you can get out of this place, right?"

"Psst," said Amy.

She nodded briefly past my shoulder. I looked, and there was the guard, looking sleepy and surly and definitely suspicious.

I said heartily: "So as soon as I fix it up with the Major, we'll arrange for something better for you. Meanwhile, Arthur, you're doing a capital job and I want you to know that all of us loyal New York citizens and public servants deeply appreciate—"

Thundering crashes, bangs, gongs, hisses, and the scream of a steam whistle he'd found somewhere.

Arthur was mad.

"So long, Arthur," I said, and we got out of there—just barely in time. At the door, we found that Arthur had reversed the coal scoops and a growing mound of it was pouring into the street where we'd left the MG parked. We got the car started just as the heap was beginning to reach the bumpers, and at that the paint would never again be the same.

Oh, yes, he was mad. I could only hope that in the long run he would forgive us, since we were acting for his best interests, after all.

Anyway, I *thought* we were.

*

Still, things worked out pretty well—especially between Amy and me. Engdahl had the theory that she had been dodging the Major so long that *anybody* looked good to her, which was hardly flattering. But she and I were getting along right well.

She said worriedly: "The only thing, Sam, is that, frankly, the Major has just about made up his mind that he wants to marry me—"

"He *is* married!" I yelped.

"Naturally he's married. He's married to—so far—one hundred and nine women. He's been hitting off a marriage a month for a good many years now and, to tell you the truth, I think he's got the habit Anyway, he's got his eye on me."

I demanded jealously: "Has he said anything?"

She picked a sheet of onionskin paper out of her bag and handed it to me. It was marked *Top Secret*, and it really was, because it hadn't gone through his regular office—I knew that because I was his regular office. It was only two lines of text and sloppily typed at that:

Lt. Amy Bankhead will report to HQ at 1700 hours 1 July to carry out orders of the Commanding Officer.

The first of July was only a week away. I handed the orders back to her.

"And the orders of the Commanding Officer will be—" I wanted to know.

She nodded. "You guessed it."

I said: "We'll have to work fast."

*

On the thirtieth of June, we invited the Major to come aboard his palatial new yacht.

"Ah, thank you," he said gratefully. "A surprise? For my birthday? Ah, you loyal members of my command make up for all that I've lost—all of it!" He nearly wept.

I said: "Sir, the pleasure is all ours," and backed out of his presence. What's more, I meant every word.

It was a select party of slightly over a hundred. All of the wives were there, barring twenty or thirty who were in disfavor—still, that left over eighty. The Major brought half a dozen of his favorite officers. His bodyguard and our crew added up to a total of thirty men.

We were set up to feed a hundred and fifty, and to provide liquor for twice that many, so it looked like a nice friendly brawl. I mean we had our radio operator handing out highballs as the guests stepped on board. The Major was touched and delighted; it was exactly the kind of party he liked.

He came up the gangplank with his face one great beaming smile. "Eat! Drink!" he cried. "Ah, and be merry!" He stretched out his hands to Amy, standing by behind the radio op. "For tomorrow we wed," he added, and sentimentally kissed his proposed bride.

I cleared my throat. "How about inspecting the ship, Major?" I interrupted.

"Plenty of time for that, my boy," he said. "Plenty of time for that." But he let go of Amy and looked around him. Well, it was worth looking at. Those Englishmen really knew how to build a luxury liner. God rest them.

The girls began roaming around.

It was a hot day and late afternoon, and the girls began discarding jackets and boleros, and that began to annoy the Major.

"Ah, cover up there!" he ordered one of his wives. "You too there, what's-your-name. Put that blouse back on!"

It gave him something to think about. He was a very jealous man, Amy had said, and when you stop to think about it, a jealous man with a hundred and nine wives to be jealous of really has a job. Anyway, he was busy watching his wives and keeping his military cabinet and his bodyguard busy too, and that made him too busy to notice when I tipped the high sign to Vern and took off.

FREDERIK POHL

VI

In Consolidated Edison's big power plant, the guard was friendly. "I hear the Major's over on your boat, pal. Big doings. Got a lot of the girls there, hey?"

He bent, sniggering, to look at my pass.

"That's right, pal," I said, and slugged him.

Arthur screamed at me with a shrill blast of steam as I came in. But only once. I wasn't there for conversation. I began ripping apart his comfy little home of steel braces and copper wires, and it didn't take much more than a minute before I had him free. And that was very fortunate because, although I had tied up the guard, I hadn't done it very well, and it was just about the time I had Arthur's steel case tucked under my arm that I heard a yelling and bellowing from down the stairs.

The guard had got free.

"Keep calm, Arthur!" I ordered sharply. "We'll get out of this, don't you worry!"

But he wasn't worried, or anyway didn't show it, since he couldn't. I was the one who was worried. I was up on the second floor of the plant, in the control center, with only one stairway going down that I knew about, and that one thoroughly guarded by a man with a grudge against me. Me, I had Arthur, and no weapon, and I hadn't a doubt in the world that there were other guards around and that my friend would have them after me before long.

Problem. I took a deep breath and swallowed and considered jumping out the window. But it wasn't far enough to the ground.

Feet pounded up the stairs, more than two of them. With Arthur dragging me down on one side, I hurried, fast as I could, along the steel galleries that surrounded the biggest boiler. It was a nice choice of alternatives—if I stayed quiet, they would find me; if I ran, they would hear me, and then find me.

FREDERIK POHL

But ahead there was—what? Something. A flight of stairs, it looked like, going out and, yes, *up*. Up? But I was already on the second floor.

"Hey, you!" somebody bellowed from behind me.

I didn't stop to consider. I ran. It wasn't steps, not exactly; it was a chain of coal scoops on a long derrick arm, a moving bucket arrangement for unloading fuel from barges. It did go up, though, and more important it went *out*. The bucket arm was stretched across the clogged roadway below to a loading tower that hung over the water.

If I could get there, I might be able to get down. If I could get down—yes, I could see it; there were three or four mahogany motor launches tied to the foot of the tower.

And nobody around.

I looked over my shoulder, and didn't like what I saw, and scuttled up that chain of enormous buckets like a roach on a washboard, one hand for me and one hand for Arthur.

*

Thank heaven, I had a good lead on my pursuers—I needed it. I was on the bucket chain while they were still almost a city block behind me, along the galleries. I was halfway across the roadway, afraid to look down, before they reached the butt end of the chain.

Clash-clatter. *Clank!* The bucket under me jerked and clattered and nearly threw me into the street. One of those jokers had turned on the conveyor! It was a good trick, all right, but not quite in time. I made a flying jump and I was on the tower.

I didn't stop to thumb my nose at them, but I thought of it.

I was down those steel steps, breathing like a spouting whale, in a minute flat, and jumping out across the concrete, coal-smeared yard toward the moored launches. Quickly enough, I guess, but with nothing at all to spare, because although I hadn't seen anyone there, there was a guard.

He popped out of a doorway, blinking foolishly; and overhead the guards at the conveyor belt were screaming at him. It took him a second to figure out what was going on, and by that time I was in a launch, cast off the rope, kicked it free, and fumbled for the starting button.

It took me several seconds to realize that a rope was required, that in fact there was no button; and by then I was floating yards away, but the pudgy pop-eyed guard was also in a launch, and he didn't have to fumble. He knew. He got his motor started a fraction of a second before me, and there he was, coming at me, set to ram. Or so it looked.

I wrenched at the wheel and brought the boat hard over; but he swerved too, at the last moment, and brought up something that looked a little like a spear and a little like a sickle and turned out to be a boathook. I ducked, just in time. It sizzled over my head as he swung and crashed against the windshield. Hunks of safety glass splashed out over the forward deck, but better that than my head.

Boathooks, hey? I had a boathook too! If he didn't have another weapon, I was perfectly willing to play; I'd been sitting and taking it long enough and I was very much attracted by the idea of fighting back. The guard recovered his balance, swore at me, fought the wheel around and came back.

We both curved out toward the center of the East River in intersecting arcs. We closed. He swung first. I ducked—

And from a crouch, while he was off balance, I caught him in the shoulder with the hook.

He made a mighty splash.

I throttled down the motor long enough to see that he was still conscious.

"*Touché*, buster," I said, and set course for the return trip down around the foot of Manhattan, back toward the *Queen*.

*

It took a while, but that was all right; it gave everybody a nice long time to get plastered. I sneaked aboard, carrying Arthur, and turned him over to Vern. Then I rejoined the Major. He was making an inspection tour of the ship—what he called an inspection, after his fashion.

He peered into the engine rooms and said: "Ah, fine."

He stared at the generators that were turning over and nodded when I explained we needed them for power for lights and everything and said: "Ah, of course."

He opened a couple of stateroom doors at random and said: "Ah, nice."

And he went up on the flying bridge with me and such of his officers as still could walk and said: "Ah."

Then he said in a totally different tone: "What the devil's the matter over there?"

He was staring east through the muggy haze. I saw right away what it was that was bothering him—easy, because I knew where to look. The power plant way over on the East Side was billowing smoke.

"Where's Vern Engdahl? That gadget of his isn't working right!"

"You mean Arthur?"

"I mean that brain in a bottle. It's Engdahl's responsibility, you know!"

Vern came up out of the wheelhouse and cleared his throat. "Major," he said earnestly, "I think there's some trouble over there. Maybe you ought to go look for yourself."

"Trouble?"

"I, uh, hear there've been power failures," Vern said lamely. "Don't you think you ought to inspect it? I mean just in case there's something serious?"

The Major stared at him frostily, and then his mood changed. He took a drink from the glass in his hand, quickly finishing it off.

"Ah," he said, "hell with it. Why spoil a good party? If there are going to be power failures, why, let them be. That's my motto!"

Vern and I looked at each other. He shrugged slightly, meaning, well, we tried. And I shrugged slightly, meaning, what did you expect? And then he glanced upward, meaning, take a look at what's there.

But I didn't really have to look because I heard what it was. In fact, I'd been hearing it for some time. It was the Major's entire air force—two helicopters, swirling around us at an average altitude of a hundred feet or so. They showed up bright against the gathering clouds overhead, and I looked at them with considerable interest—partly because I considered it an even-money bet that one of them would be playing crumple-fender with our stacks, partly because I had an idea that they were not there solely for show.

I said to the Major: "Chief, aren't they coming a little close? I mean it's *your* ship and all, but what if one of them takes a spill into the bridge while you're here?"

He grinned. "They know better," he bragged. "Ah, besides, I want them close. I mean if anything went wrong."

I said, in a tone that showed as much deep hurt as I could manage: "Sir, what could go wrong?"

"Oh, you know." He patted my shoulder limply. "Ah, no offense?" he asked.

I shook my head. "Well," I said, "let's go below."

*

All of it was done carefully, carefully as could be. The only thing was, we forgot about the typewriters. We got everybody, or as near as we could, into the Grand Salon where the food was, and right there on a table at the end of the hall was one of the typewriters clacking away. Vern had rigged them up with rolls of paper instead of sheets, and maybe that was ingenious, but it was also a headache just then. Because the typewriter was banging out:

LEFT FOUR THIRTEEN FOURTEEN AND TWENTYONE BOILERS WITH A FULL HEAD OF STEAM AND THE SAFETY VALVES LOCKED BOY I TELL YOU WHEN THOSE THINGS LET GO YOURE GOING TO HEAR A NOISE THATLL KNOCK YOUR HAT OFF

The Major inquired politely: "Something to do with the ship?"

"Oh, *that*," said Vern. "Yeah. Just a little, uh, something to do with the ship. Say, Major, here's the bar. Real scotch, see? Look at the label!"

The Major glanced at him with faint contempt—well, he'd had the pick of the greatest collection of high-priced liquor stores in the world for ten years, so no wonder. But he allowed Vern to press a drink on him.

And the typewriter kept rattling:

LOOKS LIKE RAIN ANY MINUTE NOW HOO BOY IM GLAD I WONT BE IN THOSE WHIRLYBIRDS WHEN THE STORM STARTS SAY VERN WHY DONT YOU EVER ANSWER ME Q Q ISNT IT ABOUT TIME TO TAKE OFF XXX I MEAN GET UNDER WEIGH Q Q

Some of the "clerks, typists, domestic personnel and others"—that was the way they were listed on the T/O; it was only coincidence that the Major had married them all—were staring at the typewriter.

"Drinks!" Vern called nervously. "Come on, girls! Drinks!"

*

The Major poured himself a stiff shot and asked: "What *is* that thing? A teletype or something?"

"That's right," Vern said, trailing after him as the Major wandered over to inspect it.

I GIVE THOSE BOILERS ABOUT TEN MORE MINUTES SAM WELL WHAT ABOUT IT Q Q READY TO SHOVE OFF Q Q

The Major said, frowning faintly: "Ah, that reminds me of something. Now what is it?"

"More scotch?" Vern cried. "Major, a little more scotch?"

The Major ignored him, scowling. One of the "clerks, typists" said: "Honey, you know what it is? It's like that pross you had, remember? It was on our wedding night, and you'd just got it, and you kept asking it to tell you limericks."

The Major snapped his fingers. "Knew I'd get it," he glowed. Then abruptly he scowled again and turned to face Vern and me. "Say—" he began.

I said weakly: "The boilers."

The Major stared at me, then glanced out the window. "What boilers?" he demanded. "It's just a thunderstorm. Been building up all day. Now what about this? Is that thing—"

But Vern was paying him no attention. "Thunderstorm?" he yelled. "Arthur, you listening? Are the helicopters gone?"

YESYESYES

"Then shove off, Arthur! Shove off!"

The typewriter rattled and slammed madly.

The Major yelled angrily: "Now listen to me, you! I'm asking you a question!"

But we didn't have to answer, because there was a thrumming and a throbbing underfoot, and then one of the "clerks, typists" screamed: "The dock!" She pointed at a porthole. "It's moving!"

*

Well, we got out of there—barely in time. And then it was up to Arthur. We had the whole ship to roam around in and there were plenty of places to hide. They had the whole ship to search. And Arthur was the whole ship.

Because it was Arthur, all right, brought in and hooked up by Vern, attained to his greatest dream and ambition. He was skipper of a superliner, and more than any skipper had ever been—the ship was his body, as the prosthetic tank had never been; the keel his belly, the screws his feet, the engines his heart and lungs, and every moving part that could be hooked into central control his many, many hands.

Search for us? They were lucky they could move at all! Fire Control washed them with salt water hoses, directed by Arthur's brain. Watertight doors, proof against sinking, locked them away from us at Arthur's whim.

The big bull whistle overhead brayed like a clamoring Gabriel, and the ship's bells tinkled and clanged. Arthur backed that enormous ship out of its berth like a racing scull on the Schuylkill. The four giant screws lashed the water into white foam, and then the thin mud they sucked up into tan; and the ship backed, swerved, lashed the water, stopped, and staggered crazily forward.

Arthur brayed at the Statue of Liberty, tooted good-by to Staten Island, feinted a charge at Sandy Hook and really laid back his ears and raced once he got to deep water past the moored lightship.

We were off!

Well, from there on, it was easy. We let Arthur have his fun with the Major and the bodyguards—and by the sodden, whimpering shape they were in when they came out, it must really have been fun for him. There were just the three of us and only Vern and I had guns—but Arthur had the *Queen Elizabeth*, and that put the odds on our side.

We gave the Major a choice: row back to Coney Island—we offered him a boat, free of charge—or come along with us as cabin boy. He cast one dim-eyed look at the hundred and nine "clerks, typists" and at Amy, who would never be the hundred and tenth.

And then he shrugged and, game loser, said: "Ah, why not? I'll come along."

*

And why not, when you come to think of it? I mean ruling a city is nice and all that, but a sea voyage is a refreshing change. And while a hundred and nine to one is a respectable female-male ratio, still it must be wearing; and eighty to thirty isn't so bad, either. At least, I guess that was what was in the Major's mind. I know it was what was in mine.

And I discovered that it was in Amy's, for the first thing she did was to march me over to the typewriter and say: "You've had it, Sam. We'll dispose with the wedding march—just get your friend Arthur here to marry us."

320

"Arthur?"

"The captain," she said. "We're on the high seas and he's empowered to perform marriages."

Vern looked at me and shrugged, meaning, you asked for this one, boy. And I looked at him and shrugged, meaning, it could be worse.

And indeed it could. We'd got our ship; we'd got our ship's company—because, naturally, there wasn't any use stealing a big ship for just a couple of us. We'd had to manage to get a sizable colony aboard. That was the whole idea.

The world, in fact, was ours. It could have been very much worse indeed, even though Arthur was laughing so hard as he performed the ceremony that he jammed up all his keys.

CPSIA information can be obtained
at www.ICGtesting.com
Printed in the USA
BVHW031334061019
560014BV00005B/358/P